NEW YORK SOCIETY, CIRCA 1940

There's brisk, bulging Mrs. Arleus Stroud, an executive committeewoman of imposing command. There's lovely, fluffy and furred Lucy Emden spreading femininity among the bazaars. There's Henry Livermore, the austere ambassador burdened with a Henry Adams complex. And finally there's sensitive, overbred Sylvia Tremaine, whom Beverly perhaps—but perhaps not—loves.

Smiling, charming, always pleasing and usually pleased, Beverly Stregelinus is a fixture of a charmed way of life. Mindful of Europe's agony, he dines for Greece, dances for Norway, cocktails for Poland . . . until Pearl Harbor.

Pearl Harbor marks the beginning of Beverly Stregelinus' long-delayed education. Auchincloss catapults his mannered hero out of an artificial world into the grim realities of danger, passion, and commitment. Whether Naval Officer Stregelinus can adapt to the naked forces of life and survive as an individual is one of the most intriguing dilemmas ever posed by this brilliant and perceptive novelist.

Other SIGNET Novels

LOUIS AUCHINCLOSS

The
Indifferent
Children

 A SIGNET BOOK

Published by The New American Library

In loving memory of Malcolm Strachan

Published as a SIGNET BOOK
by arrangement with Prentice-Hall, Inc.,
who have authorized this softcover edition.
A hardcover edition is available from Prentice-Hall, Inc.

FIRST PRINTING, SEPTEMBER, 1965

This book was originally published in 1947 under the author's pseudonym, Andrew Lee.

SIGNET TRADEMARK REG. U.S. PAT. OFF. AND FOREIGN COUNTRIES
REGISTERED TRADEMARK—MARCA REGISTRADA
HECHO EN CHICAGO, U.S.A.

SIGNET BOOKS are published by
The New American Library, Inc.
1301 Avenue of the Americas, New York, New York 10019

PRINTED IN THE UNITED STATES OF AMERICA

Foreword

When I read over this novel just before its publication in 1947, I decided to my dismay that it had failed in its basic purpose. It was too late for me to withdraw it, but not too late to substitute a pseudonym for my own name. "Andrew Lee" was borrowed from a clerical ancestor on the distaff side who, according to family legend, had cursed those of his descendants who should ever smoke or drink. Just what had been in my mind in affixing this stern ecclesiastic's name to anything as repugnant to him as a work of fiction would have been, I do not recall, but I know that my basic purpose in writing the book had been to create the most absurd young man I could imagine. He had to be wrong in everything: in his philosophy, in his tastes, in his friends and above all in his estimate of himself. I would then suddenly surround him with people as absurd as himself, just at the hour that he hoped would be everyone's finest: the beginning of World War II. As Beverly Stregelinus would come to see his own absurdity in the absurdity of his fellow bureaucrats, he would be redeemed and emerge as a serious person. But he simply refused ever quite to do as he was told, and in the end I threw a bomb at him.

In reading over the novel almost twenty years after I started it, it is still apparent that Beverly fails in his redemption, but it strikes me now that there is enough honesty and vitality in his efforts and in his story to justify its inclusion in the little group of books that bear my name. I hope that its picture of our military bureaucrats behind the lines (the real allies of the Axis powers) remains amusing enough to give pleasure today.

Louis Auchincloss

CONTENTS

Hamlet:	Good lads, how do you both?
Rosencrantz:	As the indifferent children of the earth.
Guildenstern:	Happy, in that we are not over-happy; On Fortune's cap we are not the very button.
Hamlet:	Nor the soles of her shoe?
Rosencrantz:	Neither, my lord.

Hamlet. Act II, Scene ii.

The
Indifferent
Children

Part I

Beverly

CHAPTER ONE

"Ah, but what a sense of order they had!" exclaimed Mrs. Livermore as she bent down to examine the detail of a large portrait of the *Grand Dauphin* and his family. "They knew how to live." Her small, sharp eyes pecked at the canvas like a bird's beak. "*L'ordre*. There you have it. They knew what happens to life when you forget the pattern. It may have been dull. Granted." She straightened up, her stocky, firm figure reforming into a line of black silk, and glanced around at the exhibition of the *grand siècle*. "The best you could hope for was a post at court and interminable hours of waiting. But then they knew how to wait."

"What were they waiting for?" the young man with her demanded. He was wearing grey flannels with a shabby brown coat and he constantly tugged at his long, blondish hair.

Mrs. Livermore seemed at first to ignore his question. She moved on slowly and came to rest before a painting of Madame de Maintenon in sepulchral black, her eyes fixed on a small child with an adult's face standing by an open window through which appeared a corner of the *orangerie* at Versailles.

"I don't see what that matters," she said. "After all, how many things are worth waiting for?"

"Oh, Gladys!" The idealist in him, and this was a major part, rebelled.

"Well, how many?"

He looked past her out the window at a green tree that bloomed precariously on a terrace above Fifty-seventh Street and Park Avenue.

"Spring's worth waiting for," he said happily.

She shrugged her shoulders.

"Maybe. It's all in how you wait."

"Do you have to wait in stiff whalebone, staring at an *orangerie?*"

She smiled and then nodded.

"You don't mind so much, then, when it doesn't come."

He snorted.

"Why not?"

"Because you're in the pattern. It all fits. Each part is like the other." She took out her lorgnette to examine a bronze of Louis XIV, the warrior, in heroic style. "You don't think he ever looked like that, do you?"

"Never!"

"But that's the way they thought of him."

"Oh, come. They loved to write memoirs about his stinking teeth." He brought the adjective out with pleased emphasis.

"You're talking about gossip," she reprimanded him. "I'm talking about art."

He accepted the rebuke. Everyone did from Gladys. She had such stores of energy—one could feel it in her, pressing its enclosure, but still held, a jungle growth behind a privet hedge. The same energy in her big square grandfather whose portraits she almost comically resembled had made him in the last century one of America's great accumulators. Yet she was stiff, poised, accurate.

"Are you and Henry still waiting?" he asked. "Or have you heard?"

"Oh, we've heard."

"Gladys! How exciting! Where is it?"

"Panama."

He thought.

"Where they make the hats?" But she didn't smile and he

quickly added: "What does that make Henry? A minister?"

"Ambassador."

He stared at her for a moment and then gave a little cry of enthusiasm.

"At last! Oh Gladys, I'm so happy for you!"

The deprecating nod and smile that she gave him did not in the least conceal the intense pleasure that she obviously felt.

"Well, I have worked for it," she admitted. She turned from the picture and sat down on the couch in the middle of the gallery while he perched on the edge beside her. Leaning suddenly against the back of the chair she contemplated her black purse clasped in both hands on her lap. "My daughters think I've overdone it, I know. They think I care too much about *décor*. They think I'm stuffy." She smiled a bit grimly. "If they only knew that I sometimes think of their lives." The very whiteness of the powder on her cheeks intensified his sense of her latent power.

"I was sorry to hear about little Gladys and Ned," he murmured in perfunctory sympathy. "What ever has got into her?"

"My dear, she wants to marry someone else. She can't 'live without him.' " Mrs. Livermore bracketed the words in a sneer. "She has 'to go to him.' Ibsen. Or is it Hollywood? And they laugh at me for caring about the seating of my parties. Ah, well." She stood up. "I must be on my way. This is just a last look around."

He stood up beside her.

"Are you taking your pictures to Panama?"

"Heavens, no. I've got to see the embassy first."

"Will you find a brilliant society down there?"

She laughed.

"Rather dark than brilliant, I fear. But we can't complain. We've had eight years in Paris and seven in Rome. And with Hitler sitting on every legation in Europe . . ." Again she shrugged her shoulders.

"How about buying yourself a going away present?" he suggested. "What about the Poussin?"

She stopped before it.

"It's nice," she said. "But charmless. No. Not even to help you keep this job, Bev. And, anyway, what about you? Army? Navy?"

He smiled a bit sourly.

"Oh, I'm going up to Bar Harbor to organize a Plattsburg

among the umbrella tables." He hated talk about his military future. The vaguer he left it the more it assumed the billowy aspect of a great pillow in which to bury his head.

"No, but seriously, Bev," she pursued. "Aren't you doing anything about a commission?" There was nothing in the least humorous to Gladys about commissions and the obtaining thereof. It was, as one might say, or rather as she *did* say, the clear duty of every man in "their class."

"Gladys, what's the use? I'll be drafted in no time," he said hastily to change the subject. "Does Henry think we're going into the war?"

"He hopes. As do we all. It's shameful to be so inert." She reached out a hand. "Well, good-by, my dear. Come and see us if you ever come through the Canal. We'll need you to cheer things up."

He saw her to the door and went back to resume his seat on the couch. Stretching out his long legs, he rubbed his forehead with nervous hands and smoothed his hair. To the less observant of the visitors who strolled by to look at the great French canvases he may have appeared younger than he was, in the early twenties perhaps, but to the occasional person who stared at him more closely, attracted by the uncoördinated indolence of this so seemingly at home young man, it was obvious that he could be no less than thirty. There was something curiously inconsistent in the impression that he conveyed; his build was good but certainly not that of an athlete; his square chin, his long, oblong face, his grey eyes and high brow should have been more suggestive of character than they were. The picture had somehow never been coördinated. Yet the overall impression was far from unpleasant; when he got up, as he now did, to explain to two bewildered ladies that Colbert was not John Adams, that the colonial exhibition had ended the week before, he did so in such a way as to make them happy they had come this week and not last. He was about to conduct them to the next room for a further examination of the quiet little Poussins that they had so suddenly admired when he felt the full, warm presence near him of the gallery owner. Felix Salberg smiled and took a few steps towards a corner, nodding to Beverly a summons that he should follow. He wore heavy, convex glasses that made his eyes look like great beetles. Yet nobody, Beverly reflected as always, was more truly kind than Felix.

"It must have been quite a party, Stregelinus," Felix began in his flat, quiet tone. "You were even later today than yesterday."

Beverly flared in sudden, unreasonable exasperation.

"If you ever went to parties, Felix, you'd know there aren't any in June."

Felix never blushed when he was hurt but one could tell. His smile broadened a little.

"I thought it was the month for debutantes," he said.

"I'm much too old for that sort of thing."

"Then what kept you this morning?"

Beverly almost stamped his foot.

"Do you expect me to account for every minute?" he exclaimed. "I suppose you keep entries of when I come and go!".

Felix looked at him curiously.

"Why so excited? I was just going to say some people had been in and asked for you."

"Well, what does it matter? Are you afraid I missed a sale? Really, Felix?"

Salberg shrugged his shoulders sadly.

"You have no patience, Bev. I don't understand."

Beverly turned away and went to the front room. He couldn't bear to hurt Felix again any more than he could bear to apologize. For some reason he had taken it into his head to hold a grudge against Felix. Could he be getting neurotic? So many people did. He caught himself sometimes spending minutes on end picturing how crestfallen, how utterly dejected and *down* his mother and sister would be if he ever declared his independence and told them . . . but told them what? He ran his hand quickly through his hair and tried to smile. Good Lord, what a beast he had been to poor Felix, Felix who for seven years had tolerated him in the gallery, put up with his interminable telephone conversations and late arrivals, Felix, who really was as good a friend as he had.

He grabbed the straw hat with the red and yellow band and hurried out of the gallery for lunch. For lunch was always the savior of his New York day; it bristled attractively at the end of a morning with a refreshing vision of *vichyssoise* and gossip. Indeed on those dim days, few and far between though they were, when he found himself without a luncheon engagement his mornings were sallow and his afternoons interminable, and if such a day, poor skeleton that it was, had the added misfortune to end on the dull note of a family evening, why then . . . well, it was a day of non-existence, a little glimpse into the after eternity of extinction . . . but no, certainly not! He pulled himself up. He believed profoundly in heaven in the deepest Victorian sense of the word, a heaven that had the comforting unreality of a dark lithograph full of grey angels' wings. Yes, he could write a poem on that, he reminded himself as he swung along, if only he didn't have to concentrate every moment on another poem already planned— even this very moment—for it was in walking to and from work that his best lines came to him. For example that one of yesterday, a perfect gem:

"If roses had not faded,
And frosts had never come . . ."

But there, as always, the inspiration stopped. He could go on, go on indefinitely, but the mood was lost:

"If daffodils not withered,
Nor . . . nor . . ."

No, anything would spoil it. And why add to it anyway, he mused as he crossed Madison Avenue against the light. Why not make a collection of his best lines? What was John William Burgon, that eminent divine, remembered for except that single, perfect one-hundred-and-thirty-second line in *Petra:*

"A rose red city—half as old as Time!"

To have written that! Could one really ask more from the few years one was fated to spend in crawling cities between . . . between:

"The hurried sandwich, the degenerative disease."

But that was good! It had a genuine Eliot ring. He increased his pace and put his mind happily on other things. There was no point, he reflected, over-taxing the muse.

New York at the end of June was a city that he loved. The big heat hadn't come yet, but the doors of the shops were all open and overhead the curtains of the windows were sucked gently inward by the breeze. Edith Wharton had said that New York in summer was always in its shirt sleeves, but she was not alive in 1941. He loved the new sidewalk restaurants, the air-cooled banks and movies, and the big dark houses of his friends, closed for the season but still occasionally reopened for cocktails in a pleasant atmosphere of slip covers and aimlessness. The orderly pattern of winter was gone; people did what they wanted and saw their friends. He turned into the Chantilly and made his way through the tables to the little garden in back where he was to meet Mrs. Arleus Stroud. He heard her loud laugh as he stepped through the door and his eyes spotted her instantly amid the jam of crowded tables. She was certainly conspicuous. She had large amounts of flesh not too well distributed and rather bulging beneath her smart, tight-fitting suit; her grey hair escaped in undisciplined strands from beneath her big hat, and her face, wide and pleasant and puffy, gave an appearance of cheerfulness and force. There was, however, in her noisy and hearty laugh something essentially grand. Sitting with her was a tall, awkward girl whom Beverly had not expected to see but whom he waved at happily. It was Sylvia Tremaine, Mrs. Stroud's daughter by a long-forgotten marriage, and together they offered the rather absurd contrast of the old nursery rhyme of Jack and Mrs. Spratt. For Sylvia had the painful thinness of semi-invalidism. Her lank, black hair fell straight to her shoulders providing a thin frame for her pale, angular face and small features that seemed to bunch together into a scowl. She moved jerkily, twisting her head around as she talked, but there was unexpected feeling in her eyes.

"We've been waiting an age," Mrs. Stroud told him as he came up to them. "Syvvie's already finished. I've ordered for you."

"I must have a cocktail," he protested as he sat down.

"Oh, Mother's ordered that too," Sylvia said.

"How are you, Syvvie?" he asked with enthusiasm. "What brings you of all people to town? It couldn't have been to see me, I suppose?"

"Dentist," she said flatly.

"Ah, yes. How romantic." He turned to her mother. "Angeline, isn't that Mabel Sehrens, you know, the one who married Toni's husband, over there in the corner with Mrs. Emden?"

"Really?" Mrs. Stroud put on her glasses and turned heavily around to inspect the little restaurant. "I do believe you're right. Isn't it incredible the people Lucy Emden sees now?"

"Oh, we'll all come to Mabel Sehrens in time. It's a natural process of decay."

"Maybe she'll buy a picture from you," Sylvia observed sourly.

"Really, Syvvie!" he remonstrated, taking a martini from

the tray offered by the waiter. "Somebody must have got out of bed the wrong side this morning."

"But what do you see in these people? Why do they even amuse you?" She looked around the restaurant with a little shudder.

"Syvvie's always so violent," Mrs. Stroud said to him. "If she'd only do something besides read and mope in the country." She turned to Beverly as though her daughter weren't there. "I don't know what to do about her, Bev."

"Come and see our exhibition after lunch, Syvvie," he suggested kindly. "You'll like it. It's right down your alley."

"I've been," she said. "I went this morning at ten. Of course, you hadn't arrived yet."

"At that hour? I should say not. But did you like it?"

"Yes. But then a lot of idiots started coming in and murmuring: 'Lovely, lovely.' So I left."

Mrs. Stroud and Bev exchanged glances. But any comments they might have made were interrupted by the apparition looming suddenly by their table of Mrs. Goodhue Stroud, her sister-in-law, but younger and beautiful. Everything about her was long and white except the famous blonde hair that flowed smoothly from under an open-head hat to a tight knot at the nape. Her cheeks, her forehead, her fingers suggested something phantasmal and Rossettiish; her clothes, with a drape here and a loop there, conveyed the idea of a Gallicized Greece.

"You've heard the news?" she inquired softly, but in a voice unaccustomed to interruption. "It's terrible. They have all of Byelorussia. They'll be in Moscow before August." Her gesture implied a sense of despair that had become habitual. "And what are we doing about it? Roosevelt, I believe, has sent another stirring message. If they only had a plane for every word. Bev, I want *you.*"

"Me? Where? In Byelorussia?"

"On my 'Intervention Now' Committee. Rufus Henderson's."

"But I bundled for Britain all last winter, Bella."

"Well, you can bundle for America now," she said archly. "Bundle to get us in."

"You're so bloodthirsty."

Bella Stroud smiled and turned to Sylvia.

"I need you too, my dear. There you are, down on Long Island, doing nothing at all."

Sylvia stood up abruptly and picked up her purse.

"You and I in all probability aren't going to be killed in any war, Aunt Bella," she said, pulling on a glove. "I think we might leave the choice of 'getting us in' as you put it, to those who will be. Good-by, Mummie. Bev. I am going to catch the 3:15." Her mother was protesting when Bella Stroud said in a voice that had a faint tinge of sarcasm:

"Don't tell me, Sylvia, that you've gone 'America First.' "

Sylvia turned back to her.

"Are you America last, Aunt Bella?" And she walked on out of the restaurant.

Beverly clapped.

"Oh, perfect! She has you there, Bella."

But Bella only gave an incomprehensible little nod of her head as she turned away to join a table of waving hands in the corner.

Angeline Stroud and Beverly lunched slowly and at length and sat on over a brandy. She was the busiest woman in New York when she wasn't the idlest; her pleasure lay entirely in extremes. Her morning had started at eight with a drive into town; it had been filled to bursting with hospital committees and funds. For four hours her mind had been pleasurably racing up and down its executive channels. She was big; she was useful. And it wasn't, either, that she was ignorant of how the world sneers at officious middle age. She knew the universal caricature. But who, after all, would do the work? And when the sun had climbed to its meridian, when throughout the city a thousand waiters were bringing a thousand martinis, then it was time to leave the board rooms, the hotel lobbies, the high posters, and foregather in a French restaurant with someone like Beverly and talk for hours about nothing at all.

"What do you think of Syvvie?" she asked. "I mean really. Forgetting that I'm her mother."

He took up the cause warmly.

"I think she's one of the dearest, sincerest people I know. I love her just like a sister. You know that."

Angeline paused and twirled her empty brandy glass by the stem.

"Like a sister," she repeated.

"Exactly."

"Well, when a girl looks like Syvvie I guess that's the most she can expect."

"Oh, Angeline!"

"My dear, Syvvie's twenty-eight."

"But some people are late bloomers," he protested. "Look at me."

"And some never bloom," she retorted with a tiny show of impatience. "Bev, I can't get through to Sylvia. That's what worries me. I never could, really. She has always despised my life and the things I do."

"Envied them, you mean."

Angeline sighed.

"Well, maybe. Isn't it the same thing? She's all full of repressions. You know how it is: I'm such an extrovert and she's not, and the psychiatrists are simply in seventh heaven telling me what an awful home I make for her. At a hundred dollars an hour, of course."

He shouted with laughter.

"Angeline, what would any of us do without you?" he cried. "But you're wrong about Syvvie. She's full of generosity."

"Yes, she's all of that," she conceded. "But what a grown-up daughter really wants is a knock-down, drag-out row with the family, ending with Ma carried bleeding from the ring. And the trouble with me is that I always find myself winning."

He nodded.

"You couldn't even pretend to be beaten, Angeline." But even as he said it, and he laughed as he did so, he felt a little chill, as if the thin, bleak wind of Sylvia's reproach was between them.

"No, I don't suppose I could," Angeline continued. "I get too mad. God knows I try to put myself in the wrong. But then when I come back from a hot day in town, and Sylvia who's been sitting for hours in a cool library just looks at me as though I were the biggest damn fool in creation, I explode."

"Mothers have such problems," he said reflectively. "I was just talking to Gladys Livermore."

Angeline tucked a hair back under her hat.

"But Gladys' girls have too many men," she protested. "My Syvvie hasn't even one."

"Not even me?"

"Not even you, you dog," she said signaling a waiter. "Though, of course, she's crazy about you. And always has been."

He blushed very red.

"Angeline!"

"You don't have to be shy with me, Bev," she said tartly. The waiter approached. "Will you have another brandy?"

"But it's so abandoned!"

"Well?"

They had another brandy.

"It's just that she has a kindly feeling for me because I was nice to her at parties when she came out and had such a sticky time," he explained awkwardly.

"Oh, shucks!"

He couldn't argue with her successfully because he knew that what she said was true. He succeeded finally in switching the conversation to Mrs. Livermore, and they passed a pleasant half hour discussing her dismal prospects in Panama. It was past four o'clock when he returned to Salberg's, his brain slightly emulsified by the last brandy and his red and yellow tie showing a large spot where he had earlier spilled tomato juice. He found a note from Felix asking him to see him and a series of telephone messages, but these he deposited in the waste paper basket and started vaguely to consult a timetable. He had to leave town early that afternoon to get down to Glen Cove in time to help a friend in last minute preparations for a dinner dance that she was giving for two of her great-nieces. As he scanned the columns of the timetable he reflected nervously that he had planned to work that night on his verse play, *Lamballe and the Queen,* and that he couldn't work the following night because he was taking his sister to the theatre . . . God, would he never have time to do the things that he really wanted to do?

"Will you see Mr. Salberg in his office please?" one of the office boys told him. He sighed and went to the back of the gallery to the big velvet-walled room where Felix sat at an empty desk with canvases stacked on the floor beside it. The only other furniture were two chairs and an easel for showing pictures. Felix looked at him for a moment with quiet severity.

"I particularly asked you to be in early this afternoon, Beverly," he said. "Do you realize what time it is now?"

"I was lunching with Mrs. Arleus Stroud," Bev retorted airily. "I didn't think you'd want me to dash off and leave her."

"You're always lunching with Mrs. Stroud," Felix pointed out. "She may have infinite amounts of money but to my certain knowledge she has never bought a picture in this gallery with the exception of a twenty-five-dollar print of couples skating in Central Park."

"I didn't know you expected me to pick my friends for their purchasing power."

This remark, totally without justification as it was, exasperated Felix to the point of slapping the surface of the desk with his hand.

"I don't give a damn what you pick your friends for," he snapped. "It's what I pay you for that I'm wondering about."

Bev rather drew himself up at this.

"Perhaps under the circumstances," he offered for the hundredth time in seven years, "it would be better for all concerned if my services were dispensed with."

There would be a last time for everything, for Gladys Livermore's picture buying, for Angeline's committees and lunches, for Bev's poems, but now, alas, the last time had come for Felix's patient refusals to accept the offer.

"Perhaps they could be," he said. "We'll try it that way, anyway."

Beverly did his best not to betray his surprise, but he was obviously staggered. He blinked for a moment and stared; then he pulled himself together and held out his hand.

"Well, Felix," he said, somewhat conventionally, "thanks for everything."

CHAPTER TWO

IN 1910, THE year of Beverly's birth, the Stregelinus family, few though its living members may have been, was generally regarded as one of New York's "oldest" and "best." That is, it was so regarded by those who were aware of its existence at all. The Stregelinuses were by no means rich or even prominent, but their respectability was uncontested; they antedated in Manhattan the rush of new money brought by the seventies and eighties, and most important of all, for in this respect one's opinion of oneself forms that of others, they were vocally conscious of the excellence of their own pedigree. They were the kind of family that brought out privately printed memorial biographies, slim but uninteresting, of each deceased male member who had to any extent dabbled in business or law; they carefully kept their family charts up to date, and the deprecatory smile which convention required at each conversational reference (and such were frequent) to the supposed founder of the line, a fourteenth century Sir Hugh Strogylinus—"such a character," "crazy old boy, you know"—covered a well of ancestor worship almost Chinese in its depth. Beverly at school and afterwards received a constant reassurance from the heavy, solid weight of his gold signet ring with its engraved shield and motto, *"Pro Patria Strogylinisque."*

Of the actual identity of Sir Hugh we know nothing, but we do know that the family came to America as late as the end of the eighteenth century and settled in Newport, Rhode Island. Hugh Stregelinus, Beverly's great-grandfather born in 1805, went to work in New York as an auctioneer, but the fact that he always spent his summers in the place of his birth gave his social position in that community as he accumulated wealth a peculiar sanctity. He was a native who had become a summer resident. From auctioneering he went into shipping and from shipping to banks. He became rich and eminent and like so many of his contemporaries he spanned his century. As a young man it is recorded in the family testimonial that he met Lafayette on the latter's triumphant American tour in 1825; as an old one he disgusted his conservative daughters by going as the "Grand Turk" to Mrs. William K. Vanderbilt's fancy dress ball. He was a figure wherever he lived.

A widower early in life, he married in his fifties the obedient daughter of an old friend who bore him five children and quietly died. These children, too, discovered it was a man's world. Left in Newport winter and summer under the care of a spinster aunt they rarely saw their ancient and magnificent father and were terrified when they did. Their clothes were black, for somewhere there was always a cousin who had died; their utmost exercise, archery, and the great amusement of a winter evening game called "corpse" in which a rubber glove filled with sand was handed at random about a darkened room. Hugh in Manhattan extended the list of his directorships; he became president of the Bank of North America; he corresponded with Lincoln during the war. He swelled in girth; his beard lengthened; he became one of the dominant figures of a pre-Gould Wall Street. But it was an era of pygmies before the age of giants. Hugh Stregelinus is a lost name; his estate amounted to less than a million dollars, and his great-grandson, Beverly, who never forgot about him, who had been to the Public Library to search for details of his life in old newspapers, had gleaned few more facts than have been shown above.

Hugh, Jr., Beverly's grandfather, not only wrote his father's life along "testimonial" lines, but conducted himself for seventy years as if to provide an easy subject for any son who might undertake a similar volume on himself. One of them did. His portrait by Pierre Troubetzkoy, showing him in middle age, seated, a silver-tipped walking stick balanced between his knees on which majestically rested a hand displaying the signet ring that Beverly now wore, was the overdominating decoration of his mother's small living room in New York. Beverly had always admired the soft eyes, the glossy brown hair, the drooping, silky mustache of this portrait; he liked to be told that he took after his grandfather. Hugh, Jr., was indeed a perfect gentleman. He moved elegantly through the boisterous age of monopoly with only the dimmest conception of what was happening; he smiled and bowed and sonorously spoke, and so well did he carry off the pose of the cultivated gentleman of law, so easily did he seem to rise in the world of corporate finance, that nobody knew till his death that he had not practiced at all but had used the paneled office in Wall Street solely for the purpose of answering his voluminous personal mail. Living on a large scale, larger than his father would have ever dared, he used up most of his own capital and all of his wife's. Beverly was fourteen when his grandfather was buried in Woodlawn in 1924. It was a date he always remembered because after it none of his relatives ever seemed to have any money. His private youthful conclusion was that his grandfather had been the only one with brains.

Hugh, Jr.'s children made an imprint on society even less marked, but they maintained the forms. The old, over-gabled house in Newport with its big lawn had to be sold, and of course the house on Fifth Avenue, but the family, making up in discrimination what they lacked in cash, went in for small apartments in the east seventies and "charming" cottages on the fringe of summer colonies. It was the old grim struggle of the *nouveau pauvres,* but the Stregelinuses brought plenty of spirit to bear, all except Amy, Bev's mother, who was, anyway, slightly removed from the others by the fact that her husband, Charles, had died even before his father.

Amy Means Stregelinus was a tall, bony, New England woman with abundant hair, virgin to the permanent wave, and a very white, prematurely old face with timid eyes and firm, thin lips. She had a haggard look as though a fury were on her trail. Most who met her classified her casually as a dull, dowdy woman, a good enough mother probably but nervous and worn. Yet she was really a highly intellectual and intelligent being. Before her marriage, as secretary and companion to her father, Bishop Beverly Means of Massachusetts, she had been the true administrator of the diocese and had composed a goodly part of his better-known sermons. She had never expected to marry; painfully aware of her lack of charm and looks, and intensely shy she had looked quietly forward to a life of care with her father and after that to the drudge of Boston charitable activities. She was twenty-nine when she met Charles Stregelinus during one of her father's many visits to Newport, and whatever it was that indolent and rather cynical young man saw in her, it was enough to induce him to propose. She in her turn fell totally and gratefully in love with him, transferring on the spot the vast and honest scope of her loyalty to the more confined areas of the Stregelinus cosmos. She accepted her father-in-law, Hugh, Jr., on his own plane; she accepted also, and unquestioningly, the round of little dinners, the summers in Newport, the distrust of the intellect, and the abiding faith in those Wall Street financiers whose "vast responsibilities" were a theme for constant sympathy and admiration. With her husband's tragic early death from typhoid all this was blown away. Amy, numb with grief—and she was one of those who never quite recover—was left with two young children and a list of securities infinitely shorter than her husband's habits had led her to anticipate. When the help came that enabled her to send Beverly to Chelton and Madeleine to Miss Tilden's, it came, not from her father-in-law towards whom, with his large houses and general appearance of ease she had naturally looked, but from the carefully saved funds of the generous old Bishop. When Hugh, Jr., died not long afterwards the shocking state of his affairs provided a ready answer for his earlier stinginess, but Amy did not forget that her parents-in-law had been paying the wages of ten servants out of capital that might, unimpaired, have proved her children's fortune. Her disillusionment with the Stregelinuses, which she extended to all New York, was sharp and decisive. But she did not return to Boston. She had too strong a sense of having made her life in Manhattan, and she was not one to go back on her choice. The devotion that had so assisted her father and that had been so lavished on her idle husband fell, a heavy weight, on her two children; for them she would carve out a safe little corner in an alien world. Her husband's death had unsettled her last sense of security, and she was constantly clutched with the fear that something terrible was going to happen. Safety became her obsession, and the Bishop once sourly remarked: "You treat the children as if they were vegetables, Amy. Remember, they have souls. Even if they *are* Stregelinuses."

Beverly was a bright and cheerful child, the favorite of his grandfather Stregelinus and the apple of his mother's eye. His attitude towards the universe appeared to be benign and sunny, but his mother, a doubter even in idolatry, noted an early manifestation of the Stregelinus temperament in his enthusiasm for summers with Mr. and Mrs. Hugh, Jr., in Newport and his distaste for the rambling seaside pile of shingle in which Bishop Means gathered his big family for Cape Cod Julys. He liked the stately stillness of the Newport house and being called "Master Beverly" by the numerous maids; he enjoyed the eternal breast of chicken that was served at lunch and the long, hot afternoons when his grandparents rested and when, instead of being made to p'ay games with rough-housing Means cousins from Boston, he could sit unmolested in his grandfather's cool library and read, one after another, the entrancing novels of Harold Bell Wright. Yet he was not an unsociable child at all. He simply knew the atmosphere that he preferred. His mother was afraid that he would be wretchedly homesick when he was sent to Chelton at the age of twelve, but this Massachusetts church school modeled on the religious and social lines of Dr. Arnold's Rugby provided what were perhaps the six happiest years of his life. At first he was terribly teased as a sissy; he had the misfortune to be clumsy at football and he was generally considered "unChelton," a damning indictment in that small, standardized world, but in due time the natural friendliness and obvious sincerity of his disposition together with a sense of humor so rare in the very young defied the rigid classifications of his formmates and ultimately blunted even the spite of small boy mob rule. From then on he knew something like popularity though he was never to be a leader. His romantic and religious temperament absorbed happily the atmosphere of idealism in which the school was drenched. The veteran headmaster whom Beverly worshiped was a great, strong, holy man, whose absolute leadership was felt by every boy and even, in after life, by the most abandoned graduate. He thundered principles of civic responsibility from his pulpit; he vainly urged public life to boys who, though impressed, were already earmarked for Wall Street; and Beverly, his eyes tightly closed as he knelt in prayer before partaking of the communion cup and wafer, a warm, roseate glow throughout his body, throbbed with the splendor of his preparation for a life devoted to the advancement of his fellow men.

Outside the chapel he plunged busily into a round of extracurricular activity. In his third form year when he was fourteen he had accepted by the "Cheltonian" a poem beginning:

> "What is it all? What does it mean?
> Human cogs in a big machine?"

—a proposition that was triumphantly flouted in a final stanza that fairly bristled with apostolic fervor. At sixteen, more sophisticated but still ardent, he was one of the editors of the magazine, stage designer for the dramatic society, and held the coveted position of rober for the headmaster in chapel. He developed passionate friendships, took long walks in the countryside, and composed gobs of poetry including a forty-page effort in blank verse to deplore the execution of the last Czarina of Russia. When Beverly graduated he had one clear ambition: to return to Chelton after college as a teacher and spend his life in the pure simplicity of its atmosphere.

At Yale he elected, almost exclusively, courses in English and French literature and the history of art, read a vast number of moderately worthwhile novels, and went to New York on the weekends. It was the age of the "super" debutante party, and he attended them all. He even managed to supplement the slender allowance that his mother made him by drawing up lists of eligible extra men with confidential annotations for an entertainment bureau that supplied Manhattan hostesses with the additional number of guests necessary to swell their parties to accepted size. For nobody could know that many people. A more substantial increase in income, however, came during the long college summers. Through one of his aunts he got a job as tutor to young Arleus Stroud, yes, *the* Arleus Stroud he always had to add when people looked up at the name, or rather his son, and thus became an intimate of the indefatigable Angeline. He was always to be met at her large, hard, formal dinners and gayer weekends; he was one of the "inseparables," too, of her beautiful blonde sister-in-law, Mrs. Goodhue Stroud, whose face and complexion were so well known to the greater public, lost in the massages of a facial cocktail or looming through clouds of Camel smoke. It was the beginning of an established life in a Stroud world beside the splendidness of which the Stregelinus tradition seemed dowdy and mildewed.

At Yale he was elected to Psi U, along with other Cheltonians, but the tenor of his life, even taking into consideration a few poems that had appeared in the "Lit" and attracted some admiration in undergraduate circles, was not felt to be sufficiently in the Eli tradition to warrant his elevation to any of the austere secret societies and "Tap Day," to his extreme disappointment for he was an enthusiastic wishful thinker, passed him by unnoticed. Like hundreds of others he believed himself a failure for a whole week.

As graduation approached he was obliged to face the future. The headmaster of Chelton had recently died, which dampened his enthusiasm about teaching there even assuming that the new administration would accept him. What he wanted to do was to be a poet, but how could one settle down at home right after graduation and just write poems? It was unheard of. He hadn't even developed a style. His best work, written in conscious imitation of Christina Rossetti (*When I am dead, my dearest* was his favorite English lyric) was permeated with a standard melancholy, distinctive only in occasional touches of "whimsy" that recalled Emily Dickinson's less successful nature poems. His worst consisted of heavy, adjectival Swinburnian lyrics on the seasons of the year and the tumults of love. He could write also some not unpleasant Browningesque monodramas in blank verse, narrated usually by an American heiress unhappily married to an Italian duke or an aged society dowager looking dreamily and philosophically back on the intrigues of a long and busy life. His favorite modern poet was Amy Lowell, and he hoped some day when he had time to write her life. But all this didn't add up to an occupation that his mother would recognize as such.

He decided to postpone the problem by going to law school, a decision which pleased such Stregelinuses as were still interested, but he evaded the sordid grind and competition of northern schools by selecting the University of Virginia. For a year he rode and dined out and drank. Needless to say, he read very little law. At Charlottesville the University, the hunting set, the countryside, and the town blend into a strange and, delightful cocktail of white columns, red brick, and conviviality, and Bev was not one to allow what he considered the senseless casuistry of appellate courts to stand in the way of his enjoyment of life.

After his first year he decided to anticipate failure by resigning and accepted a job that had been offered him by the Salberg Art Galleries through the auspices of Mrs. Henry Livermore. It was just such a job as he had dreamed of, offering as it did a daily association with beautiful things, short hours, and a lot of time for poetic reflection. His knowledge of art was limited but his knowledge of the customers was profound, and thus, despite his incurable lateness, his blatant two hours off for lunch, and his interminable

personal telephone conversations right in the main gallery
while buyers stood about waiting he managed to hold down
the job for seven years. The tall figure in unpressed grey
flannels and a sport coat in defiance of all sartorial custom,
with the long, messy, blondish hair and the loud laugh, spinning about amid Renoirs and Manets and loudly greeting
friends at the door became well known in the social and art
world. At home he lived with his mother and sister. Amy
didn't approve at all of his job or his social life, but she
loved having him with her and safely employed. She even
submitted to a reversal of their roles and allowed him to
accompany her to dress shops where he made valiant but
vain efforts to improve her appearance. He protested feverishly about her clothes, her hair, her lack of make-up; he
tried to make her go out more; he wanted her to learn
bridge, but though she made no protest and took his interest
for the genuine manifestation of love that it was, yet in her
quiet Boston way she managed to change not one iota of her
serene schedule.

An extra man is proverbially sought after, and Beverly was
the ideal extra man. People knew he didn't come because he
needed the dinner, as was sometimes the case, especially
with refugees, and they knew he didn't come for any advantage, social or financial, or even because he was bored. He
came because he liked them, and he made their dinners
"go." Bev liked everybody it seemed. He had, and what a
case of symbiosis it was, a particular leaning for that great
giver of dinners, the lady of middle age; he could enjoy the
most interminable tête-à-tête with Mrs. Livermore on the
subject of her wayward daughters; he could chat excitedly
with Mrs. Kingsland on the question of her lost faith. Yes,
dowagers adored him. He exuded an atmosphere of genuine
good humor and optimism; he made everyone, even the hostile, have a good time, conveying somehow a contagious
feeling that the present was after all a time to be enjoyed.
His loud laughs and bad jokes were irresistible. Oh, of course,
he was called a butterfly and worse; he had plenty of ene-
mies, but nobody thought him a climber. It was obvious that
he had no plan or ambition. He gravitated naturally to the
atmosphere of large drawing rooms; he floated easily and
carelessly from country house to country house. And he knew
everybody. He was an intimate of the inner rim, what he
called the "Seventieth-Street crowd," the very rich and active
bankers and lawyers who lived in large houses on side streets

and shunned the flashier summer colonies and rotogravure sections—a world in which Mrs. Stroud and her sister-in-law were noted figures; he appeared frequently at Elsa Maxwell's parties and knew all about the unrooted souls who came to be called "cafe society"; nor did he neglect those elderly remnants of the last century's great industrial names living amid the moldy rococo of their Fifth Avenue turrets. With some of the latter category it was pure kindness, for he was always kind. When he went to the large and chaotic receptions at Mrs. Emden's, considered by the uninitiated press as "the last stronghold of Knickerbocker sociey," it was out of genuine affection and sympathy for that ancient and addled lady, then so surrounded by sycophants. He extended his activities to Europe. On one trip to England taken vaguely in connection with art gallery purchases, he stayed for a month with the Duchess of Baymeath and was said to have talked all one evening with the Queen on her favorite topic of old china. "I'm nothing but a mite of observation," he happily declared to his friends; "I skip about and gather material." He told himself sometimes that he would store it all up for an epic poem; he even visualized himself as a sort of rhyming Proust, but he had no plan. Time went by.

He continued to write poetry but in decreasing amounts. He had on nine or ten occasions during his seven years at Salberg's had poems published in magazines of varying repute, once actually by the *Atlantic Monthly*, and it is impossible to exaggerate the reassurance which this gave him. He had to think of himself as something, and he liked the idea of being a poet; only thus could he square in any fashion the persistent sense of duty that remained from his Chelton days. He still clung to the idea that at the favorable moment (he was not in sympathy with the new headmaster) he might return to Chelton and revolutionize the presentation of poetry to young minds. But he had his uneasy moments. Was there time? In 1939 came war in Europe, in 1940 his thirtieth birthday. It was rather unsettling. He even began to worry about the slender quantity of his poetic output. Could his muse, like Matthew Arnold's, have atrophied?

He was still a bachelor, which intensified his growing sense of speeding years and small accomplishment. Furthermore, he was not only without sexual experience but he had never really been in love. The period of hero worship in boyhood had lasted for a long time with him; it had even survived to his adulthood in the form of an intense and sentimental affection for his male friends, definitely tapping the amount of emotions readily accessible for the opposite sex. He had believed himself in love on two or three occasions; he had even fancied himself imbued with a guilty and hopeless passion for Mrs. Goodhue Stroud which had been the subject of his less happy Swinburnian odes; but the thin quality of emotion combined with a strong natural timidity in such matters and the pleasure of romantic self-pity were sufficient to keep him from mentioning his indiscretion. Bella Stroud enjoyed such silent veneration; it titillated and never embarrassed. But Bev in time began to worry about himself. He invented robust tales for masculine consumption which were, of course, disbelieved. It was odd, he often reflected, that he should be so self-conscious in sex and so brash in everything else. The long maternal association had something to do with it. Amy was a prude. She knew this and knew instinctively that she must conceal it or be called old-fashioned by her children. She never, therefore, talked about love. She was above it. She made it seem immature, if not sordid, by her scant and deprecatory references. Bev had grown up in the firm belief that people like his mother were never bothered or tempted by sex but waited serenely for the great spiritual bond of married love which in due time came to all who were worthy. He had been ashamed of the secret perturbations that went on inside him. This reverence for the maternal attitude did not survive Yale, but upon his return to life at home after his year at law school more of it revived than he ever suspected. Amy's was a strong personality despite all her nervousness, and Bev was nothing if not impressionable. At thirty he had stretched the many postponements of his life as far as he possibly could without becoming too different a person from his dreams, but the experimental period of youth was over, and dimly, he felt that it had been wasted. Then misfortunes seemed to crowd upon him. The war abroad tarnished the luster of the party world; his mother's trust fund suffered an alarming loss and in June of 1941 he lost his job.

CHAPTER THREE

IT WAS ON a July afternoon in the middle of the week not long after the unfortunate episode in the gallery that Beverly was sitting with his mother on a private club beach on the North Shore of Long Island watching the ships idle down the Sound. It was a hot, hazy day; the shore of Connecticut was barely visible as a grey line, and the stillness in the air was broken only by the sudden, cackling hysteria of gulls as they circled over the beach. Most of the members were working in town or had left for New England vacations; the beach was almost deserted except for two or three groups of children with their nurses playing on the sand. Beverly and his mother were in bathing suits under a large yellow umbrella; they had just finished a salad lunch, and the plates lay aimlessly beside them.

"What are you going to do this afternoon?" she asked.

It was certainly a harmless question, but he had been waiting for it just as he waited now for all her questions. He could feel so strongly that she was only veiling her concern over his idleness in the little, timid, apparently casual interrogations that followed one another through the hot days that he and she were spending in the gatehouse cottage which the Strouds had loaned them on their place in Westbury.

"Oh, nothing in particular," he answered impatiently. "What does it matter?"

"It doesn't matter," she said quickly. "Not at all."

He glanced up at her and saw the studied effect of indifference. She acted so badly, he reflected miserably, and he was such a brute to make her. But there seemed to be things in his ego which his better nature could only contemplate in subdued dismay.

"You know I have nothing to do," he said with pointless self-pity.

It was she now who withdrew. It was clear that she didn't

like to encourage this line of talk. She ignored his remark by turning her large eyes towards the sea.

"I hear that Sylvia and her mother are still here," she said.

It was perfectly obvious that she must have known this.

"Yes. I'm going there this afternoon."

Mrs. Stregelinus took a cigarette out of a rather battered case.

"I suppose they'll be going off to Maine soon."

"I suppose."

"Madeleine was asking me if you and Sylvia were engaged."

He looked at her suspiciously.

"And what did you say?" he asked.

"I said of course not." She got her cigarette lighted on the second match.

"Oh. Why so sure?"

"Well." She smiled. "You may be a little past the age of impetuousness. But you haven't reached the age of desperation."

He sat up angrily. She was really becoming uncomfortably frank as she grew older. As an adult son he felt instinctively that the parental attitude though pardonably possessive should be blindly admiring.

"Mother, I wish you'd make some effort to like my friends! You never approve of the things I do. You don't care a hoot about my poetry. I don't know what it is. We seem to scrap all the time this summer."

Amy could take this in all serenity. She loved her children, but she never truly believed that they had more than a transient affection for her, or for that matter that any children ever really cared about their parents. The idea seemed entirely natural to her.

"I don't do any more scrapping than I used to," she pointed out calmly. "It's you, dear. Besides, you don't ever show me your poetry now. Have you been writing much lately?" She leaned back against the umbrella pole in an attitude that suggested a perfect willingness to listen.

He stared uncomfortably, hating to confess his lack of productivity and knowing that she was aware of it.

"I wish you'd let me read your new things," she continued. "I promise that I won't even open my mouth about them unless you ask me."

"But, Mother, you don't care."

"Don't care about what?"

"About the poems. They don't seem important to you. You're always comparing me with Shakespeare or Wordsworth. And, Lord, how can I stand up to that?"

"They were great poets."

He groaned.

"I know. Everything that's not Homer or Shakespeare or Tolstoy—out the window. If you can't be the tip top why bother? That's it, isn't it?"

"I don't like to see you making yourself unhappy with your own dissatisfaction," she said earnestly. "It's not worth it. You should think of your health."

"Health!" he exclaimed. "There you go again. I don't think you'd care if Madeleine and I were absolute dunces as long as we were in good health." He stood up and stared at the water. "If you could turn us into two contented cows with guaranteed longevity you'd do it like a shot. Then you could tie us up on the lawn and watch us chewing our cuds and say: 'There are my children—all well.'"

She only laughed at him and the fantastic injustice of it.

"I care about your happiness as well as your health, dear," she said more seriously. "After all, what else besides those things really matters?"

"You don't really think I'll ever amount to anything, do you?" he asked aggressively. "You don't ever think I could write a really good poem?" He was acting like a small child determined to find a grievance. He and his sister took an unconscious daily revenge for the past exercise of the maternal power that their mother had once held over them. They had been overdependent as children and instinctively they now resented the molding influence that they knew she had had. They kept her constantly under analysis, examining each tick in her make-up, discovering in her least actions the reminder of some interference with childhood plans that could now be coherently resented.

Amy put out her cigarette and smoothed her rumpled hair.

"I've never said you wouldn't be any good," she answered. "I don't think whether or not you could write *good* poetry is the issue. It's really whether or not you want to write poetry at all."

"Want to write at all!" he exclaimed.

"Certainly. I don't think for a minute that you were satisfied with your job at Salberg's. And I certainly don't think the New York social scene has been an adequate outlet for your energies. But you do have an ego, and a good deal of suppressed ambition. That you get from my father, I think—"

"I suppose you're going to say I should have been a bishop."

"I'm going to have my say, dear," she continued firmly. "You and Madeleine are always having fun with me. Fair is fair. I think you feel that whatever else you do is going to be justified by this poetry which is to get you the recognition that the gallery has failed to supply. You see I've thought this out carefully, darling," she said, noticing his thunderstruck expression. "Your poems will be the apologia for a type of life that doesn't really satisfy you. But that isn't a sufficient basis to write poetry on, is it? So the issue is as I say not whether you will write good poetry but whether you'll be able to write any at all."

There was a considerable silence during which Bev tried to collect himself. The rout had been complete.

"Mother, dear, you're wonderful," he said at last with emotion in his voice. "As your friends say, you're always right. But what to do about it?"

He sat down by her and she put her hand on his shoulder.

"Wait till you get really interested in something, my darling," she said. "Or even someone. All these problems will fall into line." She reached down and patted his hand. "Let's go and get dressed, dear," she told him. "If you're going to see Sylvia we'd better get started."

In the bathhouse as he climbed out of his damp bathing trunks and into his rumpled seersucker suit he reviewed carefully his long association with the Strouds. Mother and daughter certainly offered a curious contrast. Angeline Stroud his family had always known, but he and she had not become real friends until the summer when he got the job as young Arlie's tutor. Arlie and Beatrice were the children of her second marriage; her first, to a much older man, Livingston Tremaine, had lasted for only a few years and was little mentioned. She, the only daughter in a large, rich, dowdy family whose amiability and ugly mansions had covered Atlantic summer resorts before the First World War, had been married when very young and taken off to live in Paris. Tremaine had been, apparently, a person of exaggerated taste and exaggerated sensibility, a collector of Van Loo and Lancret, a hypochondriac who snuggled down deeper each year into the large, empty bed of his self-pity. It was a life that Angeline made valiant but rarely successful efforts to understand, and the sudden infantile paralysis that struck the little family after the war, killing Tremaine and leaving the baby Sylvia maimed for life, at least had the beneficial result of bringing her back to her native shores.

Her reaction had been a strong one; the Van Loos and Lancrets were speedily auctioned, and she settled down in the tasteless comfort of her big family house in Westbury and the somber ostentation of her wide brownstone in New York. But she had conceived, even through the tiny Tremaine microscope, a vision of what her life might be on a cruder, more magnified scale. Her second husband, Arleus Stroud, the senior partner of Stroud Dubrotnick, a firm of lawyers that guided as well as advised corporate clients the world over, was a man more of her choosing. Energy was the keynote of their lives; they worked and entertained and traveled; they became of all couples in New York the one that most immediately charged a gathering with an air of seriousness and distinction.

Sylvia Tremaine on the other hand had always been "poor Sylvia," a little, dark shadow of a step-child growing against the pageantry of her mother's life, peering reluctantly at guests from the top of stairways, envying her younger brother as he pounded a ball against the backboard of a tennis court. Not indeed that she had been neglected. Angeline did her best to make her interesting and personally attended to her wardrobe, rightly insisting on a note of the exotic and European. The net result: a Sylvia attired in shiny and expensive black with very high heels, heavy, gold jewelry, and a huge chain bracelet that clanked on her left wrist had something of the lugubrious fascination of an El Greco. It was a mystery too that was rarely elucidated to the observer, for Sylvia, morbidly shy and self-conscious, educated entirely at home, opened up her heart to only one or two friends. She had few enough of them though, Lord knows; she had met enough people, and Bev was perfectly aware not only that he was the closest of the friends but that her feeling for him was probably of a deeper nature.

It had all started that summer ten years ago. The sight of Sylvia, timid and lonely, in that active household had appealed to his sense of pity; he had forced himself on her attention and had made her tell him about the books she was reading. Aided and abetted by Angeline he used to drag her out of the library and make her go dancing at roadhouses up and down the North Shore. At first she hardly opened her mouth—it had been impossible for her mother even to make her come out the year before—but under the spell of his noisy friendliness she gradually warmed. It was not long before it even became a pleasure to him. Sylvia like so many shy people talked with unusual ease and candor to anyone who could break through the barrier and her intelligence was certainly clear. The world she lived in was very small, but she applied all her accurate machinery of observation to people in her immediate vicinity, her mother and step-father, her Aunt Bella, her half-brother and half-sister, and ultimately Beverly. She was constantly re-analyzing and re-testing her conclusions, and except for Arlie, Jr., whom she blindly adored, she could be intensely critical. This, however, arose not from any smallness in her nature but from the height of her standards; she breathed the isolated air of a sincere idealism and was genuinely stricken at the so frequent deviations that she found even in her own little world. Sylvia had no use on earth for the shoddy or the second rate. In the poverty of her emotional life it may have been easy for her to eschew compromise, but at any rate eschew it she did. She had an independence that was as fierce as it was undemonstrative; with it she fought her solitary battle against the steady encroachments of ill health and despair. Bev learned to admire her totally, though he was often uncomfortable at the freedom with which she criticized him. The friendship which they formed that summer had lasted through the years.

But now, he reflected, as he straightened his tie and went outside to wait for his mother, now perhaps it was different. There was the undeniable sinking of his prospects; there was the fact that all his friends were married, many of them twice. One could go on, batting around aimlessly, but where did one get? The Strouds were his closest friends. In the crumble of his hopes it seemed only natural to be on "real" terms with them. Not just a "visitor," he thought almost angrily as he walked up and down the cement pavement outside the bathhouses, not just a person who always had to leave after a friendly call and be discussed, however much liked, after his departure, but—

But there was his mother, dressed and coming towards him, and a moment later they were getting into his car. He drove in silence the five miles inland to the Strouds; his mother seemed to realize that she had given him enough for one day for she sat perfectly quiet and looked out the window. He stopped just beyond the big grey pillars that marked the Stroud driveway and let her out at their little cottage. Then he gave her a little wave of his hand and proceeded on up the gravel drive.

Angeline's house was big, square, and plain; it stood boldly naked surrounded by lawn. It consisted of two grey stories of oversized Gothic built around a courtyard and a fountain that was never turned on. Bev parked his car near the great stone porte-cochere and went into the dark, cool front hall, its huge table covered, as he could dimly make out, with red boxes of tennis balls. From here he crossed two living rooms, their dim walls cluttered with the wrong Corots, over-framed, to a long game room where he found Angeline and three other ladies playing bridge. She fluttered a hand at him; he was too much one of her household for formalities and introductions.

"Is Syvvie outside?" he asked.

"Waiting for you, my dear. Remember, don't take her for a long walk. She's not feeling too well."

He nodded and stepped out on the back terrace. Sylvia was practicing croquet shots on the lawn. She was wearing a white and spotless dress, a red bandana drawn tightly over her head, small, tightly laced sneakers and a pair of large sun glasses. Her lips, isolated with her upturned nose and oval chin, twitched as she waved to him.

"Ready to start?" she asked.

"Where are we going?"

"Over to the pasture and back."

"Syvvie, it's so hot!"

"You promised," she retorted with a characteristic jerk of her shoulders, "that you'd take a walk with me today."

"Oh, I'm game."

And they walked across the lawn and into a path through the woods. She talked very little as they went along; she needed her breath and concentration for the physical effort involved. As for Beverly, his mind was throbbing with the question of the opportuneness of the moment. He wanted to emphasize his loneliness and need of her and to stress their underlying congeniality and friendship without invoking the hues of a romantic sentiment which, try as he would, he was only too conscious of not feeling. But he had read enough about love to know that women expect emotion or at least a pretense thereof. He hated to be a hypocrite, but if it was the only way to conclude a step that was perfectly obviously not merely for his own happiness but for hers, and if, after all, the existence or nonexistence of passion was a purely subjective question, wasn't it perhaps justifiable to dash a little powder on the pale face of his proposal? As far as sex was concerned, he knew that he was more attracted to Sylvia's seventeen-year-old half-sister, Beatrice, than he was to Sylvia. But why, he reflected bitterly and irrelevantly, did he always take it so for granted that girls like Beatrice wouldn't look at him? Well, anyway, if they once might have they wouldn't now; he was thirty-one—and was he going to sit back and chatter for Angeline forever? They came suddenly out of the woods and found themselves in the pasture. Bev found a moss-covered rock on the top of a little incline from which they could watch the sluggish Stroud cows. He spread out his sweater for her to sit on and sat down beside her, chewing a long blade of grass.

"The brown and white one over there—the big one, I mean—looks just like Lucy Emden." He pointed.

"Must you come over to insult our cows?" she asked.

"That's being a little rough," he protested. "Even on Lucy."

She glanced at him impatiently and then looked back at the cows.

"What *do* you see in people like that?" she demanded.

"Oh, they pass the time."

"They pass your time."

"They amuse me then."

"Why don't you write something about them? They ought to be put to some use."

He didn't of all things want a repetition of the devastating conversation that he had had with his mother that afternoon on the subject of his writing.

"Why don't you write?" he retorted.

"Write what? Or doesn't it matter?"

"Well, say, a novel." He was cautious about permitting himself the assumption that any novice could write poetry. "I should think you could write a very good novel."

"But I don't like novels. Modern ones that is."

"That's a silly thing to say."

"Why?" she asked. "It's true."

"They're not all alike."

"Certainly they are." She crossed her legs and leaned more comfortably back against the rock while he lit a cigarette for her. "They're all erotic. Full of ordinary everyday, rather self-conscious people being erotic. It's part of what I suppose Wolfe would have called their 'teeming, sweating, earthy vigor.' And the heroines are always looking at their breast in the mirror and feeling their hips."

She laughed as she said this, her usual labored gasping laugh, exposing her long upper teeth with a facial expression that for purely muscular reasons seemed to personify a lonely and superior disdain. Bev felt a stab of irritation as he looked at her; he reflected cruelly that a contemplation of herself in the mirror could hardly bring her much satisfaction.

"Maybe heroines do look at their breasts in mirrors," he retorted.

"Maybe. They do other even less attractive things. But why is it a subject for fiction?"

"Don't you think ordinary people have a right to some place in fiction?"

"A 'right'? No, not a 'right.' "

"Well, who would you want novelists to write about?"

She inhaled deeply and appeared to think. She held the cigarette away from her and kept constantly tapping it to remove the ash.

"Oh, Hamlets, Lears," she said. "Remarkable people. Great people. Of course I know we live in an equalizing age where it's snobbish to be different, but what's that to me? If I don't choose to be interested in Mr. Man-in-the-Street or whoever he is, that's my affair. I want to look up, not down."

"The way they do in Germany?"

"Don't be idiotic."

He looked at her in some perplexity.

"Well, why don't you write a novel about remarkable people then?"

She laughed again.

"Because I don't know any."

"Make them up."

She pondered.

"I have them in my mind. Why put them in a book?"

"So I could enjoy them."

"But when I write about them they turn into little people."

He pounced on this.

"So you *have* written?"

"I confess to you, I did write a novel once."

Bev became quite excited at this.

"What was it about? You never told me. Did you try to publish it?"

"Lord no."

"Why not?"

"Because I found I had nothing to say that Mrs. Wharton hadn't said better and, of course, I couldn't stand that."

"I like Edith Wharton."

"I'm sure you do."

He let this pass.

"Tell me what it was about."

"Oh it was too silly."

"Please, Syvvie."

She looked at his earnest face and smiled.

"Can't you picture it? A lot of apathetic young people, cultivated and living on capital, talking intelligently, so intelligently, about the cosmic forces that are destroying them. And finally after a series of inconsequential incidents which they take with appalling seriousness and a great many elephantine witticisms, Peter Trevor and Evelyn Pierpont find their salvation in a decision which to them is fraught with implications—something like spending the summer in town instead of the country—and I leave them on a garden bench, their souls at last opened, their eyes filled with an infinite understanding. Satisfied?"

He was not altogether comfortable as she unfolded her little plot. The ridicule in which she drenched her simple story was vital enough to cover wider and analogous fields; it was after all an assault on a certain recognized concept of beauty and one which he himself deeply shared. Besides, it provided an atmosphere in the highest degree uncongenial for the matter that he had in hand.

"Shall we go back?" he suggested without commenting on her novel.

"I suppose."

He reached down and helped her up.

"We mustn't be too late. Your mother will get ideas about us."

He bit his tongue after he had said it.

Sylvia turned to him at first with a little smile, painfully forced. Then she looked away.

"No doubt. Mothers never lose hope," she said dryly and walked on ahead of him.

"Oh, my mother never wants me to get married," he said, following her.

She didn't turn around.

"Let's hope you gratify her then," she said over her shoulder.

He walked on in silence. Rarely had an opening seemed less auspicious.

"But if I don't want to?" he called to her.

"Don't want to what?"

"Gratify mother."

"Then let's hope she consoles herself."

He drew a deep breath.

"Which is more important: to please your mother or mine?"

She drew up and turned around her lips quivering.

"Really, Bev, you can be insufferable."

"I was only asking—"

"My mother has nothing in the world to do with my life."

"Oh, Sylvia!"

"With my emotions then."

She turned to walk on.

"Syvvie, you're making it very hard for me."

"What?"

"What do you think?"

He had assumed the injured role, but he could see by the white, drawn intensity of her face as she turned back on him that the whole matter was on an unpleasantly factual basis.

"Beverly, are you proposing to me?"

Her voice was clear and angry. He had never seen her look uglier.

"And if I am?"

"Nothing," she said curtly. "Nothing at all."

"You mean 'No.'"

"I mean 'Certainly not.'"

He bristled with sudden pique.

"Am I so repulsive?"

"You can be. You are now."

"Perhaps you will explain your fantastic lack of manners, Sylvia," he said with ill-timed iciness.

"I will," she retorted her shoulders jerking as she spoke. "It's because I resent the role you've selected for me. It's because I don't give a damn about the things you care about, if you must know. I don't want any part of that tasteful flat in the 'right' younger married area off Lexington Avenue just filled with the lamp shades and silver and Steuben glass ash trays that your friends have sent. And I don't want your 'well served dinners of eight' with 'good food, good wine, good talk,' as you once so nauseatingly expressed it. And Aunt Bella playing hostess in my own home. And Mummie just beaming at the whole thing and throwing her filthy money at both of us!"

"Sylvia!"

He had flushed hotly and clenched his fists. He felt something like hate for the gawky girl who stood there so imperiously flinging insults.

"Well?" she asked.

"Is that all I mean to you?"

"It's all *I* mean to you," she retorted with a catch in her breath.

"Husbands don't grow on trees, you know."

"No. But you ought to."

He would have made an answering retort had he not been surprised and ashamed by the sudden apparition of her tears. She quickly recovered her emotion in a simulated sneeze and a large silk handkerchief and turned away abruptly. The rest of the way they walked in silence.

CHAPTER FOUR

BEVERLY'S NEW YORK in the autumn of 1941 was an unsettled town. It was a a city of rumors, of draft stories, of applications for commissions, of a gaiety that seemed the fruit of an almost deliberate effort to cash in on a "what the heck" war fever, of a sense of doom so strong to us in retrospect that in some anomalous fashion it has become part of the time before the event occurred. The young men of his acquaintance and numbers of the older ones were on the verge of "getting into something"; in lunch clubs, in bars, and after the ladies had left the dinner table, conversation throbbed with the excitement of impending change. Some of the patriotism was genuine of course, but predominantly the atmosphere was one of getting "fixed up." Gone was the evanescent feeling of the winter before that even the ranks had their allure, that a commission should be preceded by the liberalizing experience of enlisted life. Now the talk bristled with "my uncle, Colonel So-and-So says there's an opening in—" and "Of course, if there's a war he wants to be right in the thick of it, but there are so few people who know what he knows about—" There was an increasing consciousness of special aptitudes and a higher value set on the dimly remembered courses of college days. Everyone had a horrible tale on his lips of a friend who had been drafted and given a most unfitting assignment. "A perfect waste, you know."

Different types of commissions had their waves of popularity. The Navy with its policy of granting them directly to civilians was always in the lead. One month Bev's friends would all be going to PT boats; the next Naval Intelligence would be the organization most whispered among the clink of glasses. Motives, pure, mixed, and snobbish permeated the atmosphere. And the amount of medical talk was phenomenal, of bad eyes, poor feet, lung trouble, and the impossibility of obtaining waivers. Bev was interminably button-

holed to be interminably told of the number of applications
So-and-So had made, and how if it only weren't for color-
blindness or a heart murmur of flat feet he would now be
in the RAF and bombing the cities of Germany.

There had been nothing in Beverly's autumn in the way
of a job to call him in from Long Island—for he had not
made up with Salberg—but he had made his vague promise
to Bella Stroud to work for Rufus Henderson's Intervention
Now Committee after the summer season and to his surprise
he found himself very definitely taken up on this in a letter
from Henderson himself. It was practically a summons, and
he docilely left for New York, just as glad as a matter of fact
to leave the vicinity where Angeline and Sylvia were still
lingering. His casualness, however, was destined to be replaced with an electric ardor. Henderson was tremendous;
he was an ex-newspaper editor who was touring the country
to sign up as many as possible in favor of an outright declaration of war against Germany. Tall, grey, and determined,
he gave an impression of Old Testament force which he had
no hesitation in intensifying by the use of loud-speakers, spot-
lights, and large numbers of refugees who trooped in and out
of the halls he spoke in, bearing the banners of their now
occupied nations. He would point a long finger at the delighted
crowd and thunder: "Ye are like the Laodiceans; ye are
neither hot nor cold, and the Lord God will spew you out
of his mouth!"

Bev was completely impressed; he was always happiest
when swept away in the tumultuous current of all-out enthusiasm for a "great" person and this was an opportunity he
had no intention of losing. He couldn't indeed afford to lose
it, for his prospects had never looked more dismal. He
leaped to catch the chance and gratefully undertook to handle
correspondence in the New York office. It wasn't difficult
and it involved a good deal of seeing and arguing with angry
people which he enjoyed in his new conviction of the glory
of the war. His mother proved a definite opponent for she
was strongly isolationist, so the conflict that raged all day
stormed into the home at night. But all the chatter on all
sides, so full of "life lines" and "aid short of war" and
"Britain fighting our battles" was ninety-nine parts emotions
and only one part brains, and Bev was able to romp happily
in the midst of it, blissfully ignoring statistics and communi-
qués. He even became impatient with emotion not related
to the war and had a slight falling out with his dear, old,

beautiful friend; lovely, fluffy, pearled, and furred Mrs. Emden with whom he had from earliest days shared a faith in the potency of beauty.

"Don't forget," she said firmly at an exhibition of Renoirs that they attended together, "that we still have this." She pointed to a small canvas of the beach at Dinard and tapped him on the wrist with her lorgnette. "The patch of sun on a wave. They can't take that away, can they? Not with all their Hitlers and Communists."

He could still clutch at it, the rapturous melancholy of the romantic, all that was in him that could "yearn" still tried to "yearn," but the patch wasn't enough. And his nose wrinkled at the unmistakable evidence that she was, poor dear, still drinking.

"But one needs more these days," he said. "Don't you think?"

"Of course you have the war," she answered. "Oh, yes. *You* have that."

Yes, he had it. He dined out in large hotels for stricken Greece; he danced for Norway; he drank for Poland and Czechoslovakia. Beautiful Bella Stroud swept him along in her world of bazaars and bundles, of appeals and ambulances. But, like the patch on the wave, even Bella and Henderson failed after a couple of months to occupy in any substantial way the void he felt aching in him, the void that all the preceding years from Chelton up had so noisily assured him would never come to anyone who "cared." And yet he "cared" so much!

He went through many crises. At moments he was on the verge of signing up for ambulance driving in Africa; he reveled in the vague picture of assisting the wounded under a tropic sky, of an intelligence confused but finding a noble escape in submersion in far off scenes of effort. But he didn't. And there were times when he almost welcomed the draft, the idea of slipping into the vast anonymity of army life, fading away as his adored Keats had said "into the forest dim," and quite forgetting the weariness and the fret. Sufficient details, however, reached him from his many acquaintances of crowded army lavatory facilities to effectively destroy this latter mood. His mother too contributed, for she was quite candid about her lack of faith as to his happiness in army ranks. And Angeline Stroud and Bella and all the others incessantly badgered him about "doing something" and not "just going in the draft." At the Armory

Club bar he heard more of the same, and the desire grew also to have his own small application to talk about amid the general dither.

So one day he went down to 90 Church Street, headquarters of the Third Naval District, though with a feeling of shyness at the prospect of the demands of the military and his own general unfitness. He knew plenty of men down there, but mostly of the robust elderly variety who would clap him on the back with an "I know what you want, Bev, old fellow" and have him chopping about on the mid-Atlantic before the month was over. No, he visualized some other sort of job, something that might take him abroad after a bit but that would definitely leave him on dry land. He didn't, however, like to say this, and certainly not to anyone he knew, so he sat disconsolately on a long bench with other applicants who had filled out forms, each with a red identification tag tied to his lapel. The questionnaire had certainly not encouraged him. He knew nothing of any field remotely scientific; he had no experience in office management, journalism, law, or advertising. His only language was French and he could hardly boast of it. He was reduced to the absurd hope that they might want him for a subsidiary art course to broaden the naval midshipmen at Annapolis.

He finally passed behind a counter into a room filled with desks and the buzz of typewriters and found himself facing a tall, spare, lanky naval officer whose desk was littered with forms similar to the one he had filled out. The latter waved to him to sit down, and he did so, wishing the audience were less public. He looked hopefully through the window at the tugs on the Hudson; it was a beautiful, clear day. At least we have that, he repeated to himself.

"I've read your questionnaire, Mr. Stregelinus," the officer said, "and I'm not sure that I know exactly what sort of a commission it is you want. Did you want sea duty?"

Beverly paused miserably.

"Well, isn't there some mathematics requirement? I'm not sure what it is but I'm afraid I couldn't satisfy it if it's more than two times two."

The officer conceded only the stoniest ghost of a smile, perfunctory at that.

"That's for the reserve Midshipman's School. But you're too old for that. Commissions are sometimes given directly to men with some navigational experience. But you have none?"

"None at all," Bev said quickly, with as gloomy a look as he could muster.

"Then what exactly did you have in mind?"

Bev stirred in his chair in discomfort.

"I thought you might need someone in personnel work or something like that. And I speak some French—"

"How much?"

"Oh, I get along."

"Yes, but we need more than that. What sort of personnel experience do you have?"

Bev smiled sheepishly.

"Well—none, really."

"I see. Well, there you are."

But here Bev hazarded a smothered protest.

"I don't think this is quite fair."

"Fair? What do you mean?"

"I see people all over with commissions." He waved a hand vaguely. "And I know they haven't any more experience in anything than I have."

"Who for example?"

He grew bold.

"Commander Dunlap. He was a broker."

The officer showed a flicker of interest.

"You know Commander Dunlap?"

"Very well."

"Of course he was in the last war. That gives a lot of them a chance at higher ranks. Did you ever think of trying for Naval Information?"

Beverly beamed. He had no idea what it was but it sounded quiet.

"Do you think I might have a chance?"

"All I can do is send you over. Hold on." He dialed a number on his phone and looked Bev up and down as he waited. "What's your situation with Selective Service?"

"Oh, they'll get me eventually."

"Not right away?"

"No."

The officer suddenly swung around on his swivel chair and leaned both elbows on the table. "Oh, Doug," he said into the phone. "Sorry to bother you. I have a Mr. Stregelinus here, and I thought you might possibly be interested in talking to him." He glanced at Bev's application blank. "Yale graduate, aged 31, and worked in an art gallery. Knows Commander Dunlap. Shall I send him over? O.K."

He hung up and turned to Beverly. "100 Church Street, eighth floor, and ask for Lieutenant (j.g.) Keyo. Good luck." And he stretched out a hand which was gratefully taken.

Bev hurried out in a flutter of nerves and a sense that somehow he was already "in." Infinitely further in anyway than the long line of woebegone waiters outside in the corridor that he now traversed with so brisk and lighthearted a step. He would have liked to have had lunch, to take time out as it were to celebrate, but prudence directed him through the Church Street throng to No. 100. Here was the same crowd of red-tagged young men, but the offices were dingy and the wait longer. Mr. Keyo had just gone out for lunch, which struck Bev as quite in keeping with the exalted rank of the people behind the marine sentry's barrier. He never even considered going out himself and returning later; patiently he read the columns of yesterday's *Daily Mirror*.

But the interview, when it finally came after following a Marine through long corridors to a squat little room with three desks, a filing cabinet, and an enormous poster showing two battleships and a rather antiquated observation plane, was not at all as he had so blithely expected. Mr. Keyo was young, blonde, and sarcastic; he seemed totally unimpressed with Bev's pitifully small list of post-graduate achievements. He showed a most suspicious curiosity in Bev's reasons for leaving Virginia Law School and almost threw his hands in the air when he discovered his lack of proficiency in languages.

"But you can see for yourself, Mr. Stregelinus," he said in a mild, reasonable, chilling tone, "that you have no background for this sort of work or for liaison work abroad. And you don't have a specialty like photography or cryptology or even law. Where do you think you could be used?"

Bev would like to have retorted that he *could* be used to make unfortunate applicants feel even less fortunate. Instead he said meekly that he quite agreed, that he hadn't really expected anything, that he had only hoped there might be a small slot he could fit into to be of service, and that he was sorry to have taken up Mr. Keyo's valuable time.

Back at home he plunged into his old life with almost a feeling of relief. He had tried; he too had made his application and now he could resume the role of inertia so easy to him and postpone all thoughts about the inevitable draft until it should actually come. Live in the present, he urged himself passionately. Tomorrow is no more real than yesterday. And so he existed until one weekend which he spent at Bella Stroud's exquisite little octagonal white house in Glen Cove. Bella did everything "just right"; her parties were *choisis* to an extreme. Seven or eight friends would come for a weekend to crowd her and her little guest house, but never uncomfortably. They were selected like the ingredients of a salad: one for his war information, usually a foreign correspondent, another to furnish the political motif, another the literary. But all had to have the "light touch"; all had to be able to swing easily from massacre in China to matrimony in New York. And they had to be "human"; that was Bella's great forte. They had to be genuinely devoted to a cause, or a wife, or a child, but never obsessed. Bella herself loved to show off her two lovely blonde youngsters in the parlor but she always dismissed them before the first hint of languor appeared in anyone's eye. One had to be "kind," "genuine," "sincere," at Bella's; one had to "relax," "to feel at home." Yet the chintzes were always bright and colorful and unstained; the martinis were dry and delectable; everything went smoothly and one dressed for dinner. The only flaw in the picture was that Goodhue Stroud, a decade older than his wife, being like his brother Arleus somewhere in his early fifties, looked from time to time just a tiny bit fatigued.

"But, darling, a commission is so nice," she told Bev when she had heard the sad little tale. "It isn't a thing at all to give up on. One must push and push. We'll see Mal Dangerfield at the Club at lunch tomorrow. Just you leave it to me."

"Oh, Bella, I don't want to pull a lot of wires—"

"Who's going to?" she interrupted. "My dear friend, don't you know the difference between pull and push?"

He confessed his ignorance.

"But it's so obvious," she protested. "Pull is using connections to get yourself somewhere you're not entitled to be. Push is just using a little pressure to get yourself in the slot you belong in and that you would be in except for red tape. My dear, you've *got* to use push these days, or you'll simply be trampled to death!"

"And Mal is the man to push?"

"Of course he is. Mal simply *is* Church Street."

It all seemed quite simple, and Bev felt his spirits rising with the decline of the drab prospect of army khaki which, however endurable in melancholy and escapist moments, assumed the sharpest aspects of division from all that was smooth and velvety and golden in his life as he sat in Bella's stiff but comfortable little *Empire* parlor. This warm, consoling feeling of being "in" was intensified the next day when at noon they sat with martinis on the terrace of the Club looking out over the gold course at the glory of autumnal woods. Malcolm was there, very strong and ruddy, very big and beefy and overpowering, as he winked Bev over to a corner and signaled the waiter for another drink.

"Bella tells me you're interested in the Navy," he began pleasantly.

"Yes, but they seemed to be so little interested in me."

"Who did you see?"

"Someone called Keyo. He said I wouldn't fit."

Malcolm threw back his head and gave a booming laugh.

"Keyo!" he exclaimed. "How could you? He's nobody. Why didn't you come and see me?"

"May I?"

"Tomorrow morning. The earlier the better."

So it was that Bev started the laborious business of filling in forms. Because he was slated for work in the information line these were particularly copious; he was confronted with the necessity of a complete and comprehensive review of his whole life. Reduced as it had to be, to dates of schools attended and jobs held, to times of residence in different places and to ranges of travel, it proved a very sparse and meager affair, relieved only by the glowing generalities of five letters of recommendation from five carefully selected sponsors. These latter he was quite proud of, for the writers were eminent, their indorsements warm, and their field of endeavor various; he read and reread the complimentary type with feelings of the greatest reassurance. Rufus Henderson wrote of his good work in the "cause"; Ambassador Henry Livermore commented on his "tact and seriousness"; Felix Salberg had been induced to be generous about his services at the gallery; Goodhue and Arleus Stroud were enthusiastically vague as to his "general eligibility." A well informed investigator would start out by knowing in advance who at least three of these sponsors were: Arleus Stroud, Henderson, and Livermore, and they would inevitably, he hoped, shed some of their glory on him. After the submission of all the papers, making up in toto a file that was nothing if not impressive, a great void appeared in his life. He was impatient for results while at the same time rather dreading the interruption of his civilian routine. He continued to work a couple of days a week for Henderson and he tried to take up his writing. His mother urged him to consider biography and offered to help him on one of her father the Bishop, which idea was for a while vastly appealing to him and drove him to go so far as to take out of the Public Library everything he could find on recent ecclesiastical history. But on both sides enthusiasm flickered with the discovery of how carefully this had all been covered by others, and the idea never found further form than an essay of which only seven pages were written. Mrs. Stregelinus, like her son, had a mind that liked to snatch the essence or some approximation of it from any subject and hurry on; neither had patience for the detail that must be mastered for complete understanding. He continued to dine out, to play bridge, to attend the theater, but it occurred to him more than once, and forcibly, that the Navy which had come into his life so recently was now the sole coördinating factor that he had left, a realization that intensified his still only so reluctantly conscious sense of the sorry pass things had come to with him. In such moments he liked to think that the Navy would take him far away, to new experiences and new melancholies which he would beautifully record, that the punctuation which the blue uniform would put in his present life would be definite and conclusive.

In the meanwhile his case was being investigated. Rufus Henderson told him that a Navy person had been around to interview him, asking hopefully about alcoholic addictions, and his mother was informed one morning by her alarmed grocer that a young man in a tweed suit had come snooping in to inquire about her "credit and standing" in the neighborhood on Sixty-seventh Street. Mr. Arleus Stroud had also been called upon and had been interested enough at this reminder of Beverly's existence to telephone his wife and tell her about it, supposing it would interest her if there was anything in the rumor that had come to him the summer before that her daughter and Beverly were engaged. Angeline *was* interested; she promptly asked Bev around to dinner to find out what he was up to.

"What sort of naval commission?" she asked pointedly as they sat over cocktails before dinner.

"Well, I'm not supposed to be too explicit—" he began.

"Oh, I see," she said. "Intelligence."

He smiled weakly in an effort to be non-committal.

"That's it," she went on, "the one they're not meant to talk about. Do you think you'll be happy in a desk job?"

There she was, he reflected angrily, with her usual blatant lack of tact treading all over him.

"It's not necessarily a desk job," he protested.

"Oh, pooh!" she retorted. "You know it is."

"Mummie, leave him alone." Sylvia had come in quietly during their talk and was standing behind the sofa that faced the fire. "Bev knows best what he's doing. We can trust him."

Her smile as she said this was very wonderful; it was full of sympathy and friendliness and warmth. He had not really believed her, poor twisted creature that she so often seemed, quite capable of such radiation, but it cut him now with a sharpness. It was as if the whole fabric of his now so organized future had collapsed at a touch and that nothing was there, nothing but a half-consumed martini offered him jointly by a grinning Bella and an even more boisterously grinning Dangerfield. He blinked to shake off the image that gripped him; he looked at Sylvia and her mother and simply smiled.

After that night history seized him. Japan struck, and in New York every last man at the Armory Club, where Bev was having Sunday lunch, quivered with self-righteous indignation. He rushed ro Rufus Henderson's where others of the faithful had already preceded him, and they toasted together the finally achieved participation. It was a day for the emotions, and he returned home for supper quite exhausted to find his mother by the radio in tears. She was too upset to argue with him and they went to bed early. The next morning Lieutenant Keyo called him up and told him that everything had been hurried up and that although his commission as Lieutenant (junior grade) might not come through for a few weeks, the Navy wanted his services in Church Street right away as a "special agent," which was nothing but an officer in mufti. Bev hurried down there to report; he was sworn in after only a three-hour wait and found himself in an office of very nice and agreeable young men from the Wall Street area working the normal hours of eight to five investigating the private lives and characters of other nice young men who were trying to get into the same sort of work.

As a job it had its advantages. It consisted largely in interviewing sponsors and checking on school and college records, and he spent a good deal of time on the subway shuttling from point to point around greater New York. He met and talked to interesting people and occasionally very prominent ones: the Mayor himself, and at another time, the Governor. It was always a question of some young man they knew and whom often enough Beverly also knew; he became adept at extracting information as to damaging particulars by puncturing the bubble of ten minutes' laudatory generality, mutually offered, with a fact gleaned at a former interview, a fact harmless enough in itself maybe but symptomatic of a deeper and undiscovered layer in the subject's character. The sponsor would look perhaps just a bit startled; an "Oh, you know about that, do you?" expression would settle truculently on his features and the conversation would thenceforth be conducted on more realistic lines.

It was obviously impossible for the office to check on the time he spent for he often had to wait indefinitely in outer offices before interviews could be granted, and he and his friends usually managed to rendezvous for lunch at a good restaurant and to take time out during the day to call on friends at other offices. Yes, it was pleasant enough and easy going; it was even fun after a case had been completed to dictate his findings and recommendation in copious detail into a dictaphone, but he did feel just a bit futile when the "case" turned up at the next desk a few days later to engage in exactly the same occupation. Well, this was only temporary it was explained; they would all be sent far enough and soon enough. They had only to wait.

He had seen very little of Sylvia during the fall, but since the evening at her mother's when she had so trusted him he called her up more often, and frequently of a Saturday night they took up their old haunt of La Rue. She was working in one of her Aunt Bella's organizations; she did something for refugees, but she showed very little interest in it and seemed to take the war very hard. Arleus, Jr., was in the Navy and already on the Pacific Coast preparing to leave for further points; she was very worried about him. It was too early in the war for more than a few to have suffered, but she had a tremendous sense of its stretching on and on. They never referred to the scene on Long Island of the summer before; it seemed tacitly agreed that they would continue good friends. But the absurdity of their situation was still apparent to him: that she, the loving should be the loath. One night he called her up to ask her out; it was the day of the fall of Singapore. She was going to say no, but something in his voice impressed her.

"You've had news?" she asked.

"Orders in fact." She knew by his tone it was far.

"Oh, Bev! Where?"

"If you'll come out with me, I'll tell you."

She gave a little gasp when she caught sight of the blue uniformed figure at the front door.

"A j.g.!" she cried. "And Arlie's only an ensign!"

"Age before beauty," he retorted. "I'm only amazed they gave me so little."

At La Rue, very self-conscious in his new uniform but desperately casual as he waved to friends at other tables, he told her that the commission had arrived with orders to Panama.

"Panama!" she exclaimed. "Good Lord."

He took a strong gulp of his drink before answering. He was excited and a little bewildered.

"Well, it's good to be going somewhere," he said at last. "Particularly with this news today. One can't win the war sitting in New York. Especially," he continued with a smile, "when you've done as much shouting as I've done on Henderson's Committee."

She nodded.

"I wonder what sort of duty you'll have there?"

He shrugged his shoulders.

"No idea," he answered. Then he laughed, but not too convincingly. "Mother's all upset. She's sure the Japs will strike the Canal next."

"Very likely."

"I tell her the Germans will bomb New York so I'll really be safer there."

She smiled at him.

"That's likely too."

Bev looked past her at La Rue and the dancing couples, the waiters, and the tables. He seemed to be unconscious of color and detail. They were nothing to him now but waiters, couples, and tables, yet it had been for so long his focal point. Now it was all filmy as if he were looking at it from under water. Good-by. It was really that. Postponements were over; the only reality lay in a future that he did not leap to embrace. Yes, it was certainly a kind of death. When he took Sylvia home he kissed her good night but it didn't mean anything at all. And after that it was all a confused blur of Norfolk, of long grey passageways on a Navy transport, of ringing annunciators, of strange and unsympathetic faces at the mess table, and finally one hot, clear morning, the long, green, mountainous coast of Panama.

Part II

Audrey

CHAPTER ONE

THE LONG, CURVING snake of land that connects the American continents is pinched at its narrowest point, where the isthmus holds the two oceans only fifty miles apart, by a little strip of United States territory stretching ten miles down each coast which forms the setting of the Panama Canal. The traveler approaching the Canal Zone by land either from north or south comes equally through the Republic of Panama; he passes through country heavy with jungle and dotted with thatched villages and sees little enough of anything like civilization until he enters the narrow federal strip with its sudden burst of macadam roads, well-screened houses, huge engineering shops and its ultimate view of the great ascending locks of the Canal itself. The Zone divides the jungles like an antiseptic bandage; it is wilderness reclaimed, and high-crested tropical birds scream in vain cacophony as they flash from tree to tree along Gatun Lake where the shipping of the world passes imperturbably from one ocean to the other.

In 1942, however, imperturbability was hardly a characteristic of life in the area. The year had opened amid fear and gloom which seemed only to deepen in the ensuing months; the fall of Singapore and the Philippines had caused alarm for the very safety of the Canal; sabotage was widely suspected and actual invasion feared. Troops by the thousand were poured into the Zone and anti-aircraft batteries established everywhere; light cruisers, though old ones, were deployed to guard the Pacific approaches; blimps were raised over the locks on long cables; planes droned overhead in seemingly lazy patrol. Wives and families of army and navy men were sent back to the United States; hours of work were extended and a strict blackout imposed. Lieutenant (junior grade) Stregelinus, driving from Naval Headquarters to the beach at Amador for a late afternoon swim, would stare out to sea as he sped along the highway and picture, not without a slight but pleasurable thrill, the horizon bobbing with the approaching dots of a Japanese flotilla.

The capital of this active bureaucracy was Balboa, situated on the Pacific side of the Isthmus, where the explorer had first sighted the then new ocean. Here the Commanding General of the Caribbean Defense Command had his headquarters, constructed appropriately on the summit of the hill known as Quarry Heights, while further down as rank required was located the huge, many-windowed, red-roofed, white stucco building which contained the civilian officers of the Zone governor. On the other side of Quarry Heights stretched the vast white, yellow, and red of Panama City, the Republic's capital, located, uniquely for an independent government, within the very borders of the American zone.

Beverly's life was directly concerned with a modernistic green building situated some miles from Balboa in the midst of a reservation of barracks and officers' quarters, for such was the structure that housed the offices of the Admiral-Commandant whose mimeographed signature controlled such various activities as the routing of convoys, the organization of naval patrol flights, the servicing and repairing of fleet units in transit, and the vast administration of naval shore-based personnel within the limits of the Zone. It also housed less known to those who simply came to cross the Isthmus but intimately felt by those in the headquarters area, the Director of Naval Information for the District, one Captain Nathan Darlington, USN (Ret.). He was a short, stoop-shouldered, eagle-beaked old man with long, white hair who had discovered that with the exception of the Commandant he outranked all local naval officers and had decided to take full advantage of the fact. Too old, alas, to go to sea, he was in the very prime of life for governmental organization. He had developed in Washington a dim and insufficient idea of what the Navy meant by "information" and he had started in pre-war Panama with a meager staff, but in the rich flood of wartime allowances his little weed had thrust itself sturdily and rapidly upward until it had become a factor to be reckoned with in army as well as navy circles. Just what its mission was was hard to explain, but misty as may have been the conception its realization in plaster, desks, and personnel was as concrete as the stoutest naval heart could have desired. The office occupied almost an entire wing on the third "deck" of Headquarters, consisting of a chain of rooms centering around the large sanctum of the Captain himself.

Information was not to be confused with operational intelligence or communications. Information enjoyed a field of convenient breadth, the breakdown of which into sections, one section to a room, was largely deceptive owing to the frequency and bitterness of jurisdictional disputes. The plan, however, was clear enough. The two main sections, "Section Red" and "Section Blue," which occupied the long, oblong rooms on either side of the Captain's office, represented the essence of the information plan and symbolized with their differences the two major aspects of life under Darlington's command. Section Red, the larger of the two, having within it some thirty officers and as many yeomen, dealt with information on the Republic of Panama and adjoining republics, logistical, political, or personal; it dealt presumably with any problem involving the Navy and Central America; it kept the Navy informed of such political changes as appeared in the daily paper and kept a watch on foreign shipping that transited the Canal.

Section Blue on the other hand was responsible for the administration of the Office. With only four officers but with fifteen yeomen and civilian stenographers, it handled interviews, personnel reports, office equipment, and public relations; it sorted and distributed the official mail. Section Blue was all order and smiles. Lieutenant-Commander Sheridan Gilder who presided over it was a handsome forty; his long, black glossy hair, neatly combed and matted to his scalp with a liberal dose of tonic, his trim little mustache, his small, straight nose and tight lips, his excellent build would have made him a decorative addition to any organization. His shiny maple leaves and well pressed khakis sounded a keynote that was cheerfully supported by the little flower bowls which he permitted on the desks of the women stenographers. Section Red, however, was as serious as Blue was gay. It was barricaded behind a great sign which read "Keep Out" together with several "Careless Talk" posters depicting ships in various stages of maritime disaster. Once past the barrier one was confronted with a large room in which an extraordinary amount of typing seemed to be going on and where yeomen were dashing from desk to desk with armfuls of files. As Mr. Gilder set the motif for Blue, so did Lieutenant-Commander McShane set it for Red. His messy hair and big, ever active mouth, his bull-like profile, his sloppy desk and frayed shirt collar lent to the atmosphere of premeditated disarray and activity.

It was natural for the officers in Red to say that Blue was full of Harvard men who, when not under pressure of minor clerical details, which it was claimed comprised their entire field of endeavor, spent their days in open and blatant perusal of *Life* and *Time*. Lieutenant-Commander Gilder, the Red men openly said, was a "professional reserve," an unsuccessful, social-climbing, New York stockbroker who had obtained his present rank by taking Navy cruises in long, idle summers while his busier contemporaries were attending to their civilian jobs. An elementary psychological case, it was claimed: he found in the Navy the self-respect that life had withheld. The Blue men, on the other hand, maintained that Section Red was an idle and conceited affair which produced, under a rumbling cover of false activity, items of information derived from Saturday night gossip at the Union Club bar. Mr. McShane's lack of polish, they insisted, far from being an indication of industry and efficiency was simply the outer manifestation of the inner man. Had he not started life as a smuggler before entering the maritime service? Had his twenty years in Latin American bars and along wharfs really qualified him to deal with delicate political issues? And wasn't his appalling grammar and ignorance a disgrace to the naval service? And so it went, on and on, while Captain Darlington rained upon all alike, the just and the unjust, the inexhaustible and daily torrent of his wonderfully sustained wrath.

CHAPTER TWO

THE CORNER CLOSEST to Captain Darlington's office in Section Blue was occupied by the large, neat desk of Lieutenant-Commander Gilder. His was the face that the eyes of a visitor met, and his was the line of vision that had to be crossed before access could be had to the inner sanctum of the Information Officer himself. It was, as he admitted to his intimates, something of a front job, but nobody denied his qualifications. He sat with a wholly admirable imperturbability over the expanse of a wholly unspotted blotter; his eyes sometimes wandered to the window and sometimes exchanged a twinkle with one of the secretaries; occasionally he even smiled at the other officers, but it was evident that he was holding himself in constant reserve for those more significant moments when Captain Darlington wanted to consult him, or, more accurately, when somebody wanted to consult Captain Darlington. Everything else could be delegated, in fact should be. Wherefore else the junior officers? Mr. Gilder straightened his tie for the hundredth time that morning and touched one of his long, black locks lightly with a fingertip. He allowed himself the faintest trace of a wink at Miss Emerson who was typing busily at her desk by Miss Sondberg, Captain Darlington's secretary. Even, he reflected, if the Captain was grouchy there was no denying that Section Blue was a smoothly organized unit. He cast his eyes over the division of labor in the long, oblong room with its row of windows that showed the distant prospect of the Bay of Panama. The officers sat at a line of desks with backs to the windows facing the wall where the main door was located. There were only four of them; it was not a quarter as large as Lieutenant-Commander McShane's Section Red, where the actual ground work was done behind closed doors amid the roar of typewriters, but the sections were of equal rank on the organizational chart, and Mr. Gilder liked to say that his three officers, fifteen yeomen, and four girls accomplished as much work as all McShane's "snoops" combined. For what is anything in the Navy if it is not administered? There before him was Lieutenant Amos Lawrence, of Bostonians the most respectable, who handled public relations and dealt with the Panama Press; there was Lieutenant (j.g.) Beverly Stregelinus, an attractive young New Yorker with the largest collection of first names among his acquaintance that Mr. Gilder had ever heard, who routed the office mail and composed office directives; and there was Ensign Malory, a dour-faced, thin lad who censored the office personal mail and procured office equipment. The yeomen, of course, typed; the Chief Yeoman politicated; Mrs. Soleliac was the mail clerk; Miss Sondberg the incredibly efficient right arm of the boss, and Miss Emerson filled in wherever a gap appeared. It was something to be a little proud of, Mr. Gilder reflected, and besides not only in efficiency did his section excel but in appearances, which a front office can hardly disregard. He had the prettiest girls, the handsomest and cleanest yeomen, and the best bred officers.

Miss Emerson, who attracted him particularly, was not exactly pretty, he reflected, but the nearest thing to it. She had neat, brown hair that fell straightly and smoothly to neck level and then curled up; she had large, intense, brown eyes, a curled-up nose, and a square, rather determined chin. She had, indeed, a determined look all about her; it showed itself in her trim figure, in the calm, assured way that she moved papers about on her desk, and in the very plain, very neatly cut brown dress with the wide red belt which acted, Gilder thought, as a first faint warning of danger. She was very intelligent, he knew, a college graduate, a girl who thought of everything twice. Gilder had tired of philandering in Panama City since his wife had left the Zone; he wanted something whiter for his off hours, and he was debating. Of course, with a girl like that it would take longer, but—

A nervous ensign came in the door and stared vacantly about. Mr. Stregelinus looked up and beckoned to him and a few minutes later brought him over to Mr. Gilder.

"Ensign Sutter, Commander," he said. "Just reporting in."

He left the embarrassed young man standing before the desk, twisting his cap, perspiring freely in the unaccustomed isthmus heat. Mr. Gilder asked him to sit and started the preliminary questioning. It had long been decided by Captain

Darlington that all new arrivals would be assigned duty by
Mr. McShane, which had been a great victory over Gilder;
but the latter still clung to the empty form of the interview
to which Section Blue by operational plan was entitled
with all the tenacity that characterizes jurisdictional disputes.
Carefully he went through the story of the young man's
education, nodding without much enthusiasm at the mention of a little known college.

"You live in New York?" he asked.

Ensign Sutter leaned forward in his chair. The harried enthusiasm on his fat, young, big-featured face was touching.

"Yes, I worked my way through college. I majored in
Romance languages. I was particularly interested in French
diplomatic history. I had hoped to be able to use some of
what I learned in the Navy. I put in for North Africa—"

Gilder listened vaguely.

"And they sent you here," he concluded for him.

Sutter allowed himself the mistaken liberty of a friendly
laugh.

"Well, I guess that's the way it is. Ask for the North
Pole and you get the South. That's the Navy."

Gilder perceptibly stiffened.

"I think the Navy," he said loftily, "can be depended on
to assign ensigns where they are best fitted."

The ensign in question colored.

"Oh, I didn't mean to criticize, sir. I'm very happy to
be here."

The Head of Section Blue nodded more affably.

"We have French problems here, too," he said comfortingly.
"After all, Martinique and Guadeloupe are not so very far
away."

"Oh, sir, do you think you could send me there?"

Mr. Gilder coughed.

"Well, hardly for a while. You'll be in Section Red. That's
our department for the compilation of information. Their
job is, broadly speaking, the relationship of the Navy with
Central America. I'm sure you'll find it interesting work."

The ensign looked hopeful again.

"I know I'd love any sort of investigative work. And I
do speak some Spanish, but I guess it'll be a long while
before I can talk as well as the other officers."

This remark though made in good faith was unfortunate
as neither Mr. Gilder nor Mr. McShane nor even Captain
Darlington for that matter could utter a word of Spanish.

Mr. Gilder, though in part mollified by the young man's more respectful attitude, had become quite clear as to his need of further indoctrination on the point of naval things first and foremost.

"Spanish doesn't matter so much here, Mr. Sutter," he said a bit severely, "nor does investigative work of the type you're probably thinking of. A lot of young, romantically minded fellows come down here with the notion that they're going to chase spies across graveyards on moonlit nights." This was Gilder's favorite and most used description. "But you've got a harder job," he went on more heavily. "We're a receiving center for all kinds of information. We are the Navy Department's liaison with the Republic of Panama. Getting the information is a matter for the Army and civilian agencies." Here Mr. Gilder with a deprecatory gesture managed to suggest that such work was more fitting for the lower orders of military society. "We receive it and control its naval dissemination. News is nothing in itself. It's who gets it that counts."

But the little smile of satisfaction with which he got off his familiar lecture was apparently not enough for Sutter whose face had fallen.

"But if the Army gets it, sir," he protested, "why don't *they* disseminate it?"

Gilder smiled again. His patience was infinite.

"They do. They send it to the Army in Washington or any other relevant addressee, and they send it to us."

"And we send it to Washington, sir?"

Gilder shrugged his shoulders.

"Or any other interested addressee," he repeated.

Sutter was leaning forward in his chair again.

"But doesn't it go to Washington twice then?" he asked.

Mr. Gilder snapped around in his swivel chair.

"Mr. Stregelinus," he called, "will you take Ensign Sutter into Section Red and introduce him to Mr. McShane?"

As he settled back in his chair he reflected with some irritation on the growth of this attitude of "pushing coöperation" as he called it. There seemed to be more and more commissioning of bright young men who after the scantiest indoctrination went aggressively to work in their specialized fields with an absolutely civilian disregard for the niceties of chain of command or correct jurisdiction. Of course, one needed specialists, but there was no reason for them not to be taught that Navy ways and customs came first. An ensign just reporting who was lucky enough to be received by a lieutenant-commander should be very stiff, very respectful, and *very* flattered. Sutter was without doubt the kind of young man who would inwardly evaluate officers according to their ability to investigate or speak Spanish rather than according to their rank. It was not only, Gilder told himself in an effort to be honest, because he himself would be lost by any such criterion that he objected to it; it was because of its deteriorating effect on the hierarchy of ranks and numbers. Discipline was bred of respect; respect of form. The system had to stand. He shook his head and reached into his "In" basket for something to read and initial; he picked out the Chief of Staff's new directive against the use of navy station wagons for private purposes and settled back to peruse it. Miss Emerson at this moment pulled a sheet out of her typewriter and came across the room to place it on his desk.

"Any more?" she asked.

"Oh, yes, Audrey. Sit down, won't you?" He rummaged around again in his "In" basket for something to dictate, but all he could find was a handful of suspect cards that looked as though they might be improved by retyping. He read two or three off to her and stole glances at the curve of her figure against the back of the chair. Miss Emerson, however, did not seem aware of him. She sat book in hand with expressionless serenity, jotting down occasional notes from his slow and halting dictation. It wasn't that she seemed bored so much as patient. She had a strong sense of the dignity of office hours of which he approved, but he always believed that an exception could be made with himself. When she did quicken, however, it was oddly contagious. He could feel suddenly the concentration of her stare. He glanced up now and followed her eyes across the room. She was watching Helen Drinker, one of the stenographers from Section Red who had just come into the room with a basket of cards for the mail desk. But he could see now what Miss Emerson was looking at. Helen was chatting with the young sailor who drove one of the information station wagons and who sat between assignments on a bench by the wall.

Miss Emerson looked at him and back at her book.

"She does that all the time," she said.

Mr. Gilder stared.

"Does what?"

"Carries on with that driver."

He looked over at Helen Drinker again and saw that she and the sailor were laughing. It was obviously a highly convivial laugh. Helen was not a particularly pretty girl and in her upper twenties, but her clear blue eyes and long, pre-Raphaelite chestnut hair gave her a distinguished air. The sailor, not more than eighteen, was a coarse young lump of freckles and stringy hair.

"Do you call that carrying on?" he asked dubiously.

"That's not all."

He straightened himself up a bit and tried to think of the rest of his dictation.

"It just doesn't seem right to me, Mr. Gilder," she continued, looking at him. "It's hard enough for us girls working in an office with so many enlisted men without Helen Drinker making herself cheap with a boy like that."

Gilder stared.

"You think I'd better do something?" he asked.

She shrugged her shoulders.

"Not you, sir," she said in her quiet tone. "You can't be expected to do everything. Somebody like Mr. Stregelinus. He's good with people."

"Does Helen Drinker have dates with that boy?"

"I suppose."

"You don't know?"

She looked at him with a mild surprise.

"I can find out. And tell Mr. Stregelinus."

"You seem awfully anxious about Mr. Stregelinus."

She smiled.

"Well, if you think Mr. Malory would be better. . . ."

"No, no." He folded his hands on his desk in discouragement. Nobody in the office could be pleasanter at a party than Miss Emerson but her quiet officiousness during the working day did have its trying side. She was always ready with a criticism discreetly put; if she didn't volunteer it she would sit looking so full of it that he would eventually find himself asking her. He sent her back to her typewriter but he soon found that he couldn't seem to take his eyes off the couple across the room. Really, it *was* outrageous. Miss Emerson was quite right. There was that girl from McShane's section wasting her entire morning with that little slug. And how dared he talk to her? Really. He was just turning impatiently to call Stregelinus when Helen Drinker appeared to conclude her conversation and left the room.

Inwardly he fumed. It was just the kind of thing that was most provoking because it was so hard to put one's finger on. Suddenly and unpleasantly he became aware that Mr. Stregelinus, his cheerful but irrespressible assistant, had noted his preoccupation and was smiling at him. He felt obliged to smile back, but he knew he was blushing and knew he was about to lose his temper when just at that moment the air was rent with the muffled roar from the inner office that he so dreaded: "Gild—*er!*" He snapped himself out of his chair and hurried into the sanctum.

Captain Darlington was sitting in his big, empty office in his usual pose, huddled up, his shirt sloppily open at the throat with no tie. His expressionless grey eyes moved constantly about while his head with its long white hair and great aquiline nose remained at rest, for all the world like a bird of prey, probably vulturine, waiting interminably on a dead branch. Captain Darlington, everyone knew, had been a good naval officer in his day; it had been said of him that nobody had a firmer touch on the bridge of a battleship, that nobody could turn a cruiser with more deftness; but he failed to reach flag rank because of his violent temper and now in his old age, called out of retirement for emergency, this temper had eaten up his whole personality. Poor Gilder was his whipping boy. He was mercilessly treated even in the presence of junior officers, but his hopes of placating the old man were never downed. Gilder was a reserve but as a "professional reserve" he felt like a regular. Captain Darlington, however, made no distinction between reserves and "professional reserves"; he despised them all and despised the personnel in the information office, entirely reserve-manned. His only satisfaction lay in running the office as though it were a battleship, keeping the personnel at their desks regardless of where their jobs would seem to call them, having "Attention on Deck" brayed out whenever he entered Section Blue, and devising elaborate watch schedules to keep the office efficient even in the middle of the night. This morning he looked slightly less fierce.

"The Commandant was in," he growled, "and he liked your map." He waved a hand at a large map of the Russian war zone which had been one of Gilder's little surprises. It had a cellophane cover so that the entire battlefront could be erased and chalked further ahead or back and was a project inspired by the Captain's once commenting at lunch that he could never find any of the towns mentioned in the communiques. "Matter of fact he spent about ten minutes studying it. Said he never had been able to figure out where Kharkov was."

Gilder beamed.

"Would you like another, sir?" he suggested quickly. "What about China? Or the Middle East?"

"All right. Good idea. Then I won't have to read these spic newspapers at all. That won't take too much time off other things?"

Of course it would, but both men knew the necessity of official reassurance to the requesting senior.

"Certainly not, sir. It'll be easily done."

The captain nodded and picked up a letter.

"Colonel Paulsen is writing me about that political crisis in Guatemala. Says our Lieutenant Stoner knows a bit about it and wants him to go up there with his officers. Tell him no. We can't have our officers tearing all over Central America. Besides, that's an army job and they get the credit. No use our messing in it at all."

"I quite agree, sir."

"That's all, Gilder. Except too damn many officers are going to lunch at the same time. Break the thing into shifts."

"Yes, sir." Gilder stood there hesitating. He was wondering if the moment was propitious.

"Well?" the Captain snapped.

"Oh, sir—" he began with embarrassment, "I thought I'd better—well, I wondered if you were aware—I had noticed myself that—"

"What the hell, Gilder!"

"Well, sir, it's about Miss Drinker."

"Miss Drinker?"

"She's one of the stenographers in Section Red. She's been behaving, I fear, not as you would want your young ladies to behave, and—well—"

"Well?"

"With an enlisted man, sir." He stared helplessly at the Captain, realizing too late the full extent of his error. The old man glared for a moment and then, with his iciest sarcasm:

"What do you want me to do? Marry her?"

"No, sir. I—"

"For God's sake, Gilder," the Captain thundered at him, "do you think I have nothing to do but chaperone sailors and sluts? What do you think I have people in this office for? You bother me with the God-damnedest details I ever knew. If you had your office properly organized these things would be settled by subordinates before you even heard of them. Now clear out of here, and when I next hear of this thing I want to hear that it's settled and somebody's transferred!"

Mr. Gilder made a silly little bow and hurried out.

Miss Emerson's eyes quickly dropped to her typewriter as he passed her desk. The door to the Captain's office was always open and it was easy for her and Miss Sondberg to hear every word that was spoken. Miss Sondberg, however, though she undoubtedly listened herself, took a rather superior attitude about Miss Emerson's listening and while continuing her own typing would cast an occasional glance of disapproval at her neighbor. Miss Sondberg it need hardly be said was as thin and plain as she was efficient; her hair was straight and tied in an unbecoming bun on the back of her neck. She looked upon Captain Darlington as her own property and as an "old dear" which in the manner of many elderly military men he really was where women were concerned, making as he did a daily show of his "Good Mornings" and his "Good Evenings" and frequently bringing a rose from the garden plot by his quarters to adorn the little glass vase on Miss Sondberg's desk.

Audrey Emerson noted all this; in fact, she noted everything. She was twenty-five and a perfect spyglass of observation. She knew just how Mr. Gilder stood with the Captain; she knew how Mr. Gilder pawned everything off on Mr. Stregelinus; she knew that Mr. Lawrence always kept a letter to his wife under his blotter and added chapters to it when not watched; she knew that Mr. Malory, though very thin and ascetic looking, was really as sex crazy as an adolescent and made constant dates under the pretense of official use of the phone. She had noted the occupants of Section Red as well, but of all these varied subjects it was Mr. Stregelinus on whom she lavished her most absorbed attention. She had never seen anyone quite like him. He fascinated and outraged her at once. He was effeminate in his mannerisms; he had long hair which he was constantly pulling and tugging as he telephoned emitting from time to time a great screech of a laugh that resounded through Section Blue. Yet there was a natural warmth and gaiety in this laugh that disarmed as much as it irritated and Mr. Stregelinus completely without reticence was always cheerfully rushing pell-mell past the iciest social barriers and melting the whole igloo with a sudden assault of familiarity. Not that he had been this way with Miss Emerson herself; he had simply tossed papers at her to be typed, all in great confusion, and laughed pleasantly when asked to explain, making a series of abominable jokes on her possible relationship to the "Concord Sage." But she could see how easily he treated Mr. Gilder and how he never even seemed to be in trouble with the Captain. And then the people he seemed to know! At least once every three or four days he would exchange gossip on the telephone in a strident voice with Mrs. Livermore, the Ambassadress, while Mr. Gilder listened in awe. Audrey had spent almost her whole life in the Canal Zone except for four years at Hollins College, Virginia; the people she knew were cheerful enough when they went to a party but nobody in or around Balboa ever thought of bringing such an impertinently contagious *joie de vivre* into their office routine. But how simple it was, really. He was from "the world." And it was with Mr. Stregelinus in prospect that she turned over in her mind the odd little dialogue that she had just heard.

"I'll go to lunch now, Ruth," she told Miss Sondberg. The latter didn't look up from her typewriter.

"With Laura Smith?" she inquired in a chilly tone.

"Who else?"

Miss Sondberg banged the folder back viciously.

"Have a nice cat."

"We will."

Laura Smith, the daughter of the Canal Zone's Lieutenant-Governor, worked the next floor up in the Commandant's office. She was Audrey's oldest friend which meant that they had been mutually jealous and competitive since childhood. The rivalry was at the moment in temporary suspension owing to Laura's recent victory in her father's elevation. Audrey's father was still only a semi-prominent Zone engineer. Laura furthermore had gone to Vassar and developed the long, careless curls, the drawl, and the sloppy posture of a debutante. Unfortunately, she couldn't wear a sweater in Panamanian heat, but she did her best to convey *Town and Country* on the campus with moccasins, pleated skirts, and a stick of gum lazily chewed. Audrey, arriving at the sign "Operations" on the next floor, walked into the big room, one wall of which was a giant painted map of the Caribbean dotted with ship-shaped pieces of wood representing convoys.

The senior and junior watch officers sat at desks literally covered with telephones; there was always a good deal of bell ringing and rushing to and fro. Laura emerged from the Chief of Staff's office notebook in hand, gum in mouth, sauntering but nonetheless noticeably a figure to be taken into consideration. Her cold, confident, grey eyes gave a needed sense of cohesion, and her large nose balanced the receding chin and the long, pale cheeks.

"Wait till I lock this stuff up," she said and proceeded to put the notebook in a drawer and turn the key. One of her greatest pleasures was in giving Audrey a proper sense of the importance of operations work. "I'm always afraid," she continued as they went down the corridor together, "that I'll blab some top secret 'info' at home. I hear it all day of course and I get so I can't remember what I heard from the Chief of Staff and what I've read in the papers."

"Do your mine sweeps and fishing boats ever get in the newspapers?"

"Fishing boats?" Laura laughed in scorn. "Good Lord, you don't think we bother with them, do you? That's Inshore Patrol. We're concerned with the ultimate defense of the —but there I go. In a minute I'll be blabbing something I shouldn't."

Audrey let this pass because she had other information that she wanted from Laura. Her friend was the greatest repository of gossip in the Isthmus, but to coax any item from her, even conceding her desire to impart it, was a laborious process that required a preface of flattery. It was almost noon now and the stifling heat was beginning to pervade the great green building. She said nothing · but followed Laura through the linoleum hall where all the marines were, out of the building and across the lawn to Ship's Service.

CHAPTER THREE

WHEN AUDREY LOOKED back into the past it always struck her that she had no real background at all. She had never felt the product of any one place or environment. Most of her days it was true had been spent in the Canal Zone, but since childhood she had resolutely refused to regard it as home. The elimination of Panama left two possible alternatives: Springfield, Massachusetts, where her father had worked as an engineer until she was nine years old when they had moved to Balboa, and Charlottesville, Virginia, her mother's family home where her aunt had kept a boardinghouse for University students and where she had spent a great number of rather dreary summers. But neither of these places had left much of a stamp on her; Audrey was essentially the product of a mental environment created by herself. Her parents had never been congenial companions, and as she had grown older and acquired the independence that comes with emotional frustration she had begun to look down on them. Her father, Vance Emerson, had been a fairly spirited engineer in his youth but he had deteriorated in the tropics and at sixty was a methodical, prematurely old man who either said nothing or else told interminable anecdotes of early Balboa. He had arrived at a moderately high rank in the Zone, being one of the heads of mechanical planning with a house on Quarry Heights not far from the Governor's own residence, but it was generally felt that he was too slow and stodgy and would be retired at the earliest possible moment. Audrey was well aware of this and it did little to improve her general satisfaction.

She had if possible an even less congenial companion in her mother who had first met Mr. Emerson in Springfield while she was the paid companion of the aging mother of a textile mill owner. Though Mrs. Emerson had been obliged to earn her living at that time it was despite a southern background of some slight distinction. Born in Charlottesville

Miss Martha Ellen Miles, she had been able to point with
pride all during her childhood to the big house in Keswick
owned by the Harold Blooms of Jersey City and remind
anyone who needed to be reminded that it had been built
by her great-grandfather and that Mr. Jefferson himself had
been his architect. Indeed, some of his descendants were
"kin" to Mrs. Emerson, her aunt having married a Keith
who was an own cousin to the Randolphs. Fortune, however,
had endowed Mrs. Martha Ellen Miles Emerson with little
but the memory—and it was her mother's memory at that—
of "Montaverde" the Bloom estate; as for cash, there had
never been any of that in her lifetime, nor indeed in the
lifetime of the preceding generation. And the bitter truth
of such a situation is that the charm and grace of an old
family will not survive indefinitely the loss of a luxury income.

The Miles sisters had never lived in an old house with
lovely decaying things; they had been brought up in a very
ordinary and small red brick suburban home in Charlottesville; they had always done the housework; they had always
taken boarders. Old Mrs. Miles who remembered the ante-
bellum days had had the air of a lady, but her plain, large,
simple, industrious daughters never gave the slightest impression of distinction. When the old lady had died Betty
and Martha Ellen carried on her boardinghouse for University students and managed with it considerably better
than she had done, but they eventually quarreled and Martha
Ellen at thirty-four left her forty-year-old sister and took
the previously mentioned job in Springfield. Her marriage to
Vance Emerson contained no incident worthy of note; she
made him an efficient and uninquiring wife without taste
and without nerves, who enjoyed knitting as a pastime and
could maintain a steady flow of small talk which divided
itself into gentle homilies to her two daughters and reminiscences of better times in Dixie. She rarely moved except
for marketing from the dark, shady living room of her Balboa
house decorated with brown lithographs of old masters and
one large and blurred water color of the rotunda at the
University of Virginia.

Audrey had been a lonely child. Her younger sister was
not born until she was almost ten. Her parents, though
properly affectionate, had no imagination about asking other
children to the house or creating any sort of an atmosphere
for young people. They were old as parents for her and

almost grandparental for her younger sister. Audrey went to school and high school in Balboa and for a long time she was shy, not mixing well with other children. Her marks were very poor; her adaptability worse. She took a natural refuge from home and school in an escapist cosmology; she constructed for herself an entirely imaginary continent which she populated with figures drawn largely from the biographies that she borrowed so constantly from the Canal Zone Library. Her mother could never understand why Audrey would curl herself up on the porch in the middle of the afternoon to read *The Martyrdom of an Empress* or *The Love of an Uncrowned Queen*. Or why Audrey answered her suggestions to go and play with the little girls next door with such bitter protest. At thirteen and fourteen her world was populated with the lovely ladies of Imbert de Saint-Amand; she lived with the Duchesse de Berri, the Princess de Lamballe, Madame Elizabeth, and the Archduchess Marie-Louise, in a world glittering with the chandeliers of Versailles. Her great ambition was to grow up and write a biography of Marie-Thérèse-Charlotte, Filia Dolorosa, the daughter of Louis XVI and Marie-Antoinette. But an escapism of such obvious nature could not forever clog the path of a girl whose essential intelligence was so keen and whose ego so strong. At thirteen her marks began to rise; at fourteen she led her class; at fifteen she led the school. The Principal never quite understood, nor did anyone else, what caused such a radical change. It was probably nothing more than the sudden coagulation of her personality, over-delayed by isolation and discontent. Never before or since had she enjoyed anything as sharply as she did those high marks. It was a pity they had come so suddenly. From an inferiority complex and a frustrated ego that sought relief in a vision of powdered wigs and high red heels Audrey swept on to a remarkable conceit. She presumed that other girls were impressed with her brains, and when children who had formerly been mean to her now made overtures of friendship, motivated not by admiration, as she believed, but by interest aroused in the change in her which itself had changed the marks, she tended to reject them.

Laura Smith had been her only friend before, and in proud loyalty she clung to her with an unnecessary exclusiveness. Laura had a mind as narrow as a slit, a good sense of humor, and a curiously deep worldliness. She was just the wrong person for Audrey to associate with at this time. But Audrey was beginning to live, to step across the threshold; it was an intoxicating experience and she found Laura a superb confidante. They became inseparable. They strolled to the movies together in the afternoon arm in arm; they formed mutual crushes on Joan Crawford; they bought magazines on interior decorating and furnished beautiful, white, swimming-pooled houses for themselves on Long Island's North Shore. They treated their parents with an extreme of condescension and enjoyed the drama of domestic quarrels. Whenever Mrs. Emerson asked Audrey to stay home from the movies to help her with the housework, she was made to feel that she was a cross and unsympathetic mother, an unfit parent for such a sensitive and prodigious child. Audrey got out of housework not because her mother considered her a genius but because her mother was afraid of her.

None of Audrey's pleasures, however, were allowed to interfere with what she considered her "career." She enjoyed the position of being first in the school too much to let it slip and to hold it she was obliged to do more work than those with comparable marks, for although she had a good mind for the rapid grasp of general ideas she shrank from prolonged concentration and could be remarkably obtuse about quite obvious details. Hers was certainly not a first-class intellect. But she supplemented her losses in mathematics by doing odd sorts of extra work in English, by getting permission to write additional themes for credit, by cultivating the teachers with the most disarming flattery. And as she was ultimately to be a biographer—she never forgot that—or some type of literary critic she did a large amount of reading on her own. At fifteen she had covered almost the entire field of the Victorian novel and had an appreciation of Shakespeare and seventeenth century French drama. Completeness with her was a virtue. If she started an author she would read all of his works whether she liked them or not, mostly in order to be able to say that she had read them. Her reading, her school work, her movies, her interior decorating sessions with Laura were all elaborately worked into the pattern of her week. She did everything for a purpose, real or imaginary. Her education, her taste, even her enjoyment of gossip she insisted upon regarding as factors that would ultimately pay off during the course of her long climb to recognition. She couldn't bear the idea of wasting time on things that wouldn't get her anywhere, and so when engaged in what would appear to be a non-educational activity such as a walk with Laura she would rationalize it until she had found some peg of utility on which to hang it. Wishful thinking was rampant in her most innocuous pleasures to make them seem rungs in the ladder of success. Moreover her concept of success was entirely a material one. Though the development of the intellect was to her way of thinking the prime goal of mankind she had an enlarged sense of what the dollars and cents reward of the intellectual should be. Voltaire at Ferney and Lord Tennyson at Aldworth were to her examples of how authors *should* be treated and would be too if they took pains with their public. The unrewarded vacuum of intellectual abstraction was anathema to her; her vision of the literary world was one of best sellers and opening nights, of "rave" reviews and autograph seekers. Yet she never doubted for a moment that she was an idealist and living on a far higher plane than the dumpy Zone people who lived from one day to the next. For these she had nothing but the most scathing contempt developed at an early age and willfully sustained. Her dream of success always included a row of astounded, admiring Zone faces.

At home she became increasingly selfish. She felt herself entitled to relax there and she meant this with a vengeance. She 'loathed exercise and took none. She hated helping her mother and avoided it. She loved going to Laura's house and discussing personalities and indulged in it constantly. This was Audrey shortly before she went to college: precocious, ambitious, hard, sentimental. And perfectly happy. She was never again to feel as vitally alive as in that fine first flush of self-satisfaction.

It was a foregone conclusion that she was to go to college in the States. Any peace in the family atmosphere would have been otherwise impossible. For some time she had regarded the fact that she would be away in the big world for four years as an adequate reason for not bothering with the Zonites. Life was to begin with the University. And so at seventeen she was packed off to Hollins in Virginia where her admission had been arranged by the importunities of her Aunt Betty in Charlottesville. She started life there somberly enough. She knew nobody and plunged into an elaborate curriculum of work. But deep down she was a gregarious creature, and though her old exclusive attitude of intellectual snobbery still operated to repel the pleasantest companions she developed a little clique that read Ibsen aloud and talked of going into the advertising business. Ultimately she dominated this group. She was elected to Phi Beta Kappa and wore her key on a little gold bracelet. But it was not the same as in school and she knew it. The girls who had higher marks than she, and there were several, seemed to give themselves to their subjects with a completeness that she had never seen before, and so many of those who had poor grades turned out to be surprisingly interesting people. As late as junior year poor Audrey was just beginning to realize that her concept of intellect, its development and its function, had been astoundingly immature. Life had gone bustling by her with complete indifference to her forlorn austerity. In her first two years at Hollins she did not have a single date. True she hadn't wanted one but she realized now that sex had been included with athletics and parlor games in the bundle of "non-counting" activities that she had eschewed.

The summer vacations passed with her Aunt Betty in the boardinghouse at Charlottesville were periods of desolate but valuable self-contemplation. Miss Miles, like her sister a good woman, was also larger and stronger and older. She was hopelessly plain except when she smiled, and then her big nose and chin were lost in a radiant pleasantness that centered in her large brown eyes. Unfortunately she was aware of this. She was convinced that hers was the smile of the old southern hostess, that it compensated for her size, her tousled grey hair, her octagonal glasses, and that to do anything further to improve her looks would be a type of cheapness. But though she looked "like a cook" she was a "character" in Charlottesville—as indeed was almost everyone else after fifty. The boys who ran in and out of her house all day liked her well enough. She took a motherly interest in any of them who would sit on the porch long enough to get some inkling of her family's role in plantation days and on more than one occasion had been known to give boys financial assistance through college. All Charlottesville knew her, and she could be seen any morning shelling peas on a rocker on the porch of her house on University Circle.

Audrey had a room on the ground floor back next to Miss Miles' for vacations, and they took their meals at a table for two in a corner of the big dining room packed even in summer with students who behaved very noisily in blatant disregard of the placid countenances of Miles ancestors on the wall, copied from the portraits now owned by the Harold Blooms by an ambitious amateur friend of Miss Miles. It was not fun. The students associated her with her aunt and barely acknowledged her existence. She herself was self-conscious about the boardinghouse to a point of absurdity. She fell in love twice with students; each time it was a harassed unreciprocated feeling that made her wretched and caused her indigestion. In one case it was a boy who did not even know her name, a golden-haired youth with a large Buick who was retaking two courses during the summer and resenting it intensely. Alone in her room she wrestled with herself; she burnt with indignation; scathingly she talked to herself about his paucity of intellect, his contemptible lack of ambition. But there it was. The image gripped her for two long months before it faded.

Miss Miles found her a docile but disquieting companion; it was always evident that the real Audrey was unknown to her. But Audrey was nice enough. She had the intelligence to recognize her obligation (Aunt Betty assisted her with her tuition). Financial kindness she was always to understand. And it was true too that her disposition was softening. Her concept of herself had cracked a little and she was beginning to see that others lived in the universe.

Her last year at college was a happy one. She found new friends and the old barriers seemed absurd. She was introduced to boys and she quite frequently "double-dated" in Roanoke. Her appearance improved, and her marks dropped—which gave her less pain than she had anticipated, though undeniably it gave her pain. She had relaxed for once in her life—and then it was all over. Graduation. Aunt Betty smiling through her tears arrayed in a large blue hat with a red flower. It was the end for both. Aunt Betty was almost seventy and her gout was bad. She had decided to accept her sister's long proffered invitation and move for a year or so at any rate to the Canal Zone. She had been offered a surprisingly large sum for her boardinghouse and her eyes, like those of Jefferson Davis, had always turned to the American Tropics. Audrey was to accompany her because Audrey had been away for four years, and her parents felt that before anything was done about this job in New York that she was always talking about she owed them a full year at home. It was a request that it would have taken a harder girl than Audrey to refuse.

But once back in the hot devitalizing air of the Isthmus she could feel the exits closing one by one. Aunt Betty despised the Zone from the start and the climate disagreed with her frightfully, but after a mild stroke she was afraid to leave the really devoted care of her younger sister and stayed on disconsolately, turning more and more to the solace of the brandy bottle in the silence of her room. Mrs. Emerson was tired; Audrey's younger sister was a nervous case; Mr. Emerson had only two years before retiring and then they could all go back to Charlottesville—couldn't Audrey stick it out till then? What could she do? She had no money of her own, and she did have a conscience. Wearily she took a job in the Canal Zone Library in Balboa; in the evenings at home she studied typing and shorthand and read by herself in her room. It wouldn't be forever. And then in a burst came the war and the postponement of her father's retirement. She began to suspect the gods of conspiracy but she faced the change at least with resolution enough to look about for a better job. She found one through Laura with the Navy.

CHAPTER FOUR

WHILE AUDREY AND Laura Smith were in the Ship's Service Store having a sandwich and while Section Blue was happily relieved of the presence of Lieutenant-Commander Gilder who never took less than two hours for lunch, Beverly Stregelinus and Amos Lawrence relaxed from such vigil as they pretended to maintain during the morning. Beverly's long legs were stretched out with his feet on the desk; his nervous hands were occupied in rubbing his high, broad forehead and smoothing his hair. His desk, however, was adequately impressive; he had no fewer than five wicker baskets, heaped two and three feet high with paper, and lists and charts and naval booklets were strewn over his blotter; but this disarray, it must be confessed, gave an erroneous picture of the extent of his activity. He was the router. Yeomen brought him the vast office mail each morning and he busily stamped the initials of the cognizant officer on each slip and sent it flying on its official path. Sometimes he would give a particular paper an extra-office routing, sending it as high as the Commandant himself or the Chief of Staff or over to the Ammunition Depot or Legal Officer, and if some offensive sheet defied classification altogether it could be routed to the District chaplain, a most minor echelon of the bureaucracy who had a mere table in a corner of the Hydrographic Office and two unpainted boxes that served inadequately as "In" and "Out" baskets but who was always pathetically grateful to be on a routing stamp and never committed the gaffe of sending the paper back. All this routing, however, even when stretched hardly filled Beverly's morning. Like a true bureaucrat he ignored this entirely and even from time to time demanded an assistant; the job was vital he would tell Gilder. The router had the power of life or death over any section; he could either so inundate its baskets with paper that the day itself would hardly suffice for its mere initialing, or he could dry a section up entirely and leave it, inert and atrophied, panting for a single drop from the well of mimeographed production. Gilder, though sympathetic, simply pawned off other jobs on him. Beverly drafted office directives; he acted as officer messenger between Navy Headquarters and Quarry Heights and in spare moments he was supposed to be preparing a *Who's Who* of prominent Panamanians for the benefit of those naval officers whose functions involved some mingling with the elite of that little republic. Amos Lawrence on the other hand had an absolutely clear desk and a single job, that of releasing naval district news to the Panama press, but his work took him no more time than Beverly's. They both at the moment had their heads together having approached their swivel chairs.

"And then what did you say?" Amos was asking. "He does seem to take it from you."

Beverly gave a big tug at the hair in back of his head and switched about on his seat. He only seemed at ease when indulging in that monstrous laugh.

"Well, he didn't like it this morning. I asked him if he'd give me time to get an answer from Dorothy Dix. He told me not to be disrespectful. Oh, he couldn't have been more the commander. He even told me not to call him 'Sheridan' but 'Mr. Gilder.' So, of course, I clicked my heels and aye-ayed."

Amos shook with laughter. When he did this he made a strange cackling sound like a hen; his shoulders twitched, and he also scratched his head. There was something slightly ridiculous about Amos, probably because one saw in the angular face, the thinning black hair, the little beak, the ever-so-tightly set small mouth, the familiar and more formidable features of his late great father, the Dean of Harvard Law School. Amos was the image but on a minor scale. He was awkwardly thin where his father had been stout; he twitched where his father had been still and grave. But Amos at thirty-six was a lovable creature, intense but inadequate, noble but comic, striving but impracticable, and Bev had found in him the one congenial soul in the whole naval district.

"What are you going to do?"

Beverly shrugged his shoulders.

"I'm supposed to get some dirt on them and have him transferred to the other side. You know Gilder. He wouldn't change his blotter without a memorandum in the files showing why. Oh, and another thing." Here Bev suddenly screamed with laughter. "I have to do another of those God-damned maps! Can't your department take one over?"

Amos held up both hands.

"I've only got one yeoman."

"Well, what else has he got to do?" Bev protested. "After he's finished one of your famous morning releases: 'The Commandant has announced that the rumor that officers in the district would be allowed to go without ties is utterly without foundation. He further states—' "

"Oh, shut up," Amos interrupted. As a bureaucrat he realized the necessity of not shaking all the tenets. "I wouldn't expect you to understand. Go back to your *Who's Who*. That'll win the war."

He pushed his chair back to his desk and was about to take out from under the blotter the letter that he was writing his wife when a voice boomed:

"Do I have to do all Section Blue's work?"

They looked up at the familiar rumbling voice of the common enemy and saw him standing in the doorway, the big-lipped, three-hundred-pound Irishman who headed Section Red, Lieutenant-Commander McShane. Behind him was the younger man on whom he leaned in jurisdictional disputes, Lieutenant Peter Stoner who had been a labor lawyer in Portland, Oregon before the war—a sturdy, stocky man with a vast bumpy circle of a face. Mr. McShane advanced to Bev's desk brandishing a memorandum.

"What about this map?" he roared.

"Map?"

McShane had to pause for a new breath.

"Gilder sends me in this memo saying my section is going to be responsible for keeping up some fool map on China!"

"That's only fair," Amos interposed from his desk. "We do Russia and the Middle East and it keeps two of our yeomen busy all morning."

Bev blandly opened a drawer. "Some people like to put in the battlefront by a red ribbon with thumb tacks," he explained, showing some specimens of this, "and some like putting isinglass over the map for pencil inscriptions."

McShane was speechless.

"But, damn it, I—" he began.

"Or you can just use erasable crayon," Bev continued imperturbably. "I'd recommend the isinglass. That China front keeps wobbling back and forth so and sometimes with those names you'll find a whole section has been put in as much as a hundred miles out of line. But it's interesting."

"Damn it, Stregelinus. I'm trying to tell you I have no intention of touching the map at all! What do you think we do in Section Red all day? Picture puzzles?"

"Make a note of that, Amos," he said. "It was the Commander who answered that question. Not I."

McShane stared at him with baffled distrust. In all previous conflicts with this impertinent and idle young man he had come out rather the worse for Stregelinus seemed to find invariable backing from Mr. Gilder and even on occasion from the Captain himself.

"You'd better watch your step, Stregelinus. I'm a lieutenant-commander," he exclaimed with childish pique.

"In that case," Bev threw back at him, standing up as he did so, "you should deal with those of equal rank. Mr. Gilder will be back at one. There's no occasion for you to waste the time of his junior officers."

He watched in satisfaction as McShane stamped out.

"That's telling him, Bev," Pete drawled with a wink, "but one of these days you'll go too far. Come on, Amos. Lunch. Bev can guard the holy portals of Section Blue." Bev turned away to his papers and didn't look up until Pete and Amos had gone. Then he glanced around to find someone to take his dictation. Miss Emerson had come in from her lunch and was working at her typewriter.

"Miss Emerson, would you take a memo?"

"Certainly, Mr. Stregelinus."

She came over and sat down briskly in the empty chair by his desk, pencil and pad ready.

"Memo to all officers," he began in a businesslike tone. "Subject: Use of District station wagons for recreational purposes. Paragraph One. Officers are reminded that District station wagons will be available on Saturday afternoons for the purpose of transporting—yes, transporting—organized parties of enlisted men to sites—make that places. Sites or places?"

"Places."

"Places of historic interest in and near Panama City." He paused after this effort and looked around at her. She remained expressionless. "The trips cannot extend further than fifteen miles from Headquarters, and a list of the departing party—no, I guess, the excursion party—together with serial numbers and rates will be furnished the District

Transportation Officer with one copy for the driver of the car—"

"Only one?"

Beverly looked up in surprise to see the young bright face of Esmond Carnahan beaming down at him. This young man, only twenty-five, had come to Panama as third secretary at the embassy of which his maternal uncle, Mr. Livermore, was in charge. He was a person of easy charm and quick friendships, of passionate if immature idealism. He looked more like a child than a man as he stood there, so short and just a tiny bit chubby, in a spotless white linen suit with a red rose in his buttonhole.

"Only one," Bev answered smiling. "What brings you Navywise?"

"Only one!" Carnahan exclaimed again. "But the driver of the car will need one for his files, won't he? And he'll need one for the garage. And the embassy should get a couple of copies if you're going to be driving sailors all over Panama." He looked at Audrey and smiled brightly. "I see," he said, turning to Beverly, "that you keep lovely girls chained to this paper factory. At the embassy we treat our young ladies better. None of these sordid directives." He flicked his fingers contemptuously over the papers that littered Bev's desk.

"What do you want, Carnahan?" Bev exclaimed. "Or did you just drop in to annoy Miss Emerson and myself? Go stamp your visas."

"My mission to Headquarters," the young man answered sententiously, "was to confer with no less a dignitary than the Chief of Staff. My mission in *your* office is the slightest of afterthoughts, a matter of the deepest inconsequence."

Beverly caught Miss Emerson's eye and smiled.

"Well?"

"My beloved Aunt Gladys," Esmond continued with a slight bow, "my greatest support in life—in every way—has commissioned me to ask you a question. It appears she had a dispute at dinner the other night with the British Minister as to whether Admiral Mountbatten is a grandson or great-grandson of Queen Victoria. Bets were placed. She has mislaid her Almanac de Gotha and knows that you are the only man who knows it by heart and therefore prays—"

"Of course. Great-grandson." Such thorny questions as the number of Hesse-Romanoff alliances or the inter-mixture of Mecklenberg and Coburg blood strains were the A B C of

Bev's daily speculations. "There's always confusion about him," he explained. "You see, he was a grandson of the Princess Alice, but his father's brother, Prince Henry, married Princess Beatrice, her sister. That bothers people."

"It bothers some people more than it does others," Esmond answered, winking at Audrey. "You'd better draw me a little chart to take back to Aunt Gladys. I'll never remember that."

Beverly took this entirely seriously and began to draw lines on a piece of paper.

"Such an efficient office," Esmond remarked to Audrey. "I'll come to the Navy for everything."

"We try to oblige, Mr. Carnahan."

"Give this to Gladys, Esmond," Bev said, handing him a piece of paper, "and run along now. We have work to do."

When Carnahan had gone, Beverly finished the memorandum on station wagons and looked in discouragement at the piles on his desk.

"What next?" he asked.

"There's your schedule of officers' lunch hours," she suggested.

"Yes. And the memorandum about compulsory acceptance of Panamanian invitations. But I don't feel I can go in for those today."

She closed her notebook and slipped the pencil under the leather catch.

"There is one thing," she said, looking directly at him.

"And what's that?"

"It's the question of what you're going to do about Helen Drinker."

He stared at her in embarrassment.

"Oh, you know about that?"

"Who doesn't?"

"Yes, I see what you mean. Everyone seems to. But I mean you know about my being stuck with it?"

"Oh, I know everything."

His expression became interested.

"Then you know all about it?"

"I don't know what you mean by *all* about it. But I've just typed a little memo on what I do know." She handed it to him. "Mr. Gilder told me that you would be handling the matter."

He took the page and glanced through its short concise sentences with a growing feeling of disgust.

"How did you get mixed up in this?" he asked sharply. "Aren't you a friend of Helen's?"

She did not show any abashment.

"Perhaps that's the reason."

"But if you'll pardon me, Miss Emerson, there seems to be something so underhand about this. So like this office," he added indiscreetly, looking about him in revulsion at the white, stainless, pictureless walls. "Is this the way you always do things down here?"

"I suppose you could look at it that way," she said quietly. "But if you really thought it would be the best thing for a friend wouldn't you do it too?"

"I'd go and tell her first," he said stoutly.

She shrugged her shoulders.

"Do you think I wouldn't?"

He looked with interest into her wide brown eyes.

"I wonder."

"Do you want me to?" she asked, half rising.

"No, no!" he exclaimed hastily. "It's too late for that now. I'll write the orders. The boy will be transferred."

She settled back in her chair.

"She's simply lost her head," she went on. "She's a good ten years older than him and he doesn't give a hoot about her. It's all most unseemly."

He made an effort to laugh.

"We were all young once," he said. "Tell me one thing, Miss Emerson. Why in God's name when you think of all that goes on in this Isthmus do we have to worry about this one isolated affair? Have we gone moral?"

She appeared to reflect.

"Well, her father's a colonel, you know."

"No, I didn't know," he said impatiently.

"Oh, yes. And a friend of the Commandant's."

"Dear, dear!"

"And I know Mr. Gilder doesn't like the girls in the office to be on those terms with the enlisted men."

"He wants them all for himself, I suppose?"

But she only smiled, and, picking up her notebook, returned to her desk. She had hoped for a better reception and her disappointment was considerable. Quite unreasonably she made bitter reflections on the gossiping propensity of her bosom friend and companion, Laura Smith.

CHAPTER FIVE

AUDREY WOKE UP very early the following Sunday morning and went out on the little porch by her room to sit on the comfortable wicker chair that had the best view of the hill. Here she lit a cigarette and sat in contemplation. The two hours after dawn were Panama's most endurable; there was a tingling damp freshness in the air which she clung to, always conscious of how soon it would be dissipated by the solid heat of the day. At the bottom of the hill way below her lay the big, shingled houses of Balboa with their heavy screens and raised first stories; just beyond them was the vast dock area and she could see the ships anchored in Balboa Basin. An Argentinian vessel with the painted flags and national letters of neutrality was moving slowly westwards on its way to sea; one of the old American cruisers of the *Concord* class, a unit of the Southeast Pacific fleet, long and grey and dotted with white-uniformed sailors was passing it on its way to dock. Audrey watched them and thought of the picture in the history textbook of her childhood of the young Columbus, restless and yearning at the docks of Genoa watching the big galleons depart for distant lands. Through another screen she could see the Smiths' house only a few doors down the road, covered with leaves, a mellow and comfortable combination of green and grey with a neat little lawn and a faded stone deer in the center. She liked Quarry Heights; with the exception of the big Union Club in Panama City on the other side of the hill it was the only place on the Isthmus that she really did like. Its isolation was aristocratic up on the side of the hill by Army Headquarters and overlooking the huge, white, stuccoed Zone Administration Building with its long red roof. The road borders were neatly cut; the little patches of jungle which screened each house from the others were kept under rigid control and gave more the effect of a conservatory than an equatorial wilderness. The Emersons' was the meanest house on the hill, a square, shingled two-story affair that could never excite comment—but still it was on the hill. Things could be worse. If only there was hope she could live.

It was Beverly whom she thought of as she went upstairs to dress. It was Beverly whom she thought of in relation to every object on her dressing table. And when she looked over at the bookcase in the corner where she had gathered the faded and tattered first editions of her favorite author, George Eliot, those decomposing volumes of *Romola* and *Middlemarch* purchased for ten dollars apiece by correspondence with New York secondhand book stores, it was the contrast of Beverly's nervous vitality that destroyed what pleasure she had formerly found in their contemplation. The vision of him seemed to redouble their dimness as the memory of the young hero of *Romola* seemed only to intensify the smudged green of the novel's covers.

She put on her green and white dress and twirled around the room, holding her wrapper behind her as though it were a train, waltzing, as she imagined, at the embassy. She drew herself suddenly up in front of the mirror and stared at her image in dismay. For here she was twenty-five years old, she thought with disgust, and rhapsodizing about a man whom she hardly knew. Whom she didn't know at all as a matter of fact. Could she ever be happy in a life full of Esmond Carnahans and Beverly Stregelinuses? She tried to answer "yes" because she didn't see happiness anywhere else; she made the effort deliberately to close her mind to any vision of life at and beyond the embassy that didn't fairly glitter with a variety and a charm that admittedly she had no knowledge of. She knew perfectly well the inevitable disillusionment that always followed her own strange habit of deliberate romanticizing, but if dreaming was the basic structure of anything approaching happiness and if it was impossible for her, as she well knew it was, without even making the effort to weave a dream out of the thin material suggested by her home or job, or mother or aunt, wasn't she almost obligated in fairness to herself to allow herself the dream and pursue its realization? The loss of illusion might be implicit in this realization, but what could she do?

Life always seemed to spin around in these silly little circles of desire, attainment, and disillusion. Life was manifestly unworthwhile to anyone who gave it a thought. It could not but be. Some people, she reflected, like Tommy Sondberg, Ruth's brother whom her family wanted her to marry, and Mr. Stoner in the office got an apparent satisfaction out of the glow of their own animal consciousness, the awareness of their own bodies, a sort of turkey strut. There were moments too of sheer desperation in which she toyed with the idea, not altogether without its fascination, of submerging her problems and her ego in the flood of sexual mastery which marriage with a person of Tommy's heavy and physical temperament would involve. But where would be the abiding satisfaction?

Which brought her as always, she reflected sourly as she went downstairs and took a seat on the main porch, back to the question of God. She was not by temperament a religious person, but where else could a sense of the worthlessness of life and a terror of annihilation afterwards lead her? She had followed the evolution of Aldous Huxley's spiritual thought through its various and highly published stages. She had felt drawn to the logic which, starting from the premise that materialism was a curtain between the soul's eye and God, moved on to the ultimate denunciation of everything in life that did not assist directly towards the unclouded contemplation of the deity. She had enjoyed the dimensions of the junk heap which this created. Love of family fell in with love of money. It clouded the eye. "Let the dead bury the dead." "Behold my mother and my brethren!" The fact that she felt so little emotion towards her own family contributed, she supposed, to her pleasure in finding family ties relegated to so low a level in the Christian life. But to dispose of duties and not ambitions was hardly in accordance with even Huxlean precepts. She would have to live in mystic, ascetic adoration and to her there was no chillier concept. If she had to suppress personality to attain peace how did this differ from extinction? She had no urge to be a pulse in an infinite sea of love.

Oh, life.

She heard her Aunt Betty's heavy step on the stair and forced a smile as the large, beshawled figure appeared at the door. Miss Miles leaned heavily on a cane and stared around the porch through her octagonal glasses. Her grey hair piled on top of her head seemed to be escaping in longer looser strands than usual.

"What you doin' up so early, Audrey?"

"Thinking."

"What's a young girl like you got to be thinkin' about at this hour? Before she's even had her breakfast?"

Audrey surveyed her with detachment.

"Sin."

Miss Miles was seating herself slowly and laboriously in a wicker arm chair, but the unexpected word startled her into what was almost a drop for the last two inches.

"Gracious me, what do you mean! At seven o'clock?"

"Isn't seven o'clock a good time to think about sin? Besides, it's Sunday."

"I never heard of such a thing."

Audrey appeared to consider this.

"No," she answered slowly. "I don't suppose you did."

"What sort of sin? Nothing on your conscience, I hope?"

Again Audrey was silent for a moment.

"Well, that's just it, really. Does it matter what sort of sin?"

Miss Miles gave a snort.

"It used to where I come from."

"That's what you thought. But did God?"

"Did God what?"

"Did he make any distinction? Isn't goodness unattainable? Aren't we all sinners?" She got up and walked to the screen door. "We all care about something more than God, don't we? Look at Mother. She cares about running this house. And Daddy thinks all the time about engineering."

"Why not? Aren't those fine useful things?"

"And you, Aunt Betty," her niece pursued, "what do *you* care about?"

Miss Miles stared at her without answering. Then she seemed to enter for a moment into something like the detachment of Audrey's mood.

"It's hard to say," she answered. "I suppose I care about my memories most. All the beautiful things I've seen. The blue hills in Virginia. The Lawn at the University." But the interest in Audrey's eyes brought her back to the point. "And I care about my nieces living useful lives and marrying good men," she finished gruffly.

"I see. You care about our learning not to care about God."

"Land sakes! What sort of talk is that?"

"Just talk."

"It's irreverent, that's what it is."

"I suppose."

Miss Miles looked at her in perplexity.

"Well, what do *you* care about?" she inquired. "Books?"

"Oh, I guess I care about joking with amusing people about people who are less amusing."

"Gracious me!"

"Why not? If not God why not that?"

"I don't know what's got into this daughter of yours, Martha Ellen," Miss Miles continued, turning to her sister whose placid, even face had just appeared at the door. "Talkin' about reverent things in some smart-alecky modern way at this hour of the mornin'."

Mrs. Emerson went over to the table by Audrey's chair, picked up the ash tray, and emptied it carefully into the wastepaper basket.

"You shouldn't smoke before breakfast, daughter," she observed quietly. Then addressing Miss Miles in the same even tone she continued: "I expect the child's been readin' too much. That's all young folks do these days. Read, read, all the time. Breakfast's about ready."

Audrey got up to go into the dining room. She looked at her mother pityingly. What *was* the use?

"That's right," she said. "Everything's a problem of generations, isn't it? Look at Laura Smith. I'm sure she's read a book. Maybe two. What are we coming to?"

Her mother, helping Miss Miles out of her chair, didn't even listen to this, and they all passed into the dining room where Mr. Emerson whose bald head and round perspiring face made every room that he was in seem doubly equatorial was already seated at the head of the table, being served by the colored maid. The dining room walls were decorated by two small mirrors and a lithograph of President Taft inspecting Culebra Cut; the furniture of dark oak wood was heavy and utterly simple but seemed too strong for the light matted walls. The china dishes were painted with a startling variety of cats and dogs; the unstemmed water glasses were of different sizes. In a cabinet in the corner jumbled glassware clinked at each step on the floor. Audrey sat down in silence and poured herself a cup of coffee. She could see that her mother, who was inclined to disregard her moods entirely, had been vaguely disturbed by Miss Miles' account of the pre-breakfast conversation for she was casting searching looks at her. In a moment, she knew, her mother would ask her father to confirm her suspicions. Yes, here it came.

"Vance," her mother said, "don't you think Audrey looks a bit tired?"

"Oh, Mother."

"Perhaps she does a little," Mr. Emerson answered, surveying her through his spectacles with a backward tilt of his head. "Maybe she's been goin' it too hard over at the Navy. Those battleships won't sink if you take it a little easier. Eh, daughter?"

"I'm all right, Daddy."

"This gettin' up early and talkin' about reverend things before breakfast don't look right," her mother continued imperturbably. "It shows strain. Maybe you ought to exercise more."

"Audrey doesn't exercise at all," Miss Miles contributed.

"And I don't intend to." She turned more resolutely to her father. "Daddy, will you please tell Mother not to fuss about me? I looked after myself for four years away from home and I can certainly do it now."

"If you ask me," Miss Miles continued, "she ought to get out more in the evenings. A young girl shouldn't be home with a book. Why, the Zone is swarming with attractive young officers."

Audrey put down her cup, stung.

"You wouldn't think they were so attractive if you knew what they were all after, Aunt Betty," she retorted. "Balboa isn't Richmond in 1861, you know. I don't know any Jeb Stuarts or John Pelhams."

"Don't be snippy with your aunt, Audrey," her mother reproved her. "You know as well as I do there must be plenty of nice officers over at the Navy."

"In my section," Audrey answered in exasperation, "we have Mr. Lawrence who is married and always writing his wife. Then we have Mr. Stregelinus, a New York blue blood who never thinks of me except as a typewriter, and Mr. Malory who likes to jitterbug. Of course, there's Commander Gilder who wants to sleep with me——"

"Audrey Emerson, you be quiet!" her mother exclaimed with sudden energy. "Don't you dare use that sort of talk in this house!"

Mr. Emerson stared into his plate and Miss Miles nodded her head approvingly at her sister. Audrey shrugged her shoulders.

"If you don't want to hear the truth," she said.

"Oh, the truth!" her mother retorted. "I don't know what

all you have over at the Navy but I do know your habit of exaggeratin'. And anyway there are plenty of nice clean boys among the families we know down here and don't you try to tell me the contrary."

"If you mean, Mother," said Audrey in a silly, cool, sarcastic tone, "why don't I go out with Tommy Sondberg I think it would be as well for you to say so."

Miss Miles and Mrs. Emerson exchanged glances of exasperation.

"I mean no such thing," Mrs. Emerson snapped. "Don't you go putting words in my mouth. I think Tommy Sondberg is a fine upstanding boy and I'd be glad if I thought you'd ever marry anyone half as nice."

"Really," Audrey remarked, feeling in herself the throb of excited but inevitably regretted pleasure that comes with hurting those who love us, "I can't but marvel at the adaptability of you and Aunt Betty to modern-day conditions. You're always extolling the departed grandeur of the Miles. Yet you could reconcile yourselves to a Sondberg. I congratulate you but I struggle with a less noble nature." And crumpling up her paper napkin she got up from the table and went to her room.

She stayed there with the door closed until ten o'clock at which time she put on her best straw hat with the green flower and slipped down the stairs and out of the house. She walked down the road to the Smiths'. Laura was going to drive her to church. She found her in the big dark dining room, sipping orange juice and reading the *Star and Herald*. General Smith, very thin and grey in an immaculate white suit, was at the other end. He asked Audrey how her father and mother were and when she and Laura were to be made admirals, his usual joke, and then reverted to his newspaper. Laura drawled on about a "divine" lieutenant colonel she had been out with the night before and said she really didn't know why she went out so much—really she *was* going to stay home a few nights soon and catch up with all the good books—and then took Audrey upstairs while she finished dressing and showed her two new photographs of army officers on her bureau. She did everything she could to postpone their church going, but it was a habit to which Audrey firmly adhered and eventually they drove off to the little white pseudo-Spanish Episcopal church that stood so primly at the bottom of the hill.

She knew that Beverly usually went there to get away,

as he put it, from a naval God and she glanced around
after they were seated to find him sitting alone in a back
pew looking very hot in his tight white uniform. She smiled
at him only to get a rather stiff nod and she didn't look
around again. The Helen episode, she reflected sadly, had
been most unfortunate. It had not occurred to her oddly
enough that he would be repulsed by her behavior. It had
seemed much more probable that a gossipy nature like his
would warm to the problem suggested and amalgamate its
energies with hers in the search for a solution. So she had
reasoned anyway when she had scraped together the pieces
of Helen's dreary story to hold them hopefully under Sherry
Gilder's snout. And to have run instead into an uncompromising integrity had certainly proved an unexpected humilia-
tion. But if one worried about all these wretched little things
could one live at all? She sighed almost in boredom and,
catching sight of Helen's wide-brimmed hat in the front of
the church, reflected strangely with what impunity she regarded her own role in relaying to Gilder that rather colored
version of Helen's romance. The time had been when she
would have suffered nervous pangs from such a thing, time
when her conscience had been a rather hysterical mentor
sticking its head up at the oddest moments, but now its
visits were rarer. Lethargy had descended over her feelings,
lethargy and detachment. She roused herself with a slight
shudder as the congregation rose for a hymn. Could she
never think of anything but herself? When all the world was
full of poetry and beauty and ambition—and even war.

Laura nudged her.

"Look at Helen," she whispered. "Looks as though she's
been crying her eyes out. What did they do to her boy
friend?"

Audrey only shook her head and put her finger to her lips.

Helen followed Beverly out of the church, breaking into
what was almost a run when she saw him quicken his step
as he walked down the flag-stoned path to the road.

"Mr. Stregelinus!"

He turned to face in astonishment her flushed and worried
countenance.

"Yes, Miss Drinker?"

"Why did you have Eddie Taylor transferred to Cristobal?

He stared at her and then glanced in confusion at the

people who were crowding past them on the path. He stepped off on the grass and walked a little way towards the middle of the lawn. She followed him and caught him by the arm.

"Why did you?" she repeated.

"Eddie who?" he asked vaguely.

"Oh, don't pretend you don't know!" she cried impatiently. "The boy who drove the station wagon for your section."

"Oh, yes," he said hurriedly. "Taylor. I don't know. I guess they needed another driver over there. They're always grabbing our personnel." He was unable, however, to face the penetration of her stare.

"There wasn't any more to it than that?" she insisted. "It wasn't because I'd been going out with him? Are you telling me the truth?"

"My dear Miss Drinker, I—"

"Of course, it isn't the truth, Helen," said someone behind them in a clear level voice. "Do you really want the truth?" They both turned around to find Audrey.

"What do you want?" Helen exclaimed in sudden fury. "What business is this of yours? Clear out of here, will you?"

"I think I can handle this, Miss Emerson," said Bev in a rather lofty tone.

But Audrey looked entirely unrebuffed.

"Yes, but why should you?" she answered. "It wasn't your fault. You only did what Commander Gilder told you. I'm the one that's really responsible and I don't intend to have Helen take it out on you. If she must make a disgusting scene let it be with me."

Helen listened to this, dumbfounded. Her stiff, stubborn face turned slowly red and her large blue eyes widened.

"So it was *you* who put Gilder up to this," she gasped.

"I was one of the people who complained," Audrey said coolly. "There were others. It was for your own good, Helen."

"My own good!" Helen closed her eyes for a second at the sheer audacity of it. "I suppose I should be grateful to you," she said after a moment.

"Possibly."

"I suppose you think this will keep Eddie and me apart?"

"No. But that wasn't the point. It'll keep you from making a public spectacle of yourself, writing little notes to Eddie all day at the office and leaving little bunches of lavender on the front seat of the station wagon."

Helen's eyes showed all the fury of an only child whose parents have never told it the truth.

"How dare you?" she cried. "How dare you tell me that you did it for my good! You wouldn't do anything for anybody, Audrey Emerson. You're just as nasty and cold as they come!"

"If by cold you mean that I don't go around hysterically telling everyone I'm in love with a sailor ten years younger than I am—"

"Eight!"

Beverly tried to get between them.

"Look, girls," he pleaded, "don't you think we've had just about enough of this?"

Helen turned blindly to him looking for allies.

"It's just like her!" she said excitedly. "She's always sneering at conventions. But she can't abide people who break them. Oh, she makes me vomit. She and her friend, Laura!"

"Where is this getting us, Miss Emerson?" Bev protested.

"It depends where Helen wants to get. If she wants everyone in the Zone to know about her—"

"Oh, that!" Helen almost smiled. "I assume if you and Laura know the publication will soon be complete. If it's so bad, Mr. Stregelinus," she said, turning again to him, "maybe you'd rather have me out of the way?"

"Oh, no, Miss Drinker!"

"Maybe you could get *me* transferred to Cristobal."

It was Audrey's turn to stare.

"My God, Helen, what do you want to do? Marry the boy?"

Helen's eyes flashed as she saw Audrey's incredulity.

"It's just what I will do!" she cried. "If Eddie sees it that way."

"If."

"And if I do," Helen continued exultantly, "I'll be married right here. And if I am, I hope, dearest Audrey, that you will be one of my bridesmaids."

Audrey only smiled and gave a little bow.

"I should be honored."

When Bev finally escaped and dropped into the front seat of his car he mopped his brow and breathed deeply in relief. He couldn't, however, avoid the feeling as he started up the motor and drove down the road that in some inexplicable fashion Audrey and Laura and Helen were all still friends and that a wedding and bridesmaids as visualized might actually become a sober reality. He thought with astonishment of hymns and wedding presents, of telephone calls and thank-you notes and of the strange, big, ugly pelicans that flapped with clumsy freedom up and down the beaches of Panama.

CHAPTER SIX

AT THE OFFICERS' bar that afternoon, a varnished oval affair in a corner of the Bachelor Officers' Quarters, in a room decorated by a large clumsy mural of Panama Bay, Bev and Amos sat perched on stools, consuming the first of their ante-dinner martinis. It was Beverly's favorite moment óf the day; he had put on a clean khaki shirt; he had combed and brushed his long hair and given his face an alcohol rub, and now as he moved his olive stick about in the shining golden yellow of his cocktail he felt a sense of melancholy that was far from unpleasant. They were speaking of marine heroism on Guadalcanal.

"But it's terrific, Amos!" he was exclaiming. "It's as if the fine rare flower of true America were bursting into bloom after all these years!"

"All what years?"

"Years of Santa Claus. Isolation. 'The world owes me a living.' " Bev finished off his martini at a gulp. "Years of degenerating bureaucracy. And then a bunch of kids jump off on a beachhead and put us all to shame. Make us show up for what we are."

"And what are we?"

"Clerks, Amos." He raised two fingers to the colored bartender who nodded and started mixing two more martinis. "Clerks. You and I sit side by side and shuffle paper. They die."

He felt his uselessness big and solid inside him. But Amos was not ready to share the mood. He never was.

"I think I can agree with you about your job, Bev," he said after a pause. "Mine needless to say is one of the more vital."

"Oh, piddle!" Bev exclaimed. "Even Darlington doesn't—" Discretion stopped him. "Amos, I've got to go to sea."

"You! You don't know a compass from a roulette wheel."

"I could learn. I've sat in on some of those night courses in navigation."

Amos laughed in his own croaking manner.

"You'd be great!"

"Well, I'm going to apply anyway."

"Do your family know? Think how worried they'd be."

But Bev, ignoring him, stared unhappily into his next martini. He was always about to apply for sea duty and Mr. Gilder was always discouraging him by assuring him that the application would be rejected. And then, deep down, hateful but nonetheless present was that tiny, lurking, still-born sense of relief. He had decided anyway that he would ask permission to take a trip to Guantanamo and back on one of the convoys; this would at least remove the onus of never having been to sea—except on the naval transport that had taken him down to the Zone.

"An unmarried man," Amos continued in that assured tone which he used to carry off his major ironies, "really should go to sea. Now I, of course, would never be ashore if it weren't for my wife and children—"

"Who are sitting up in Boston learning the difference between Lawrences and Lowells," Bev cried. "And I should go to sea for them!"

"Marriage is a public duty," Amos continued. "What was wrong with you anyway? Wouldn't anyone have you? I thought in New York people were less particular."

When Amos was in one of these moods there was no talking to him. Bev even felt a desire to defend Boston from the sweeping negation of his irony.

"What about the Miss Tremaine you write to so often?" Amos went on.

"Sylvia?" Bev's eyes assumed a faraway expression. "Sylvia won't have me. Would that she would."

"Why not?"

"She thinks I'm 'tinny,'" he answered frankly. "How pathetically little she knows of the depths of my emotional involvement! I suppose it's my tragedy that I can't make her see it. She has money too. At least her mother has. I haven't and that makes me self-conscious."

"Ever try pinching?"

Bev looked at him in disgust.

"You're worse than Stoner," he retorted. That was one of the deadliest things about Panama, that one had no real friends. He thought of the sympathy of his New York circle, the people who understood his very monosyllables and knew his cousins. What was wrong in the Zone was the uprootedness of people. They didn't give a damn who you were or what you were, because you weren't "real." You wouldn't be part of their postwar world. Amos, for example, was so utterly absorbed in his absent wife that even those closest to him in Panama were only figures in a shadow world that would dissolve with the Armistice. People who didn't probe too deeply into the texture of their human relationships could be content in Panama, people like Stoner who had no imagination about others and sought in friendship a companionship for the exchange of platitudes; and no doubt such people were in a majority, but Bev from time to time had fits of loneliness that took him back in spirit twenty years to his days as a "new kid" at Chelton in the cold, crisp fall of a formidable New England. Yes, he had Mrs. Livermore and Esmond, that was true. It was a great piece of luck to have found a nearby embassy housing two such friends. But he saw less of them even than he had in New York. The naval and diplomatic circles rarely intersected. And Esmond after all had too jumpy a mind for real sympathy, while his aunt was too busy for long introspective chats. In the last analysis there was no one in the whole Zone who could understand his feeling for Sylvia or his nostalgia for the bright sparkle of Manhattan pavements east of Central Park and the broad, warm green of Long Island lawns.

There was only one thing to do and that was to order another martini. He was beginning to feel them a little now. Lieutenant-Commander McShane came up behind the two and jovially put his hands on their shoulders.

"I spoke to Gilder about that map," he brayed. "He says I'm right. You and Lawrence are to do it."

Beverly turned to him bitterly.

"With the greatest of pleasure, Mr. McShane," he said. "And may I congratulate you on a jurisdictional victory? I know what they mean to you. My mornings will now be full. I only regret that I have but one *Life* to read for my country."

Mr. McShane didn't get it; he never did. His little eyes rolled suspiciously back and forth as he looked from Amos to Bev.

"I'm not fighting with anyone," he snapped. "I'm just trying to put the office on a working basis." His eyes wandered around the room as he repeated his sentence.

Bev suddenly could feel almost sorry for him. The constant need for self-assertion must have been such a wear and tear. It was this eternal chatter that had moved McShane steadily up the ladder from truck driver to lock worker to the harbor office and at long, long last to the Navy. He stared at the big, constantly moving lips that formed the constantly repeated sentences that reinforced the almost insane ego of the man; they seemed like the two great wings of a wounded sea bird; they flapped desperately to squawking cries.

"A working basis, I take it," Bev observed, "means that Section Blue does everything Section Red can't be bothered about." Saying this he took his drink and moved sullenly away from the bar to a table by himself. There were times when he simply couldn't make the effort, when even the muscular exertion of emitting his well-known laugh seemed impossibly laborious. He glowered over his glass at Amos who was chatting pleasantly with McShane and with Stoner who had just joined them. There were no loyalties. No integrity. Nothing but frivolous insincerity in the give and take of human relations.

He stared into the hard but reassuring golden depths of his cocktail and visualized again the scene outside the church of that morning. It was Miss Emerson's extraordinary *insouciance* that kept returning to him, the calm deliberation with which she had made her strokes. If she was a part of the hypocrisy of the tropical world, and so indeed he had judged her, she was at least not small. Nor afraid. She had apparently standards aplenty, only never, alas, a guide to orient her choice amid their wide selection. If a girl like that only had a tutor—or a friend— He found himself wondering if she was lonely in the same way that he was. Somehow he felt that under her hardness there was at least the possibility of real feeling such as his. There was nothing, at any rate, he reflected as he glanced sourly over at Amos, to stand in the way of his finding out. As the burst of McShane's laughter came to him, he pushed aside the unfinished martini with sudden resolution and walked to the telephone in the corner.

El Rancho was the big beer parlor in Panama City where everybody met on week-day nights. The dance floor was

open to the sky; the tables were spread about on different
levels under cupolas and porches. On one side through many
vistas the red and yellow of the Panamanian capital
stretched itself to the eye, and further out in a long shim-
mering arc, brilliant and surrounding, lay the wide expanse
of Panama Bay.

They had been talking with some constraint about Helen
Drinker and her plans. He was tired of the subject and saw
that she was.

"Now that we're running a marriage bureau I guess we
can use first names," he said awkwardly.

She smiled quickly to cover her embarrassment.

"Yes, Beverly."

"Maybe we can even be friends."

"Who knows?"

"It's all right, my taking you to dinner this way. I mean
Gilder won't object—"

She stared.

"What?"

He flushed suddenly.

"I mean officers and stenographers, as a point of etiquette—"

She burst out laughing.

"You *are* old-fashioned," she said. Then she smiled. "No,
I think you're entirely safe. If not, I won't tell anyone."
She watched him with amusement while he ordered and the
fuss that he made with the inert waiter. It was such a curious
combination, his gesticulations, his long hair and strident
voice, his ridiculous laugh, and then, as if to counterbalance
some of the undeniable effeminacy, the likability of his
friendly grey eyes.

"I've really wanted to do this before, you know," he said.

"Have dinner at El Rancho?"

"No. Take you out."

"And why haven't you?"

"Well, I guess I didn't quite know how to go about it."

"You mean you didn't really want to," she reproached
him. "It must have been so difficult—so few opportunities,
I mean. Working every day in the same office."

"I suppose that does sound silly," he admitted. "But you
always looked so business-like and definite. As if you knew
just what you were planning to do when you left the office.
The way you fold up the typewriter drawer. With such a
click."

"You do notice people, then."

"Notice people! That's all I've *ever* done. People are my *métier*."

She looked at him with some misgiving.

"I always supposed that your people would have to be something pretty special."

"What do you mean, 'special'?" he demanded.

"Oh, you know." She shrugged her shoulders. "I supposed they'd have to be grand."

She could see by the emphatic way that he said "Nonsense!" that it was a suggestion which he was not unused to rebutting.

"I don't pick my friends," he protested. "They happen. I admit I don't hold it against them if they're what you call 'grand' any more than I do if they aren't. Well, look down here. Amos Lawrence. Is he grand?"

"Very."

"You've just got a chip on your shoulder, that's what's wrong with you, Audie."

"Audrey."

"Audrey then."

She took a sip of the martini which the waiter had just brought.

"It's not a chip," she said reflectively, "it's just being realistic. Mr. Lawrence seems very swell to somebody like me. So do you, for that matter."

"Well, I hope you're not going to be swept off your feet!"

She was enjoying it more even than she had thought she would. There was a vehemence about his friendliness that seemed to surround her and pack her into a big, fluffy, cottony box. He appeared to have emotional values and odd little standards of conduct that had no relation to the world which she had been brought up in and little or none, she suspected, even to his own. He was certainly unusual; he seemed to float above the ordinary world with an impregnability that she felt would sustain any number of hits from critical anti-aircraft below. What on earth could one do with him?

"How do you pick your friends?" he returned aggressively. "By their *un*grandness?"

"Oh, no. Not at all. I like swells. It's just that there are so few of them around."

"Don't you have friends, then?"

"I suppose. I never stopped to think about it, really.

There's Laura Smith, of course. I guess she's about my best friend. Except I hate her."

He emitted a shout of laughter.

"Audrey, you're priceless! I can see we're going to be great friends."

"No friend like a new friend."

He was going off into another spurt of laughter when the waiter arrived with two plates of oysters.

"Have you made many friends down here?" she asked. "I mean real ones?"

"It's funny. I was just thinking about that this afternoon. No, not really. Everybody's thinking of home all the time. They don't have much to give. As a matter of fact, Americans as a whole don't go in much for real friendship, do you think?"

"What's *real* friendship?"

"What is it!" He speared an oyster. "It's something you can't get on without and call yourself alive. Real friendship?" He appeared to grope for words and stared at her in perplexity. "What's the use of living, anyway, if you don't have friends for whom you'd be willing to do anything under the sun and who'd be willing to do anything for you?"

She stared back at him.

"But who does? There aren't any people like that."

"I disagree with you! One hundred per cent."

She smiled at his intensity.

"Where do you find them? You just said Americans don't go in for real friendship."

He waived this.

"I mean they don't cultivate it. But it's there in them. Just a question of bringing it out."

She hesitated. She was not in sympathy with his emotional approach to the question and she knew that when she disagreed in an argument she had a tendency to carry her point too far and too emphatically. Such was not the impression that she wanted to create tonight.

"Don't you feel though," she asked, "that most of your friends don't give much of a damn? Younger married people for instance who are all taken up with themselves and their babies. And older people who aren't really interested in anything about you except the fact that you're young. Sometimes I feel that no one *really* cares about anyone else."

His mouth opened with horror.

"My dear girl, you're so wrong! So utterly, abysmally wrong.

I can't begin to tell you. There may be something in what you say about people with babies, but older people—why probably my best friend in the world is Angeline Stroud and she's more than twenty years older than me."

"Who is Angeline Stroud?" Listening to him go on was like playing tennis with a person who lobs every third ball over the back net.

"Mrs. Arleus Stroud. And such a dear. The sweetest woman—"

"Oh, yes," she interrupted. "I've read about her in the papers. You see that's what I mean by your friends being grand."

"Oh, she's not grand," he protested. "Rich as mud, yes, but that just gives her a chance to be more generous. Why she's plain as an old shoe and twice as comfortable. You'd love her, Audrey! Take for example the time that Lillias Anesco had to auction off all her things: pictures, bronzes, the whole works. Angeline was in Europe at the time but when she came back and found out about it what did she do but go straight down to Parke-Bernet, get a catalogue and set to work to trace every last, blessed item that had been sold. It took her a year to buy them all back and she didn't let on till she had the works, and then on Christmas day—"

Audrey began to realize that she was just a tiny bit bored. It was not, however, an unpleasant sort of boredom and it was very easy to disguise. The world that he prattled on about lost most of its forbidding remoteness in the cozy ennui that settled around it in her mind and he himself if less impressive became more reachable. As she listened to successive anecdotes illustrating the great goodheartedness of Mrs. Angeline Stroud and others of her circle, their kindness to Beverly, their wonderful sense of humor and the gay, careless, *crazy* way in which they conducted themselves on occasions where the utmost formality was apparently to have been expected, she had the pleasant sense of ease that can come with splashing in a warm bath. That is, when she didn't try too hard to remember what she had expected of him. But, oh well. Did one ever really enjoy the moments in one's life that one did enjoy? She joined in his laughter over the climax of a story about Mrs. Emden at a dinner in London for Edda Ciano.

The Rancho was filling up. Army khaki and navy whites predominated, but there was a large civilian element as well, Zone couples, and even a group from Panamanian society.

Beverly waved to this person and that; occasionally officers
would stop by their table and chat. She noted that he was
almost the only naval officer there in his work-day khakies.

"But there's Lydia!" he cried, waving across the floor. She
followed the direction of his gestures and saw sitting at the
center of a table of naval officers and Panamanians the looming figure of Mrs. Schmidt, red hair, jewels and all, a familiar
sight to everyone on the Isthmus. "Shall we join her party?"
he asked. "She's such fun."

Audrey hesitated. Mrs. Schmidt was an enigmatic character.
She was not really a Zonite though she had started as one.
Her story was variously told and much of it was legend, but
it included beyond a reasonable doubt at least three husbands, one of whom, a worker on lock construction in the
early part of the century, had tumbled into the Canal and
drowned. After this Lydia was believed to have done almost
everything. That she had run a beer parlor for the Culebra
Cut excavators was known; it was less certain that she had
owned two brothels in Panama City. Her second husband had
been Panamanian; together they had obtained control of all
the cabarets in the Republic; her third, Schmidt, a German,
had helped her to extend her empire throughout Central
America. Schmidt had disappeared; he was now variously
rumored to be in an internment camp in the States, to be
in Berlin on the German general staff, and to be developing
beer markets in the wilds of Brazil. At any rate the great-
hearted Lydia had shed him. She lived in Panama City, magnificent and husbandless, surrounded by the offspring of her
many unions, running a vast business single-handed—efficient,
vulgar, showy, sensible, and kind. To be sure she was hardly
respectable. She could never have been received at the
embassy or even been friends with the Smiths. No one even
knew if she was still an American. But all Panama adored
her and her parties and her champagne; Americans of any
standing who passed through the Isthmus called on her; she
was a "character" beside whom the Zone seemed pale and
anemic. Beverly, of course, had promptly become one of
her intimates.

"I would like to," she said dubiously, "but you know how
it is—"

"I know Lydia's a great woman," he interrupted firmly.
"And what's more I think it would do you good to know her."

She nodded and smiled. The only thing that she minded

was the interruption of their talk, but she was hardly going to admit that.

"Let's join them, then," she said.

They made their way across the dance floor towards Lydia's party. She waved her big feather boa at them as they approached and flung a series of introductions around the table. Two dark Panamanian gentlemen arose and bowed to Audrey; the rest of the table nodded. Esmond Carnahan jumped up and hurried over. He was dressed in a white flannel tuxedo and was wearing a large carnation in his buttonhole.

"So you've brought your lovely secretary at last," he exclaimed with a bow. "I thought you kept her imprisoned behind those green naval walls."

"Oh, Miss Emerson gets about," Beverly answered.

"No thanks to you."

"She doesn't need me. Or you, Mr. Secretary, for that matter."

"We'll see about that. Miss Emerson, don't you need me?"

"For what, Mr. Carnahan?"

"Well, at the moment for a dance."

But Audrey only thanked him and sat down between Amos Lawrence and Lydia. Amos was holding a large bumper of champagne from which he offered her a sip. Lydia turned to her with an appraising but not unfriendly eye.

"Aren't you the girl I see at the Union Club sometimes with General Smith and his daughter?"

"I have been there with them."

"Do you like them?"

"Don't you?"

"My dear, they won't even know me."

Audrey hesitated.

"Then I guess they won't be knowing me either," she said.

"Why?"

"Because I seem to have joined your delightful party." She said this with the necessary smile of polite irony.

"But, Bev, I adore this girl!" Lydia cried, turning to him. "Where did you find her?"

"Miss Emerson is the mainstay of our office," Amos answered for him. "Not only does she do her own work but she has mine and Bev's as well."

"Oh, crushing load!" cried Esmond, slumping forward, his

arms outstretched on the table. "Fifteen minutes added to every day. I wonder Miss Emerson doesn't have rounded shoulders."

"It's having the embassy work too that's the real burden," Audrey answered quickly. "Isn't it, Beverly? Answering questions from third secretaries about the ramifications of the British royal family."

"Exactly!" Bev exclaimed in delight. "Carnahan, Lydia, comes sniveling into our office with a mental shopping list from his Aunt Gladys."

"Questions I really want to know the answer to I take to Lydia," Esmond rejoined with a wink, only to get his hand slapped. "Miss Emerson, won't you please dance with me?"

She nodded and got up. Esmond followed her on to the crowded dance floor. With his smooth round cheeks and bright smile he seemed to have stepped out of the lacquered prose of an Elinor Wylie tale.

"Can't we go somewhere else?" he asked.

"I thought you wanted to dance."

"Yes. But afterwards."

"And leave Beverly and Mrs. Schmidt?"

"Oh, you don't want to sit with that gang, do you?"

They were dancing together now, but she stepped back and looked at him in surprise.

"But I came with Beverly," she reminded him.

He laughed happily.

"Of course you did," he answered. "But he'll be contented with his Lydia. They'll have a perfectly ducky time swapping dirty stories."

"Don't you like Beverly?"

"Oh, sure. But what a moth-eaten old primrose he is!"

Audrey stiffened. She was surprised at how much she resented the insinuation. And from such a porcelain cupid, too.

"I don't agree with you at all," she said warmly. "I couldn't agree with you less. And what's more, Mr. Carnahan, I don't think you should talk that way about an old friend."

But Esmond only laughed again.

"Oh, it's that way, Miss Emerson, is it?" he said with provoking joviality. "I *see*."

Back at the table Beverly glanced towards the floor in search of them.

"Who is she, Bev?" Lydia asked with a snap of her small

black eyes. They blinked and rolled, her eyes, with an energy all the more marked for its contrast to the plaster deadness of her heavily powdered face. With her red wig and huge body Lydia seemed not only ageless but sexless. "Such a sweet little thing," she continued, gazing at Audrey through a lorgnette. "Not really pretty, of course, but attractive in a mousy sort of way. Just the thing for you, my dear, if Carnahan doesn't ruin her."

Bev was filling his glass from the bottle in the middle of the table.

"I didn't think anyone could be ruined nowadays," he said.

"Don't you believe it!" Lydia exclaimed. "Certainly they can."

"People like Lydia always turn out to be the greatest sentimentalists," Amos said.

"What about you, Lydia?" Bev asked. "Could you be ruined?"

"Me? Oh, I'm indestructible," she declared gaily. "I came down to the Isthmus in the old French days when I was sixteen."

"When men were men," Amos commented dryly.

"When men were men," she repeated warmly. "Exactly. Not like these days. If you could have seen Bev and Esmond at my house the other night, Amos! They practically tore each other's hair out. Bev called Esmond a 'decadent' and Esmond made a terrible fuss, saying he'd been horribly insulted. What he really was, he kept yelling, was a 'degenerate.' "

Amos nodded.

"A fine manly quarrel."

"Esmond can be such a baby," Bev protested.

"You ought to get married, my dear," Lydia told him seriously. "Of course you're the type who ought to marry money, but pick yourself a little girl down here, someone like the one Carnahan's just run off with and after the war I'll fix you up in business. Or maybe I have a daughter the right age for you. Do I, Amos?"

"Granddaughter most likely."

"Oh, Amos, you are a brute!" she cried and covered him with her feather boa.

Beverly laughed, but he was moved. He knew she meant it. There was no better friend in all the world than Lydia. She would go to any pains to help him make money, and as he bethought him of his rather wrinkled past, and as he gazed about at the gaiety of Panama, particularly just then as a sea breeze fluttered over the dance floor and cooled the air he wondered if, married to somebody like Audrey and working for Schmidt Cabarets, he wouldn't really be happy for perhaps the first time in his life. This was sentimental but what had the rest of his life been but that?

"Of course, I'm not entirely unattached," he said moodily.

"Some girl in New York," Amos explained to Lydia. "But she turned you down, didn't she? Sensible girl."

"Yes," Bev answered. "She turned me down."

"Now didn't you like Lydia? Really?" Bev asked Audrey two hours later when they were dancing and the others had gone on to the Union Club.

"Yes, I suppose I did. I guess I'm a bit of a prude about some things still, but give me time. I'll get over it."

He looked at her approvingly.

"You're awfully intelligent."

"Why do you say that?"

"You read George Eliot in the office and that sort of thing."

"So I do. I suppose that makes me awfully intelligent."

"To me it does. And then there's something repressed about you. Something smoldering. You're quiet but down deep you're really not a bit shy. Are you?"

"I am shyer than you are."

"Didn't it take me all this time to ask you for a date? I'm a terribly shy person."

She laughed at this.

"Well, I like it," she said.

"You're really great fun, you know."

"Because I listen to you?"

"Well, that's a huge virtue. But you have others. Were you really born down here? How long have you lived here?"

He took her over to a table. He had forgotten his questions by the time they had sat down, but she gently steered him back. There were some impressions to correct.

"I went to college in the States," she said. "I'm not entirely dredgified, you know."

"Oh. Where?"

"Hollins. I used to live in Virginia."

"Really?"

"Yes, I know I don't seem particularly Southern. But Mother's family were all poor Virginians. You know the type. A tattered present with an illusory past. They lived in Charlottesville."

He gave a little gurgle of excitement.

"But I went there to the University for a whole year!" he cried. "Law school. Ten years ago. What was your mother's name?"

"Miles. Aunt Betty ran a boardinghouse for students."

"Miss Betty Miles!" he exclaimed. "Why, of course. I remember seeing her on her porch at University Circle day after day. Well, I'll be damned!"

It was just as well, she reflected, that she had not attempted to impress him with the picture of old family houses on the James that she sometimes used with indifferent success on her friend Laura.

"Aunt Betty lives with us down here now. Why don't you come around and see her some afternoon?"

"Listen! Don't think I won't. I'd love to. Of course, she won't remember me but we could have a wonderful time talking about the old days. And by the way, talking about swells, where did you ever get that chip on your shoulder? The Miles are howling swells. I wonder that you'd even go out with Yankee trash like me."

"Swellness wears off," she explained. "After a few years of taking in washing."

"But you can always tell breeding."

"I wonder if you can transplant it though," she murmured, looking around El Rancho. "My memories of Virginia aren't particularly happy."

"But you don't like it here do you?"

"Now why do you say that?" she asked him, turning to him. "Do I seem discontented? I'd hate to think that."

"Oh, no. But you give me a sense of having larger fields to conquer. You weren't born to stifle down here."

"That's always nice to hear. What shall I do about it?"

"Go north."

"I haven't any money," she rejoined flatly.

"Neither have I."

"You and I probably mean different things by that."

"There you go with that chip. Will you please knock it off?" He reached over and pretended to brush something from her shoulder. "I mean by no money that I have no income other than my naval salary. Which is less than you get, my dear."

"But your family has money," she suggested hopefully.

"Mother has about nine thousand a year of her own which is considered penury among her friends. And she needs every penny of that for herself and my sister. Now have I been sufficiently specific?"

She was careful not to betray the unpleasant surprise aroused by this piece of information.

"Well, you have connections then," she said. "What sort of a job could I get in New York?"

"Any job you wanted."

She smiled with a touch of impatience.

"But what's the use now?" she protested. "We're both stuck here in war jobs."

"Oh, yes, I'm talking about after the war."

"Oh, after the war," she said wearily. "Yes, after the war we'll do lots of things. But in the meanwhile you'll go on sorting cards and I'll go on typing them."

"And reading *The Mill on the Floss*."

She smiled.

"And reading *The Mill on the Floss*," she repeated.

"What do you want?" he asked with sudden earnestness. "What do you *really* want?"

She hesitated. "Will you help me if I tell you?"

"Yes."

"I want to go home. It's after midnight."

He took her hand as they crossed the street to where Amos' car was parked and she let herself give his a small and friendly squeeze. But this action, she quickly saw, was premature. There was an observable delay of some seconds before she received any answering squeeze, and that was possibly only part of the necessary pressure by which he kept her out of the path of a passing car. It was a bit awkward but she was quick to learn. She saw that he was not to be hurried, that he was easily scared away. Unusual, perhaps for the Canal Zone but by no means impossible. She knew fortunately that she could atone for what he might regard as the brashness of her conduct by sparing him the embarrassment of debating the equities of a good-night kiss, and so when he had arrived at Quarry Heights she said suddenly:

"Right here, Bev. Stop. I'll hop out here." And slipping out of the car she closed the door and leaned for a moment on the window. "Good night. And thanks loads. I'll see you tomorrow."

But as she turned to go he called after her.

"Audrey. You know what we hardly discussed at all?"

She turned back.

"What?"

"Helen."

"Oh, Helen," she said with relief. "She'll keep."

CHAPTER SEVEN

WHEN BEVERLY ARRIVED at his desk in Section Blue the following morning his head was aching from his over-indulgence in Lydia's champagne. He had been in such a good mood the night before that he had forgotten to take his seltzer tablets before going to bed. Staring vaguely at the vast pile of paper in his "in" baskets he leaned forward to rest his head on his hands. The early morning cool was still in the air but his skin was beginning to prickle in anticipation of the dreaded heat of the day. With a slight shake of his head he blinked and reached into the first basket. As usual: a new district directive on mimeographed paper reminding naval personnel that a salute was a mark of courtesy and not of social inferiority; an elaborate report from a Panamanian legislator on recent disturbances between police and American servicemen; and a long, chatty, official letter from the naval attaché at Guatemala about a man whom he had met at a cocktail party who had said that his uncle, highly placed in Argentina, predicted an Axis split before June. He threw them back in the basket, picked up the *Panama-American* and leaned back in his chair. His eye, however, lighted on a front page picture of the Chief Justice and a second later, galvanized into action, he had his scissors out of the drawer and was carefully cutting it out. He had recently decided in conference with Mr. Gilder to illustrate his Panamanian *Who's Who* by pasting newspaper snapshots alongside each typewritten paragraph, a decision incidentally which had given him the pleasantest excuse for scanning the newspaper during working hours.

Amos was editing a Panamanian press release about a group of officials fishing in the Bay of Panama and had just crossed out the name and rank of the American naval officer who had made the biggest catch. He peered over at Bev's desk.

"Just as I thought," he murmured. "Paper dolls. I knew you'd come to it."

"Not at all," Bev retorted.

"Are you going to fill them in with crayon?"

"Maybe."

"That'll be pretty. And does each one get a name, like Reddy Fox or Old Mrs. Quack?"

Bev took out a handful of newspaper pictures from a drawer and surveyed them admiringly.

"I've only got obvious facts about them now," he said reflectively. "Birthdays and official positions and things. How do you think I ought to label them?"

But Amos wasn't listening. He glanced over at Audrey's desk and back.

"I'm encouraged to see you've started dating," he said with a wink.

Bev flushed.

"I don't see why you use that word, Amos," he said with unnecessary sharpness. "I don't think it's becoming."

" 'Dating'? What's wrong with 'dating'?"

"Oh, never mind."

"You needn't be so sniffy."

"Will you drop it please? The whole subject," Bev snapped. He could have bit his tongue off for betraying such absurd sensitivities. Now, of course, Amos would be really curious.

Amos, however, turned silently to his press releases and Bev started looking around in his top drawer for some glue to paste his pictures to cards. His eyes fell on a penciled memorandum, his application for sea duty.

"Oh, Miss Emerson," he called over to her in a voice that trembled with assumed calm, "could you take a memo for me?"

She came over looking offensively fresh and neat, her pad and pencil in hand.

"You look fine," he muttered.

"I feel fine," she answered cheerfully. "I enjoyed myself last night."

"That's good," he said skeptically. "Did you like Esmond?"

"Very much."

"He's a bit of an acquired taste. A nice boy though. His grandmother was a cousin of my father's and I've always sort of kept an eye out for him."

"Oh, really? How nice of you."

He glanced at her sharply.

"Your memorandum?" she asked with a smile.

"Oh, yes." He cleared his throat and leaned back in his

swivel chair. "A memo from me to Gilder. Subject: Temporary sea duty, request for. Paragraph one: it is hereby requested that I be assigned to temporary duty aboard an escort vessel on the Guantanamo convoy for the period of one round trip between Cuba and the Canal Zone. Paragraph two: in view of the repeated requests for sea-going officers made by the Bureau of Personnel and in view of the navigation classes at night school in Balboa that I have attended—that sounds well anyway—it is felt—no, damn it, *I* feel—that the experience would be of the utmost value. Paragraph three: I have no duties in the District that would suffer during my absence. That'll do it, I guess."

She nodded and closed her notebook but made no comment, to his disappointment, on the subject matter of the dictation.

"I saw Helen this morning," she said.

"Oh?"

"She has astonishing news."

She appeared to expect from him the liveliest interest but he felt only an unreasonable and bitter disappointment. How could she after the cheerful intimacy of their talk of the night before revert with such fatuous ease to the sordid topic of Helen? He made an abrupt gesture of impatience and half turned away.

"What news?" he asked sourly. "Has she found another sailor?"

"She doesn't have to. Taylor's going to marry her!"

He turned back in genuine surprise.

"He really is?"

"He really is. And I am to be a bridesmaid." She smiled as she saw the cloud of irritation lift from his face. "But I have to do your application now," she said, getting up. "I hope it will be successful. And I hope," she said in a lower tone, "you won't mind my saying that I think it's very big of you to make it."

When he came back from lunch the same day he found his application returned with a penciled note on it : "Rejected. No relief available. S.G." Angrily he walked over paper in hand to Mr. Gilder's desk.

"Sherry, you're always urging us to take one of these trips," he protested. "And now you won't let me go!"

Mr. Gilder smiled his nicest smile.

"Who'd do the routing?"

"Oh, the routing," Bev said disgustedly. "One of the yeomen could do it."

"It's an officer's job, I'm afraid, Bev."

"Well, Amos, then."

"Amos has a big job of his own."

"Oh, you know he does nothing."

Gilder's eyes looked stern.

"I think that's about enough of that, Bev," he said firmly. "Maybe in a month or so we'll be able to arrange something."

He smiled as he watched Bev returning disconsolately to his desk. Yes, they all wanted to get out, and who could blame them? Darlington was not a man to make one love one's work. Even he, Gilder, had had a similar application rejected with a snarl and a bite, and all he had asked for was command of one of those converted yachts that crept up and down the coast of Central America. He, a lieutenant-commander! But never mind. There was the *Sardonyx;* it was commanded, he knew, by a "mustang," and already there were stories. . . . If he bided his time he might yet have his reward. He pictured himself free of Darlington, as flag officer even of a few YP's, with Bev and Amos perhaps on his staff, not, to be sure, on the rough convoy work which was highly unsuitable for such vessels but on a slow and delightful offshore patrol up the Caribbean coast with stops in Limon, in Puerto Castilla, in Belize, in a world with uniforms and fishing and women with gold earrings and champagne.

CHAPTER EIGHT

AUDREY FOUND THAT her old nervousness was returning these days to replace the phlegmaticism that had marked the preceding two years of her Zone life. She never came home after an evening spent with Beverly in Panamanian night clubs without reviewing in agony her conversation and demeanor. There was always present her feeling of a gulf between them and that some careless if not deliberate action on her part might shatter the seemingly slender bridge by which they precariously communicated. She was well acquainted with her own innate leanings to iconoclasm. How many times in the past had she not devoted herself, step by step, to the achievement of some precious plan only to find herself, on the very brink of fulfillment, suddenly and unexpectedly but with a certain undeniable, fierce little pleasure at the very irrevocability of what she was doing, sweeping away the whole fabric of her painstaking creation. It was for this reason that she was scared of that lurking, uninvited critic within her who laughed at Beverly, was bored by Beverly, wanted to contradict Beverly, this critic who was always jumping up and down inside her during the very moments when she was trying hardest to live in the cloudless world of his gusty emotionalism. For once in her life, she vowed with determination, she was going to make herself live in somebody else's pattern. It was the old conflict between poetry and prose. Beverly viewed as poetry, was full of bad rhymes, Heaven knew, and of broken meters, but if one concentrated on the rich morocco binding and the wide empty margins one could see that it was poetry. There was an undeniable excitement to being with him. She had never known a feeling quite like it before, and the fact that it was interfused with periods of ennui when she had to listen to his interminable chatter about Chelton School and Gladys Livermore was simply part of the price, she knew, that one had to pay in any human relationship. The idea of the Zone without him was already an impossibility—seasonless Panama seemed to have developed a spring.

She was not, however, in love with him. Nor did she particularly try to persuade herself that she was. His mental and physical sloppiness appalled her. The violence of his wishful thinking amazed her. But he took her out of herself and Panama on a rambling, ticketless jaunt through a world of "beautiful" things and "beautiful" friendships, a world of a thousand cocktails and canapés where one lunched with Angeline and dined with Bella, laughed with the gay and suffered—exquisitely—with the suffering. Before the impact of this her harsher standards bent, and though she could still feel them, taut and straining and ready as it were to spring back with destructive force, the interlude was hers to prolong. They went out two or three times a week to dine in Panama City; they had long, wonderful discussions in isolated bars on remote topics. She had never before met a person who drew no border lines between art, history, and life. They found a rich field of mutual interest in eighteenth century memoirs and a constantly renewed excitement with each discovery that this or that marquise, long a favorite of one, was equally admired by the other. Particularly engrossed in the drama of the Revolution they would elaborately compare notes on the conduct of their heroines on the scaffold.

"*My* favorite picture," he would tell her, for example, "is the gallantry of the Noailles ladies. Moving! You can't imagine. The old *maréchale* and her daughter and granddaughter, all in the same tumbril." He put his best into the accentuation of occasional French words with an accent that was as spirited as it was abominable. "And when the brute of an executioner tore their bonnets, the pins caught in both the *duchesse's* and the *vicomtesse's* hair! They bled terribly. Wasn't it unspeakable?"

"Horrible," Audrey would agree. "And do you remember Madame Elizabeth?"

"Ah, that saint!"

"Do you remember how Madame de Montmorin recognized her in the tumbril and told the others who she was? And as each one went up the steps to the guillotine they bowed or curtsied to her. Wasn't that magnificent?"

"Madame Roland was wonderful."

"Bev, a Girondin!"

He quickly dropped Madame Roland.

"Du Barry was the real scandal," she added. "Kicking up that terrible row all the way in the cart."

He nodded vigorously.

"Bad blood. How it shows."

Where would it all end? She tried not to let herself speculate too much. One thing she was already learning from the war was that life has to be considered in individual segments and not as a whole with a beginning, a steady rise, and a gentle decline. There was a pleasant unsubstantiality about these days that she was later to look back on with nostalgia, but she was always careful, even in moments of greatest congeniality, not to spoil by any betrayal of her own less elevated nature the picture that he appeared to have conceived of the prim, demure, little Zone girl with strong suppressed undercurrents of imagination and temperament that only he, Beverly, could appreciate.

If her life was brightened by their friendship, his was no less. He had never before had a friend who was so completely willing to be on the receiving end of his confidences and stories, and the fact that he had discovered her of all places in Panama and directly under his own nose never ceased to intrigue and delight him. He would sometimes bring along a handful of manuscripts and read aloud to her from his poems. There was a little restaurant on the second floor of an old house in Panama City with a small balcony that had a view of the harbor, and they took to going there with a brief stop at El Rancho on the way home. She was a highly attentive listener and could like almost anything she decided to like. Her comments were apt to be somewhat technical but he found them helpful. She never, like his mother, compared him unfavorably with Wordsworth and she had a way of remembering the poems afterwards that was flattering. He listened, too, to the problems of her proposed life of George Eliot and even became enthusiastic enough to wonder if he could write a book on Edith Wharton.

"I knew her, you know," he told her once.

"Mrs. Wharton? Why, Bev, really? What a privilege."

How different, he thought with sudden bitterness, from Sylvia and her easy habit of debunking.

"Not well at all, but I dined a couple of times at the Pavillon Colombe and I have an autographed copy of *Twilight Sleep*."

"Oh, Bev!"

"Do you like her books?"

"I love them. I've read the whole shelf in the library here."

There was a thoroughness about her that never ceased to amaze him. He had learned that when she said she had read a whole shelf she meant just that. And nothing was impossible to her, which was the way he himself had been and felt until recently, until Sylvia and the gallery and the war.

"But do you think anyone would read a book about Edith Wharton today?"

"Loads of people. You might start an Edith Wharton revival. I'll help you with it."

He felt entirely relaxed with her. There was no uneasiness about whether or not their friendship should evolve into an affair. She gave every appearance of being satisfied with the status quo and he could enjoy himself with impunity. He was slightly disgruntled, however, at the chilly reception which he got from Gladys Livermore when he called her up once to ask her if she would invite Audrey to a cocktail party at the embassy.

"But you promised to come early and help me," she told him.

"Well, I will," he answered. "She can come later by herself. She doesn't have to be brought. And you'll be crazy about her, Gladys. She's a find."

The pause at the other end of the line implied every kind of skepticism.

"Oh, I dare say," she said finally. "Well, bring her if you want."

It was the beginning of his realization that to a woman like Gladys, Beverly encumbered was not by any means a friend equivalent to Beverly single. He did not, however, transmit any of the chill of her invitation to Audrey, and she cheerfully promised that she would come.

Audrey indeed was cheerful to everybody these days. She would even occasionally play cribbage with her Aunt Betty on a Sunday afternoon instead of retiring firmly to her own room with a three-volume Victorian novel. Her patience with her mother and with her younger sister was much commented on in the family circle, and she failed even to resent the comment. She had not as yet had Beverly to her house, but this was not so much from snobbishness as from a strong, almost passionate reluctance to mix her two lives, the dull past and the almost miraculously agreeable present. It was a positive superstition that made her keep them apart.

One relationship that she gave a good deal of time to was her rather precarious one with Helen. Helen had resigned from the office and was making elaborate preparations for her wedding with Seaman Taylor. She had given a defiant publicity to the whole affair: she had become engaged in both newspapers; she had chosen bridal attendants, including Audrey, and she was planning a large and fashionable reception. Laura had even been maneuvered into offering to give a cocktail party in her honor the Saturday before the wedding. "What shall I do?" she had protested to Audrey. "He's not even a petty officer!" Audrey had reassured her by telling her how democratic it would be thought. Nobody, of course, outside Mr. Gilder and others in the Information Office saw anything particularly wrong in the marriage, but Helen's thinking had been conditioned by theirs, and she couldn't get it out of her head that she was scoring a tremendous point in the general advancement of freedom. Audrey saw this clearly and with her redeveloped sensitivity had begun to feel conscience stricken at her rôle in forming Helen's point of view. She determined not to notice the irony of Helen's inclusion of herself in the bridal party and pretended that everything between them was on the pleasantest possible basis. She dropped in frequently on the Drinkers of a late afternoon and made herself useful to them in dealing with lists and presents. Few people could be more helpful than Audrey when she tried. Beverly on one or two occasions came with her and was at his nicest with Seaman Taylor. This poor boy, bewildered by all that was happening to him, was at first in no way reassured by the appearance at the house of Lieutenant Stregelinus, but Beverly in his usual style and with his usual warmth simply crashed through the barriers and got him chatting happily enough about life in Colón and at his home and how soon they would be sent to the Far East and where they would go. Audrey, watching them from her corner with Mrs. Drinker, began almost to hope that she was making up for what she had done.

CHAPTER NINE

THE UNITED STATES was building a new embassy in Panama, a big, red brick affair on top of a hill in Baya Vista, and pending the completion of this residence the Livermores had rented the largest private house in Panama City. This was a white, two-storied, many-courted, multi-fountained structure with innumerable little rooms full of lacquered furniture leading into one another through moon doors. In the big, central, flag-stoned court Gladys Livermore lay stretched one afternoon on a chaise-lounge drawn under the wide shade of a canvas awning that covered one corner of the court. She was alone; her book lay open, its face turned down, on the little glass table beside her; she was fanning herself with a large cardboard fan. She was a big woman and not made for equatorial climate but she did not give in easily and rare indeed were such moments as this when she gave way in any degree to her general sense of let-down.

There was a letter half read in her lap from her sister in Washington; it spoke of the charm of Georgetown life where the dollar-a-year group had settled in small brick houses with lots of flowers and lots of cocktail parties, an exciting picnic existence where flourished the best of war talk and war rumors. It seemed to poor Gladys as she fanned herself that all the world was full of stimulus outside her own secluded corner. Well, it had been her choice. Nobody had had more opportunities or more means with which to implement them. With money and brains she had been in a position to choose her life, and she had chosen the diplomatic and with it a husband of definite charm if definite lassitude. She it was who had always pushed him and she it was who had managed the job. Her houses and her dinners in Paris, Rome, and Prague had sustained him on the slow road up through secretaryships and consulates, but now when success had really come to them in their fifties, it had brought them Central America and not Europe; it had brought them this awful sprawling house, this heat, these bureaucrats, and the dubious amusement of Panamanian society. It was a challenge no doubt, and hers was an enterprising soul, but it was not a challenge that carried with it any elation. It was, alas, a grim business. She was thinking of her Renoirs and Manets stored in New York. It was the first time in her life that she had been without her own things.

"Gladys," she heard from the next court. It was that high, familiar voice.

"Oh, Bev! Come in, my dear. How nice that you came early." She sat up and shook hands with him as he approached her looking unusually neat in his white uniform. He sat down beside her.

"Exhausted?" he asked. "I am."

"Well—you know." She smiled at him. "Panama has these moments. I wouldn't confess it to anyone but you. But you're one of the only people down here I can really talk to."

This was true enough. Twenty odd years made little difference between them, for so many of Bev's friendships were with older women. He had even been once in her employ; from time to time in the old days Felix Salberg had loaned him to her to assist her in her purchases and they had spent wonderful days together in big art galleries chatting side by side on red plush chairs while dealers brought out canvas after canvas in the hope of adding them to her impressionist collection. Gladys's taste had always been perfect; she had really taken him along because she liked his chatter while she concentrated. In Panama she liked to see him and gossip about New York, but her sense of duty as a hostess made her prefer seeing him alone; he had a tendency to monopolize her when other guests were present. In fact, he had frequently been offended at his exclusion from some of her larger parties.

"And vice versa," he cheerfully agreed.

"I feel there are a lot of people here who might be fun," she said, "if I could receive them. But, of course, one is more tied down here than any place. The Panamanians are so sensitive. I'd like to have the smugglers and people like that."

"You do have the people who make their money out of it," he said laughing.

"Yes," she agreed. "But that's different. They're no fun. As long as I can't have the genuine article the way we did in Paris I'd much rather skip what's in between and get down to the bandits and pirates."

"And the Lydia Schmidts."

"Yes, I'd give anything to know Mrs. Schmidt," she said with real enthusiasm for there was nothing false about Gladys's human curiosity. "But there you are. Her husband's on the blacklist, and besides she's had far too many of them. Of course, you can have a good time as a free lancer."

"Like Esmond."

"Oh, Esmond." A little frown appeared on her brow. "Esmond has too good a time. He'll never make a diplomat."

"You don't think so?"

"Not unless he buckles down. He can't get over the idea that when he goes to a party it's to enjoy himself. Now that certainly is no help to me."

Bev lit a cigarette and dropped the match box on the floor. It was the kind of thing he was always doing.

"You don't really like Esmond, do you?" he asked as he leaned down to retrieve it.

Gladys rather drew herself up. Bev's great trouble, she reflected, was that he never knew where familiarity ought to stop. She said firmly, "One doesn't talk that way about one's husband's nephews."

He hung his head.

"I'm sorry."

"Now let's talk about you, my dear," she said lightly with a quick change of tone. "Who is this Miss Emerson who's coming in this afternoon?"

He blushed.

"She's a girl who works in my office. Very intelligent. Not a bit Zonish. You'll like her, Gladys."

"There you go. When men say that I know they want me to and are afraid I won't."

"That's perfectly silly," he protested.

"Is she a lady?" Gladys and Bev each knew what the other meant by this. It was a technical term.

"Essentially, yes."

"You mean she's not."

"Gladys, you're so unfair!" He was sitting bolt upright on his chair now. "Of course, she doesn't have a terrific background but she's a hundred times better than most of the girls we know would be if they'd been brought up down here."

"How abstract you're getting."

"And she comes from a very good family on her mother's side," he continued. "Southern."

"Ah, my dear, but what good does family do you if it's buried in the past?"

He was too serious however even to smile.

"She's a Phi Bete," he concluded triumphantly.

"Oh, really now, Bev!" Gladys roused herself from her posture of relaxation. "I can see you're far gone."

"Far gone? What do you mean?" His tone was highly irritated.

"I mean you're very taken with the girl."

"Women always think that."

"Because it's always true."

"You've never said it about me before."

She laughed and lay back on the cushions.

"Because it's never been true about you before," she said teasingly.

He got up uncomfortably and started pacing up and down.

"Watch out, my dear," she cautioned him. "I know everybody plays around down here, but you're just not the type. Instead of taking a girl into the bushes you take her to the embassy. Which is much more dangerous."

"I think I can look out for myself, Gladys," he said with a touch of impatience.

"One never can tell when a person like you is going to make a complete donkey of himself," she said seriously. "That's where people like me come in handy. Is Miss Emerson self-conscious?" She could never get away from the idea that people outside her group were ashamed of the fact.

"A little."

"That's bad."

He was about to answer this when Henry Livermore appeared across the courtyard in a dignified, well-pressed grey suit with a white flower in his buttonhole. He was a remarkably handsome man for fifty-five but his air of austerity and the slight stoop in his walk made him seem older. His head was small; his hair sparse and grey though still covering the vital spots; his nose large and Roman, and his eyes the clearest blue. His face was far more masculine than that of his nephew, Esmond, but both suggested the final bloom of an old plant. Beverly used to say about him that he had a Henry Adams complex and was burdened with the weight of an imagined ancestry. Certainly he and his nephew were interesting examples for theorizing on decay. One felt their antecedents went back at least as far as Rome; one felt at once their charm and ineffectiveness. But where Esmond was passionate and aspiring his uncle was cool and dogmatic; Mr. Livermore could deliver well-phrased, balanced opinions on literary and historical subjects, but whenever Bev prodded him further anticipating a provocative discussion from the nature of his opening remark he would find that all had been said and the master was waiting in dignified patience for the next question to be resolved.

"Good afternoon, Beverly," he said a bit frostily. "I think our guests are beginning to arrive, my dear," he continued to his wife.

Gladys got up and a moment later some Army officers came in. Shortly after this came the first secretary of the embassy and his wife, and in a few minutes a small chatting circle had gathered around the Livermores. The colored servants appeared from various doors with trays of drinks and the little reception was under way.

Esmond was in a petulant mood because his uncle had just told him that he would be expected after the party to escort the younger members of the Hernandez family, visitors from Peru en route to Washington, to *Pride of the Yankees* at a Panama cinema. His lips curled downwards like a small child's. Audrey stood beside him uncomfortably in her best green and white dress wearing a hat with big, wavy, conspicuous flowers that she now realized was a dismal mistake.

"They say it's not a bad movie," she said consolingly.

"A lot of grubby sentiment," he retorted. "Imagine! Filming the life of a man who's just dead! They say his wife helped direct it. What unspeakable vulgarity."

"Anyway, it's your job."

"Oh, damn the job!"

"That's nice."

He eyed her critically.

"You worship jobs and success and things like that, don't you?" he said peevishly.

She stared in surprise.

"What makes you think so?"

He shrugged his shoulders.

"Maybe Beverly will straighten you out. You knew of course that you were being chiseled into a cosmopolite?"

He raised his eyebrows as he said this, and the amateur sardonicism of his tone grated on her.

"You mean he's my Pygmalion?" She couldn't help a certain stiffening. He laughed.

"Except he seems to have made a statue out of a woman," he said more playfully. "A beautiful cold statue."

She was afraid someone would hear him.

"Look. There's Beverly now," she said and waved.

"Oh, damn Beverly."

"And you're supposed to be friends!"

"Friends? What does a person like Beverly know of friendship?" He twirled the gold knife at the end of his watch chain round and round. "Yes, Bev and I are friends in the modern sense. We drink together and say mean things about each other's acquaintances."

Audrey gently drew his attention towards Mrs. Livermore who was casting glances in their direction. He could see by where his aunt looked after their eyes met that he was being propelled towards the clump of Hernandezes across the room.

"Come with me," he said.

She shook her head.

"No. Your aunt wouldn't want you to seem attached."

"What'll you do? Do you know anyone here?"

"I know Bev."

"Well, he knows everyone."

Saying which he moved reluctantly off to do his duty. Audrey stood miserably alone for a few minutes pretending a great and sudden interest in the Chinese ivory statuettes on the little table beside her. If only she knew nobody at all, she reflected, it wouldn't be quite so bad. It was the presence of Beverly standing in the middle of the room talking to the Ambassador, one hand on his hip, his shoulders slouched, his square jaw working away as he expounded noisily and inaccurately no doubt some vaguely conceived but passionately adopted theory of Latin American politics. He commanded, however, she could observe, more attention than one would expect from the quality of his opinion. It was perhaps his tallness and his high brow, together with his energy and sincerity—but now he had seen her. He was waving to her again beckoning her to come over and join them; his kindness was certainly beyond dispute. But she suddenly felt that she wouldn't take advantage of it, that anything was better, and to show him her independence and her courage, she smiled back, shaking her head just the slightest bit and turned, to her own amazement and certainly to his, to walk directly over to where Mrs. Livermore was sitting.

Mrs. Livermore and Señora Fernando Alvarez were conversing alone by the tea table, the former leaning slightly forward to catch the old lady's words, a manufactured smile on her lips that was somehow pleasant without even pretending sincerity. It was a mannered, exaggerated, "old New York" smile; it was put on for company like an evening dress and the initiated guest recognized it as a compliment. The señora was very old and very distinguished; the long, yellow, wrinkled hands that she clasped and unclasped on her black satin lap had applied chastisement in years past to two sons who had later been presidents of the republic. As she was speaking Mrs. Livermore saw Audrey approaching and gave her a distant smile, but the latter, desperate with the loneliness that comes only at parties, read too much into it. She actually went over and sat down by them. Mrs. Livermore visibly froze. She continued her conversation in Spanish but the señora stopped her.

"My Eengleesh ees poor," the old lady said, "but perhaps it ees good eenough for theese young lady."

In fact Audrey's unhappy expression was an easy betrayal of her linguistic ignorance. She blushed.

"Oh, please don't stop for me," she stammered.

"But certaynly, my dear. It ees good to practiss my Eenglish."

Slowly it dawned on Mrs. Livermore that this girl not only had the impertinence to interrupt her conversation and change the language in which it was being carried on but that she was actually going to stay and chat. She waxed so indignant, a state of mind it may be added not entirely unpleasant to her, that she almost forgot the señora.

"I believe you know Beverly Stregelinus," she said icily.

Audrey gave her a little smile.

"Oh dear, yes," she said sweetly. "Mr. Stregelinus and I are quite old friends. He's often talked to me about you."

The impudence of this was enough to make Mrs. Livermore turn altogether from the old lady. Even the "Mr. Stregelinus" had an ill-bred formality to it. Had Audrey said "Bev," she would have thought her familiar; she was not in a mood to be pleased. And the idea of their discussing *her!*

"We're talking about a young friend of mine who's an art critic," she explained to the señora. "Well, not so young at that," she added by way of an afterthought, glancing at Audrey. "He's older than he looks."

"It must be so interesting for him to live down here a while," Audrey said, to fill the gap. "Such different concepts of art and architecture."

Mrs. Livermore looked at her suspiciously and decided to set a few things straight.

"Oh, it takes more than Panama," she said with a little wave of her hand. "More than South America too. An art student hasn't really cut his teeth until he's been in Europe for at least three years. It's a long training, Miss Emerson. People talk about doctors having a hard start." She gave a little snort and toss of her head at the very preposterousness of the contrast. "But the poor art critic, unless indeed he's a very rich one, can't even think of marriage until he's at least forty. Of course Beverly has nothing at all of his own." Here Mrs. Livermore became suddenly aware that she had arrived at the very borders of vulgarity, and she turned in some embarrassment to the señora. "I was just saying," she repeated in a louder voice, "how hopeless it was for young artists to marry young."

But the señora had not quite understood. She knew it was something about marrying and something about money. She nodded vaguely.

"Yes, I understood you geeve a great fortune to Meester Leevermore when you marry him."

This brought a quick blush to Mrs. Livermore's cheek, and Audrey had to work hard to conceal her smile. She turned boldly to Señora Alvarez.

"Mrs. Livermore makes me feel as though I could never be the wife of an artist," she said loudly. "I have no money and I can't even speak Spanish."

The old lady gave her a wonderful smile.

"But, my child, you have charm," she said. "What more ees it you need?"

"Thank you, señora."

Mrs. Livermore moved restlessly in her chair.

"As if anyone would really want the life of an artist or art critic's wife if they could choose," she began, flashing a smile of "as we two know" on the old lady. "There's certainly nothing easy about it. So many people think it begins and ends with the first act of *La Bohême*. They don't see the miserable hours in tiny apartments and bad restaurants."

"Oh, but I think I'd love it!" a devil made Audrey exclaim. "I think it would be wonderful!"

"Then I suggest you learn your languages," said Mrs. Livermore coldly, and turning to Señora Alvarez in a not-to-be-denied manner she firmly continued the conversation in Spanish.

"Henry, I have a bone to pick with you," Bev cried as Mr. Livermore approached the little group of Army officers with whom Bev was standing. The Ambassador smiled gravely.

"Pray pick it, Beverly."

"What about the picture of you in the paper last week with General Alfarista?"

The Ambassador's brows knitted.

"What about it?" he rejoined. "It was taken during my Central American tour."

"The picture showed you arm in arm," Bev continued indignantly, "and the caption was full of slop about democratic leaders meeting to reaffirm Atlantic Charter principles."

"And you think perhaps our friend, the General, is not heart and soul in accord?" the Ambassador queried with a rather studied smile.

"I think what everyone thinks, that he's the bloodiest dictator of them all!"

This was strong and Mr. Livermore didn't like it. He preserved, however, his collected mien. There were no Central Americans in the immediate group who might take offense and he couldn't give Beverly's challenge the icy silence that it deserved in the presence of service men whose minds after all might be full of these generalities. He utterly deplored the continued and growing interference of abstract thought with diplomatic routine and at the moment he actually loathed this brash young friend of his wife's for his tactless and violent assault.

"We all of us have to do a lot of things that we don't entirely approve of," he began heavily. "After all, we're at war and allies are allies."

"But do we have to call Alfarista brother?"

Mr. Livermore promised himself that this unbearable creature would never be asked to the embassy again, Gladys or no Gladys.

"There's such a thing as a 'little white lie.'" He brought the phrase out with pompous felicity as though it were his own invention. "There's a lot of loose talk about the principles of democracy these days. Some people seem to feel that one can't be democratic unless one is constantly screaming the fact into the reluctant ears of a Latin American neighbor."

"It seems to me though, Henry," Bev went on, "that the talk is never looser than when General Alfarista is characterized as a democrat."

Mr. Livermore shuddered at the repetition of his own first name. He remembered that his wife had authorized this revolting familiarity, but he had not thought it was a privilege that would be abused in public. As he glanced around the group to see the effect of Beverly's last remark he was pleased to observe a glazed expression on every eye. Bev had only succeeded in boring them. It would be safe now for him to retire to another part of the court, and retire he did.

When Audrey got up this time there was again the question of calling on Beverly for help. Esmond was hopelessly involved with the Hernandezes, and she didn't know another soul on the terrace. Her sense of isolation and misery was acute, but no more really than she had expected. She was not one to tremble at the first step or to be routed by the foolish display of bad temper in which Mrs. Livermore had just indulged. To rise meant to suffer; no doubt to be on top was to suffer still, but this seemed to her the most natural of natural things in an unequal world. There were some happy souls like Beverly who seemed to float effortlessly through the halls of their own desire, but to most, even to Esmond, steps were necessary. Unhappiness at the top and at the bottom, but in life we climb. There was perhaps some pleasure in the actual succession of altitudes. She went over to Bev finally and gave his white coat a little tug from behind.

"Will you take me home?" she asked when he turned around.

"You want to go now?"

"If you're ready."

"Aren't you having a good time?"

She looked at him reproachfully.

"You know I'm not."

He glanced in the direction of Mrs. Livermore and then frowned.

"Let's go," he said.

In the open taxi which he hailed at the embassy gate he contemplated the quiet figure beside him.

"You didn't have a row with her, did you?" he asked.

She turned to him with dignity.

"Whom do you mean?"

"Why, Gladys, of course."

"Mrs. Livermore? No, I didn't have a row with her. But she insulted me."

Bev emitted a whistle.

"So? You must have said something."

"I didn't say anything," she retorted irritably. "It's just that she dislikes me. Dislikes me so much that she can't even keep it under control."

He stared at her for a moment and then forced a smile.

"I suppose she thinks you're trying to marry me," he said lightly. "Women always think things like that."

The look on her face, however, was serious.

"But, of course," she said, "I am."

He was about to emit one of his loud laughs when something in her face stopped him.

"Audrey, what do you mean?"

"Just that. I want to marry you."

He stared at her in absolute astonishment. She looked away without apparent embarrassment; she gazed at the Spanish stucco of the residential section as they sped by. It was the calmness of her resolved mood that most struck him and stirred, far down, an entirely new sense of excitement.

"You couldn't be serious," he said hurriedly with self-conscious emphasis. "You don't know what you're saying. Me! But, Audrey, I'm the worst bet in the world. I'm thirty years old—I'm a bit over thirty as a matter of fact—and what have I got? Why good God, Audrey, I'm really the worst sort of flop, I—"

"You needn't look so alarmed, Bev. I'm not trying to force you into anything."

"No—but—well, *goodness*, Audrey!"

She smiled at him in her nicest way.

"I shouldn't have ever said what I did, I know. It's one of those remarks there's no answer to."

"But what do you see in me?"

She smiled again at his earnestness.

"Oh, that takes a woman," she said. "I see all I could

make of you. If I could ever get all that scattered energy strung together."

"You make me feel like a broken necklace. Spilled all over the floor."

She nodded.

"And rolling all hither and yon."

"Really, what complete nonsense we're talking," he protested.

She shrugged her shoulders.

"Yes, I suppose we are."

He swallowed hard.

"You mean you didn't mean it then, what you said about wanting to marry me?"

She smiled.

"No, I didn't mean it."

Again he stared, with a sense of slowly subsiding excitement.

"Oh, you didn't."

"Do you mind?"

"Well, you could do worse you know."

"Yes, I suppose. Of course you say yourself you have no prospects."

"What absolute tosh!" he exclaimed vehemently. He was sitting bolt upright on the old leather seat. "Just because I have no money doesn't mean I have no prospects you know."

"What *are* your prospects, Bev?"

"Don't you think I could be a diplomat?"

"Yes."

"Or a poet?"

"Well—maybe."

"You're so contrary," he said in exasperation. "A moment ago you said you could make anything out of me."

"Something. Not anything."

"Oh, you!"

He subsided into silence the rest of the way to her house and certainly thought of nothing but this conversation during the eight to twelve watch that he had that night in the office and afterwards during the restless two hours that he put in before he fell asleep. He was not sure which of the several things that she had said she really meant, but it was perfectly clear that she wouldn't have said as much or in the way she had said it if she hadn't felt a more than ordinary interest in him. And this alone was quite enough to give him a thrill, a thrill which he realized to his chagrin was all the more recognizable for being so rare in his experience. One of the few things about himself that he admitted to himself was the fact that he did have a fixation and one that he knew he dramatized about his not being attractive to women. But there it was. He could never quite get away from the idea that it was a little bit incredible to him that any girl should think of him seriously in *that* way. All the women with whom he had at one time or another imagined himself in love had been outstandingly beautiful or attractive and, being usually older than himself and having affections already preempted, they had looked upon him in the light of another and delightful intimate and confidence-exchanging friend.

Sylvia of course was different, but then Sylvia was always different. He didn't really think of her as a woman at all. Poor lonely thing, the very idea of sex seemed to clash with the harmonious velvet of general kindness in which he draped her. Sylvia might be in love but who could really— in all honesty—be in love with Sylvia? And he wanted to fall in love. He had learned to face the fact, if obliquely, that the sentiment inspired in him by such a friend as Bella Stroud was not of a robust sort. He had learned to remember with some bitterness the words of a rather sentimental English teacher at Chelton, words that he had scoffed at with the triumph of an idealistic sixteen: "Romeo and Juliet, you must remember, were very privileged persons. To few of you will come the good fortune of such an experience." To few of them, he now wondered? To any? But at least even his divorced friends had had a fling at it. Was he to be confined forever to the restricted emancipation of the passionless? Could one live and not feel? Feel? But surely he *felt* enough; sometimes he wondered if there was anything in him but emotion. Emotion, but maybe scattered, rolling over a marble floor aimlessly, like those beads—

No, she was not a romantic but she was honest and direct; he felt sure of that. She was compact where he was untied; she was intense where he was—messy. He admitted it. And he lay awake thinking of the enigmatic earnestness of her expression as she had said: "Yes, I suppose we are." Could it possibly really be that he *was* in love? Angeline Stroud had once told him that when you were in love you always wondered what the other person was doing, that you spent your time filling in the absent life with imaginary details. He had to confess that he was not particularly interested in what Audrey was doing at the moment. Probably in bed. Or out with somebody else. He didn't seem to experience the prick of jealousy. But there were other criteria. Silently he abused poor Angeline, making fun of the fictional quality of any love life that her imagination might reconstruct. Everyone learned to love after his own individual fashion and everyone learned it differently. He might not care terribly what Audrey was doing at the moment, but he knew that he cared about seeing her in the office the following morning. He had learned to look forward to her reserved, almost impertinent little nod of greeting which seemed so firmly to repudiate the friendly familiarity of the evening before. Audrey in the office was all business.

He sat up suddenly in bed. There was no denying it: he was thinking, actually thinking, of asking her to marry him! After the war, of course—even in a moment of the wildest insanity he could never have contemplated incurring the jovial ridicule of the naval district by an office marriage. One simply didn't marry on a foreign station in the middle of a war. But afterwards, that's what he now confessed he was thinking of, after it was all over, coming back to Panama in civilian clothes and going to the Emersons and—the sudden vision of Bella Stroud and her laughter over the cocktails tightened his every muscle. "But his was a *real* romance," she was saying; "Gladys Livermore tells me he met her in a naval office down there. Isn't it something? Our Bev! Yes, of course, Angeline's giving a party for them. You know what a saint my sister-in-law is."

How they'd all laugh! He wouldn't be allowed to take Audrey quietly up to Chelton where he had already in his imagination provided himself with a job; he would have to run the gamut of all the friends. He would have to watch his graceful mother "making the best of it"; he would have to put up with the hearty congratulations of friends who would ask them to dinner once, almost immediately, and thereafter on a "next time you're in town, old boy" basis. He would have to put up with Angeline's genuine kindness and her "But I *really* like her, Bev," and Bella's inevitable little cocktail party for them and her condescending flatteries to Audrey like "Ah, down there I'm sure you all read everything."

He got out of his bed and sat on the chair by the window, leaning forward to press his nose against the screen. It was almost a full moon and the Canal glittered beyond the square hulks of the officers' barracks. He stared up at the moon and kept staring until he could feel the tears in his eyes. What did he care anyway? For Bella or his mother or for Angeline or, for that matter, anything in his whole miserable past? The books and poems that he had read all his life seemed to be about people who suddenly woke up to the fact that their lives had been wasted. Might this not be his turn? And yet, he reflected miserably, it seemed hard that he had to make all the decisions himself. That there wasn't in him a turbulent, frothing cataract of early nineteenth century passion to run hissing over all his doubts and half-doubts and sweep him away willy-nilly in the gushing current of aliveness.

CHAPTER TEN

IT WAS WITH these speculations in mind that Beverly decided to see the Emersons at home. Audrey had never asked him to the house but she had told him that he would be welcome at any time, and so one afternoon in the following week he presented himself in khaki blouse at their front door at exactly five o'clock.

Audrey heard the bell and jumped up to look at herself in the mirror. Her family were expecting a few friends, including the Smiths, for cocktails—a rare occasion for them —but she had not expected anyone so soon. She hurried to the hall to answer the door and forestall her mother's inevitable shouted injunction; but as she approached the screen she and whoever it was on the outside could hear the dreary wail from upstairs: "Oh—Aud*ree!* Will—you—answer—the —door." Like all her mother's infuriating habits, it could never be controlled by anticipation. She would intone this even when she saw Audrey actually hurrying to the hall.

Her face dropped a little when she saw who it was.

"Oh, hello," she said. She couldn't but notice his informal khakis and remember General Smith.

"My, aren't we glad to see me!" he exclaimed. "Now I know how the Fuller brush man feels."

"Don't be silly. Do come in." She opened the door.

"Well, just for a minute." He followed her through the living room and out on the porch.

"Aud*ree!*" came the voice from above. "Who—*is*—it?"

She controlled a gesticulation of anger and walked to the foot of the stairs so she would not have to shout.

"Nobody for you, Mother dear," she called up in a rather frosty tone.

"What?"

"A friend of mine, Mother," she shouted. How rather awful, she reflected as she returned to the porch, absolutely to loathe one's own mother.

Beverly missed none of the rasp in her tone and enjoyed it.

"Busy day?" she inquired brightly. "I got off at noon."

"Yes, as a matter of fact. I must have added twenty names to my *Who's Who*."

She emitted a low whistle.

"You must be exhausted."

"I am."

But she couldn't keep it up today, the constant little tone of banter about the futility of the office. She was provoked at her mother; she was sorry Beverly had picked this particular day to come and she was worried about the general impression that her family's friends would create in him. Besides, she had to type the ridiculous *Who's Who*.

"Isn't it disgraceful," she began in that irritating tone that seems to anticipate accord, though both sides know it will not be forthcoming, "that they keep an able-bodied man like yourself tied up in such a piddling, social-gossip job?"

It was all very well for Bev to describe his job that way himself, but this way it stung. Besides she was only a stenographer in the office and not meant to evaluate.

"Of course, it's a good deal more than that," he said stuffily.

"Oh, pish."

"Pish, nothing!" he retorted. "Without us how would the Navy know what was going on down here?"

"*Time* magazine."

She could see by his tightened lips that he was mad. Why did she do things like this, she asked herself. Why?

"I don't see why you work for the Navy if you feel that way," he said peevishly. "After all, you can get out whenever you want. I can't. And besides you shouldn't talk about the office outside the office."

"Who brought it up?"

"Maybe I had better go." He got up and fingered his cap. "We seem to be on the acrid side today."

"Oh, please sit down." She stood up and gave him a little push at the elbow. "Don't get all huffy about the office. You know I don't mean it. We're too good friends to quarrel. Anyway, about that."

He sat down mollified but definitely surprised. Was she always like this at home?

"I still don't think you should talk that way," he protested.

"Very well." She smiled obediently and sat down beside

him. "I'll remember that the enemy is always listening. And they might send a wireless to Berlin. 'Lieutenant (junior grade) B. Stregelinus has just finished his *Who's Who*. Ach! Himmel! Get Goebbels! Get Goering! Dees man must bee stopped!'" She concluded her painful parody with a look of defiance. It was an effort to justify her mood of idle destructiveness.

He laughed wryly.

"You might tell me one thing," he observed. "Why do you get this way with me? With everyone else in the office your conduct leaves nothing to be desired. 'Oh, that nice Miss Emerson,' they all say, 'so quiet and polite and efficient.' But with me you're a fury."

She laughed.

"A fury?"

"Yes," he insisted. "Maybe it's because you see that I see into you. That under that quiet front it's all seething. Is that it? Is that why you don't really like me? Even when you say we're friends?"

She didn't like this at all.

"But Beverly, you know I like you."

"We'll let that pass anyway. Why then do you pitch into me so?"

She reflected.

"Because of all you take for granted, I guess," she said more seriously. "I see you every day sitting at that desk with all those stacks of paper piled up around you arguing in your Chelton accent with Mr. Lawrence about nothing at all, and I say: 'How *can* he do it?' But you go on, working busily, telephoning the ambassadress, scrapping with Mr. McShane, having the most marvelous God-damn time—"

A heavy clump was heard on the stair and then the sound of a large person coming down one step at a time. Audrey looked around to see the massive figure of her Aunt Betty, curiously swathed in a long wrapper made the dowdier for dabs of old lace, standing in the hall and looking at them doubtfully.

"Oh, Aunt Betty, do come out here. I have a friend I'd like you to meet."

After the routine grumbling that she wasn't going to make a "pesk of herself" with "young folks around" she came out and planted herself solidly in a wicker chair for the remainder of the afternoon.

"It's not the first time we've met, Miss Miles," Beverly began enthusiastically.

"Audrey tells me you were at the University for a year. Was that while I was there?" Her eyes blinked behind the square rimless glasses and her hands, so reddened, fingered the lace nervously.

He turned to Audrey.

"Maybe your aunt and I should both keep how long ago it was under the cuff," he said laughing, "but it was ten years ago. I love the way you call it *the* University, Miss Miles. I haven't heard it called that for so long. But down here you must say the 'University of Virginia' or people will think you mean Balboa Junior High." And he emitted one of those well-known screams of laughter that were so impudent and so tiresomely bound up with his own jokes. "I adored Charlottesville. I can't ever have too much of the red brick and the rotunda. And you all have such a delightful sense of the futility of effort. Do you remember Ken Mason?"

"Why I should say I do," Miss Miles gasped in surprise. "Ever since he was a baby. His mother was a Marinooper and kin to my Aunt Agnes—"

"Of course," Bev interrupted, "and he was the boy who took me to dinner one night at your house on University Circle."

"Fancy!"

"Oh, Miss Miles, you and I are old friends. I don't suppose you remember, but we spent all dinner talking about Ken's family place in Keswick and what they could do to keep it from tumbling all to pieces."

"Well, I declare!" Miss Miles' face was wreathed with pleasure. "Do you know Idleworth? It used to belong to the Caskies when I was a girl. Why I used to go there every Sunday for lunch. Some people called McCrea have bought it now."

Beverly burst into a peal of laughter.

"Some people called McCrea. Oh, Miss Miles, you're marvelous! Audrey, can't you just feel the old dominion blood boiling when your aunt says that? It's superb. Some poor white trash called McCrea!"

Miss Miles blushed but not uncomfortably. The nice young man seemed to concede her background its proper importance and yet treat her with the flattering intimacy that he would a contemporary. It was gratifying. More than that. It was heaven.

"Oh, now you're putting words in my mouth, Mr. Stregelinus. They're very nice people, I hear. Not a bit flashy with their money like some of our Yankee friends. Their son went to the University too."

"Charlie? Certainly he did. He didn't go to *the* High School in Alexandria, but he belongs to *the* country club there. And he culminated his career by marrying one of *the* Stuarts and settling down in the shadow of *the* Mr. Jefferson." All this to shouts of laughter. "But I'm not making fun of any of it, Miss Miles. Really, I'm a most ardent admirer of the whole system."

At this point the bell rang and General Smith and his daughter, Laura, came in accompanied by his aide and an elderly couple whom Audrey didn't recognize, and she had to go up to tell her mother and father to come down. When everybody was assembled she detached Beverly from her aunt and asked him to help her in the pantry with the cocktails.

"Listen, I love your aunt," he said to her as he opened a bottle of gin and started measuring with a jigger. "She's a great character. Looks exactly the way she used to sitting on the porch of her house on University Circle. Do you remember that house?" She nodded with a slight shudder that he failed to notice. "Of course you told me. You used to spend your vacations from college there. Your Aunt Betty is my idea of the old South."

Audrey might in another mood have expatiated at length on the Virginia side of her family. She had studied it with great care, all with an eye to those details that she could work—oh, how casually—into the largest number of conversations. Those great-uncles whose drab, small-town lives defied romanticization even in her determined mind were labeled "interesting" or "unique." If they couldn't be given carriages they could be given vices. She satisfied her conscience by telling only true details but isolating them from their context so as to create a picture of the unusual. Thus her great-aunt Tillie's fear of thunderstorms which used to drive the old lady into a closet was told in such a way as to leave the impression of an eccentric, beautiful, and many-acred lady who would retire during tempests to a specially constructed room without windows in the center of her house. But this afternoon Beverly seemed to have brought himself to the proper point of appreciation, and she could afford to indulge in the more compatible role of debunker. She pulled the cork out of the bottle of Argentine vermouth.

"Doesn't it make you mad that Aunt Betty should look down on the McCreas?" she asked.

"Hasn't she a right to?"

"A right to? Oh, Beverly. Think of Mrs. McCrea. That beautiful woman. Every talent. Every grace. And with money to give Idleworth a needed dash of Long Island. And there's Aunt Betty, an ex-boardinghouse owner, sitting on the porch ranting about a civilization that was dead before she was born. And the nerve of it, Bev. The nerve. She actually believes that she's more of a lady than Mrs. McCrea." The name was like a dope injected into her and spreading through her veins. She stopped, checking herself on the verge of indiscretion, realizing that her debunking had gone far enough. But her memories kept flooding back. Charlie McCrea had gone to the University; he had come to her aunt's and taken a room; and she could remember his mother and Miss Miles touring the house on the former's inspection trip. Yes, how she remembered them: Mrs. McCrea, her critical but kindly eye taking in every monstrosity and reserving comment until at last she spied a portrait copy of an early Miles about which she could allow herself to speak with some element of sincerity, and then saying so smoothly: "Oh, Miss Miles, how charming that is. Those eyes. What real distinction" (or something), and Aunt Betty, so sweaty, so from the kitchen, so constantly adjusting her glasses in a manner that gave away her self-consciousness in the face of elegance, smiling with such tiresome delight and saying (Oh, God!): "Well, I reckon it's not unusual for a Miles to look distinguished."

There was no suffering in the world like that, Audrey knew. It was cruel beyond any torture to know that Charlie McCrea and his friends, when they came bounding down the stairway and saw her in a corner in the hall, would register on her for a fraction of a second and rush on, having automatically in that moment classified her as something that came with the landlady, lost forever in the steam of the kitchen. Somehow it could have been borne had they been peasants in a Greek tragedy and groveled low on a board stage before gods from whom injustice was to be expected and to whom a surly respect had to be paid. But never. They were better. They were the Miles, and the back was always stiff and the impression conveyed a bad one. Audrey had sometimes looked out her window towards the moonlit rotunda at night and cursed "Mr. Jefferson."

When they went back to the porch Audrey introduced Beverly to Laura and moved on herself to talk to the general's friends. Laura crossed her legs in a stiff, affected way and fixed on Beverly a steady stare, the fascinated absorption, as she meant it to be, of a mind accustomed to roaming focused on an insect that has won its temporary curiosity. And indulgence.

"You know the ambassador and his wife I believe, Mr. Stregelinus," she said.

Beverly rose to the occasion.

"Yes indeed," he responded. "Intimately. Couldn't like them more. Are they friends of yours?"

Laura stirred uneasily at his warmth. No trick to it, so she could hardly say anything cutting about the Livermores. And her sense of accuracy, like Audrey's, her linen-closet mind usually prevailed over her desire to be grand except where the self-delusion was genuine.

"No, Father and I don't know them personally. But Mrs. Livermore has a nephew, Esmond Carnahan, who works at the embassy. We've met him around and about, you know, and I've heard him speak of you as a friend of his aunt's."

Bev nodded perfunctorily. Laura's desire to irk him by this association with a woman so much older missed fire completely. As a matter of fact this often happened with Laura. Absurdly oversensitive herself, she always expected others to be.

"Esmond is a great friend of Bev's," Audrey told them from across the room.

"Oh?" Laura turned to Beverly and dropped her voice. "I can't say I'm glad to hear it, Mr. Stregelinus. Father and I both thought him very snobbish. Like his uncle. They're not popular in the Zone, you know. Not at all."

"You don't say."

"They're too good for us apparently. They never make the slightest effort."

Beverly began to warm up to the defense of the Livermores and of Esmond.

"They're not accredited to the Canal Zone," he pointed out. "They're our emissaries to the Republic of Panama. They don't even have to speak to anyone in the Canal Zone if they don't want to."

"Oh, Panama." She shrugged her shoulders in disdain. "Of

course, if they're so crazy about Panamanians. Not that I don't like Panamanians myself. I have many acquaintances in Panama City naturally. But they don't do for friends."

Beverly could see the hopelessness of their discussion.

"But that's their job," he said.

"Whose job?"

"The Livermores'."

"Oh." Her mind reverted with a snap. "Tell me," she said in an even lower tone, "I wonder if there's any truth in the rumor one hears about Carnahan. That he's a little—well, you know." She flapped her hand. "Has wings shall we say?"

He almost choked with revulsion, not at the rumor or the idea of it which he had often heard and which invariably followed people who looked and acted like Esmond, but at the slimy nastiness of her approach. At least he could disappoint her.

"Why, I never heard of such a thing!" he exclaimed. "I've known Esmond for a long time and there's never even been a breath of that sort of thing. Good Lord! Who'd you ever hear that from?"

"Oh, no one in particular," she said hastily. But she wouldn't retract the remark and it did not decrease his temper any to realize, as he suddenly did, that she ascribed his spirited defense of Esmond to a partnership in bad habits.

"You should get to know Gladys—the ambassadress, I mean," he said coldly to change the subject. "She's a marvelous person. I know you'd love her."

Laura put down her cocktail glass on the table and shook her head several times.

"Oh, no, Mr. Stregelinus," she said briskly. "You don't understand. You see, Father and I don't care for that sort of people at all."

The chip on Laura's shoulder had now become a log.

"What sort of people?" Beverly retorted. For a second he was fascinated by the idea that she was going to ascribe some fantastic sex life to the Livermores.

Laura gave the faintest shrug of her shoulders and reached for her glass.

"That provincial type of moneyed New Yorker. I can't bear their stupid conceit. Don't you get awfully tired of it, Mr. Stregelinus?"

"I don't know what you mean," he retorted angrily.

"Oh, the people you must have seen all the time. Vanderbilts and things."

Audrey had overheard the last few sentences of this conversation from across the porch while she listened to General Smith expatiate on the problems of union labor in the Canal. She set her teeth in vexation, but at the same time she felt almost compelled to admire Laura's independence, her very blindness to the dreadful impression she invariably created. She heard Beverly's heated argument to the effect that his friends were, after all, his friends, and that he didn't consider them in any one category, and what did Miss Smith mean anyway by calling them all "Vanderbilts and things," and suddenly she relaxed and remembered that it didn't matter what Beverly thought of Laura. One couldn't live and care about such trifles.

At this point some more people came into the room and Beverly was able to escape from Laura. He discovered Mrs. Emerson all by herself in the middle of the room and took up his stand beside her. She was not, however, a woman with whom it was possible to maintain any sort of conversation; she simply stared and nodded. He noted, indeed, that her self-preoccupation was such that she did not appear to have any inkling that there was a special relationship between him and her daughter.

"Audrey tells me she always has such a good time with you in Panama City, Mr. Stregelinus," she said. "It's nice of you to take her out. She doesn't get much change down here."

"Nice of me!" he protested. "It's nice of her." How could any woman be so obtuse? He felt a prickle of disgust. But he was seeing the worst anyway—there was some comfort in that—this was her family and it wasn't *too* bad. He kept watching her across the room where she now sat talking to a young major, General Smith's aide; she looked so cool and interested. The new sharpness with which she had greeted him earlier operated only to make him think of her as an individual removed from himself, and as such suddenly and frighteningly distant. Perhaps she had already classified him as good only for gossip and was now beginning to realize the extent of her own boredom. What after all had he given her in all their evenings but a bubbling sense of his own chatter? Other men weren't that way at all, particularly in Panama and in wartime, and such other men were probably the men she was used to. He had had the brief charm of novelty and nothing more. He felt as he reached his empty glass again and again to Mr. Emerson's hospitably passed shaker under the bulging eyes of her mother, that he was discarded, relegated to regions of upper shelves and lower drawers. It was again that recurring feeling that he himself was an insufficient offering, that something substantial or contractual, a kiss or proposition or proposal, had to be tendered if their relationship was not to founder in the shallows of fraud.

"You don't have to bother talking to me, Mr. Stregelinus," Mrs. Emerson said in the voice of one long accustomed to self-effacement. "Why don't you go talk to Laura or Audrey?"

The remark brought him back to his senses with a start. It was the remark that had been made to him all the time in one form or another years ago when he had first started to go out and before he had become finally identified with the older middle-aged. He had never done anything but rebuff it, but reassure the speaker with obvious sincerity of his obvious interest, but now with a funny, shy little feeling of elation, he realized that it was an injunction that he was going to obey. He nodded gratefully to her and moved out to the porch where he had seen Audrey go.

She smiled at him and sat down on the hammock which creaked and swayed. He took the rocking chair beside her and balanced his cocktail precariously on the arm. His uniform looked more crumpled than ever and there was a large spot under his left chest pocket. She wondered at his preoccupation.

"You're certainly putting away those marts," she remarked, looking at his glass. "Is my friend Laura as bad as all that?"

"Your friend Laura, my dear, is quite definitely as bad as all that, but it so happens that I have other things on my mind."

He was certainly solemn. There were big beads of perspiration all over his high forehead and his hair looked unusually messy, but then he was always pulling at it, and particularly so this afternoon after his drinking. She felt irritated with him and irritated with herself.

"You look cross," he said.

"Do I? Well I am, a little. The Smiths get on my nerves too."

"I don't think I've ever seen you really cross before today," he continued. "I guess you were cross the other day with Mrs. Livermore. As a matter of fact, I'll bet you can be really acid when you want."

She surveyed him dispassionately.

"Why do you go around dressed that way? Can't you have your uniforms pressed?"

He bridled.

"What's wrong with my uniform?"

"Everything. It's all wrinkles and crinkles. And look at that spot."

She reached over and put her finger on the stain. It was a relief to do it, to let herself go, but she shuddered a little as she sat back on the hammock with the realization that she was risking total alienation.

"You're just ashamed of me because that old dodo, Smith, is here!" he exclaimed angrily. "I never knew you were so rank conscious, Audrey."

"Well now you know."

"Who gives a damn what those people think?"

"I do."

He snorted.

"Apparently. I guess that's why I've never been asked inside this house."

"Oh, no, Bev!" She looked in sudden alarm at the unhappy expression on his face and in a moment her irritation was gone. "How can you be so silly? I admit my not asking you here was deliberate, but it wasn't because of you. It was just—well, what was the use?"

"The use?"

"Oh, you know. You can see how Mother and Aunt Betty are. I have to put up with it, and I'm not complaining, but why should you?"

"Are they so difficult?"

"Oh, they mean well."

"Nobody gets on with their family all the time."

"Don't they? I picture you and your mother as always on the most wonderful terms." It was quite true. She was sure that he simply didn't have other people's problems.

"Don't you believe it! We have awful rows."

"Oh, rows."

"You shouldn't feel though that I have no place in your family life," he protested. "I don't want to be just another El Rancho friend."

"What sort of friend do you want to be?"

"I want to be a friend for bad times as well as good. I'd like to come up here and read to your aunt in the evening when she's lonely."

She looked at him skeptically.

"You'd better get yourself a copy of Mrs. Gaskell's life of Charlotte Brontë then."

"I will."

She laughed and patted his hand.

"You're sweet, Bev. You really are. But I can handle this end."

She could see by the way he was staring at her that he really did have something more to say. Her heart seemed to miss a beat. Not now, she thought desperately, not now, not so *soon*—

"Audrey," he said, leaning forward in the rocker and placing his cocktail glass on the floor, "I've been thinking so much about what you said in the taxi the other day. Coming back from the Livermores'."

"Oh, that."

"I just don't know what you meant. I've been wondering all week."

"Maybe I didn't mean anything."

He edged the rocker laboriously closer.

"But, Audrey, why shouldn't it be, someday? Why shouldn't we—after the war—if we still feel the same way—?"

She studied the embarrassment on his face and tried to smile.

"There's no reason at all why not, *if*, as you say. Life's always simpler than people make it."

"Then you—?"

"Yes, I—" she mocked him and stood up. "Don't let's get too serious, Bev. The others will be wondering where we are. And you know what a cat Laura is."

And sure enough, there was Laura coming out on the porch and over to them.

"Daddy's being too depressing," she chirped to them. "I had to come out. He's saying it'll take us ten years to clear the Japs off all the islands."

Audrey scarcely heard them as she turned away towards the porch door. What in God's name was the war to her or Laura, she thought with sudden impatient self-distrust, but a stupid job in a stupid office, a longer sentence in Panama, and occasionally the purely sentimental pleasure of looking around at the young pilots in El Rancho and feeling a catch in the throat when the orchestra played *Coming in on a Wing and a Prayer?*

CHAPTER ELEVEN

IT WAS AT Helen's wedding the following week that Beverly
had his sharpest seizure of doubt. Helen had insisted from
the beginning that this be a large and social occasion in
defiance of any criticism that might lurk in the minds of her
family and friends. She stood up proudly before the altar
with her bashful-looking sailor and seemed to be saying triumphantly to the six self-conscious bridesmaids arrayed in
unbecoming pink: "So it was convention that you all valued,
was it? Is this conventional enough for you?" Beverly in the
back of the crowded little church, desperately uncomfortable
in his tight white uniform, mopped his brow and shuddered.
Everything seemed horribly confined and twisted. The stiff,
empty-faced saints on the windows in the white walls, the
wide-brimmed hats in the congregation, the fussy lace dresses
matted around the big bodies of the matrons, the stiff collars
that some of the older men *would* wear—all these details
synchronized in a fetid atmosphere that seemed to negate
any slightest hope of spirituality. He had literally to grip the
back of the pew in front of him to keep himself from turning and rushing from the church and revelling exultantly
in the strip of green grass which he could descry outside the
open door at the end of the aisle. If there was a God,
surely he was out there and not in this steamy interior at
the celebration of such a rite.

Resentfully he watched Audrey standing so calmly by the
altar, so apparently unmoved by the atmosphere that exasperated him. There was nothing in the ceremony that re-
volted her; she was an integral part of its smallest ramifications. After all, hadn't it been through poor Helen that their
intimacy had first flowered, hadn't it been over her dissected
romance that those first evenings at El Rancho had been
blissfully spent? He felt soiled by the very thought. Audrey
lived in a different world and suffered, if at all, from a very
different sensitivity. It was entirely natural, perhaps, that he

should visualize himself in a similar trapped position before that same minister who, though a tower of respectability in the Zone, seemed now to radiate only the darkest and most malignant leer.

It was not quite the first time that he had felt this rush of panic. He had gone to bed after the cocktail party at the Emersons' full of martinis and a sense of dizzy excitement at what he had regarded bravely as his then definite commitment. He had dreamed, alas, a far from encouraging dream. All his friends and his mother and sister, who had incidentally never seemed more lovable and kind, were on a train going in one direction while he and Audrey were in one on adjoining tracks headed in the opposite way. The two trains, however, kept constantly passing each other with a great whizz and racket, yet there seemed to be plenty of time for conversation. Everybody leaned out the windows and talked and asked him and Audrey to come with them, but Audrey kept saying, no, she had always wanted to go to New York, and the others kept saying it was too bad because it was more fun where they were going and cheaper too. Then Bev saw they were all nodding and waving understandingly at him and winking sympathetically as they kept disappearing down the track, and he wanted terribly to join them and got up to leap out of the train and, of course, woke up.

At first he had stared up at the ceiling and waited in blissful anticipation for that sense of release that reality brings after nightmares, and then it had dawned on him with a sad, sick little sense of doom that the dream was true. He had shaken it off somewhat during the day but he had taken care to see less of Audrey during the following week, and now in the church the full terror of it returned to him in force.

For almost the first time in his life he contemplated the idea that there might not be a God or an afterlife. That it was all just this. Never had Panama seemed more of a fantasy or his old world, centered in Fifty-seventh Street, a more concrete reality. He knew now that he couldn't wait for the end of the ceremony or for the departure of the bride. When one suffocated one had to have air. He looked to his right and left; he nodded in a sickly way in answer to Miss Miles' blooming smile, and then suddenly he found himself with his back to the altar retreating in long steps from the church. Outside he felt only relief in the fresher air and walked with a light step to the line of taxis. And as he drove back towards Headquarters he felt a lessening of his antipathy towards Audrey. He remembered with gratification her reluctance to join in his mood of cheerful propositions for the future. When he was back at the District where he could now feel his mother's presence in the very heat of the air and Angeline Stroud's in the messy bareness of his room, he thought again of Audrey's "Yes, I—," and his feelings were warm. Poor girl, after all she must have realized that things, however bright they may have looked, could never be entirely what they promised. He, and not she, had exaggerated his involvement. Things would be pleasant enough in the ensuing weeks but perhaps it might be as well to suspend for a little while their pleasant dinners. This would provide on his part a sort of tacit apology for the alcoholic ardor with which he had offended her common sense on the porch.

CHAPTER TWELVE

SATURDAY NIGHT ON the terrace at the Union Club was magic to Beverly, for here, he thought, was the essence of life in Panama and the essence, indeed, of life in the Latin tropics. It might have been in the large, stone dance floor or the shimmer of Panama Bay; it might have been in the moonlight reflected from the deep French windows of the white club house; or in the chatter from the air-cooled room with the oval bar so filled with American officers; or it might have been simply in the rustle of Signora Allessandro Alfaro as she swept across the floor, her blonde braids piled in a giant pompadour over her pale forehead, catching the eye of the President's sister and shaking her fan. But not entirely. It was in other things. As his eye fell on Hortensia Alarias sitting at the opposite end of the dinner table that he was at, as he watched her poise, her elegance, her long, black hair with the pearl tiara, as he listened to her excited Spanish accent while she talked to Commander Gilder— Hortensia, daughter and niece of Presidents—suddenly she laughed. She laughed harder and harder; she threw back her head and gave what was almost a scream of laughter; she laughed and laughed—and then he felt uneasy; he became uncomfortable—what was it? The Union Club seemed to drop away and it came to him, that same laugh, like the laugh of a macaw, strident and free, from the steaming growth of a jungle.

"Why are you staring at Hortensia?" Lydia Schmidt demanded. He started and turned to her.

"I was thinking of how she laughed. What it reminded me of."

"Well, what does it? A parrot?"

"That's it," he said. "A parrot."

"A black parrot?"

He stared.

"Is she?"

Lydia shrugged her shoulders.

"Not altogether. But some. They've all of them got some. You can call it a sun tan if you want to be elegant. But I've been here too long."

"I know you dug the Canal yourself, Lydia," he said laughing, "and I suppose that gives you a right to shatter my illusions. But it's so mean of you. Now just think of Hortensia. Her father President, you know, like her uncle. Educated in a convent in France—"

"New Jersey."

"New Jersey?"

"Certainly. Pulaski. Where did you hear it was France?"

"From her, I guess."

"Oh, you." Lydia snapped her black eyes at him and adjusted her massive pearls. "You're such a romantic, Bev. Hortensia was educated in a convent in New Jersey and her husband is an ex-bartender. Don't shudder. Those are facts. Panama's disappointing. But if you'd seen it grow from a bunch of uncovered backsides to a club like this you wouldn't mind so much."

He shouted with laughter.

"Lydia, you're peerless!"

"Look at Marina Guardiarco over there at the corner table. Respectable looking?"

He nodded.

"Quite the lady, isn't she?" Here she leaned over and lowered her voice, winking at Amos on her right as she did so. "She owns the juiciest slice of real estate in the hottest part of the red light district."

"But, Lydia," he protested, "I thought all that was yours."

She turned to Amos.

"Shall we throw him out?"

Amos flung his hands in the air.

"You mean it's not true? Jeepers! And I was going to marry you for your money!"

"You two are the limit," she cried. "New York and Boston. Our old families." She looked from one to the other and smiled. "I'll bet neither of you has ever earned a real dollar."

"You wouldn't expect Amos or me to work!" Bev exclaimed. "After all, we never had your opportunities. There are laws now about making money the way you made it."

"And jail has become very fashionable," Amos added. "I'm sure Lydia would find it so, don't you Bev?"

"All her friends."

"If one of you dances with me," she cut in, "I can only be insulted by one at a time."

She and Beverly were soon bobbing slowly over the terrace floor.

"Your ambassadress friend is being entertained up there," she said, nodding towards the great windows of the second story which were aglow with light behind their heavy yellow curtains. "I saw them come in. General Terence must be giving a party."

"Who's there?"

"The usual 'official' crowd. The commanding general, the Governor of the Zone, the admiral, the Panamanian Secretary of State, and the Livermores. My, they must get tired of each other. Oh, look, Bev." She pointed to a corner of the terrace. "There's that little Emerson girl. Oh, my God. They're having a family party. I can't bear it. There's the mother and the father and that dreadful aunt. I'd better not wave at her because I'm sure they don't approve of me. Poor little thing. I asked her tonight, you know, and she must have declined just out of kindness to those old crows."

Most of the people at the many tables were finishing dinner and beginning to move on to the floor, and Beverly had no difficulty in following Lydia's gaze to the lone table where Audrey was sitting. She saw him too and gave him a flitting smile.

Audrey had not wanted to go to the Union Club that night. She had declined Lydia's invitation earlier in the week because she had anticipated one from Beverly and he had not told her that he was going to be one of the party. In fact he had not been himself at all in the past few days. Something had happened, but what she could not be sure, unless he had simply become scared. She remembered bitterly his impetuosity of the other afternoon. Apparently it had been regretted. Saturday afternoon at any rate had rolled around with a complete vacuum before her. She had been sitting on the porch with a bowl full of book oil polishing her battered editions of George Eliot when her mother had come out and suggested that an evening at the Union Club would be "just the thing" for Aunt Betty's spirits. This sort of treatment was periodically dosed out to Aunt Betty and unfortunately did appear to be successful, so Audrey had been unable to offer a better criticism than a groan. This, of course, she had been immediately asked to explain.

"I really don't think your father and I demand so much of you, my dear," her mother said, "that you should grudge us one evening of your company at the Union Club, especially when you have nothing else to do. Maybe you're ashamed of the way we look. Well, I can't help it if I'm not as smart looking as Laura Smith." She always assumed a great admiration on Audrey's part of Laura which was entirely unfounded. "But I will say this for myself. I think your aunt and I cut a more distinguished appearance than that painted Mrs. Schmidt you talk so much about."

"Yes, Mother."

And, of course, it was an unusually gay evening at the club. Everybody she knew was there; everybody waved at the table where the Emersons and Miss Miles so placidly sat. Her father ordered some wine with a great many remarks · such as: "We only do this sort of thing once in a while. I don't think a few dollars will bankrupt us if we don't make it a habit, do you, Nelly?" and a good many winks at the unresponsive Panamanian waiter. Her mother made very few comments but watched the dancing with a staid madonna stare, one arm, resting on its elbow, raised to her chin in an attitude of "So this is what you young people are so crazy about." Miss Miles as usual was drinking too much and remembering oft-repeated anecdotes of her uncle's place, "Rougemont," now a gas station. Audrey felt a distinct sensation of nausea. She could eat very little and whenever a remark · was addressed to her she felt an irritation so bitter that she had to pause to keep the temper out of her voice before she spoke. She kept trying to relax herself mentally and physically and had almost succeeded when she saw Beverly waving to her, and her stomach muscles contracted again.

Esmond Carnahan was one of those persons who always turned up at the right moment. It was one of the best things about him. Suddenly there he was, arrayed in a white flannel tuxedo with a red bow tie and cummerbund and a red silk handkerchief just peeping out of his breast pocket. His hair looked more tonicked than usual and the curls, flattened the least bit, glistened. He smiled at her and started across the floor to their table. She felt herself going weak with gratitude.

"Good evening, Mrs. Emerson. Miss Miles. Mr. Emerson," he said with his friendly smile. "Miss Miles, you're looking very well. Would all of you mind too much if I took Audrey away for a little dance?"

They nodded enthusiastically at the charming young man whom they could not seem to remember meeting before, probably because they never had. A sense of names and when to use them, Audrey reflected, was probably Esmond's only asset to the diplomatic service. She followed him happily on to the floor.

"Are you at Lydia's party?" she asked.

"Yes. It's one of my nights off. At the embassy, you know, we're like chambermaids. We have our nights out."

"Is Beverly there?"

"You don't think Lydia would give a party without Bev, do you?"

"No, I don't suppose."

"I know you've been going out with Beverly," he continued, "but you couldn't be serious about him, could you?"

She felt too tired to retort.

"Why couldn't I?"

"Oh, Bev." He laughed brightly. "It would be just like catching a beautiful butterfly in a garden. When you opened your hand you'd find it was all legs."

She shuddered.

"Aren't you awful," she said.

"Perhaps."

"What would I find if I caught you?"

"A cocoon, my dear, that would sprout into an even more beautiful butterfly."

She felt nothing but disgust.

"Who'd want to catch any of you," she said bitterly. "I'd better go back to my family."

But he stopped dancing and tucked her arm under his.

"You need cheering up, I see. How about a drink?"

She said nothing and they went over to the bar.

In a corner of the room which contained the oval bar, on a red, leather-backed, circular seat, Lieutenant-Commander McShane and Lieutenant Bill Ellis, commanding officer of the U. S. S. *Sardonyx*, were drinking scotch and sodas. Ellis had just arrived from the last Guantanamo convoy and had come over to Balboa for a discussion with operations officers in the District. Saturday night was "all out" with him and he had wandered down to the Union Club to get started.

He was a handsome man in his early thirties but his looks provided little key to his character. Long, smooth, brown hair, a sharp chin and nose, and eyes that gave a penetrating effect from under arched eyebrows—so far he was very much the naval officer. But more revealing perhaps was the suggestion of puffiness about his eyes with its faint implication of indulgences, past and present, the playful, half-sneer on his lips, and a marked tendency to wink at everyone he saw. Ellis had been a sailor for twelve years before he had been commissioned; he was still at heart a chief. McShane had buttonholed him at the bar; his preferred occupation on Saturday nights was to impress the sea-going men with his own importance in the overall operational picture.

"Yes, sir," he was saying, "I wanted a ship. I did indeed. I told them I didn't care what sort of a ship. Naval transport or auxiliary or even one of these amphibious things. The point is I can handle ships, and God damn it I can handle men. I've been around. But they said to me: 'Mac, how old are you?' Well—heh, heh," here he reached over and gave Ellis a little poke. "I snapped right back at them and said: 'Anyone who says I'm a day over forty's got to prove it.' I never had a birth certificate. And what did they do? Damned if they didn't tell me to let the young guys do the sailing. 'You're for the big job, Mac,' they said. 'Headquarters.' "

He subsided for a moment into his scotch. Ellis stared into his glass in a dazed fashion.

"I'll tell you, Mac," he muttered finally, "what I'll do." Again he was plunged into thought. "They need another convoy commodore on my run. A convoy commodore," he repeated. "You know, to go along on one of the merchant ships. Merchant ship boss. Just the sort of thing you can handle, McShane. Allison's getting old and wants to quit. Swell job. Different ship every convoy. I'll speak to Captain Michalis about you. That's the thing. Convoy commodore." He looked at McShane glassily but with perfect comprehension. Drink affected his speech long before his mental coördination. McShane was too old a hand at the boasting game not to have anticipated this suggestion.

"You put your hand right on it!" he exclaimed enthusiastically. "The one job of all of 'em I could really do up brown. But, what can I do about it? I've been dogging Michalis' office for months. 'Why, you old fart,' he says, 'you've got a job, and you can stick to it.' Hey waiter, two more scotches here." The waiter stopped and eyed him blankly. "Two more scotches," he roared, "and make it snappy. So much nonsense," he continued, when the waiter had hurried off, "this business of learning Spanish. All you have to do is to yell at these Spics and they understand."

Ellis stared at him and wondered how far he could be induced to go.

"It's a great comfort," he began slowly, "for the boys at sea to know that there are guys like you on the beach. I don't mind telling you, Mac, we sometimes get worried."

McShane beamed.

"We do what we can. Why, when I came into that office first you wouldn't have believed it but there were only three officers and one old card index. And now we're spread all over the place." He looked around and lowered his voice. "I'll bet we have seventy-five thousand secret file jackets alone!"

"No!"

"On the level. This whole damn part of the world is honeycombed. I wouldn't be surprised if there were six secret bases for refueling Nazi subs along the coast from Yucatan to Colombia."

"What do they get? Bananas?"

But all was lost on McShane. He shrugged his shoulders.

"God knows what they may be getting," he said earnestly. "God knows."

"You'll catch 'em, won't you, Mac?"

McShane looked serious.

"If they can be caught we'll get 'em."

At this point the waiter arrived with the drinks, and Pete Stoner came by. McShane waved him over to introduce him.

"I'd like you to meet one of my best young men, Ellis," he said jovially. "Pete Stoner. We're sending him along with you on your next trip. Just for a bit of sea indoctrination. I guess you know how to give him that, eh?"

Ellis glanced up at Pete.

"Glad to have you along," he said.

Mr. Gilder, immaculately white, his ribbons in precise array, his slick, black hair in perfect formation, was watching this introduction from the other side of the bar. He was talking to Hortensia Alarias, but he kept one eye alert on Ellis.

"I'll be right back, Hortensia. A moment of business," he explained and walked around the bar to McShane's group.

"Hello, Ellis," he said, "may I join this pleasant little group for a moment?"

McShane looked disgruntled but Ellis nodded, curtly perhaps, and Gilder, hoisting his trousers to save the crease, seated himself beside them.

"I see you're meeting your new skipper, Pete," he said to Stoner pleasantly enough. "May I drink to a very good cruise?" He raised his glass. "I wish you came over to this side more often, Ellis. We need to hear more from our convoy friends."

Ellis looked from Gilder to McShane in fascination.

"You know how it is," he said. "I'd like to. But on the whole," he continued illogically, "I like to stay out of the God-damn Zone as much as I can. Panama City and Colon —well, they're O.K. If you like Spics, and I guess I do. But these dredgers. You can have 'em."

McShane's face assumed a suspended expression. Mr. Gilder smiled.

"I think we can all second you on that thought, Ellis," he said.

This was too much for the Chief of Section Red.

"Just a minute, Sheridan," he interrupted, his eyes moving swiftly back and forth as they always did when he was nervous. He started to tap the table with one hand. "I don't at all mind saying that I think a lot of you guys go too far in this prejudice against the Zone. Now I happen to have lived in these parts for twenty-five years. I know these people well. They're fine people." •

"Hear, hear," Stoner put in. "Tell 'em, Mac."

"And I don't mind saying," McShane went on, his Irish blood warming, "that in all these petty disputes between the Navy and the Zone my first loyalties are with the Zone." This was directed at Gilder who merely smiled at Ellis. But Ellis did not smile. He had finished his drink, and any of his crew could have warned them that his steady, silent stare was the prelude to something much worse.

"What's that?" he asked thickly. "You're against the Navy?"

"I didn't say that," said McShane hastily. "I was only saying that my first loyalties—"

"What about your navy loyalties?" Ellis interrupted. "Or don't you have any?"

McShane blinked in consternation and looked at Pete, but Pete wasn't going to stick his neck out by arguing with his prospective commanding officer. For once Section Red was alone.

"I think you'd better remember that I'm a lieutenant-commander," McShane said as fiercely as he could.

Ellis stared blankly at him.

"Nobody can give orders who's disloyal to the Navy," he said heavily. "There's Captain Michalis. Let's ask him."

This, however, was the last thing that appealed to McShane. The episode had been sufficiently distasteful without adding to the picture a disgruntled staff officer who was highly unpredictable in his likes and dislikes. It was almost unbearable to retreat before Gilder but with a firm swallow and a "Let's go, Pete," he made the best of it.

Gilder, left alone with Ellis, radiated a quiet satisfaction.

"I've been wanting someone to do that for months, Ellis," he said. "My congratulations. Any time I can do some little thing for you, just say the word."

But Bill Ellis was intent now on the uncrumpled whiteness of the other's uniform and his blood, already up, was tingling.

"You're all alike," he snarled. "Desk sailors. Always knifing someone in the back. Jesus!"

Gilder's lips narrowed into a thin line.

"I can see you want to be alone," he said acidly and getting up returned to his friend, Hortensia.

Beverly was standing by the main door of the club arguing violently with an attendant over the admission of some naval officer who he claimed was coming to join Mrs. Schmidt's party when Sheridan Gilder came up.

"But no guests Saturday night who are not members," the attendant repeated stubbornly.

"You know that's absurd," Beverly almost shrieked. "Half the people here tonight aren't members. Now will you let this gentleman in?"

Gilder waited until he had succeeded, which took only ten minutes, and then spoke to him.

"Could I have a word with you, Bev?"

"Certainly, Sherry." They moved in and stood at the fanning bottom of the great stairway to the private entertainment rooms. "What's on your mind?"

Gilder looked grave and confidential.

"You remember, Bev, a few days ago you said you'd like to take a convoy trip?"

"Yes. But it went to Pete." He felt his heart beating. Couldn't things ever be settled?

"That's right." Gilder locked his hands behind his back. "But things have changed a bit. Pete's still going. Except I'm thinking of sending you too. How about it?"

"You know I'd love to."

"There's another thing. And this is under the cuff. Strictly. Keep your eye on the skipper. There's been some talk about him. Just keep your ears open and let me know when you get back."

Beverly looked at him sharply and then nodded.

"I understand," he said. "Surely."

Mr. Gilder suddenly stepped back to clear the steps and Bev, looking up, saw the official party descending the stairway. Half way down and leading was the commanding general, ablaze with ribbons, and Mrs. Livermore. She was very grand in green lamé and pearls, erect and interested, moving her head around with that jerky movement so characteristic of her like a crane about to take wing, her intent, short-sighted eyes trying to take in the club and who was there. And tonight she had a lorgnette—she rarely carried one—that she was using with much effect. He stepped back assuming that she would not speak to him on such an occasion but hoping, nonetheless, because of Gilder's proximity that she would. They were at the bottom now and he heard her loud voice which divided speech into groups of run-together syllables, punctuated by pauses, right in his ear:

"Good evening, Beverly—so nice to see you tonight—General, do you know Lieutenant—is that right? I never know." Here she inserted one of those friendly but pointless laughs that made unintelligent people think her silly. "Or do I say, Lieutenant, junior grade, Stregelinus?"

Beverly stepped forward and shook the general's proffered hand.

"Good evening, sir."

He stepped back. But to his surprise Mrs. Livermore instead of walking on with the general swung around to address him more directly. It was rare, for she had not an exaggerated or snobbish but a highly realistic sense of comparative rank and importance.

"Will you do me a favor, Beverly?"

"Most certainly."

"Will you find my nephew and tell him—don't ask him, *tell* him—that he must come to the *Presidencia* and join me and his uncle. Mr. Ellery has had some sort of seizure and has gone home. So we have to cancel Esmond's 'leave.'" Again that laugh. "I'm asking you because you can always find people. Isn't he here tonight?"

"Yes. I just saw him."

"Oh." She appeared to reflect. "Are you with your little girl tonight? The one we talked about the other day?"

"No."

"No? You've thought better of it?"

He hesitated.

"I've thought about it."

She nodded.

"Good for you, my dear. Don't forget what I said about the dangerous age. It comes long before forty."

"I'll get Esmond," he said.

"Will you?" And she gave him the broad but mannered smile, the hearty tilt of the head which though evidently a social gesture still managed to convey a certain warmth. He sometimes wondered if Mrs. Livermore had any way of particularizing her friends; her exuberance and energy where people were concerned seemed almost to preclude intimacy, or rather to extend it, stylized, to all the social world. She moved on and Bev turned to where Gilder was trying unsuccessfully not to look impressed.

"I have to go look for Esmond Carnahan, Sherry," he said, "and give him a message from his aunt. But let's talk more about the *Sardonyx* business. You know I'm all for it."

Mr. Gilder, however, appeared to be preoccupied with Mrs. Livermore.

"Was that Miss Emerson she was referring to?"

Bev looked startled. He hadn't realized they had been overheard.

"No."

"I suppose it's some other friend of yours."

But Bev ignored his sarcasm.

"Do you think I have only one?" he asked and hurried off to find Esmond. He hadn't time really to worry about what Gilder might or might not think for his mind was principally occupied by what it was going to be like on the *Sardonyx*. He was already envisioning the most sensational kind of wreck with a picture of himself picked up at sea, a ragged survivor, by some splendid destroyer, asking with a nonchalance worthy of a Stregelinus: "Did we get Guadalcanal? I've missed the news for a bit." But there were also sentiments of discomfort. He would have to pack a bag and lug it to the train across the Isthmus to Cristobal which would mean intolerable sweating; he would probably not be able to use his electric razor on board, and then there was the inevitable embarrassment of being an officer ignorant of the sea confronted with enlisted men who were not. Decidedly it had its bad side.

He met Audrey and Esmond walking down the terrace.

"Your aunt wants you to go on to the *Presidencia,* Esmond," he said, not without a trace of satisfaction. "She told me to *tell* you, not to ask you."

"Damn!" Esmond was all indignation. "Jack Ellery's going to do that."

"Sick," Bev explained tersely.

Esmond had an immediate sense that Beverly was enjoying it.

"Well, I won't do it!" he exclaimed. "She can't order me around that way."

Beverly shrugged his shoulders.

"Go ahead, Esmond," Audrey said firmly. "You know it's just one of those things. They happen."

"But I've got to take you home first." Audrey's family had already left.

"Audrey can join Lydia Schmidt's table with me," Bev interposed. "I'll see that she gets home."

Esmond went off in a temper and Beverly and Audrey returned to Lydia's table and sat down. Everybody was either dancing or in the bar and there was no one at the table except two of Lydia's sons at the other end. The older, by the Panamanian husband, was in a state of complete inertia from drink; his long, greasy, black hair was falling over his forehead in streaky lines, and the younger, Peter Schmidt, aged fourteen and precocious, who should have been at home in bed, was sitting on the table yelling insulting things at the dancing couples whom he recognized and sometimes at ones that he didn't.

"Little darling," Audrey murmured under her breath, and then turning to Bev: "You've been quite a stranger."

"I thought you must be getting sick of me."

She appeared to debate this.

"But I don't think I am."

"It's bad for people to see too much of the same people all the time," he said confusedly. "Don't you think?"

Deliberately she kept herself from looking up at him too suddenly.

"Why?"

"Oh—they get stale."

So that was it, she reflected. Now she was in for it. Her life seemed to be taking on a pre-war international note. There was crisis after crisis and a single inevitable outcome.

"You mean *you're* stale," she said. Her effort to keep the tenseness out of her voice did not succeed.

"Oh, no, Audrey."

"What else could you possibly mean? Go ahead. Say it."

He scratched his head and looked around miserably.

"It's not that, Audrey. Really. It's just that I don't think I ought to—"

"What?"

"Ought to lead you on."

She stared.

"Lead me on to what?" she demanded.

His embarrassment was painful to see but pity was the last thing that she felt at the moment.

"Lead you on to think that I could marry you," he blurted out finally.

Her mouth opened in astonishment at his way of putting it.

"Are you a prince in disguise?" she asked acidly.

"We don't really like the same things," he hurried on to explain; "our lives are too different. I'm tied down to all sorts of things in New York that would bore you to tears."

"Such as?"

"Oh—everything."

As she looked into his troubled unhappy eyes the thought of what she was going to say to him came near to compensating for the disappointment of her failure.

"You don't have to go through all that, Beverly. It doesn't matter that much. If you want to back out, back out."

"But it isn't like that, Audrey. Can't you see—?"

"Of course, I see," she answered sharply. "Don't you think I have my pride?"

He put his elbows on the table and rested his forehead on his hands.

"I can't bear to think I've hurt you," he murmured.

"Oh, don't talk like a movie star!" she retorted impatiently. "You haven't done that much damage. What do you want? A written release? Maybe there's a notary public at the club." She pretended to look around in search of one. "Of course it is a little late."

"Oh, Audrey, don't be like that."

"What do you expect?"

"I don't know. I just feel that everything's gotten out of hand. There seem to be so many me's. If you knew how I stayed awake sometimes and wondered about myself."

"No more fascinating occupation I'm sure."

He lifted his head and gave her a desperate look. Her very sarcasm seemed to provide the anchor he needed, for he exclaimed with returning ardor:

"Audrey, I've gone crazy! Forget everything I've said tonight, will you please?"

But this unfortunately was only the blow that loosened the last wedge in her self-restraint.

"What you need is a nurse!" she snapped.

He looked very hurt.

"How can you be so mean?"

"Because I'm not going to sit here all night listening to you shift your ground and all the time taking me for granted. If you think you're breaking my heart, you're crazy!"

"Oh."

"Let's get a few things straight, Beverly Stregelinus," she continued in a tone that was a tense mixture of unease and satisfaction. "You were a very exotic being to me when I first saw you. I confess that I was terribly impressed by those first names and that accent. And the way you seemed to be able to twist Mr. Gilder and the others around your little finger. Everything seemed easy and pleasant about you. I decided right then and there that that was what I wanted."

It was his turn to be astonished.

"What?"

"You. And anything that went with you."

"When?"

"From the very beginning."

"But you hardly looked at me in those days."

"Oh, I had my plans."

"I don't believe it!"

"Don't you? Do you remember how we first became friends?"

He thought.

"You mean the Helen business? Yes, I know that's what

started us. Oh. But—" He stared as the idea grew. "You don't mean that that was the reason you took the matter up?"

She nodded,

"Certainly it was. You don't think I was interested in Helen, do you?"

"You weren't. No, of course, you weren't."

And the vision of her remorseless little ego tearing away with sharp fangs at Helen's secret suddenly sickened him. It wasn't possible—but, yes, yes, it was only too credible. And she, seeing it for the first time in his wretched eyes, became panic-stricken.

"I'd have done anything. Anything," she repeated fiercely. "But what difference did it make after all? When we did become friends, I couldn't take it."

He looked up with sudden triumph.

"You're just making all this up because you do love me!" he cried.

She laughed with sheer incredulity at the vanity of it. Then she cast everything aside.

"Now we have gone Hollywood!" she exclaimed. "Except in the movies the hero doesn't bore the girl to tears every time they go out with dull, rambling, incoherent anecdotes about all the rich old ladies he's wasted his life with!"

He turned very white and started to get up.

"If you're going to be nasty," he said.

"Wait a minute," she said, restraining him with one hand on his arm; "I'm not going to let you off as easily as that. You're going to have some idea about what I've been going through. I think I should die if I had to listen to one more story about Angeline Stroud. But I will say this about your conversation. You're the only person I've ever met who's always wrong. You're wrong about books. You're wrong about facts. You're wrong about people. But most of all, my dear, you're wrong about yourself. Every now and then I get a peek into the mirror that you see yourself in. I see that warm, big-hearted poet who loves goodness so much that he can be forgiven his brilliant vulgarities. But where is your heart?"

He was not listening to her now; he was only looking at her sadly.

"Then you never cared at all," he said.

There it was. She felt it in her side, a stab of real remorse.

"Oh, a little," she said impatiently. "But what is there to care about? You're all airy laughs and art for art's sake and beauty being a joy forever. You and Esmond. And Aunt Betty."

He gaped.

"Aunt Betty?"

"It's the same attitude. Any way you look at it. You all rhapsodize about the beauty of a turn of phrase or a spot of sun on the wall or some damn thing like that." She waved one hand in the air. "Things that have a deeper meaning. Dear, yes. Like those verby sonnets of yours. And Aunt Betty's nostalgia for relics of the old South. She's the last stage, that's all. She can get a jag out of anything now. She sits in her rocking chair with a double bourbon in one hand and an old button hook in the other and hiccups about the associations it brings back to her. You'll come to that. So will Esmond."

He was interested enough almost to forget the personal insult.

"My, my. What an extraordinary picture. Does she really drink?"

"She really does."

"And I thought she was so wonderful."

"Oh, everyone's 'wonderful' to you," she said wearily. "I want to go home."

He stood up.

"I'll take you."

She shook her head.

"No, please. I'll ask Pete. He told me earlier he would."

"Pete?"

"Didn't you know that Pete was one of my best navy friends?"

And giving him a little smile and nod she got up and went over to the bar where Pete Stoner was sitting alone.

"Will you take me home now, Pete?" she asked him.

"Sure."

"Are you ready?"

He looked at her and smiled.

"Ready for what?"

She gave a little laugh at her own obviousness.

"Ready for anything. Let's get out of here." She turned to the door, and Pete, heavily, slid off his stool and lumbered after her.

They drove towards El Rancho in the open and ancient Cadillac that Pete shared with Amos. Audrey rested her head on the broad leather back of the seat and enjoyed the wind in her hair and the stars over the narrow streets. The cathedral in the plaza loomed white and enchanting as they sped by. This part of the city had a high-portaled splendor in moonlight that was a mellow contrast to its blatant color at high noon. All she wanted was to avoid contemplation and decision; she only wondered vaguely if she would follow irrevocable words with irrevocable acts. Beverly, of course, was gone forever and she felt nothing but a strange exaltation at the candor with which she had blotted out the past months of her life.

Pete stopped the car in the parking lot by El Rancho.

"Cover charge," he said and kissed her. It was his only remark since leaving the club. He leaned over and put a thick arm around her shoulders. She made no move and he kissed her again.

"You don't mind tonight," he said, opening the door.

"No," she answered. "But how did you know I wouldn't?"

"Oh, I know."

They went in and sat down at a table near the floor. Pete ordered two scotch and sodas.

"You think you know all about women, don't you?" she asked.

"Not all. But enough."

"Enough for your purposes. Is that it?"

"Oh, Audrey," he complained, "why do you girls always try to make a wolf out of me? I'm just a lonely naval officer in the tropics. All I want is a little companionship."

"I suppose that's why you keep that little apartment of yours in Panama City," she said. "Long after your wife's gone back to the States."

"There you go," he protested, "hammering away again. I'm trying to sublet it."

"Oh, Pete." She stirred the drink that was just then placed before her. "I suppose I should say you're just a nice, shaggy sheep dog and trust you." She thought of herself with a vague surprise. To be so abandoned and so utterly indifferent. But excuses were rampant. After so much talk, so much discussion and talk, so many half-truths and half-everythings—

"That's right, Audrey."

"What about your wife?" she asked suddenly. "What would she say?"

"What do you think?" he asked with a shrug. "But a man's a man. You're smart enough to know that. If she knew it would hurt her. But she won't know. I'm not trying to trap you, Audrey. You weren't born yesterday."

She stared at him, fascinated at her own depravity.

"No," she said. "I certainly wasn't."

"All right then."

"I don't have to be persuaded," she said with assumed pride. "If I want to be seduced, I'll be seduced."

"Well, while you're making up your mind, we could be driving over to my apartment." He raised his eyes inquiringly.

"So we could," she said, putting out her cigarette. "To see if it's ready for subletting."

He called for the waiter and asked for the check.

Part III

Sylvia

CHAPTER ONE

WHEN BEVERLY WENT down to the Cristobal train with
Pete on the Monday following the events at the Union Club
he had just the sinking feeling in his stomach that he had
been afraid of. It was all very well to dissertate in melancholy
fashion over martinis at the District bar about the miserable
futility of the mimeographed life and to feel, no doubt, the
sincerest pangs of intellectual despair, but when the actual
break occurred he found himself facing it with all the reluctance and physical shrinking of an invalid in a hospital
who has been yearning for release yet who upon sight of the
valise and the strange clothes laid out so uninvitingly on a
white chair by his bed turns instinctively back to the empty
and loathed bliss of his pillow. But having Pete was a comfort
and he consoled himself as the train rattled across the
Isthmus by fixing his eyes on the speeding vision of dense
jungle and saying to himself: "Why do you worry so? Why?
Remember that it doesn't matter. It doesn't really matter.
Not even the most awful things." But then his mind would
leap ahead to envision how hot and prickly he would be after

carrying his bag down the long dock, how miserably he would feel if he saluted the wrong end of the ship, and how people would laugh at him if he got mixed up between port and starboard.

"Pete," he said excitedly, "let's run over again exactly what we have to do when we come aboard." But Pete who was absorbed in a movie magazine and whose aloofness to the entire subject was unfathomable only replied: "On these old yachts if you so much as salute the captain he'll think you've been to Annapolis," which was all very well, Bev thought, but could he be sure? He remembered that he might be seasick and when he tried to think of the pages in Knight on seamanship so laboriously learned he knew now, he positively *knew*, that he didn't remember a thing. "Binnacle list," "Charley Noble," "by the deep six," "Capstan," "whirlwind"—the dreadful terms spun around in his mind connoting a rough and uncomfortable world of anchors and chains and heaving decks. As the train slid out into a field all heads turned to the Canal and exclamations filled the car for two new heavy cruisers were visible standing down Culebra Cut on their transit to the Pacific. Pete moved to the other side of the car to watch them and Beverly, staring at the hulks of grey as they moved slowly along, again composed himself.

What a joke, he told himself, to get excited about a cruise in the Caribbean on a converted yacht! And he became reflective in what he liked to think of as Matthew Arnold's mood of "high seriousness." He remembered in his highly emotional childhood during the last war when he used to wake up at night and burst into tears over the suffering in the trenches that his mother had told him that no suffering was unbearable because men fainted or died before it became so. How he had clung to that in his passion, so strong and vicarious, that nobody should suffer more than he. "Tell me, Mother, are you happy, Mother?" His had been a fierce little ego that wanted other people's moods to synchronize with his own that there might be no discordant element to spoil the atmosphere. But that was it, he thought; it will be over. It must be over some day. Nothing is unbearable. And with a sick but calmer sensation he stared over the tops of the trees and thought of himself and of his mother, thought of them shopping, thought of them sitting on the porch in Long Island and discussing flowers and books. That was real and he had seen it and this mirage of cruisers and "Charley

Nobles," whatever they were, would pass away or he would pass away, but anyway it would end.

They got off at a station before Colón and managed to get a ride in a station wagon going to the Submarine Base where the *Sardonyx* was tied up. Bev felt his calm disappearing again and a strong impulse to be sick; he shut his lips tightly and prayed that the dock was miles away. But it wasn't, and only the briefest minutes seemed to have gone by when the unmoved Pete said, "There she is!" and directed the driver to pull up right beside the ship despite Bev's absurd protest that it would look less showy if they arrived on foot.

As Pete had predicted the *Sardonyx* was hardly a terrifying sight. A pleasure yacht not over two hundred feet in length, the sole aspects of war visible upon her were a three-inch-fifty gun on her forecastle and four fifty-caliber machine guns clamped to her upper deck. And, of course, the dull grey paint which covered her from the tip of her single broad stack to the waterline, obscuring with military drabness all the brown and gold and gleaming white with which Bev liked to think that she had glistened in former days in the blue harbors of Newport and Miami. Indeed, the grey paint pouring down from infinite sources over all the world could be the symbol of the war itself, extinguishing, obliterating the Rivieras, the color, the gaiety, and swamping all individuality in the uniformity of organized death. So Beverly reflected anyway as he took it in, the paint and the ship, his eye running anxiously over the long deckhouse with its square windows, the wide deck on top with two boats in the davits, and aft to the circular fantail where he noticed two racks of depth charges in place of the broad leather couch that usually characterized this part of such pleasure craft. She was not a beautiful yacht; her lines lacked the grace of the *Moonstone* tied further down the dock, but she had a capacious and sturdy look as she sat stolidly in the water and he felt somehow reassured.

The gangway watch saluted them casually and examined the orders which Pete handed him.

"I'll keep a copy of these for the moment, sir," he said, "to enter them in the log. I think you'll find the O.D. in the wardroom," and he pointed through one of the windows. They went around the fantail and opened a screen door in back which admitted them to a large, paneled room with a green-covered table in the center. An officer in khaki, his shirt open in front, was lounging on the sofa with a magazine.

The victrola was playing *Deep in the Heart of Texas*. He looked up when Pete and Bev came into the wardroom.

"Don't tell me," he said heartily, "I know. From the District for a sea cruise. Temporary duty to last approximately two weeks." He got up and took the papers Pete handed him. "My name's Winston," he said after giving the orders a casual glance. "Both of you had better bunk together, for the trip out anyway. Make yourselves at home. We probably won't be getting under way till tomorrow." Winston was a strong and very thick-set young man with small expressionless eyes that belied some of the heartiness that appeared in his broad flat face and air of aggressive self-confidence. "We have supper at 5:30," he continued, looking at his watch, "and then the others'll probably go to the Strangers' Club. Except me. I've got the deck, damn it all."

Pete entered easily into conversation with him while Bev moved shyly around the wardroom. Two Negro mess attendants had come in and were moving silently about setting up the wardroom table for supper. He drew courage from the gleam of the silver as they laid the knives and forks noiselessly down on the white table cover. His stomach muscles, so contracted, began to relax and he wondered if he wasn't after all going to have a good time.

But now two other officers had come in and he turned nervously to meet them. They were talking to Pete and nodded at him pleasantly enough. One of them, a short, middle-aged man with long thinning hair and stooped shoulders, came over to him with the friendliest smile.

"How are you?" he asked. "My name is Foster. I'm the Engineer Officer," he continued ungrammatically. "These junior whippersnappers call me the 'Chief Snipe.'" He put one arm under Bev's and looked around at Winston with a wink. "But that's because I'm the only one who works here. These ensigns don't do nothin' but sit in the wardroom and wait till it's time to go ashore. Except the Exec. This is our Exec, Mr. Calloriac."

None of them wore any insignia on their open khaki collars but Bev rather imagined, with that familiarity that comes after a few months of rank consciousness, that the "snipe" was a "j.g." obviously commissioned from the ranks during the war and that the Exec was a full lieutenant. The latter, who advanced to shake his hand, was thick-set as Winston was but taller and inclined to be stout; he had wavy, thick black hair and strong handsome features. His eyes were friendly and Bev felt much encouraged. There was nothing, however, particularly sympathetic in his first words.

"I don't know just what they expect you guys to learn when they send you out this way with us," he observed. "I suppose it's just the idea of getting a little spray on those neat caps of yours." He must have been confining himself to Bev, the latter reflected, for no one could have worn more battered head gear than Pete. "Well, you're welcome to learn anything you can. I'm the navigator and if you care to shoot stars with me and work them out, why fine. Only you've got to get up pretty early." "Oh, that would be perfect!" Bev cried enthusiastically. He felt his shyness slipping away in his desire to convey the full force of his eagerness. "We've been taking a night course over at the District but the only time we ever shot stars was one night in the field by the Commissary."

Calloriac didn't smile; he simply said:

"I get a fix every morning and night if I can." He went over to the victrola where the needle was grinding away having finished *Deep in the Heart* and cut it off.

Bev and Pete went down to their rooms with Mr. Foster who showed them all over Officers Country, including the snapshots on his own bureau of his wife and daughters and an invalid aunt who, it appeared, resided with his family in San Diego. He was very kind and appeared like an anxious landlord with a tentative lodger for he busied himself opening drawers and even examined the medicine closet in Bev's room, removing odd bits of toilet articles to make more space. The rooms were all interconnecting and bore the remnants of an attractive yellowish painting job; actual beds fastened into the deck had not been ripped out in favor of naval bunks and there was a variety of bathrooms. But everything showed signs of the rough life to which this pleasure craft had been submitted; the doors either stuck or failed to close; the tiles on the bathroom floors were cracked, and a vigorous stream of red rust liquid answered one's pressure on the tap. Bev on the whole, however, was dazzled by the luxury and he peopled it in his fancy with former occupants as Foster rambled on.

"You ought to like our Exec if you're from New York," he was saying. "Mr. Calloriac used to teach in some private school for boys up around there. He's smart, too. Reads all the time and plays a lot of them fancy records. I never had much time for those things but I guess you don't if you spend twenty years in the Navy. I used to be a Chief Machinist's Mate. Spent twenty years in the Navy and seventeen of them at sea. Always on big ships too. Nothin' like this. There's nothing to running little ships like this. Easy. I guess that's why they make people like me Chief Engineers on them," he went on in complete unconsciousness of any inconsistency. "They need experienced men for these old engines that are always breaking down."

Bev surveyed him with the amazement that he always felt in the presence of those who had actually been able to survive two decades of military life, but it was the remark about Calloriac that impressed him most. He looked at his watch and then hurried up to the wardroom to make the most of the fifteen minutes which he had before supper. He had a feeling that Calloriac was a person whom he was going to like very much and one whom he wished to establish as his guide and mentor before the trip began. The wardroom, to his relief, was empty except for the Exec who was standing in the same spot looking out the window and listening to the victrola. It was just at the end of what Bev luckily recognized as one of Rachmaninoff's piano concertos.

"How interesting that you should have that piece on board," Bev began. "It's always been one of my favorites."

Calloriac looked around with just the least impatience and picked the record off the machine.

"It's all right," he said laconically. "I play it about once a week. I wait till I get just so fed up with all this." He indicated a greater environment than just the vessel with his broad gesture. "And then I play it."

This remark was enough in Beverly's imagination to augment the figure before him to the dimensions of a Byronic hero. He could see now in the lonely lieutenant the romance of the early nineteenth century, the strength, the remoteness, the bitter, sarcastic temper of the Corsair, the infinite superiority of the attitude, yet such a heart beneath it all, such a *person* if one ever got to know him. These impressions bubbled over in him; he was delighted with the fullness of his conception.

"It makes all the difference in the world," he burst out, "to find someone in Panama to whom Rachmaninoff does make a difference."

Calloriac looked at him queerly.

"You've been in Panama long?" he asked.

"Months." Bev managed to put a century into the word.

"At the District?"

Bev nodded gloomily. "In information," he said with a deprecatory smile, "or, as we call it, the 'Office of Naval Misguidance.' "

Calloriac shrugged his shoulders.

"Oh, I suppose," he said tolerantly, "it takes all sorts to win a war. Don't get the idea that I think we do anything. I mean on board here. We couldn't any more sink a sub than we could a battleship." And he went into a brief explanation of the inadequacies of listening gear when attached to the bottom of a ship that could only make ten knots, which wasn't at all what Beverly wanted to talk about. He listened politely.

"Gosh," he interrupted finally, "it must be wonderful to understand those technical things so well. I never went to a navy school."

But Calloriac was not an easy person to flatter.

"Neither did I," he said brusquely. "It's nothing but a question of common sense and picking things up as you go along. Naval officers belong to the same company of frauds as anyone else."

"Frauds!"

"I don't care what you call 'em," Calloriac went on, shrugging his shoulders. "It's the same old myth of the administrator. The idea that the man who says 'Jones, you do this' and 'Arbuckle, you do that' is more important than the guy who actually does the damn thing."

Bev took refuge in platitude.

"But surely we can't get along without administrators," he protested. "You can get a Jones or an Arbuckle anywhere, but the man who directs them and coordinates them and frames the policy—he's the one who's hard to get, he's—"

"That's just the myth," Calloriac interrupted. Clearly, it was only his conviction in the matter that was overcoming his lack of interest in Bev. "I'll be damned if he is. Look. Suppose our gyro compass goes on the blink. I can find a hundred Captain Ellises to scream around the bridge and threaten everyone on the ship with a court-martial. But I have to scout all over hell and high water to get a gyro electrician who can understand the thing and fix it."

"Ah, but you see," said Bev triumphantly, "you do get him in the end. There's the administrator for you. Who else could get him?"

Calloriac snorted. He had obviously tired of the subject and tired of Bev.

"I take it," Bev said softly, "that you were not an administrator before the war."

The Exec looked at him sullenly for just a moment and then laughed. He sat down heavily on the couch.

"God no!" he replied. "I was just a poor damn school teacher."

"Where?"

"Oh, near New York. You'd never have heard of it."

"I might have."

"Elmhurst. It's a small private boarding school. Eighty boys. Nothing like St. Mark's or Chelton."

"Yes, I've heard of it," Bev lied unconvincingly. "It has a marvelous reputation. What did you teach?"

"I was Physical Director."

"Oh." If he had said janitor he could not have more effectively shattered the Byronic picture which Beverly had been so carefully filling in. "That must have been interesting."

"I liked it," the Exec answered. "I was just starting to teach mathematics too when the war broke out."

But Beverly had quite lost interest in the school now that the prospect of a conversation about teaching the arts to young boys, among whose number, had the school turned out to be something more hopeful than Elmhurst, might have been found some mutual acquaintance, some child of one of Beverly's friends, had disappeared.

"Mathematics," he murmured politely. "I suppose that's where you got your background for navigation."

"More or less."

There was a pause during which Beverly seated himself in a chair at the end of the table.

"It certainly is quite a ship you have," he remarked looking around. "So unexpectedly comfortable for the Navy."

"You been on other ships, Mr. Stregloonus?" This was from the engineer who had just come up the circular stairway from the sleeping quarters. "Or is this your first duty at sea?"

"I was on the *Semiramis* for a little while. Nothing to speak of."

"The *Semiramis*? That's interesting. I know a lot of officers on her."

Beverly decided bravely to correct the false impression.

"I meant I was only on her for transportation down to the Canal Zone."

"Oh."

He noticed Calloriac raise his eyes for just a second to examine him. He stirred miserably and changed the subject.

"Is Captain Ellis on board?"

Calloriac looked up again, this time with a note of suspicion, perhaps even of hostility.

"Do you know the Captain?" he asked.

"Well, I've met him. At the Union Club in Panama. He seemed awfully nice."

Calloriac and Foster exchanged glances.

"Yes, he's on board," the latter said. "He'll be up in a minute."

They sat in silence after this. Calloriac immersed himself in a magazine but Foster came over and sat near Beverly in a more friendly fashion. Pete Stoner came up with Winston and through the door Bev could see two younger looking officers, probably ensigns, talking on the fantail.

"Who owned the *Sardonyx* before the war?" he asked Foster. It was a question he had been very anxious to ask but did so now in a low voice in fear that Calloriac would overhear and disapprove.

"She was owned by someone called Stroud. Maybe you've heard of him; he was a sort of lawyer—"

Arleus Stroud. The name like an arrow went winging into the rich curtain folds of the past, piercing and tearing a great gap through which all the blue and gold of Long Island Sound came surging in indistinct tumult and beyond which he seemed to see the sunlight leaping on the pavements of Fifth Avenue.

"You mean this is the *Tamburlaine?*" he gasped.

"That's it. Do you remember her?"

Beverly paused, his mind too full of associations.

"Yes," he said finally, "I do. Mr. and Mrs. Stroud built her just before I graduated from college. I guess about twelve years ago." Yes, he had a picture now of her riding at anchor in Cold Spring Harbor off the club house. "I think the family sold it after a couple of years. She never cared much for yachting—"

But he was interrupted.

"For Christ's sake!" came a voice from behind him, "can't I even get my own chair on this Chris-Craft?" And Beverly rose in horror from the Captain's seat to confront the Captain. "Oh, it's you," Ellis continued with a brief smile. "You and this other officer are the two who are coming aboard for this trip? O.K." He waved them into seats and sat down himself, slipping his napkin out of the ring on his plate. "Let's eat, boys." And then turning abruptly to Calloriac he said: "You'll have to do something about the ship's office. It looks like a pig pen. The yeoman and storekeeper don't do nothin' except make love to each other."

This remark was followed by a general silence which seemed, however, to cause no particular embarrassment.

"No soup," the Captain muttered as a steward's mate served him a platter of ham. "Wasn't soup on the menu, Mr. Quimby?" This remark he sent in the direction of a very young, blonde ensign at the end of the table.

"It was, sir."

"What happened to it?"

"Stokes told me, sir, that the paprika gave out, and . . ."

"Always a lot of damn excuses," Ellis interrupted violently. "But I can tell you this." Here he tapped the table with his forefinger warningly. "There are going to be a couple of busted cooks in that galley if things don't pick up. It's a hell of a thing to serve slop like this. Take it away," he snapped at the steward's mate, "and bring me some beans. Here I worry all the time. I don't know why. No one else does." Each remark, half muttered to himself, was followed by a glare around the table, his handsome features pulled together in a sullen knot, his eyebrows arched in a high curve. Bev suffered alone; the other officers went on eating as if the Captain wasn't there. He felt, mistakenly, that somebody should say something.

"Are we getting under way tomorrow, Captain?" he asked.

Ellis shrugged his shoulders and bit off the end of a celery stalk.

"I haven't got a crystal ball," he retorted. "No one tells me nothin' around here. If the signalman on watch isn't doping off on the bridge or playing checkers and condescends to answer a signal, and if the officer of the deck will get out of the wardroom long enough to read it, we might get under way. Who knows? I never get told nothin' till I hear it from a mess cook!"

CHAPTER TWO

ELLIS AND FOSTER, as Bev was soon to discover, represented two very different types of Navy "mustang." The differences between them were largely characteristic in exaggerated fashion of the great cleavage between the bridge and the engine room. On the bridge in an atmosphere of clear skies and blue waves, of flag officers pacing to and fro, there is a consciousness of centralized control and a tremendous emphasis on appearance; it is a world of sharp commands and quick maneuvers where speed means more wind in your face and causes more rippling of the many-colored signal flags that soar up to the yardarm and fall away with such grace, and the rudder is something far below that at a touch of the hand swerves the big ship in column with her sisters. But in the engine room these concepts are associated with sweat and heat, and the hard working machinist's mates who labor on the throttles to produce the outward show are more constantly in juxtaposition with the caverns of ugliness that, in most things, sustain the fragile and beautiful exterior of life.

Bill Ellis knew nothing of the world he lived in. He had joined the Navy at seventeen and until the war he had always been in the bridge gang of capital ships, attaining at last the smug elevation of chief quartermaster. He had been handsome, almost dashing, as a boy; one need not linger on the details of his introduction, in full innocence, to the routine naval liberty in tropical ports. Perhaps if he had had a family atmosphere behind him or even some slight extra-naval interest, intellectual or otherwise, with which to combat these impressions he might have been rescued, but as it was he embraced the life of bars and brothels without the slightest hesitation. And as every man must have some pattern in his life, some sort of skeleton to hang his varying impulses and excursions to if his personality is not to degenerate to that of a tramp Ellis turned to the Navy more and more.

No man presented a neater appearance on the bridge; no one was more intent with binoculars on the flag ship's signal halyards or cried "Execute" with more alacrity, and none saluted the colors with more gymnastic snap. Small wonder that when so many enlisted men were raised to temporary commissioned rank to meet the war's increased needs Ellis should have been recommended by no less than a vice-admiral. He knew his Navy; at least he knew the bridge. Life was a simple matter. On shore it was a succession of bars where girls could be picked up; at sea it was a series of deftly executed signals and carefully checked chronometers. His health record, dotted as it was with venereal entries, contrasted curiously with the neatly entered commendations in his service jacket.

It was easy to see why he made a poor officer. He lacked the remotest understanding of the why in life or even in the Navy and, stripped of the snap and polish of the peace-time battleship, he found on the small patrol craft to which he was now assigned only a constant reminder of how nice things had been when they were done right. This, added to the panic which he felt when he began to realize how un-qualified he was to handle or fight a ship, produced a temper almost permanently bad which in turn resulted in the type of absurd reaction that in a crisis, say an imminent collision, would make him suddenly turn to a signalman on the bridge and yell: "Don't you know you can't wear white socks up here?" And then, the crisis averted through the quick thinking of his officer of the deck, he would rush below to his cabin and in the neat, distinguished hand that had been molded by his old navy log writing, produce memorandum after memorandum on the wearing of the correct uniform of the day. His moods lifted and fell with remarkable speed and variability and his junior officers never knew what to expect or where to expect it. With them he was utterly at a loss and he alternated between giving them complete authority and treating them with the contempt that he had meted out in former days to signalman strikers on the *Colorado*. Yet, rather pathetically, he liked them all, wrote them excellent fitness reports, and wanted to be liked in return. They smiled when he smiled and said nothing when he growled, but all the while he was uncomfortably conscious of the unanimous dislike in which his uncontrollable temper, quite aside from the social barrier inevitably present between the college-graduate reserve and the "mustang," had caused him to be

held. He was fairly congenial with Foster, but the latter at
heart hated him for his failure to understand machinery and
his drafting of machinist's mates from necessary engine-room
duty to assist deck hands in the constant painting and cleaning
of the ship which Ellis' battleship background made him
emphasize at the expense of drills, instruction, and even
vital repairs.

Foster was a realist. He had started life from an even
lower rung than Ellis, having been the son of a poor Maine
farmer. He had never been the spoiled darling of the quarter-
deck. His life in the Navy had been a long and arduous
experience in boiler rooms, in engine rooms, amid throttles
and generators, listening always to the deafening hum of
spinning shafts. Six years a fireman, five third class, five second, two first—there had been no admirals to give him a
push. He had risen laboriously to lieutenant (j.g.) through
warrant, arriving at this incredible altitude of commissioned
rank only after one year of war at the age of forty when
he was ten years older than his present captain. But he had
taught himself. The world had some meaning. He read newspapers, magazines; he was married—happily too, unlike Ellis
—and had two children who lived near the Navy Yard at
San Diego. He reached out to people and only occasionally
now did the long jungle habits of survival of the fittest,
acquired so necessarily by the ugly farm boy kicked around
by machinist's mates and water tenders, show themselves in
some instinctive conversational stab in the back made on a
fellow officer whom like as not he was devoted to, for no
reason except that like an animal being tamed he still bit
from time to time to see, perhaps, if his fangs, long unused, were still there. And Beverly, fascinated by the contrast
between the two which came out more and more as he
talked to them and from details sparsely dropped by Calloriac,
enjoyed the Aesopian implications, the whole matter bearing
the resemblance that it did to the grasshopper and the ant.

Nothing could have been more typical of Ellis than his
conduct during the ship's getting under way the morning
after Beverly and Pete reported. He arrived on the bridge,
a broad elevated expanse of deck with a gyro repeater in
the center forward of the many-windowed pilot house, in a
radiant good humor and went over to the rail where Bev
and Pete were standing to observe the special sea detail and
to tell them in terms of the utmost frankness of his sexual
luck in Colón the night before. But just as he was getting to

where he had left the cabaret with the singer, a scared-looking signalman came up to him with a message from the escort commander of the convoy, the destroyer *Elizer Norris,* asking why the *Sardonyx* was not under way. Almost simultaneously a messenger reported that the engine room would need fifteen more minutes to warm up the main engines.

"Jesus H. Christ!" shrieked Ellis. "Does it take all day to get this Chris-Craft started? Where the hell is the officer of the deck? Cast off all lines!"

"But the engine room—," exclaimed Calloriac, appearing from the pilot house. He got no further.

"Cast off all lines!" the Captain almost screamed. "Tell the engine room to answer bells!"

The loud speaker brayed out: "Cast off all lines," and the indolent Negroes on the pier moved slowly to the bollards to pick up the heavy rope.

"Port back one."

Bev heard the jumbled bell sound of the annunciators and about twenty seconds later the reluctant puff, slow at first, then faster, of the port engine. The *Sardonyx* began to back gradually away from the dock.

"Starboard back one."

And they were under way. Slowly the little ship cleared the dock, turned to port and then, with increased speed, made for the harbor entrance and the breakwater. Bev observed to his surprise that Caloriac had taken the conn, for Ellis in a fit of temper at the slowness of the signalman who was receiving another message from the escort commander, had climbed up to the blinker light, pushed him aside, and was actually taking the message himself. No doubt to have his hand on the light again brought back his self-confidence. If he was a bad officer at least he could be a good signalman and escape for a few minutes into the happy irresponsibility of his enlisted days, but only, alas, for a few as the very message he was receiving involved a decision that he would have to make.

It was a beautiful day. To the north Gatun lock, highest of the three, rose over the pointed dark roofs of Zone houses, southward lay the crowded and colored squalor of Colón and before them the deep blue of the Caribbean. As they passed the breakwater the sea grew choppier, and Bev felt the salt damp breeze on his face. It *was* exhilarating. Two patrol craft, two sub chasers, the *Elizer Norris* and the *Sardonyx* made up the escort. They broke into a wide semicircle outside the breakwater, sweeping sectors of the convoy assembling area in anticipation of the approach of the merchant ships. Unconscious of time he watched the operation with delight and his heart leaped when Pete nudged him and pointed to the gate where the first of the freighters was passing through. With his binoculars he could make out fourteen vessels behind her.

"Another cigarette convoy," Pete commented in disgust. Bev stared at him.

"Cigarette?" he asked irritably.

"Going back to Gitmo to pick up cigarettes and movie magazines for the boys down here. The fastest ship in the convoy can't make more than seven knots. I never saw such a bunch of boneyard pickings."

Bev turned resolutely away determined not to have Stoner spoil his pleasure at being finally "in the midst of things." As for the type of cargo, well he knew how absurdly Pete exaggerated, and as for the speed nothing in life was more relative than the movement and size of ships. For obviously on a barren expanse of water any vessel created its own referent. The *Elizer Norris,* cutting back and forth ahead of all the others, a long, grey, four-stacked streak, its five-inch guns ominously silhouetted and its broad wake foaming behind, might in truth be a twenty-year-old and superannuated destroyer, but there she loomed with all the massive dignity of the newest battleship. The PC's were relegated in turn or, rather, promoted to the grade of escorting destroyers and the rusty old merchant ships seemed to form a convoy as mammoth and pregnant of possibilities as any that had left eastern Atlantic ports for the great invasion of Africa.

"Well, here I am," Bev thought, "after all the talking and the mimeographs and the petty squabbles." At long last. Submarines were operating in the Caribbean at the time, he knew, but as he faced the wind the idea filled him with none of the usual pricking sensations of fear but with a melancholy exaltation, a sense of "it had to be this way and why should I seek to avert it?" He focused his mind seriously on the possibility of the torpedo—the shivering crash, the slow, slipping death—and envisioned his last staring glance at the wide horizon and into the infinite space of the heavens where his dead and episcopal grandfather appeared, a large, beckoning, isolated figure, something like Marguerite in the last scene of a cinematic version of *Faust* he had once seen.

"And really what have I to lose?" he wondered. It wasn't

as if he had a future. As if he had even a wife or children.
No, he was simply a nervous, tired, rather foolish creature
who twisted his hair and made a grunting sound in his throat
when he was nervous. He was making it now. Then he reflected sadly but not without satisfaction how miserable his
mother would be. He had a fleeting vision of a posthumous
edition of "war letters" to his friends—letters, alas, which
he had never written. But it was the sudden recollection of
sharks that put an icy termination to these reflections and sent
him hurrying below to the wardroom to get his mind on
other subjects.

Sea routine imposed itself on the ship with such speed
that well before the day was done Beverly felt that he had
been under way for a week. Such social atmosphere as had
existed on board evaporated for the most part; the men stood
their watches, swept down, slept. The sea was calm and
the *Sardonyx,* assigned to the stern sector of the convoy
because of her slow speed and poor sonic equipment, pa-
trolled monotonously back and forth on a zigzag course,
dropping speed from time to time to stay behind the ships
that straggled. The *Elizer Norris* led the convoy, so far ahead
as to be out of sight. One PC and one SC were stationed
along each of the flanks. The convoy itself in four uneven
columns chugged precariously along.

Captain Ellis assigned Beverly and Pete as assistant officers
of the deck, each to stand watch with one particular ship's
officer. Beverly, upon request, drew Calloriac who stood a
navigator's watch from four to eight in the morning and six
to eight at night, taking the deck at that time in order to
be able to shoot stars. There were two sextants on board and
Beverly learned the simple HO 214 procedure in short order.
He was very nervous the first night and kept apologizing to
the quartermaster for not shouting "Mark" loudly enough for
the latter to hear and mark his time when the star had
been juggled to the horizon. Calloriac, however, was patient
and took considerable pains to make matters clear to him.
In fact, he kept Beverly in the hot, shut-in chart house for a
good deal longer than Beverly wanted, doing the sights first
by 214 and then by 211. Bev's first stars were absurdly in-
accurate and he felt inordinately discouraged, but the next
morning he had a triangle of only eight square miles for
the ship's position and that evening he had the exquisite sensation, no doubt because of luck, of seeing three of his lines
of position meet in a heart-warming pin point. From then

on his interest dwindled, as if the war were a circus side-show to offer the curious an opportunity to see each thing once as a process of self-enlargement and then, justifiably, to pass on to fresh booths. Obviously he had to continue his watches but nothing was expected of him in the interim, and nothing he did except to sleep and read books in the wardroom and take from time to time a little stroll on deck. One morning, however, particularly productive, he wrote a sonnet on Bellatrix and Procyon—the theme being their silent guard over a north-bound convoy in troubled waters—but he hesitated to embark on anything longer because of the possibility of losing the manuscript in a disaster.

He thought with pleasure of the routine in Section Blue going along without him. The routing of official mail and suspect cards. The completion of his *Who's Who*. The organization of the station-wagon trips to Quarry Heights. Another world. Even Audrey, strange little Audrey with her passionate dogmaticism, her quick temper, her conscience, seemed far away, but he was not too detached to notice that of all the tropical fantasy of the last ten months she alone, when outlined against what he liked to think of as the glitter of his former life, retained any substance. She seemed to have made for herself in his thoughts a permanent little niche which as distance increased between them tended to solidify into a steady and interesting source of reflection. The sharpness of their arguments, the intense competitiveness that existed between them softened in retrospect, and he mellowed in thinking that she might even be worrying about him. Perhaps it was the change in the relation of their two positions from the patently absurd picture of a naval officer at a desk opposite a stenographer to the man on the deep leaving a worried feminine heart at home that thus blunted in his mind the acid edge of their rivalry. Surely everything was on a sounder basis now.

But all was to be disturbed by the discovery of Pete's little affair.

One night at supper in the wardroom when the weather was particularly calm and an evening wind was softening up the heat of the day, Captain Ellis, in a pleasant mood, was discussing with his usual indelicacy the case of a coxswain whom the pharmacist's mate had just placed on the binnacle list for the return of an "old dose."

"These kids don't know how to take care of themselves," he commented. "Not that I'm one to talk though," he added with a knowing laugh. "I guess there's not much you can do about it in Panama."

"Most infected place I ever did see," Foster volunteered with a shake of his head. "No. Shanghai was worse. Yes. I guess Shanghai was worse."

"That's where I got my first dose. On the Eastern Station," Ellis confided. "Not many men in the Navy who don't foul up somewhere along the line."

"The Navy ought to run its own places," continued Foster, his soft voice beginning to grate with emphasis as it always did when he had a point to make. "What's the sense in letting these kids get stuck just because a lot of old women on the beach"—he invariably used the phrase "on the beach" to describe the civilian population—"got a lot of crazy old-fashioned notions? Don't you think so, Ned?" He looked at Calloriac for whose opinion he had an almost awe-stricken respect. The latter was staring at his plate with that detached and contemptuous expression which Beverly would have considered Byronic had he not known him to be a physical director. He looked up.

"Do I believe in government support of that sort of thing?" he asked. "I certainly do not. What do you take me for?"

"Oh, no!" Ellis broke in sarcastically. "What a thing to say, Fos! You shock me unspeakably! I agree with Mr. Calloriac. They ought to throw every sailor who gets a dose in the brig. Horrid, nasty things! Dear me, what an idea! Please hand me my Shakespeare. I want to read something pure."

Beverly waxed hot with indignation at the crudity of this. He saw Ned's eyelids flicker.

"I know what I stand for anyway," the Exec answered heavily. "I don't intend to feel ashamed of the fact that it makes me sick to see all these kids that we have on board, lots of them only seventeen, and what they do every time we tie up. You and Foster can shrug your shoulders when a boy like Miller gets messed up. I know how that kid feels. He wasn't interested in that sort of thing until your smutty old chief boatswain's mate sneered at him for being a good boy——"

Ellis interrupted by flinging his hands up in the air.

"The next thing you'll be telling us is that he can't go back to his sweetheart in the house next door because he's unclean. Oh, Mr. Calloriac! You're breaking my heart." The remarkable thing about Ellis as he laughed and rolled his eyes around the table was, as even Beverly could see, that he wasn't in the least bit spiteful. Yet Calloriac was obviously furious.

"Supposing it's true," he snapped. "I could believe it. A hell of a lot of gratitude you boys are going to get from some families when they see what's happened to their kids. Go ahead. Glory in it. It keeps the men happy. A happy crew. Christ!" The Exec was evidently a man of such strong convictions that he was easily worsted in argument. It was quite possible too, Bev reflected, that continuous disgust had blunted the edge of his wit, or again that he had simply become convinced of the futility of debate with such mentalities as Ellis' and Foster's. Bev began to see himself in a role that was far from unattractive to him, that of the new idealist who arrives just in time to revive and second the flagging efforts of the pioneer. He was about to open his mouth when Ellis, showing for the first time a rather nasty sneer, turned to the engineer.

"I suppose we ought to have lectures on current events," he suggested nastily, "or maybe discussion groups. Who'll serve tea? Will you, Fos?"

"No, we'll have women for that," the engineer answered, winking lewdly and pointlessly. "I'm a-wonderin' how much discussion they get done in them mixed discussion groups."

This remark, like most of the engineer's comments, seemed to vilify a not very clearly defined group. He packed a tremendous contempt into the pronoun "they." He could always be counted on to run obediently after the Captain's train of thought even when his secret urgings—if urgings he had, if indeed he was of any persuasion—were for the Exec.

Beverly could stand it no longer.

"Lots of ships have started discussion groups, Captain," he broke in, "and with terrific success. My mother's in USO work in New York and she writes me that there's a constant demand for good manuals and good books just so men can prepare subjects for debates. She feels, and I agree with her, that the service man is much more intellectually curious than we suspect. You can see it aboard here even. Why just yesterday I saw one of your signalmen reading *Diana of the Crossways*."

The effect of this excited speech, brazenly full as it was with references to mothers and strange books, completely broke up the atmosphere of gathering hostility.

"Was he reading on watch?" the Captain asked suspiciously.

"Oh, no! He was simply trying to improve himself. And isn't it wonderful that he should?" Bev exclaimed, looking around the table. He held the surprised attention of the Captain, Calloriac, Stoner and Foster, but Winston and the ensigns at the lower end of the table who had resolutely learned to ignore conversation from the Captain's area made no exception with him. "And you know the sort of junk the Navy dishes out in pretense of affording good reading: Admiral Mahan, a few emotional non-fictions like Claude Bowers, and adventure novels with emphasis on Louis Bromfield. Oh, yes, and two copies of Miss Armstrong's *Trelawney*. Every ship has them for some reason unaccountable." Here he laughed loudly. "But something like *Diana of the Crossways* a man's got to get for himself. And a book that a man will jam in his crowded seabag must be a book he cares about because he's got to carry it. Mother worked on that theory. She has a lot of imagination about those things. She got a list from Fort Dix of all the library books that had been taken out and hadn't been returned."

"Well, I guess there are always some who like to read," the Captain assented with some show of politeness. "I didn't mean them."

"Oh, yes. Nothin' wrong with reading," Foster put in.

"But what the navy man really wants when he goes ashore," the Captain continued more emphatically, "first, last, and always is—well, you know what. I don't care what you say about books and USO shows. Those things are O.K., but they don't alter the fact of what he really wants. It's always been that way and always will be."

"That's right." Foster nodded. "That's it."

"Hear, hear," cried Pete Stoner and Bev felt a fury against him as a traitor to the Information Office.

"There must be lots of boys," he protested stuffily, "who don't like to run the risk of disease that you run down here."

"And that's why the Navy ought to run its own places," Ellis announced triumphantly. "Everything could be neat and clean and legal." Here Bev and Calloriac exchanged glances in a first moment of mutual sympathy. Bev found himself thinking of some type of converted cruiser called, say, the U.S.S. *Ellis,* its sides an immaculate grey, its brass work shining, and at the gangway in the uniform of a naval officer, white gloves, spy glass and all, a leering madame. "A guy could go in," the Captain continued, "no questions asked and he wouldn't have to be worried afterwards about having picked up a dose or run afoul of the law. There'd be medical inspectors."

Beverly shook his head.

"It couldn't be."

"Why not?"

"You'd never get it past Congress."

Ellis shrugged his shoulders.

"That bunch of grandmothers."

"The laws of the several states," Pete began with exaggerated sententiousness, "are not a regulatory code but the expression of an ideal of living. The law takes the point of view that sex doesn't exist or at least that it's something uncommonly rare. Giant penalties are assigned for light offenses. To authorize what you suggest would be to admit legally that there are people who don't confine their erotic activity within the narrow limits prescribed by the marriage laws. This the great American people would never stand for."

Foster looked at him admiringly.

"Law is funny, ain't it?" he said. "You a lawyer, Mr. Stoner?"

"I can make a noise like one."

"How would you go about employing your inmates for these places?" Bev demanded indignantly.

"Inmates?" Foster asked.

"He means the girls," Ellis said impatiently. "As if there'd be any trouble about hiring several hundred thousand of them! Why, they'd go anywhere for a good job like that. They'd even come down to Panama."

"They?" Bev queried. "And do you mean to say that even if you could get enough women, females I'll call them, you would be willing to have our government actually pay out money to induce its own citizens to take up a life of sin and prostitution?" He was now fairly trembling with indignation and his awe of the Captain was completely gone.

"You see, Captain!" cried Pete. "There speaks the great American ostrich."

"It's not that bad, Mr. Stregloonus," Foster began in explanatory fashion. "Them women who lead that life is not all so bad as people make out. I used to be on shore patrol down in Lima, Peru, and I used to go in all the houses there. You know, to clear the boys out after liberty." Here there were several winks and "Yes, of course" remarks around the

table which the engineer loftily ignored. "A lot of them wom-
en I got to know like friends. They wasn't bad. They did
their job and didn't fool around after hours. And they made
a good living. Some of them retired and married respectable
men."

"But, Mr. Foster," Bev protested, "what sort of a life is
it? I don't have to argue about it. All I have to ask is, would
you want your daughter to be one? Naturally not," he answered himself rhetorically in a sudden appalled misgiving as
to what the answer might be; "it's always someone else's
daughter who you'd want to do that."

The Captain snorted.

"I'll bet you'd be amazed if you knew how many of your
big society women would fall for the first sailor that asked
them. Why, a lot of those people, they're worse than prosti-
tutes."

"It's just nature," said Foster philosophically.

"In my home town," Pete remarked, winking at the Captain, "you could have a waitress one night and the wife of
the president of the company the next. Only I preferred the
waitress."

The conversation at this point took a dip which there is
no point in following. Bev thought longingly of the great
canvases in Salberg's, of the telephone in the corner of the
main room, of his whole happy, lost life. It was as if a
filthy brown hand had smeared all the colors of the paints.

"Don't you think there are any decent women?" he asked
the Captain icily after a particularly revolting account of the
marital infidelity of one of the latter's sisters-in-law.

"Oh, your mother and grandmother, I suppose. Everybody's mother and grandmother," he answered with a cynical shrug. "But as for modern women, young women—well,
I don't know what you call decent. I don't see anything
wrong in a wife playing around a bit if her husband's away
for a long time. You can bet your last dollar he will so why
shouldn't she? She's going to anyway. Hell, they all do."

"Would you feel that way in your own case?" Bev asked
boldly.

"Sure. Except I told my wife when I left the States last
that if she ever did cheat I didn't want it to be with no
amateur. I didn't want no clumsy kid fooling around her."

This qualification to the single standard point of view, so
much more lewd and degenerate than an attitude of indifference in that it indicated some slight consideration given

the subject, reduced Beverly to speechlessness. But he fretted inwardly at the cheap familiarity that had grown up of a sudden between Stoner and the Captain, justifying his antipathy to it on the ground that Pete had forsaken his principles to promote congeniality with a superior officer, whereas actually he knew that Pete had no such principles and that what gave animus to his own reaction was the fear, barely confessed, that his world after all might be artificial, a papier-mâché house of refuge built by timidity against a universe obsessed to the exclusion of all else in the fascinated study of its own reproduction. He remembered how he had laughed years before when a neurologist at dinner at Mrs. Emden's had told him that man on the average thinks of sex in one form or another ninety per cent of the time, that if we have the courage to take stock of our own private reflections whether in the office, at the theater, during travel, even when engaged in the concentrated study of some entirely extraneous matter, we will find there like a grinning Cheshire cat that little window through which we peek at varied and imaginary eroticisms. "Just another of the natural functions," Bev had protested, "no less to be ignored, no more to be over-emphasized than the excretory one."

Yet, he reflected unhappily as he finished his dessert amid the guffaw aroused by Foster's last outrage, didn't he have to admit that the greatest works of art were lavish with intimations of suppressed pornography? And what was all the praise accorded to this person or that person's treatment of "passion" but, boiled down, the statement of a creed irrevocably interweaving art and reproduction? Why had God created beings if their sole function in life was mental and physical preoccupation with the means of reproducing it? It reminded him of the futility of his old office in New York in the Third Naval District where he had worked with a group of officers who did nothing but investigate the qualifications of applicants who, if accepted, would do nothing but make similar investigations themselves. And so the world expanded. Small wonder that Christ had been a celibate. At least, he concluded, they can't soil the beauty of the windows at Chartres.

He went up to the bridge with Calloriac but the sky was overcast and to his secret relief there were no stars to shoot. The sea was getting choppy, the same sea that half an hour before had been so infinitely peaceful, and the *Sardonyx* was starting to pitch, a fact that caused Bev not the slightest alarm, for now at the end of his fifth day he knew he was acclimatized and wouldn't be sick. Calloriac, still moody from the conversation at supper, wouldn't talk and Bev leaned idly on the rail watching the glow of the sunset through the clouds. He saw Pete come out of the wheelhouse, but resolutely looked away. The latter, however, came over and leaned on the rail beside him.

"How you doin'?" he asked with pointless amicability. Bev decided to say nothing but reflected a second later that this would be childishly rude.

"O.K.," he muttered.

"Quite a little set-to you had there with Ellis."

"Do you think so?" This icily.

"Not still mad, are you?"

This was too much. Bev turned and looked with contempt into Stoner's broad face.

"And why shouldn't I be?" he demanded. "I've never been so disgusted in my life. That man is rotten through and through. And as for your encouraging him and leading him on—well, I suppose one can't expect much more from someone who can't distinguish between a lady and a waitress." He didn't care what he said now and actually forced snobbishness into his tone in order to irritate Pete, even if only to irritate him with the picture of his, Beverly's, narrowness. But he didn't succeed. "Maybe you're right," he continued as Pete only smiled. "Maybe there isn't any difference in your home. All I know is that in New York there is."

"Sure, sure," Pete drawled consolingly. "Ladies are as pure as snow in Manhattan. Particularly *your* friends. From what you tell me most of them are past the dangerous age anyway."

Bev exploded.

"Women are no different anywhere," he exclaimed. "It's simply that you see them through the filth of your own mind."

"Bev," said Stoner paternally, leaning both elbows on the rail and looking down into the water, "there are a lot of things you ought to wake up to. You could have a much better time. Take this sex business. From the way you talk I doubt if you've ever slept with a girl."

Bev flushed to the roots of his hair with mortification and annoyance.

"It so happens," he lied in a lofty tone, "that you're entirely wrong."

Pete shrugged his shoulders.

"Maybe so," he conceded easily. "Oh, I'm not saying that you didn't go giggling into a couple of naughty houses with fraternity brothers in your old Yale days. Saturday night drunks and that sort of thing. What I mean is—"

"I'm not a libertine if that's what you mean."

"There you go," Pete protested. "You're always up in arms on this subject. Libertine! You think everyone who's the least bit normal is a libertine. Where do you draw the line? You were just boasting that you hadn't always been a monk."

"There's a good deal of difference," Bev interrupted again with dignity, "between an occasional indiscretion and a life of habitual sin." He almost wished now that he hadn't estopped himself from using, as an example that men can get through bachelorhood without lechery, the shining example of his own monasticity. But, he reflected, Pete would only have classified him as abnormal.

Pete shook his head.

"You don't understand women," he insisted. "You can't understand women until you live with them. You think they like poetry and dinner parties and gossip. Maybe they do. But all that's a drop in the bucket compared with the way they feel àbout a guy who'll—"

"I get the idea," Bev broke in hurriedly. "Please don't expose me to what we went through at the table."

"Take that little society girl in New York you're always writing to. Tremaine, isn't that her name? I'll bet you could make twice as much time with her if instead of sitting on the opposite side of the drawing room and twiddling about Shelley you'd steal over and . . ."

Bev stared at his gesture in horror.

"That proves that you could never understand my friends!" he cried. "Sylvia Tremaine! What a fantastic idea!"

Pete was beginning to be nettled by the continued sharpness of Beverly's tone.

"Well, I don't know your friends in New York," he said with the beginnings of a sneer. "They may be icicles for all I know. But as for your lady friends down here—well, if they pull the wool over your eyes they're not pulling it over mine."

"Do you mean to imply by that," Beverly demanded in a tone the frigidity and superiority of which made his other remarks seem positively friendly, "that the United States Ambassadress has morals which you question?"

Stoner snorted in derision.

"Not that old hen. I mean the little chicken you're always playing with in the office. I mean Audrey."

"Audrey!" Bev felt his heart muscles contract.

"Yes, Audrey."

"What do you know about Audrey?"

Pete could see that he had scored more of a point than he had aimed for, but the desire to overcome, so strong in him at all times, carried him forward to the swift blow that would clinch the argument.

"Whatever there is to know," he retorted.

Beverly's ears were humming; he felt sick with dislike as he stared into Pete's small, unfeeling eyes. In his confusion he was conscious of a stabbing thought that kept hissing: "Don't give yourself away," but it crumbled before bewildered curiosity.

"You mean you . . ." he stammered. "You mean you *know?*"

Indirection was not one of Pete's failings.

"I mean I've slept with her," he said brutally.

Beverly gaped at him.

"When?"

Pete smiled slightly and turned away.

"I suppose a gentleman wouldn't go into all the details," he said with sarcasm, "but since you insist, that night we were all at the Union Club just before you and I took the train for Colón."

"I remember you took her home," Bev said mechanically.

"We stopped off at my old apartment on the way. But don't take it to heart, old man," Pete continued more breezily. "That's the way the girls are. Except in New York, of course," he added with a wink, clapping Bev on the shoulder. "What you need is to get wise to yourself. After the war you can marry your lovely Tremaine. I'm sure she's as pure as snow." He said this with sincerity, anxious now that he had triumphed to alleviate the victim's distress. "But don't be a St. Francis in the meanwhile. There are too many Audreys to pass the time with. And incidentally, I think our Audrey rather likes you. Why don't you work on that, boy?" This was followed by another clap on the shoulder and another wink, and then, to Beverly's great relief, for he knew that he was utterly incapable of speaking until he had collected himself and was also afraid of further betraying how much he was affected, Pete turned and left the bridge.

CHAPTER THREE

BEVERLY DIDN'T SLEEP much that night. His mind was full of Pete Stoner's apartment in Panama City; he remembered the bathroom, the wardrobe, the day-bed covered with the musty Colombian chintz. He tortured himself with the most upsetting details of what must have gone on. From time to time he would ask himself: "Do you really mind as much as all this? If so, why? What in God's name is Audrey to you?" But each time in answer he felt that throbbing pain, so constant and so unsought, so absurdly alien to his nature. And with Stoner of all people! The very symbol of everything that wasn't himself. That she should turn out so to belong to *that* world made him feel isolated and lonely. Well, let them have their way. Let them laugh at the ambassadress, at Salberg's, at New York, his New York. Let them revel in their lechery. Let them grovel in it. For didn't it really prove that at home he had known a better world and finer people? Could anyone imagine Sylvia stopping off at Pete's apartment with so foul a purpose? Could one, for that matter, imagine Sylvia even knowing a person like Pete? Let them laugh at us, he thought bitterly. How can it hurt?

One little thought, however, kept edging into the crowded chaos of his angry reflections, a thought tempered with uncomfortable reason, one that seemed to know in advance how small a welcome it would receive from anger and to hover in consequence like a persistent but uninvited poor relation. It was the memory of Audrey's unhappiness that night and of his own prim behavior. Hadn't she been suffering under a strain and could one expect a person so encumbered to be fastidious? Ah, yes, he reasoned irritably, true, but there are limits and one has to draw the line somewhere. After all, what would his mother have to say of conduct like that? His mother! Good Lord, with what a shake of her head, with what quiet but irrevocable disgust would she turn away forever from such a girl! He thought swiftly of Mrs.

Emden, of Mrs. Livermore, even of Mrs. Stroud. Yes, the latter would at least be repelled by the sordid tastelessness, the abandon of such an affair. One could mingle with such people, he reflected savagely—the more savagely as he thought how the liberal world would laugh, and perhaps rightly, at his sentiments—but in the long run they always let one down. True, people of his acquaintance had their slips, but not with Stoners. Or even if with Stoners—well, anyway, the fact was clear that that's what he got for playing around with a Canal Zone stenographer. "Steam shovel society." He laughed acidly and ultimately fell asleep.

He woke up, feeling the messenger of the watch tapping his foot.

"It's 3:30, sir."

Beverly reached for the red goggles beside his bunk and put them on before switching the light. Then he swung his feet out and lowered them to the deck; for fully five minutes he sat staring stupidly into the mirror on the door leading to the bathroom. His body fairly ached with exhaustion. When he stood up finally a lurch of the ship flung him across the room, and he stubbed his toe badly against the bureau. God! It was the nadir of existence. He took in the inert massiveness of Stoner, snoring in the upper bunk and thought balefully of the wretched life the war caused him to lead. The dreadful hours of the early morning with which his only previous acquaintance had been at late parties had now become habitual and grim companions. Would it ever end? Oh, he knew all about the marines on Tarawa, he answered himself irritably as he got into his trousers. So they *were* having a worse time. So what?

He drank a cup of cold coffee in the wardroom and groped through dark passageways up to the bridge. Calloriac had already relieved the deck and told him curtly to check and see if all the watch had been relieved. He muttered "Aye, aye, sir" and stumbled into the wheelhouse where he bumped into the annunciator and heard a momentary jangle.

"That's all right, sir," said a voice in his ear.

He found the phone and called the forward gun. All relieved. Also in the engine room. He shouted down the voice tube to the sound room. Then he asked aloud in the dark: "Wheelhouse relieved?" Three voices answered up. Helmsman, lee helm, messenger. The quartermaster was out with Mr. Calloriac. Yes, he was told, the lookouts on top of the wheelhouse had been relieved. In fact, he discovered later, all this had been reported already but Calloriac liked to give him something to do.

He went out and reported to the Exec, who grunted.

"Doesn't look as if we'd get any stars this morning," he added a moment later.

The moon was almost full but continually obscured by great masses of clouds which were driven rapidly across the sky by a southerly wind. In the darkness for hundreds of yards he could see white caps. He picked up a pair of binoculars and scanned the horizon for the convoy. Gradually he made out the ships, shadowy spots which did not appear to be moving at all. He braced himself against the bulkhead of the wheelhouse as the ship rolled.

Calloriac turned to the open window of the wheelhouse. "Left to zero one zero."

The *Sardonyx,* equipped as she was only with listening gear, made no effort to lay down an intricate sound search on her patrols. She steamed a fairly monotonous zigzag astern of the convoy, having just speed enough to steer forty-five degrees to the right or left of the convoy course and still not drop behind. This left the officer-of-the-deck with little to do except give an occasional order to the helm. Calloriac informed him gruffly that the convoy destination had been changed by radio dispatch to Key West. Bev almost jumped with excitement. The other, however, seemed to have little enough to say about it.

"I guess a night like this makes you miss that desk in Panama," he observed.

"Oh, it's got to get a sight worse than this," Beverly answered cheerfully. "You can't imagine how bad it is there. The utter, the continual frustration. Having to work for people for whom one hasn't the slightest respect."

"You don't have to be at a desk in Panama for that." And then fearing that he had been too pointed, Calloriac proceeded to take an intense interest in some supposed scene off to starboard, training his binoculars carefully in that direction.

But Beverly welcomed a chance to discuss this.

"I think I see what you mean," he answered quickly. "But at least you move about. You've seen Colón, Kingston, Guantanamo, Trujillo, and Lord knows how many other places. And now we're going to Key West!"

"But always on the same little ship. Never forget that." Calloriac dropped his binoculars and steadied himself against the wheelhouse beside Beverly. "The same God-damned little ship."

"With the same Captain."

"Exactly. The same son of a bitch." He turned and looked at Beverly defiantly. "That may shock you but it's the way I feel. What's more, I don't care who knows it."

Beverly hastened to agree.

"I'm not shocked," he said. "He's the person who shocks me. At dinner tonight for instance."

"That's bad enough," Calloriac agreed sullenly, "but that's only in the wardroom. What I hate," he went on more vehemently, "is the interminable emphasis on looks. It's always paint, paint, paint. And when they're not painting they're swabbing. That's all he can understand. He carries on instinctively even though he knows nobody gives a damn whether this little ship is painted or not. It helps him to cover his ignorance. You and I, Stregelinus, are out of luck. Come right slowly to zero nine five!" he shouted to the wheelhouse and picked up his binoculars to sweep the horizon.

"Oh, I suppose Ellis has some justification," he continued after a moment. "It's true that not much does ever happen down here and a ship like this wouldn't have much chance to get a shot at a sub. If we ever took a torpedo not even a damage control wizard could save us. So he fills the day with cleaning programs and sacks up himself. If it's true that we spend our lives looking for some sort of order I guess even paint has its purpose."

Beverly reflected drearily that life was mostly formality. Without it, chaos. It passed the time and after a while you could die. The higher the civilization the more rigid the pattern until, as in the complicated whirl of pirouettes that surrounded the French kings, the very intricacy of the form became a *raison d'être* in itself.

"I had a friend in New York," he said suddenly, "who would never go out except to the most formal dinners. He said he never knew otherwise what he was in for: charades, or those ghastly word games, or strip poker, and what's more, he never could tell whether he'd get home at a reasonable hour. But at a formal dinner he knew when to arrive, when he could eat, whom to talk to, and the latest he could possibly stay. That's the kind of reassurance the Navy gives."

Calloriac did not appear fully to appreciate the analogy.

He walked away and examined the gyro compass repeater.

Then it happened. It wasn't exactly that they heard it; they felt it in their ears, in their noses, in every nerve. And the vessel shook.

"Depth charge!" Calloriac shouted. "General Quarters!"

Beverly, paralyzed, heard the long, wailing ring throughout the ship, the signal for battle stations, and a few seconds later the thudding of feet. Here it was. And, oh God, he had time to reflect, how he hated it! Again that sensation of impact. And again. More depth charges. Ahead he suddenly saw a bright red flare in the sky.

"Convoy turning to port. Forty-five degrees, sir," the quartermaster shouted.

"All engines ahead flank!" Calloriac ordered.

Somebody on the bridge had put on a telephone headset.

"All stations report when ready."

"Tell sound to sweep thirty degrees on either side of the bow," came the Exec's voice.

Beverly noticed Winston and Stoner coming up to the bridge.

"What the hell's going on, Calloriac?" Captain Ellis appeared from the wheelhouse, a life jacket buttoned around his blue silk wrapper.

"The *Norris* is dropping charges, sir. And the convoy's turning to port."

"Why wasn't I notified?"

"I rang the alarm immediately, sir."

"I mean before, damn it! You must have had some warning."

"None, sir."

"Christ! You were probably all asleep as usual. It would take a torpedo to wake anyone up on this bridge!"

Beverly could make out now the white clammy expression on Ellis' face in the moonlight.

"No one was asleep here, sir. There was no indication of an attack, as you would have found if you'd been up here," said Calloriac in a voice taut with anger.

"Oh, I suppose I should stand up here all night!"

"It would help, sir, if you were up here more often."

Ellis completely lost his head. He shouted now at the Exec so everyone on the bridge could hear:

"You don't seem to know who's commanding officer of this ship! You're on here to carry out my orders and don't you forget it! Not for one single little minute don't you forget it!"

"Will you take the conn, sir," said Calloriac in a low tone.

"No, I won't take the conn! I can't see a God-damn thing yet. Keep the conn!"

Complete silence followed this outburst for ten or fifteen minutes except for Calloriac's occasional orders to the helm. The *Sardonyx,* speeding at nine knots on the new convoy course, soon caught up with the aftermost ships and resumed a zigzag patrol. It had been previously agreed at the convoy conferences that in the event of attack she would make no effort to join the faster escort ships but stay behind the convoy and act if necessary as rescue ship. Beverly searched the sea desperately, his imagination boggling at the idea of suddenly perceiving a division in the waters, a bubbling and hissing, and then, long and sinister, the black shape of a surfacing sub, its five-inch gun trained in the direction of the little ship. This is awful, this is awful, he kept repeating to himself. Section Blue with his "in" basket full of censorship reports, the little violet in the glass on Audrey's desk, Commander Gilder's well-pressed trousers, flashed through his mind in a moment of sick nostalgia. He remembered the difficulties of torpedoing a ship of the *Sardonyx*'s light draft. Though it could be done. Now is your moment, he warned himself in a suddenly calmer frame of mind. Now it has come. Now you are face to face with yourself, your own little, absurd, insignificant self, with no witness but eternity. I, Beverly, no, not Beverly, but just an organism, another organism in this or that state of evolution, faced with physical annihilation. Just I, with no one to watch and no one to record, and nobody—this was the most incredible of all—to talk to about it afterwards over a martini at the bar or a cup of tea on a long Westbury afternoon.

"Do you intend to keep the crew at general quarters all night, Mr. Calloriac?" growled the Captain.

"If necessary, sir."

"If necessary!" Ellis repeated with sarcasm. "I'm getting sick of these alarms. The *Norris* drops a couple of charges on a whale or a school of fish and we have to be up all night!"

"That's what we're here for," said the Exec tight-lipped.

"Don't tell me what we're here for!" the Captain snapped.

"Main engine room reports the port engines stopped, sir," came from the man with head phones.

"Jesus Christ!"

Calloriac gave an order and the annunciators jangled. A moment later Foster was on the bridge.

"Captain, there's a bearing on the port engine burnt out. It'll take eight hours at least. It's the flank speed."

"God damn it, Foster!" the Captain shouted. "Will nothing ever work on this ship! Starboard ahead standard!" he yelled at the wheelhouse. "I'll take the conn, Mr. Calloriac," he said in a calmer tone. "Notify the escort commander by voice radio that 'Sunflower' is leaving the convoy. Use the code-word for breakdown." Ellis appeared now to have got control of himself.

The rest of the night passed swiftly. Ellis a half hour after his radio message secured the crew from general quarters and returned the conn to the Exec. In doing so and in leaving instructions that a sharp lookout be kept and that he be called if any sound contact were made, he showed no trace of his recent loss of temper. He seemed entirely to have forgotten his wrath at Calloriac for he actually patted him on the back when he left the bridge, and turning to Beverly he remarked cheerfully: "I guess you got more than you bargained for on this trip." Then he hurried below to his room, lighting up a cigarette before closing the door.

Dawn was breaking, and Bev could barely make out the dots of the retreating convoy. Calloriac, in a stony mood and furious at not having all his guns manned, scanned the water through binoculars and addressed not a single word to him. This was all right. For Calloriac, he decided, was Byronic after all. And as Bev watched the dim glow over the horizon; as he joyfully recognized that the night actually was slipping away and that good old familiar daytime was returning with safety, with Key West, with a whole future in its billowing lap; as he faced the wonderful fact that this was not only safety but safety emblazoned with the memory of a night in convoy, a night which, after all—didn't it?— elevated him permanently from the ranks of passive war contributors to those who at least could say that they had been under attack once, and what's the difference between once and ten times, the line of demarcation has been passed, hasn't it?—as he took all of this in, with or without Audrey, his eyes filled and overflowed with large drops of grateful tears.

CHAPTER FOUR

FROM THIS POINT on everything seemed to go Beverly's way. They arrived at Key West that afternoon only to be sent out the following morning to Miami where the necessary repair work would have to be done. It just so happened that the technicians and equipment for this particular diesel job were at the sub-chaser base at Miami, and it just so happened also, Beverly remembered with delight, that practically half of his friends had gone through the sub-chaser school there, the famous "S.C.T.C." and that several were undoubtedly still there. Arlie Stroud, for example, just back from a year in the Pacific was there with Helena. Sylvia had written him. Beverly paced cheerfully about the decks as the *Sardonyx* rounded the Florida Keys. The weather was cool and the day clear and incredibly beautiful. He could feel optimism and anticipation throughout the ship.

And the next morning Miami loomed before them, her colossal line of hotels visible far out to sea, sparkling and jumping in the sun. She was an enchanted city and Beverly with an involuntary gesture stretched out one hand to her. Here after a year, and such a year, was the U.S.A. again, for the brief glimpse of the docks of Key West had conveyed no impression of America. It was absolutely too good to be true. Even Captain Ellis was in the best of moods.

The signal station at the end of the school dock flashed them to go alongside Pier 7, the furthest away from the central area, and this was effected by Captain Ellis in a rather surprisingly good piece of ship handling. The pier was crowded with SC's tied up three abreast of each other but space had been reserved for the *Sardonyx* just forward of a Cuban mine sweeper. Two civilian technicians came on board immediately to look at the engines and an ensign bearing a large armful of mimeographed directives containing instructions for liberty hours, liberty uniforms, dock regulations, and so on.

Ellis took these papers and flung them across the wardroom table at Calloriac.

"Read these as soon as possible. But before we find out that we aren't allowed to let's declare liberty for half the crew until 0800 tomorrow morning. All officers can go except the OD."

Beverly and Pete lost no time in hurrying below to change into their cleanest khakis. Bev had not forgiven his erstwhile friend but he was in too good a humor now to hold a grudge. Besides, the very existence of Panama up here seemed open to question. Mrs. Livermore had some substance in retrospect, but the others—

In twenty minutes they had shaved, bathed, and were actually putting foot on the dock. They lingered for a moment before the yellow stucco administration building of .he school, watching dozens of officers hurry in and out. Bev wanted to go in to get a roster to see who was there whom he knew, but Pete wanted to telephone his wife and dragged him away. It was also Bev's intention to call his mother whose voice he hadn't heard for a year, so they strolled up the boulevard past palm trees and shops to the Miami Colonial Hotel.

Miami burst on Beverly's dulled senses like a rocket. The colors were almost too sharp, the scene too varied for one so long immersed in the Canal Zone. Miami like New York is a Levantine town, but unlike New York it has freedom in its architectural expression. There is no outlet for color in narrow Manhattan where buildings are forced up, straight and simple and soot-stained, to the sky, but in Miami the Levant expands unfettered under a golden sun and by a blue sea. It is a crazy and wonderful riot of pagodas and palm trees, of highways and temples, of hotels, white and yellow and green, endless hotels running down the beach in a long line of birthday cake artificiality. It is the naive, nostalgic creation of Western commercialism, a sort of crazy Constantinople, a possible if vague foreshadowing, as Beverly suddenly conceived it, of a culture's ultimate return towards its Mediterranean origin after a long and questionable ramble on both sides of the Atlantic.

When they arrived at the Miami Colonial, Beverly took in the crowded lobby, the large air-cooled bar, the busy-looking people hurrying back and forth.

"I don't care," he told Pete, "if people are always rushing back and forth in America with no place to go. I love it."

He sat breathlessly in his booth waiting for his call to come through. The line was full of whirrs and interrogations.

"I'm sorree. There's a two hour delay on New York."

"Cancel it please." Two hours! He fairly trembled with irritation. Of all the ridiculous things. He could see the back of Pete's head in a booth across the corridor. Obviously he had got his call through. Maybe he should try later, and then, spotted through one of the panes in the booth door, standing before the hotel desk apparently to leave her room key, in the plainest, the very plainest if most expensive of pink dresses with a straw hat that boasted an enormous brim, a brim that seemed to defy with its blatant waviness every wartime restriction, large, erect, yet somehow not at ease with the world, not entirely—it was hard to express—assimilated, was Mrs. Arleus Stroud. He burst from the booth.

"Angeline!"

She looked up, startled. Then she put a hand over her heart in a mock gesture of being overcome.

"Why Beverly Streg!" she exclaimed. "What in the world!"

"What are you doing in Miami?" he fairly screamed.

"But, my dear, you? I thought you were in Panama. I'm just down for a few days to see Arlie and Helena. He's at this submarine chaser school. But I suppose you are too. Why didn't you write me?"

"No, I'm on a ship that's just in for repairs. Came in this morning."

Mrs. Stroud had recovered from her surprise now and was looking him up and down with a swift critical eye. She took in the sun tan, the messy uniform, the frank enthusiasm on his face.

"My dear, you look a million per cent better than when you went away," she said with her usual candor. "You looked awfully sort of blotchy last year, if you know what I mean. Like an old piece of *pâté de foie gras.*" She looked at him and smiled as he screamed with laughter. "No, I mean it," she continued seriously. "But now you look like a lifeguard. I didn't realize you'd been at sea."

"Well, I was in Panama for quite a while," he admitted, "and I may go back. But I'm gradually spending more and more time away."

"What sort of a job is that? Sounds amphibious."

"No. It's just that I'm being gradually transferred to sea duty," he explained hurriedly. "Naturally I have a lot of odd jobs that I have to keep going back to finish up. But what do you think I'm on?" he exclaimed to change the subject.

"I'm sure I haven't the vaguest."

"The old Stroud yacht. The *Tamburlaine!*"

"But how remarkable!" She was obviously taken aback. "I knew it had been given to the Navy but I couldn't imagine what good it would be to them. Isn't the war too much for those old diesels? They never were any good. And how about the generators?"

"Worse than ever!" But he had no intention of getting sidetracked on a tangent of generators. With their passion for particulars there was no telling where such a topic would lead Mrs. Stroud or her son Arleus. "How's my Syvvie?"

"Syvvie's in Palm Beach with Goodhue and Bella. Now I was just thinking . . ." She paused and fixed him with her clear grey eyes. "How much longer are you going to be around?"

"I don't know. A few days maybe."

"Well, I tell you what. I'll call Syvvie now and have her come over tomorrow morning. Tomorrow's Saturday. Arlie doesn't have classes in the afternoon so let's all meet at the Bath Club for lunch. Good?"

As ever, Mrs. Stroud made everybody's plans. It was unbearable for her to see things messed up when it was so easy for her own clear mind to keep them straight.

"But I don't want to drag Syvvie away from her uncle's," he protested.

"Nonsense. She's bored to tears there. Besides we haven't seen you in an age. The boys in uniform come first, don't they?"

"You're always wonderful, Angeline."

"Tomorrow then. I'll be out there in the morning with Syvvie and Helena. Come any time. Bus 36 runs right by the entrance. Pick it up at the Venetian Hotel at the end of the Boulevard."

They shook hands, and she murmured: "Wonderful to see you again," and disappeared out the door. His being thus relegated to the next morning was no symptom of coldness on her part as he well knew but merely a characteristic of her departmentalized mind. She saw him; she registered; she consulted her schedule; she fitted him in. It was the same with a hairdresser as with a prospective son-in-law.

CHAPTER FIVE

THE BATH CLUB the following morning had as much variety and gaiety of color as any beach in an advertisement for cigarettes. The brown stucco of the club house, the white sand, the blue sea provided the elemental colors as a background for the flowering of umbrellas and bathing suits. But it wasn't so much the color that gave the scene that hue of the ideal which promoted it from reality to advertisement; it was the presence, the overwhelming presence, of youth. Age had stayed at home; age couldn't get gasoline or hotel accommodations and age, of course, had no uniform to wear. Whatever else war may have done to the beaches of Florida it certainly improved their looks. The Bath Club without age, full of the stalwart, the young, dotted with naval officers either glistening in white or brown-skinned in bathing trunks, together with their young wives was exactly like—an advertisement.

That is with the exception of Sylvia, and she was the exception always no matter what the surrounding picture. She was sitting alone under an umbrella far down the beach and closer to the water quite by herself, leaning against the umbrella pole with an enormous pair of dark glasses through which her eyes focused, with frequent glances up at the sea, on the second volume of *The Golden Bowl*. Her long, thin legs, her oval chin and small crooked mouth appearing from under the glasses in what seemed to be a point, the long, lank, black hair, conveyed to the observer a totally different impression depending on whether or not he knew who she was. To a stranger she probably suggested something undernourished, pathetic, Italianate; she seemed undoubtedly a sort of scarecrow, an unhappy, twisted thing with a strange, foreign habit of exaggeration manifested in the clanking bracelet of gold charms that she wore on her left wrist and, again, the enormous glasses on her nose. But the New Yorker who "knew"—knew, that is, that she was Sylvia

Tremaine, that New York had never in two hundred years
been without a Sylvia Tremaine, that she was a daughter
of the "fabulous" Angeline Stroud and a niece of Bella, and
all in all a fine if neglected flower of the inner circle whose
existence seems even more illusory than it actually is because
of the refusal of its members to have the routine blankness
of their daily lives photographed or reported—to such a
New Yorker she would appear as "poor Sylvia," for some
reason a lonely creature but one who had a flare for dress,
who could make her natural plainness interesting, who had a
genius for contrast as exemplified by the simple black bathing
suit of such exquisite silk and the famous bracelet with its
collection of rare items ranging from the Alexander coin
to an earring of the Empress Josephine.

Sylvia in glancing about the beach did not feel much more
part of it than she looked, but today Mr. James had not
provided the outlet for her entirely self-conscious escapism
that he so often did. She closed the book. Of course she
had read it before three or four times; she had read everything of James, shelves of it; she had even pored through
the three hundred thousand scrawled words of his notebooks
and the thousands more of his unpublished letters. She probably knew him as well as any person living. Similarly with
George Meredith, for reading to her was far more than a
pastime. The creation by James of a small fictional world,
a fairyland of vast dark lobbies where shadow people dwelt
only to feel and to appreciate the wonders of each other's
unsubstantial virtues, this final refuge of a man who found
only disappointment at the crudeness of the actual was the
source of Sylvia's fascination. For she was not under the
slightest illusion as to her own helplessness in the world;
she knew herself to be plain, anemic, and she knew too that
the black melancholy which came over her in such waves
and left her so gasping had a neurotic origin. She was cursed
always to see with a deadly intelligence everything that
surrounded her from her own squeamishness to her mother's
force. And in strange, deliberate fashion she invariably concentrated on authors who had created out of their own
revulsion to actuality a world more suitable to sensitivity, to
beauty, and to tact. Of these James was sovereign, but there
was also Meredith, and even Racine and his contemporaneous
tragic writers. Order and symmetry and the palace that
crowned the actual world in which but not of which these
last wrote—Versailles—had absorbing interest for her and

she loved of a long afternoon to steep herself in Saint-Simon until she could almost picture the wonderfully uncomfortable formality of that court, could almost feel the oppressive but protecting whale-bone of seventeenth century dress. But now, she reflected, how platitudinous but how true to say that the war broke in, had to be faced. Not that she wasn't entirely willing to face it herself. It was how it might change the few who were dear to her that was worrying her. Beverly for example. That chapter had been resolved, closed, but could she bear it if it had all to be thrashed out again?

She shut *The Golden Bowl,* her whole body suddenly taut with a nervous spasm, her heart pounding, and lived over every second of the horrible day in Westbury. It would never do this way she warned herself, panting; it was absurd to be so excited and besides there was Helena, her sister-in-law, so blonde and thin and lovely, walking over the beach to her. With Arlie. She felt herself calm down as she watched Arlie; he waved at her so cheerfully. She smiled back and thought sympathetically that he was getting fat. It wouldn't be bad for years yet nor would he be bald for years either, but the future was written there. Yet he was still handsome; his small features and clear skin gave the effect of something finely chiseled that would ultimately if not soon be too broadened, but that pleased for the very reason, perhaps, of its transiency. And his smile was radiant. He was a boy again and her baby brother.

"Hi, Syvvie! How was Palm Beach?"

They both sat down by her.

"It was my vacation," she answered smiling. "That is from PC's and SC's and whatever else you have here. You wouldn't believe you were in the same world at Auntie Bell's. But Arlie darling," she continued patting his hand shyly, "I'd much rather be here with you. And your friends. Everybody's dead at Palm Beach. They're old and pathetic; anyone who's over forty is old now and they know it's absurd to be Palm Beaching in war but they don't quite know what else to do. There isn't anything really. So they apologize all the time. Uncle Goodhue didn't talk about anything but you."

"But why do they go there?" Helena asked picking up her knitting. "I thought Aunt Bella was much too busy with her Nurses Aide. She's always speaking somewhere in uniform."

"Oh, they always have time, the Aunt Bellas, don't they?" Sylvia asked with a shade of malice.

"Syvvie!" Arlie exclaimed. "I thought you admired her so!"

"We've always been supposed to, I know," she said with a little laugh. "But since you've come back, Arlie, I somehow see the whole family in a different light."

Helena nodded.

"But why?" he protested. "Do you think of me as criticizing them?"

"No, no, dear," Sylvia said hastily. "You're much too kind."

"But I don't feel that way at all!" he exclaimed. "I'm not like these guys who come back and scream every time they see a civilian taking a drink. I don't hold it against Uncle Goodhue for going to Palm Beach. Why shouldn't he? He's tried to get back in the Army a hundred times."

"He's all right," his sister answered in a definite tone. "It's Aunt Bella. She was always lovely and witty and wonderfully turned out but since the war started she's been ever so much more so. It's been her great triumph. She lives and breathes war. She reproaches me every time she sees me for not being more faithful at the Red Cross. She gives the most superb dinners for Greece and then goes on somewhere to dance for Yugoslavia. She dons her Bergdorf uniform and gives charming little cocktail parties for her associates. She has carefully picked sergeants out for the weekend on Long Island. She's always turning on the radio news. But it's nothing but a game, the same game she played before. The old wretched game of charm, charm—charm and tolerance and wit and taking a proper interest in this or that and not being stuffy and pretending that it's only a delightful joke that you take your lettuce salads with the utmost seriousness when really you do. Oh," she broke off suddenly, "I'm sick of her!"

Arlie whistled.

"Poor Aunt Bella! Leave her something to wear."

"But Syvvie's right, darling," his wife put in. "I know just how she feels. We think of you all the time and we just can't take the same interest in Nurses Aide graduations or helping your mother and Aunt Bella find just the right quotation from General Monty for their speeches."

Arlie looked shocked.

"Mummie too!" he exclaimed. The other two looked at each other and smiled.

"Mummie's not as bad," Sylvia allowed. "She's got you to worry about. And then Mummie never goes in for charm the way Aunt Bella does. She likes being administrative—well, just for the sake of being administrative."

Arlie looked from one to the other.

"I'll be darned!" he said. "Things have changed when Syvvie says what she feels about Mummie."

"But what do I feel after all?" Sylvia protested.

"That she hasn't any charm."

"I didn't say that."

"You implied it."

"It's perfectly true anyway," Helena interrupted. "She hasn't. Not a particle. You can't have charm without imagination can you? She's a dear, of course, and we all love her, but Arlie I think it's a good sign that we three can sit here and discuss your mother and aunt frankly."

"Don't you really think we've changed, Arlie?" Sylvia asked.

"Well," he said slowly, "frankly, yes, a little. You all seem to take up less space in the world if you see what I mean. You and Helena though realize it."

"And Aunt Bella doesn't," put in Helena. "She's bigger than ever."

"She told me the other night," said Sylvia, "when we were having a lobster dinner at the Emdens', that she couldn't bear to see all that rich food wasted on the old and that she wanted to throw the doors open and let in the Marines to eat it all!"

"And did she?" Arlie asked.

"Certainly not!" Helena exclaimed. "Her idea of entertaining a marine is to give a little dinner at El Morocco for some captain who's shot down twenty Jap planes. But will she come down and work with Syvvie and myself at the Replacement Centre, getting a job in vital industry for some crumby sailor who's been discharged from the Navy for homosexuality—"

"Helena!" Arlie remonstrated. "Is that what you and Syvvie have been doing at the Replacement Centre?"

"Well, they weren't all discharged for that reason," she admitted. "But if the war's to be total we've got to use everybody. Discharged soldiers and sailors have to be given jobs."

"But I thought you'd just been doing clerical work somewhere."

"That's all I've been doing," Sylvia interrupted. "Helena's just being kind to include me. I was acting as a sort of useless secretary for Aunt Bella three afternoons a week when Helena came in and took me out. Now I arrange the employment cards for her and—"

"Nothing of the sort, Arlie," said Helena briskly. "She's been very helpful and when we go back next week I'm going to start her on interviewing. Except," and here she gave her sister-in-law one of her wonderful smiles, "I don't allow her to take any books to the office. I'm rescuing her from Aunt Bella and Henry James."

Arlie wanted, however, to know all about his wife's job of which she had only written him the vaguest outlines. Like his mother he had to have things explained from beginning to end.

"But every time I picked up a pen, darling," Helena told him, "I thought of Jap planes and cruisers and I couldn't bear to bore you with my silly job. The best part of it is that I've had a fight with Aunt Bella. When I took Syvvie away from her she was a bit snooty and made remarks about the Replacement Centre only wanting me for my name and couldn't I see through them and so on. So I let her have it. I told her that it might be fun for people like her to have their pictures taken playing checkers with golden-haired Guadalcanal heroes at St. Albans but that if she really wanted to be a help she could come and work with me on the misfits."

"Wasn't she furious?"

"Oh, you know how she is. Anger is such poor taste. But we still hardly speak."

To Sylvia it was a pleasure to slip out of the conversation and listen to Arlie and Helena talk. He'd been away for over a year and they were very much in love. She wrapped herself in their emotion, in their relationship, and felt protected. Helena was quite the most important thing, with one exception, that had ever come into her life. Arlie she had always adored, but he was a half-brother and five years younger and ever so objective and immature, and at Yale he had been, altogether with determination, a playboy. In fact if she hadn't carefully idealized him and if he hadn't had almost pathetic moments like their mother even in the midst of happiness when he had been naively bewildered about life, she would have found him frequently obnoxious. He had gone in very heavily for the Fence Club and the New York weekend, for Long Island and debutantes; he had had the required affair with an older woman and parted with a beautiful understanding; he had gone through the various experiences which tradition expects of anyone young and male and rich, as it were, with a check-off list. Spontaneity was not a characteristic of the Strouds but they were doubly careful to see that their lack of it didn't cheat them of anything.

Then Helena had appeared. She came from Cleveland which was pretty western for Mrs. Stroud but not seriously so; her family were of a solid Ohio variety; her grandfather had once been United States Solicitor General. She was serious but not pedantic; she was a hard working student at Smith whose New Haven weekends were gay but occasional when Arleus met her. It was a perfect match. He fell in love with the picture of loose blonde hair and glasses, the small tweeded figure with the big books, the general loveliness so indifferent to itself. And everything that was handsome and kind and idealistic and so easily redeemable in him involved Helena in depths of emotion that were utterly to obscure any personal ambition. Arleus had changed entirely with marriage; they had lived in New Haven where he attended law school. He developed a rather traditional but perfectly worthy desire to go into the foreign service, to which ambition his father, determined to be modern, gave more praise than was really called for. Arlie, however, was much gratified and felt very unselfish.

Helena came more and more into her own; she had a perfect understanding of the vulnerability of her family-in-law, that combination of sensitivity with unimaginativeness which so characterized Arleus and his mother. Mrs. Stroud, full of distrust at first, came to depend on her. But it was with Sylvia that she was most wonderful, Sylvia who, all Tremaine was all imagination, the lonely fruit of Mrs. Stroud's first union. Poor Syvvie had assumed that the kindness of her young sister-in-law would cool into family indifference after an appropriate interval, but she had found that Helena was not one to put aside anything she had started. Every time the young Strouds had come down from New Haven Sylvia had found herself included in some sort of party. Helena quite firmly and quietly saw to it that every friend of theirs should become at least a friendly acquaintance of her sister-in-law. And after Pearl Harbor when Arlie had gone away and Helena had taken an apartment with her two babies in New York she found time to telephone Sylvia every morning. She made her come down and help with the children, which Sylvia loved; she removed her from Aunt Bella and let her help in the Replacement Centre; it only remained, Sylvia had told her smiling, for her to find her a husband. "Oh, you can count on me," Helena had answered promptly. And once when Sylvia had mumbled something emotional and indistinct about being grateful at her constant inclusion in Helena's life the latter had retorted: "But you goose, Syvvie! Don't you see that Arlie and I *love* you? I couldn't manage without you." Sylvia had reflected with tears of gratitude that even though it was obviously untrue, if Helena said it this made no difference. Helena gave her that same feeling of being normal and part of everything that Beverly did, but with Helena there was less emotional price to pay.

Arlie was waving at some friends of his who came over to greet him and he introduced them carefully to his wife and half-sister. They seemed young and unprepossessing but Sylvia, since Arlie's law school career, was entirely used to the democratic habit he had acquired there of picking up people whom in college he would have referred to as "crumbs." He did this kindly and conscientiously now but there was just a suspicion of the collector in the way that he carefully picked people for individual qualities. For example, as these Miami friends wandered on down the beach he leaned over and told Sylvia and Helena:

"That tall guy is a remarkable fellow. He has the best marks in anti-sub warfare in my group. And the little one, you'd never guess it, is one of the best damn ship handlers I've ever seen. He had a mine sweep in the Aleutians."

"Well, I'm glad they didn't stay," Helena observed to tease him. "I don't think they're half as nice as our pansies at the Centre, do you Syvvie?"

"Of course not. People at sea lose all their finesse."

"Look at Arlie."

"All right, you two," he retorted. "Maybe you wouldn't like it if I moved down the beach and spent the rest of the day with those two girls they're with."

Helena smiled brightly.

"Don't let us stop you! I think the one in that charming

pink bathing suit, you see, the color of a stye in the eye,
belongs to your first friend."

Sylvia adjusted the big sun glasses on her nose.

"And the fat one goes with the mine sweeper!" she exclaimed. "Surely he found her in the Aleutians."

Arleus shook his head.

"For a pair of snobs," he began, "I have yet to see the
equal of you two."

"Arleus Stroud!" his wife remonstrated. "Speak of the
pot and the kettle! How could I be a snob? I'm nobody.
But you! You went to a snob school, snob college, joined
snob fraternities and senior societies, spent your idle years
before I met you going to snob parties—"

"The Yale senior societies," Arlie interrupted with dignity,
"are *not* snobbish."

"I suppose I'm to believe—" But here even Helena stopped.
"Yes I know, darling, that's taboo. Even in the family. And
then, of course, you're not one little bit of a snob yourself."
Here he caught hold of her hair and pulled her head gently
back. "Mercy!" she cried. "Sylvia's the snob. Not us. Everyone knows that."

He released her.

"That's right," he agreed. "It's Syvvie."

Helena shook her head to reorder her hair.

"Yes. Syvvie looks down on us Strouds," she maintained,
"from the lofty height of her Tremaine blood. Oh, my
metaphors! But, confess, Syvvie, don't you really feel superior?"

"Definitely," she answered in the same spirit. "I remind
myself day and night what the Strouds were when Van
Doren Tremaine was signing the Declaration. It's my greatest
consolation."

"Musty old Tremaines!" Arleus retorted. "Why, they were
mortgaged before Grandfather Stroud even got his start!"
And he flung his towel at her. It landed on her knees. "Why,
I'll bet when you marry you make your husband change
his name to Tremaine," he continued. "Aren't you the last
of the line?"

"I am," she said. "Isn't it Roman? But fortunately there
are plenty of Strouds. A huge, vulgar number."

"Well, there won't be any more Tremaines," he rejoined
with a wink, "unless you do something about it pretty soon.
And that reminds me. What about Beverly? Mummie says
he's a sailor now. And incidentally," he added, whirling

around at Helena, "speaking of snobs there's your A Number One."

It was wonderful, Sylvia thought, the way Helena made not the slightest effort to warn him with a nod or a poke. They had taken her in so completely that there was hardly any embarrassment in discussing before her the man they knew she was in love with. It gave her the happiest feeling of relaxation.

"Oh, I don't know," Helena said, "if he's as bad as all that. I hear he's very nice to several dowdy Stregelinus aunts."

"But, my dear," Arlie put in, "think how nice I am to you. Do not even the Pharisees?"

"Well, I—!"

"The thing about Bev," Sylvia said reflectively, "is that he lavishes affection and kindness equally and unsnobbishly within certain limits. But his original act in laying down these limits is pure snobbishness. He doesn't know anyone outside them. He doesn't first meet people and then discard them but that's because he's so careful whom he meets!"

"He must be meeting a lot of people in the Navy though."

"Oh, he is."

At this moment Helena quietly pointed at something and following the direction of her finger they saw their mother approaching them wearing a wide beach hat, her high heels sinking into the sand, accompanied by the long, gaunt commanding officer of the school, the youngest captain in the Navy, Lucius T. Arnold.

"Leave it to your mother," breathed Helena, and they all got up. The Captain nodded to Arleus whom he knew, shook hands with Helena, and Mrs. Stroud introduced him to Sylvia. He was in a white uniform with a row of ribbons; he had a pair of bathing trunks over his arm. It was obvious that he would be leaving shortly to change so they all remained standing.

"You remember that talk we had about prisoners, Arlie," his mother cried triumphantly. "Well, the Captain agrees with me. I brought him over particularly to have him tell you the story about his Polish friend that he was telling me on the bus. Please do, Captain. The children think I'm a dragon. I'd like them to know the way people who've been 'occupied' feel."

"But the young ladies," he protested with a southern smile.

"Oh, in war they must face facts."

Arleus intervened politely.

"Please tell us, Captain. I'm sure if Mother can take it my wife and sister can."

"I wouldn't be too sure of that," he said with a glance at Mrs. Stroud, and they all laughed. "But," he went on more hurriedly, "my little story was simply this. My Polish friend, a lieutenant-commander, hadn't heard a word from his wife or children since the fall of Warsaw but he had every reason to suspect the worst. I met him in London a year ago when his destroyer was operating with the British and went out with him for a month to study some new sound gear that the Admiralty had given him. During that time he sank a German submarine and there were a large number of survivors swimming in the water close to our ship. He asked me what I would do if my wife had been—" Here the Captain raised his hand. "You can guess what he said had happened to her. You can guess, too, what I answered."

Arleus stared at him intensely.

"And then, sir?"

"And then, sir," continued the Captain with slow emphasis, "he backed his ship into the midst of the survivors and cut them up in the screws."

Sylvia gave a stifled gasp.

"That," said Mrs. Stroud volubly, "is what I call a dose of their own!"

"Do you mean, Captain," Sylvia cut in with a breathless boldness unusual to her, "that you would have done the same thing?"

"I'm afraid, my dear young lady, I wouldn't have had the stuff to go through with it."

"Afraid!" she echoed. She stared at him with eyes widened by horror and then turned and ran down the beach. She ran all the way to the edge of the Bath Club section; she kept going till she saw an unoccupied umbrella and sank to the sand beneath it as though it were a refuge. Her heart was pounding again, and she ran a hand nervously through her hair. Silly, how silly, to get so agitated! Already she was sorry, overcome in fact with remorse that she might have offended Arleus' CO. But what a dreadful world! Where her mother's eyes flashed with hate for an enemy that she had never seen, knew nothing about, and where Arleus had to fight out among coral islands for trade or pride or security or some unfathomable national reason in a war that was costing more than all the Orient was worth. Oh, yes, it had to be. She was no pacifist. But inevitable as it might be it was nonetheless true to her that the war was corrosive, deeply so. The surface had been cracked and look what was within! The light in her mother's eyes and Aunt Bella's tiresome selfishness and all the poor neurotics who wandered wretchedly into the Centre with their ugly little vulnerabilities exposed by the hard glare of military life. It was all there before, she told herself; it's only that I see some of it now. But this was small comfort. Only Arlie, darling Arlie, had improved, and she felt weak with longing to be a man and go out to the coral islands with him when he went again.

"Is this how you greet me?" burst the cheerful voice. She looked up in fright.

"Oh, Bev!"

She stood up, and suddenly she knew her eyes were full of tears. He put his arm around her shoulders and kissed her on the cheek.

"There, there," he said briskly, giving her shoulders a little squeeze, "I know all about it. I just passed your mother and she told me I'd find you over here—and why."

"Oh, Bev, do you think I made him mad? Do you think I've hurt Arlie's chances for a good position? I couldn't stand that."

He took both her hands in his and laughed.

"Good Lord!" he exclaimed. "They were only amused at you. Angeline told me the Captain said 'There's a girl with spirit!' For heaven's sake, don't worry."

She smiled at him at last and put on her dark glasses again. Behind them she was secure, her emotion carefully veiled. She simply took him in for a few moments and said nothing. Yes, he did look better and his smile was just the same, just as cheerful, and she felt that it was too much, this, first Arlie back and now Bev.

"But, Syvvie, my dear, how are you?"

She just nodded. But he, of course, was wonderful and when they had sat down together under the umbrella he covered over every awkwardness with a stream of chatter that seemed to foam out and obliterate any crevice or fissure, rounding off smoothly all the knobby edges of personality. She listened to him thankfully. Nobody could do it like Beverly; nobody could so defy the universe. His gossip was like an infinite cloud of the fleeciest and thickest cotton with which she saw the gaping holes of her intellectual roof plugged, one by one. Her mood changed and little by little she began to feel a reassuring warmth circulate over her like the tingle in the veins of whiskey on a cold day. They both sat and looked at the sea and smoked cigarettes. He chatted on about how he had missed her and her mother and Aunt Bella, about the barrenness of Panama from every point of view, about Esmond Carnahan and the Livermores, about the amount of reading he had done. She half-listened and watched him intently through her glasses. His face had filled out a bit and it was apparent that the long blondish hair was even thinner around the temples. The khaki uniform which he had not yet changed for bathing trunks, the shirt open at the neck helped to intensify the air of increased self-control discernible in him.

"You keep staring at me," he interrupted a story to remark. "Am I so different? Have I lost any more hair?"

"Oh, yes."

He clutched his head in agony.

"I knew I shouldn't have asked you!" he cried. "Women have no heart about that sort of thing. It wasn't my fault that there were no scalp specialists in Panama. Have I lost much?"

She laughed remorselessly.

"Men are so vain. No, not much. But it wouldn't be true to say I hadn't noticed."

He made a face at her.

"What a Puritan you are," he exclaimed. "Can't you even tell one little white lie?"

She laughed again and then began more seriously:

"Tell me about yourself, Bev. I'm glad to hear Mrs. Livermore and her nephew are well, but there's a whole year missing in you. That's what matters to me." She had time afterwards to reflect that, however unintentional, this remark might easily be construed as a bid to him to recommence the chapter that had started in Westbury and that the failure on his part to leap into the breach with: "I haven't changed, at any rate, towards you," was proof, if proof she needed, no matter what protestations might ensue, that he *had*. Why it was that the realization of this did not hurt her as she would have expected was not at first entirely clear, but it began to penetrate, little by little, that after all she had known perfectly well in Long Island that he hadn't cared in the way that he protested, so that seeing this more clearly now was not painful when compensated as now by his increased masculinity. For that was it, she supposed ruefully; that like so many of the weak of her sex she could do easily without great feeling in men if she had in return at least the appearance of strength.

"I suppose it hasn't hurt me," he answered after some reflection. "I suppose it doesn't hurt to be made to realize how easily unspeakable people climb to power in a military setup. I guess I'd always lived in a fool's paradise. I didn't know such people could get to the top."

"Such people?"

"Syvvie, if you knew them," he protested with an earnestness unusual in him, "if you knew men like Commander Gilder and Commander McShane. Or even Captain Darlington, though at least he's a gentleman."

She picked him up on this.

"Is that so vital?"

He gave a little grunt and started to take his shoes off.

"I knew you'd say that!" he cried. "That's just the sort of thing I would have said a year ago. What earthly difference can it make whether or not a man's a gentleman? Or whether he's been to college? It's ability that counts, isn't it? Do you mind if I take my socks off?" She shook her head and he did so and buried his toes in the sand. "I'll get into my trunks in a minute but I want to have this out with you."

"This business of my thinking ability matters?" she said smiling.

"Ah, well now," he said quickly. "Wait a second. Of course it would if you could find any. But when there isn't! If it's a choice between two blockheads, I say take the one who's a gentleman. You and I have been too apologetic in the past, Syvvie. We've always assumed that we'd led sheltered lives. Why, until I joined the Navy I had no idea how broad and varied a life I'd had. Don't you agree?"

"Oh, yes. We've been a couple of Marco Polos."

"There you go," he said irritably. "Debunking everything I say. Now I know I'm home."

Sylvia mused for a few seconds.

"Well," she said slowly. "There may be something in what you say. A gentleman is at least brought up to listen to others. Politeness counts for something I suppose. We have some Army and Navy officers at the Centre and they're always getting snarled up in jurisdictional points and snapping at each other. But even so, Bev, it seems to me your re-action is violent."

"Violent is the word for it," he exclaimed. "When I think of the emotion I've wasted in the past apologizing to the world for myself, for Chelton, for Yale, for my New York friends, for Long Island, it makes me tired. When I think of the dinners at your Aunt Bella's when she and I have worried about striking too trivial a note. But that's all over now. I've seen the Canal Zone! Of all the flat, dull places, utterly devoid of curiosity—"

"What sort of curiosity is it they lack?" she interrupted suddenly.

"They don't talk about anything but sex."

"Really? And yet I'm sure you wrote me of a girl who worked in your office who had a collection of first editions of George Eliot."

"Oh, did I?" He had quite forgotten this.

"Yes. I was intrigued by the whole picture: the heat, the Zone, the rebound *Adam Bede* bought for ten dollars sitting so proudly alongside the worn Britannica." She looked at him for a few seconds with a questioning smile.

"You're thinking of Miss Emerson," he said with some embarrassment. "I confess she had aspirations. But she was exceptional."

"Tell me about her."

"I thought you wanted to hear about me."

"Forgive me," she said. "I thought it might be the same thing."

He raised his eyes to the heavens.

"Women!" he exclaimed. "The assumptions you make. Miss Emerson had her moments it is true." Here she noticed he seemed to swallow hard. "But *au fond*, my dear, she was another Zonite. She had a rather sordid affair with one of our officers. We can forget her."

"Oh." She clearly showed her sense of not having been told all. "You sound so final. I think of her now as having been cast to wailing and gnashing of teeth. Very well. We shall forget her. But I return to the lack of curiosity. I still feel that I've scored a point with George Eliot."

"Well, of course, there are always exceptions," he said impatiently.

"And what of Aunt Bella's dinners after all?" she continued in disregard of this. "Are they on such a lofty plane? Oh, they've gotten worse even since the war. You know her old habit of getting a few lions and cracking the whip to keep things moving? Well now she has at least one general or one ABC man from Washington. And she rips about dropping her little bombshells: 'Do you suppose it's true that the French enjoy their occupation?' or 'Does the marine fight harder when he's homesick?' But it's wonderful what old English silver and Bendel clothes can do to dress it up."

"You never really liked her, did you?" he said thoughtfully.

"I can't abide her. You're the second person I've confessed that to today. You and Arlie. But that doesn't invalidate my point. That you had a much sharper eye for the second rate in Panama than you ever did for the second rate at home, for all the so-called 'apologetic' attitude that you and I labored under."

He shook his head violently.

"I won't admit it, Syvvie," he insisted. "It's because your life is glutted with Aunt Bellas that you don't appreciate them. But if you'd spend a few months—well, almost anywhere except where you do spend them, you'd see."

She leaned back against the stem of the umbrella.

"What will you do after the war, Bev?"

"After the war," he repeated bitterly. "I wonder if there'll be any after. I want to go back to New York and appreciate the life I used to lead. And I want to teach at Chelton. I want to start an art department up there. I know I could do it. I'm sure I could make painting real to boys. And if I could get someone like your mother to donate a little gallery and get us started with a few pictures and photographs I'd be all set. I've written Dr. Minturn—"

She half-closed her eyes and listened to his plans. It was odd, she reflected, how little actually she minded the violent conservatism of his point of view, if one could dignify it by calling it a point of view. He sounded after all just a little more like Uncle Goodhue, and what was Uncle Goodhue but the personification of her New York? Oh, we women *are* superior, she thought easily. For a man, well he was more or less a beast of action; he "did" things, but only women knew how laughable was his point of view with regard to things done. To have Beverly less subtle was to have a less congenial Beverly, but since when, she concluded with a smile, did women care for subtlety or congeniality with men? Sylvia, she said to herself, you are degraded. For what was she getting at besides admitting to herself that it was the very possibility of his having been in love, really in love, with this Miss Emerson that made her so warm to him now. In love with him she had always been, but not by any means at all times ready to accept him. She could refuse a Beverly who was desperately clutching at security from the cracking floor of a misspent social life, a tinny, vibrant Beverly, but it had been hard for her to do, and what could help her with this one, so much less pushing and tinny, dignified even with the unhappiness of a tropical love affair? But her expression hardly changed; she simply listened to him with a small smile about the corners of her lips.

CHAPTER SIX

BEVERLY PASSED A most pleasant day. He immersed himself in the Strouds, in the beach, in the sun; he fairly wallowed in them all. He and Sylvia and her mother and Arlie and Helena simply sat on the sand all day with occasional dips in the water and of course occasional drinks. They talked about everything and everyone; never had Bev felt more one of the family. When late in the afternoon they left Miami Beach, agreeing, however, to reunite for dinner on the roof garden of the Columbus Hotel, Beverly felt infinitely removed from Panama and approached the *Sardonyx* down the long dock with a mild shudder. For despite her previous Stroud ownership the little naval vessel had shed all traces of happier eras and had shrunk, in his estimate, to its present moral dimensions, that of a squat and placid ambassador from America's little empire beyond the waters. He found the Captain and the engineer in conversation in the wardroom. They merely nodded to him when he came in. Pete was reading a magazine in the corner.

"I can fix that generator myself," Foster was saying. "The engineers on this ship can do that any time."

"But you've got a naval base right here," Ellis insisted. "What the hell have they got to do besides sit on their ass all day long? Let them fix it. Christ, man, when we have a chance to spend a few weeks in Miami let's not throw it away! I'm telling the division officers to present a list of all the stuff they want done to the ship."

Foster nodded his head several times.

"Just as you say, Captain," he answered. "I can fix up plenty of work for them to do. I thought maybe you wanted to get back to sea as soon as possible."

"Yeah," Ellis drawled sarcastically winking at Pete, "I'm crying my eyes out at being stuck in Florida for a few weeks. I can't wait to get back to Panama! Knock that stuff off, Fos. The kids on this Chris-Craft haven't been to the States for two years. Put every God-damn thing you can think of on that list!"

"I think I'll telegraph my wife to come down," Pete said. "I don't care if I spend the rest of the war here," Beverly interjected.

"Where've you been all day?" Pete asked.

"At the beach."

"How is Miss Tremaine?"

"Fine." He was surprised to note how much he still resented Pete.

"Who do you think I ran into today?"

"Who?"

"Laura Smith. Been up visiting her grandmother. Those official families get around like nothing. She's on her way back to Panama. Waiting for a plane. We're going out tonight with the Captain and some girl of his—"

"I've got a lulu," Ellis threw in.

"Why don't you and Miss Tremaine meet up with us?"

This idea was not particularly attractive to Beverly. He feared the worst in the Captain's choice and wondered that even Pete would venture to mix General Smith's daughter with such riffraff. On the other hand the idea of confronting Laura with Sylvia and of meeting Laura away from her natural habitat, the background of her usual self-confidence, was rather fun. He hedged and finally gave a tentative promise to meet them late in the evening at the Glass Bucket.

He changed quickly into his whites and a half hour after leaving the ship he was sitting at a round table in the bar at the Columbus sipping a martini while waiting for the Strouds. He was still living in a bubbly world of delight and Panama continued to retreat. He thought of Sylvia's reference to Audrey and tried to remember how he had phrased that letter and how many times in his correspondence he had mentioned her. Well—poor Audrey. He stared into the golden depths of his martini and thought: after all, there's nothing to hold against her. She was just an amusing, an aspiring little Zonite. He had found out about her and that was that. Besides she didn't really exist at all. And there now was Angeline Stroud threading her way firmly through the tables, followed by her children and daughter-in-law, looking far from visionary—

At dinner in the big dining room that overlooked Miami harbor they talked about Arlie and his future.

"You're still going into the diplomatic?" Beverly asked.

"Why do you say 'still'?" Arlie demanded.

"No reason. Except that most people I know in the service take the attitude that after it's all over they're not going to go back to whatever it was they were doing. At least the war's saved me from that, they say."

"I suppose they all want to be teachers or writers," Mrs. Stroud deplored. "Every Tom, Dick, or Harry thinks he can write a book."

"And most of them do," Sylvia agreed.

"But somebody's got to go on taking in the washing," her mother continued in her grandest tone. "Everybody can't have a job that's interesting all the time. I know what Beverly means. But I don't see that the mad rush among all your friends to get into the State Department or the Department of Justice is going to be any solution."

Because Angeline could see so clearly into the unsubstantial basis of the idealism of the younger generation she never lost an opportunity to belittle it. Her exaggerated preference for sincerity drove her continually to further boundaries of conservatism. It was an angry and artificial championship of lost causes. For her contemporaries, most of whom without really changing their views now professed every general tenet of liberalism, she felt only contempt. Yet none knew better than she herself that her reaction led her into unwelcome fields and made her antagonize the people she cared for most. It was her unfortunate habit that she felt bound to react to everything. Nothing could be allowed to pass.

"Mummie never believes in anything new," Arlie protested.

"You know that's not so," she reproved him. "You're just mad because I won't clap my hands every time a young man goes into government." She turned to Bev for support. "I can remember when going into government meant a real sacrifice. So can you, Bev. And how many nice young men did it then? But now that you can't make money any more, now that we've gone practically socialist and government's become the band wagon, all the bright young men are breaking their necks to jump on!"

"And what's wrong with that?" Helena asked.

"Nothing. Except they want all the credit of doing something unpopular and noble."

It was always a bit hard to realize that Angeline believed the things she said, Bev reflected, but there it was. She did and passionately. He knew, however, how to moderate her tone.

"Arlie doesn't want any credit," he pointed out. He saw the quick, wounded look in her eyes and was sorry he had said it. Angeline adored her only son but it was without success that she fought her tendency to contradict him.

"Oh, I'm not speaking about Arlie," she said quickly, giving her son an expansive smile. "Arlie's a fighter," she continued with admirable irrelevance. "He's not one of these young men looking for Japs under a file cabinet in Washington."

The others laughed at this, the only way as they all knew to deal with Angeline when she got heated.

"Mother thinks everyone in the States is a slacker," Arlie explained. "Even Admiral King."

"I never said that, Arlie," she remonstrated.

At this they all laughed again.

"This is only the second war, after all, when it's been fashionable to be at the front," said Beverly confident that his recent sea duty removed him from all possible criticism. "Did anybody's ancestor here fight in the Civil War?"

"Certainly," Helena answered. "My grandfather. When he was only seventeen too."

"I'll bet you can't match that, Angeline," Bev exclaimed, turning on her boldly. "What was your grandfather doing?"

What Angeline's grandfather had been doing was, as Bev well knew, a story interwoven with the history of the textile industry.

"He was a very busy man," she said a bit sharply. "He had great responsibilities. He couldn't just drop everything and grab a musket."

"Or a file cabinet," Arlie added smiling.

"Well he couldn't, Arlie!" his mother protested.

"Oh, Angeline, don't take us seriously," Bev said consolingly. "We know he was a great man."

"Greater than you're apt to find these days," she said with a nod. "I wish Arlie and Syvvie could have known him. Of course he died before they were born. But there was an energy and an integrity about him that is very rare now." Angeline lost what little humor she had when she spoke about the past. "I remember as a child his telling me how he came over from Scotland as a boy of sixteen with only two gold pieces in his pocket and went to church his first day in New York and put one in the plate."

The others, except Sylvia, listened respectfully to this oft-told tale.

"I suppose," Sylvia said with a shake of her jangling bracelet and the nervous twist of her thin shoulders that always preceded a sarcasm, "there must have been plenty of immigrants who did that and then went out and starved."

"One doesn't hear about them," Helena added.

"You're all very modern and very smart. That's all I have to say," Angeline observed sourly.

"Let's forget about Mummie's Grandpa and the war and all those things," Arlie exclaimed hastily. "This is a celebration. And here we have a second bottle of champagne." The waiter had just opened it with a particularly loud pop and was filling the glasses.

"What shall we drink to?"

"To all of us?"

Beverly raised his glass.

Whether it was irritation at her daughter for her last remark and a wish to get back at her, entirely to be expected with a mother as objective as Angeline, or whether it was purely and simply her utter lack of understanding of the feelings of others that induced her to say what she now said, it was impossible to tell.

"No, no," she exclaimed beaming suddenly at them all, "I know what we'll drink to. Arlie, you and Helena and I will drink to Syvvie and Bev. And may they stay together now that they've found each other again."

Arlie and Helena looked startled, but then quickly smiled. Beverly was aghast. He turned to Sylvia, but she clapped her napkin suddenly to her lips.

"Mummie, how *could* you?" she gasped. And then in a second she had burst into tears and was hurrying from the dining room. Helena gave her mother-in-law one look and got up to follow her.

"No, leave her be, Helena," Angeline cried. "She's better alone when she gets this way. She's really too unreasonable!"

But Helena without a word followed Sylvia out.

"Really, Mummie!" Arlie protested.

"Well, what's wrong, Arlie?" his mother asked angrily. "I declare, I've never seen anything so silly in my life. Syvvie is simply morbid half the time about herself. The slightest little thing and off she goes. Helena spoils her. There's no doubt about it."

"But you don't have to embarrass her publicly, do you?" he retorted.

"Publicly! I like that. I suppose poor Beverly here is the public."

Arlie stared down at the table cloth for a second in an effort to control his temper.

"You know what I mean, Mummie," he said more quietly.

Beverly in the meantime was experiencing as acutely uncomfortable a sensation as he ever remembered.

"No, I don't know what you mean, Arlie," said his mother defiantly. "I . . ." But here she too stopped. Even to her it must have occurred how dreadful it was to make a row during Arlie's short time back from the war. Beverly sensed this. Everything was tumbling about in his mind but he heard himself say:

"It's perfectly all right, Angeline. I think it was wonderful of you to say it. Poor Syvvie's embarrassed, but she'll get over it. After all, she may not care a rap for me. You know, I guess, that she turned me down once. But Arlie thinks you embarrassed her because I may have changed." Here he turned to Arlie. "Please don't worry about that. I adore Syvvie more than ever."

Arlie blushed deeply.

"Gosh, Bev," he murmured, "that's nice to hear. It'll all be O.K., I'm sure. I hope you don't think I've been rude," he added to his mother.

Angeline gave a little nod to indicate that, of course, she had been right from the beginning.

"Not at all, my darling," she said warmly. "It's as plain as the nose on your face that Bev and Syvvie were made for each other. A little jolt here and there is what they need. We can't pretend to be blind all the time, can we?" she said to Beverly with a smile. "Now, I tell you what. Go out in the lobby and wait for Syvvie. When she comes back catch her and take her on to some other place. She won't want to be with so many of us after this little scene."

"A good idea," Arlie said enthusiastically.

Beverly got up and said good night to them without further ado. He was about to shake hands with Mrs. Stroud when a sudden impulse prompted him to bend down to kiss her cheek. The impulse was poorly timed, for, unimaginative as always, she drew her head back the slightest bit in surprise and then with a quick "oh" presented him a cheek. He pecked it and was gone.

In the lobby he stationed himself where he could command a view of the door to the ladies' room and waited.

Sylvia finally came out, red-eyed but erect, her black satin evening dress rustling as she moved. Helena followed her and saw Beverly first. She touched her sister-in-law's arm. The latter looked around and seemed to suppress an exclamation of surprise.

"Syvvie," Bev said quickly, coming over to them. "Get your wrap and let's you and I go to the Glass Bucket. Come on."

She looked tearfully at Helena.

"Go on, Sis," the other urged her. "I'll call you the first thing in the morning."

Sylvia without a word returned to the ladies' room.

"That's a good idea, Bev," Helena said. "You know these little flare-ups she has. It's nothing. Take her out and give her a good time."

"As a matter of fact it was Mrs. Stroud's idea."

"Oh, Mrs. Stroud!"

"She didn't mean to upset her."

"Oh, I know," Helena said wearily. "She never does. Neither does Bella. But between them they'll be the death of poor Syvvie."

At this point Sylvia emerged with her coat, and bidding Helena good night without repeating, however, the incident of the kiss, Bev hurried Sylvia into the street and into a taxi. All the way to the Glass Bucket he kept up a steady flow of conversation on ordinary topics, how fortunate they were to get a cab and how they'd probably have to walk home, and how appalling the black market in Miami was; even after they had arrived and found a table in the subaqueous night club with huge fish painted on walls that were colored green and blue and spotted with a commercial artist's concept of deep sea vegetable life, he did not relax his efforts to spare her the slightest occasion of referring to the incident at the Columbus. It was too early yet for the larger crowds and their table was well removed from the very noisy and vibrant orchestra.

"I'm awfully sorry, Bev," she said at last, after he had ordered something to drink and appeared to be temporarily out of ideas. "How embarrassed you must have been."

"It was nothing."

"But it was," she insisted. "It was like this morning. I must get over it. When I'm upset by anyone I want to run away. I have the feeling that I simply can't bear it."

"But Syvvie, my dear, what was so unbearable about what your mother said?"

She shook her head slowly.

"Don't you see?"

"No. Unless it was the idea of having your name associated with mine that was so awful to you?"

"It wasn't that at all. I suppose I might as well be frank with you." She paused for a second. "Don't you see that Mother is throwing me at you?"

He didn't hesitate at all.

"But that's just where I want you to be thrown!" he exclaimed.

"Oh, Bev." She smiled at him helplessly. "You're always kind. Ever since you used to dance with me by the hour and insist that you weren't stuck. But we're up against more serious things now. Mother wants to get rid of me."

"Oh, come now!"

"But she does." She held up her hand to check his protestations. "I ought to know. She loves me in her own way but having me on her hands at my age appalls her neat mind. It just isn't right. Mummie has never understood me. I don't know how much you know about it, Bev," she went on in a more earnest tone than he had ever heard her use, "but I've always suffered from moods and depressions. They get pretty nasty sometimes and I go down to the country. I don't know where they come from. Inherited I guess, from the Tremaines. I have moments of just not being able to bear anything that strikes me as cruel and hard. The idea of cruelty assumes hideous proportions, and then I feel as if I were sitting in that room in one of Poe's stories where one wall after another closes in and the black space contracts and contracts—I can't tell you how awful that is." She looked at him with suddenly brightened eyes.

"Syvvie, dear, don't talk about it," he protested.

"But I must," she said with firmness. "Tonight. You've got to know all about it in view of what's happened. You see, Mother hasn't got a neurotic bone in her body and she just can't bring herself to believe in mental problems. She could cope with anything else but not that. When I was little she used either to scold me horribly or else send me to a psychologist. There was no in between. I remember one doctor who wanted to get me away from home for a couple of years, but Mummie wouldn't hear of it. She didn't sympathize but she was too possessive to let me go. Then I used to be afraid of her and, of course, that just made things worse. Don't look so worried, Bev," she said smiling suddenly and taking his hand, "I'm much better now. I very rarely have attacks except little moments like today. But Mummie works on her revolting, old-fashioned theories that what I need is a home of my own. She's ready to throw me at anything male."

"Compliment!"

"Don't be a goose. Not you. She thinks you're quite a catch."

Here at long last the waiter arrived and placed the drinks on the table.

"I don't see why. I haven't any money."

"No, but she has plenty of that. Do her justice. Her standards aren't that vulgar."

"But, Syvvie," he interrupted, "what does this have to do with me? I agree with your mother. I think you should have a home of your own. And I'd do anything in the world to persuade you to let me give you one." He turned and looked at her squarely as he said this, conscious at the time that his slight alcoholic glow enabled him to fix her with an expression of lustrous sincerity. His eyes didn't even flicker. "I haven't changed," he went on, "since that day in Westbury. How about it, Syvvie? Will you marry me or won't you?"

There was no repetition of the anger of the other time but her eyes were full of tears.

"Oh, Bev, you don't have to! You really don't!"

"But I think I do."

He smiled at her beamingly and there followed a moment of slight awkwardness. He couldn't very well kiss her in the night club yet the situation so obviously called for some physical manifestation of joy. His solution of taking her right hand in both of his and pressing her fingers to his lips while he looked at her was not ideal.

"We're engaged then," he said.

"I don't suppose it's legal until we put it in the *Tribune*," she answered with a smile, pulling back her hand. "But I insist that as far as you and I are concerned it's binding."

"Shall we announce it?"

"Why not?" It was wonderful how quickly she had regained her old, defensive self-possession.

"I hoped you'd say that," he exclaimed. "It may be some

time before we can get married but I'd like to feel it's all settled."

"Some time?"

"Darling, we don't want to get married until the war's over."

"Oh?"

"Don't you think war marriages are a mistake?"

"I don't see anything wrong in them for people our age," she answered frankly. "But I don't want to seem pushy. I should be hiding maidenly blushes. And I shall hide them." She took a compact out of her handbag and dabbed her cheeks. "See what an abandoned wretch you've made of me! What would Mummie say if she saw me using a compact in public?"

"I think," he said firmly, "we should wait at any rate until we get some leave. Then we can talk it over and make definite plans. Maybe my next duty will be in the States—"

"Oh," she interrupted with apparently shocked surprise, "what would Mummie say? As soon as you're one of the family she'll want to throw you into the blood bath with Arlie."

They smiled at each other.

"That's another point," he reminded her. "We're not going to worry about your mother any more."

The music was very loud now and the Bucket was filling with uniforms and evening dresses. They were young and pleasant faces for the most part, not distinctive but healthy, gathered in from the sub-chaser school and the Air Force. He asked her to dance.

Sylvia, to whom night clubs were anathema, was utterly contented this evening and was quite sure that she had never been to a more enchanting place than the Bucket. She insisted that its décor was effectively submarine, pointed out that the octopus chandelier was just such a thing as she'd like for a wedding present. She took more pleasure in dancing, more interest in the people around them than was usual with her. She became quite drunk with happiness, quite delirious at the sudden, the obvious solution to her problem. The whole tortured question of whether Beverly loved her enough resolved itself into the simple answer that he would marry her. A line from an old hymn kept dancing through her head, oddly in conflict yet sometimes in tune with the music: "Only God's free gifts abuse not." Millions of Europeans had married on no better assurance. And she, Sylvia, had always been a classicist too, had always decried the unformulated "yearnings" of the romantic school. No, no, she thought happily; this time she wouldn't be a goose.

Beverly was very interested in all the details of the announcement; he would call his mother in the morning, he told her, and when would she tell hers? At breakfast? She was about to answer that she would probably wake her mother up when she came in, when to her surprise a thickset naval officer in khakis with a pugilist's face nodded at her. He was dancing with a tall girl in a black and orange suit with a hat dominated by a large feather. Except for her height she might have been attractive, though her head and features were too small for her body and her eyes were half-closed in a disdainful way.

"Bev," she said, "do you know those people over there?"

He looked in that direction.

"Oh, it's Pete," he said with interest. "And the girl with him is Laura Smith. She's the daughter of the Lieutenant-Governor of the Canal Zone. Do you mind if I ask them over to our table? They said they might turn up."

She tried to keep the disappointment out of her face.

"Not at all. We must be nice to the Governor's daughter mustn't we?"

Bev guided her over to where Pete and Laura were and they all four stood in the middle of the floor, jostled by dancing couples while Beverly made the necessary introductions. They then weaved their way towards the table in the corner.

"Practically in the pantry, isn't it?" Laura observed to Beverly as she sat down in Sylvia's chair. It was unfortunate that she was not in a better humor; as a matter of fact she could hardly have been in a worse. Her trip home to stay with her grandmother in Cincinnati had not been a success; she had found almost all her old friends away and those who were left not particularly impressed by her father's recent elevation. Her grandmother had had a mild stroke too during her visit, and this had played havoc with what few social engagements she had managed to dig up. Now in Miami she had just been apprised that she would have to wait three days before her priority would get her aboard a plane and she had failed to get a room either at the Columbus or the Miami Colonial, being forced to seek refuge in a third-rate affair blocks from any place convenient. And tonight

on top of everything Pete Stoner, she felt, had virtually insulted her by not wearing a white uniform.

"I guess they didn't know you were coming," Beverly retorted. "It was the best table we could get." Here he went
off to fetch a waiter.

"Such fun to run into Beverly and Pete," Laura said to
Sylvia perfunctorily. "They're so amusing together."

"I've never seen them together before," Sylvia explained.

"If only Audrey were here," Laura continued turning to
Pete, "how like old times it would be."

Sylvia noted the name.

"Who is Audrey?" she asked.

"Oh, an old friend of ours in the Zone. Or, perhaps,"
Laura continued with a mean little smile, "I should say an
old friend of Bev's."

Poor Sylvia at last sensed the hostility in Laura's attitude
but she was not enlightened as to the reason. She could not
know that Pete had explained in advance to Laura that they
were going to meet Beverly's girl, a tremendous social "swell,"
a "daughter of Arleus Stroud," and that in drawing the picture he had made it seem that he and Laura alike were
quite beyond the pale of this creature's accustomed re-
treats. He had done this in obedience to the old impulse
that always motivated Laura's friends, the impulse to take
her down a peg; but this in addition to other factors previously mentioned had irritated her beyond his anticipation or
desire. Everything about Sylvia increased her spite: the quiet
expensiveness of her black satin, the exaggeration of her
huge bracelet, her air of timid reserve which Laura inter-
preted as snobbish aloofness. And she, Laura, who usually
dated with nobody under a major, caught with a mere
lieutenant and out of uniform too! Laura, to put it mildly,
was out of control.

"You and Audrey Emerson are great friends, aren't you?"
she observed to Bev as he took his seat beside Sylvia after
ordering the drinks.

"Everybody loves Audrey," he said blandly. With one glance
he saw the game "dear" Laura was up to. He hit back. "Of
course you and she grew up together in the Zone, didn't you?
You know her better than all of us. Aren't the Emersons
some sort of relation to you?"

Laura gasped.

"Certainly not!"

"I always think of everyone in the Zone as being related, don't you, Pete?"

"Oh, you do." Laura was barely polite now. "There's all the difference in the world between being a Zonite and in the Army. Daddy of course is Army. He's a major-general now," she said turning to Sylvia, "but as he's also been appointed Lieutenant-Governor he wears civilian clothes."

"That must be nice," Sylvia said vaguely.

"Of course he'd infinitely rather be in uniform with a war going on."

"I imagine so."

"What is your father doing now?" Laura asked her with the aggressiveness of a small child. There was a painful silence.

"My father isn't living," Sylvia answered in a barely audible tone. "He died when I was a baby."

Laura blushed crimson.

"I'm so sorry," she said in confusion. "I thought Mr. Arleus Stroud was your father—"

"Mr. Stroud is Sylvia's step-father," Beverly said succinctly.

"Oh."

Pete saved the situation.

"Come, Laura, let's dance," he suggested, and she got up quickly and moved to the floor. Sylvia picked up her glass and took a sip.

"Are they great friends of yours, Bev?"

"Oh Lord, no."

"I'm glad."

"Did you think she was very awful?"

"Very. I'm sure her friend, Audrey, must be nicer." Here she smiled at him.

"Audrey's out of the same drawer," he said hurriedly. "So you see you have nothing to be worried about."

"I wonder. This one would never collect George Eliot."

"Oh, Syvvie!"

"All right," she said meekly. "I'll be good. But, Bev, darling, please take me home now. I'm terribly tired and excited."

"Won't you wait till they come back?"

"No, please, darling," she insisted. "I don't want to see her again. There's something about her that gives me a chill."

"It's just because she's jealous of you."

"Jealous? Is she in love with you too?"

"No, no," he said laughing. "Laura goes by rank. Ensigns and j.g.'s bore her, lieutenants and lieutenant-commanders amuse her, commanders interest her, and captains intrigue her."

"So? And why should I do anything to her?"

"Because, my dear, you're something she calls 'New York Society' which in her own truculent way she fears may be snappier than anything on the Isthmus of Panama."

"Incredible! Come, Bev. Take me home. You can come back."

He held her hand in the taxi and reflected with some discomfort that he would have to kiss her before they got to the Miami Colonial. It was too bad, he told himself irritably, that she had no physical attraction for him at all. For that was the case stated bluntly. He was devoted to her; he pitied her; he wanted intensely to be in love with her. He had idealized, romanticized her, but he could never get away from the fact that she was so painfully thin. He scratched his head and looked at her. She seemed to be deep in contemplation staring at the floor of the cab. He wondered if it was going to be hard to make conversation now that they were engaged. They had always talked a blue streak before.

"A penny," he said.

"I was thinking of your mother, Bev. I wonder if she knows how much I admire her. I'm afraid she doesn't."

"I'm sure she does." He took her by the shoulders, leaned over and kissed her on the lips. He could see in the dim light from the street lamps that she was weeping and as he folded her in his arms and she rested her head on his shoulder it came to him with a warm reassuring throb that maybe after all he was in love.

He walked for several blocks alone after dropping her at her hotel, too much in the grip of a strong but unfamiliar elation to want to go back to the ship. He moved, he was sure, with a springier step than before; he felt a new confidence in himself. He was no longer an idle bachelor, trespassing with his asceticism on the natural fructification of life. He wanted to tell everybody he saw that he was a new Beverly, a Beverly who was engaged to be married. A Beverly who was "one of them," one with them. A Beverly who was "real." Finally. At thirty-three. A Beverly who would be the son-in-law, possibly even the father of the grandchildren of Mrs. Arleus Stroud.

The glaring lights of a Miami Beach bus were approaching him from behind. It clattered to a stop and without a second thought he jumped into it. It was impossible for him to go to bed.

Back at the Bucket he found the situation worse than he'd left it. Bill Ellis had arrived well plastered with a flamboyant Miami blonde whose noisy presence at the table and obvious attraction for Pete were proving too much for poor Laura. She hailed him hopefully when he approached the table and then got up to meet him, literally pushing him backwards on to the dance floor.

"I'm sorry," she said with a sniff, "but it's just a little more than I can take over there. You've got to dance."

"But that's my captain," he protested.

"I don't care if he's the admiral. I'm not used to associating with ladies of the 'tart' variety."

"Is she that bad?"

"My dear, she asked me if I lived in Miami. As if anyone ever *lived* here."

"And that proves she's a tart?"

She leaned back to stare at him.

"That sounds rather too stuffy for our old Beverly!" she exclaimed. "This must be the influence of Miss Tremaine. We'll have to give you a going over when we all get back to the Zone. But tell me, was Miss Tremaine very irritated with me tonight? Tell the truth; I won't mind."

"I think she was, a little."

"Was that why she went home?"

"Well—she was tired."

"Oh." Laura wrinkled her nose into a little ball. "She must be very sensitive."

"She is. But you weren't very polite."

She gave a toss of her head.

"I don't believe I have to come to Florida to learn manners," she said loftily. "If your friends can't take a little kidding they'll have to do without my society. I wasn't brought up in a graveyard."

"Neither was Syvvie."

"She looks it."

His hand released hers, and they stopped dancing.

"It might interest you to know," he said with real anger in his voice, "that Syvvie and I are engaged."

Laura looked at him with an equivocal little smile to act as a cover until her attitude should be resolved. She was aquiver with indignation but she didn't want an open break. Her smile broadened and she reached for his hand.

"Why, Bev, congratulations!" she cried, with a vigorous shake. "Of course it interests me. And don't hold my silly little remarks against me. I'm tired tonight. You know how one gets. I didn't mean a thing I said. Honest Injun."

He looked down at her grey eyes suspiciously.

"Oh, all right," he said. They went on dancing.

"Will you be married before you go back?"

"No."

"Wait till after the war?"

"I guess."

She was quiet for a few moments. Then, in a new tone: "Of course, you know I don't think it's ideal for either of you."

"What isn't?"

"Oh—this 'alliance.'"

"Why not?"

"Don't get mad, Bev." She eyed him sagely.

"I'm not mad."

"Very well."

"I simply want to know what the hell you mean."

She shrugged her shoulders as if to express that his rudeness was just another of the things that people of her intelligence had to put up with.

"I just thought," she explained, "what an opportunity you were both throwing away to broaden yourselves. Obviously you've both been brought up with the same narrow Manhattan background—oh I'm not saying it doesn't have its advantages but it is narrow. You know the same people and like the same things. You'll just keep reinforcing each other in your mutual prejudices. I daresay you'll be happy—"

"Yes, I daresay we will," he said strongly.

"But frankly," she went on, "I'm a bit disappointed. Just a bit. I can't help it. You've been coming along so well in the past year."

"I have!"

She nodded. "I've been able to see that New York—well, we won't call it snobbery—peeling off little by little in our Panama sun. You were getting to be almost human. But now you'll creep back into your shell and peer at life out of the windows of the Racquet Club."

"I don't belong to the Racquet Club."

"Well you know what I mean."

"No, I don't know what you mean," he said indignantly. "I don't know at all what you mean."

She smiled in resignation.

"How anybody who's been brought up in an oblong slot like the Army can have the gall to throw stones at a New Yorker is beyond me," he went on angrily. "I suppose you think if I married a Zone girl we'd be a couple of cosmopolitans, we'd be so broadminded."

"Well if you're going to be nasty—"

"What else are you being I'd like to know? You and your 'interest' in me."

Laura's lips quivered.

"If I were really nasty," she drawled, "I'd point out the obvious convenience of Stroud money to a post-war Beverly."

Once more they stood still on the floor.

"That does it," he said in a dry brittle voice. "Come on, cat, I'll take you back to Pete."

"The truth isn't any fun, is it?" he heard her say as he led the way back to the table, but he made no answer. Unfortunately they were met by Pete and Ellis and Ellis's girl who had decided to leave the Bucket and who refused to allow Beverly to go back to the ship by himself. They had a taxi waiting, Ellis explained heavily, and, by God, they were going to give him a lift. The taxi ride was dreadful; Beverly, crumpled between the driver and Pete in the front seat, got what small consolation he could from imagining Laura's discomfort between Ellis and the blonde in back. They stopped after what seemed an interminable ride in front of Laura's boarding house and waited while Pete got out to escort her in. She swept out of the taxi elaborately omitting to say good night to anyone, but they all could observe that while she was fitting her key into the lock Pete tried to grab a kiss and got a sharp kick in the shins that had in it no possible element of coyness. Ellis leaned out of the window and putting two fingers to his lips emitted a deafening whistle which was answered by the angry slam of the door. Pete limped back to the cab. It was all very sordid.

They stopped at several bars on the way back and the taxi driver came in and drank with them. Beverly was not nearly as drunk as the others but he was too preoccupied with all that had happened during the evening to care particularly when he got back to the ship. He sat stonily with a drink in one hand while the others swapped stories and laughed. He had a vague consciousness of its being somewhere around three o'clock when they finally drove up to the naval gate. Ellis and the blonde went right through; he turned and nudged Beverly with a wink saying: "We're going to cook some scrambled eggs in the wardroom." Pete wandered after them a bit unsteadily and Bev reflected what a gross quantity he must have drunk for ordinarily the heaviest night would not even shake his rugged bulk.

The gangway watch on the *Sardonyx* had gone below to call his relief, so at the moment they came on board there was no one to see them. This struck Captain Ellis as very lax and he swore about it for a few moments, and then they all went into the wardroom and turned on the lights. The blonde friend uttered several little squeaks of amazement when she saw the big sofa, the mahogany wardroom table, and the paneling and made all the usual remarks about the boys at sea "having it soft." Beverly went straight down the circular stairway, took off his jacket and fell into his bunk.

He lay there motionless feeling heavier and heavier. Each ounce of his body seemed to be slowly liquefying and slowly oozing towards a center of gravity somewhere in the middle. He vaguely wondered if the concentrated pressure would break through the bottom of the bunk. Everything that had happened during the day seemed very far off but very clear. It would all have been quite ridiculously easy to cope with except for the dull misery that even now he felt from Laura's hateful malice. He let his mind dwell for a moment with pleasure on the dreadful things he would like to see happen to Laura. He imagined himself slapping her nasty face in public and her running for revenge to her father only to find that he had been dishonorably discharged from the Army for incompetence in the administration of Canal Zone affairs, unmasked by the brilliant Lieutenant Stregelinus. He smiled as he envisioned her dismay. But now his head began to spin—

He woke up with a splitting headache two hours later, his mouth dry and swollen, and after a great deal of inward debate he summoned the energy to stagger up to the wardroom for a glass of water. It was dark there but he heard snoring and made out the hulk of Pete's recumbent figure on the sofa.

"Good night, sir," he heard suddenly. It was the gangway watch right outside the wardroom window but the boy was not addressing him.

"I'm just going to see Miss Martin home. I'll be right back," Bev heard the Captain's voice from the deck.

CHAPTER SEVEN

THE FOLLOWING DAY which was Sunday was, as Beverly reflected later, as full of incident as the dramatic twenty-four hours into which the French classic tragedian had to fit the events of his play. It started uneventfully enough with a severe hangover when he woke up at ten o'clock and dragged himself in clean whites wearily up to the wardroom. There he found Stoner, Winston, and Foster eating breakfast, each intent on a strip of the comic section of the Miami *Daily News*. The rather sullen silence was indicative of the way the night before had been spent. Bev drank a glass of water greedily and reached for *Dick Tracy*. The door to the fantail opened and Calloriac, who had not gone out the night before, came in, in obvious good spirits.

"My wife arrives this afternoon," he threw out cheerfully. "I just had a telegram."

There was vague murmur of congratulation. Beverly made a greater effort.

"How nice. Where's she going to stay?"

"I'll find some place."

"Pete has a great friend who's got a room in a boardinghouse which she'll be giving up soon," Bev continued looking across the table at Stoner. "She'd do anything for Pete."

The latter scowled.

"Oh, shut up," he grunted.

"Don't you think your friend, Laura, would be delighted to help you—?" Bev was asking, but just at this point the door opened again and Captain Arnold, four stripes gleaming on each shoulder, Captain Arnold, yes, he and none other, stepped into the wardroom. They all stood up. He looked around with ominous passivity.

"Do you always have breakfast at this hour on converted yachts?" he asked.

"Only on Sunday, sir," Calloriac answered. They all waited for the Captain to point out that Pearl Harbor had occurred on a Sunday, but he didn't. He simply stood there, tall and gaunt and terribly thin, his large eyes roving about the wardroom.

"I always heard this was good duty," he continued humorlessly. "It takes all sorts I guess to make a war. Where's your skipper?"

Calloriac made the mistake of smiling.

"He's not feeling exactly up to the mark, Captain, if you know what I mean."

Captain Arnold simply looked at him gravely.

"Is he on the binnacle list?"

"Well—no. Not exactly."

"Get him up here."

Calloriac hurried down the stairway.

"Please sit down," the Captain said to the others, and they did. The silence was absolute.

"A very comfortable wardroom," the Captain remarked. "Hard to think much about submarines when you're sitting in a place like this."

"Oh, we think about them," Foster volunteered, for nothing could keep him out of any conversation long. "We've been on convoy duty for two years." He grew bolder as he saw Captain Arnold nod in answer. "Since long before these little patrol craft you see down around here were invented."

Captain Arnold, USN, could see that the little man who was chattering was an ex-CPO of some sort, probably a machinist, and he softened as will a southern *chatelaine* before the picture of something old and faithful, something devoted and utterly dependable.

"Yes, you were the pioneers," he said more gently, "and we've learned a lot from what you haven't been able to do. Are you the engineer?"

"Yes, sir."

"They say that a man who can keep one of these yachts running can keep anything running. Would you like to come to my school?"

"I would, sir. But what I'd really like is to get back with the fleet."

"Oh, the fleet." The Captain shrugged his shoulders as though to indicate that heaven could not be attained in this life. There was a sound of feet on the stairway and a second later Ellis appeared. He had thrown on a khaki shirt and jumped into khaki trousers; he still had slippers on and his eyes were puffy with sleep.

"Good morning, Skipper," Captain Arnold said firmly stretching out a hand. "I've come to look you over and see about this damage."

"I'm sorry to be below," Ellis answered forcing a little smile. "It's Sunday, you know," he continued, for as Beverly was to discover, when in temper he could show surprising nerve—his ego made him forget his fears—"and we've had some hard days at sea recently."

"Sunday's the same as any other day in Miami," Captain Arnold rejoined. "Pearl Harbor, you know, happened on a Sunday." And the two went out to take a tour of the ship. Calloriac and Foster followed them; the others went on with breakfast.

But it was not long before Foster came hurrying back.

"Lord!" he said slapping his forehead. "That four-striper is poking his nose into every part of the ship!"

"What's he finding?"

"What isn't he? It's only taken him ten minutes to find that—"

The general alarm began to clatter.

"GQ!" Winston exclaimed. "Damned if it isn't a real inspection!"

The rest of the morning was a sad affair. Captain Arnold ruthlessly put the crew through all the drills and made several interesting discoveries which, although he made no written notations, one felt quite sure he would not forget. He called for a fire party on the fantail and it took fifteen minutes before they got pressure on the hose; he called away a fire and rescue party but the crew had never received instruction in this drill; he passed the word to abandon ship and the life rafts couldn't be released. All the time he said nothing while Ellis, now apologetic, now sullen, tried to explain in senseless fashion that this or that was not required by the Panama Sea Frontier. Arnold simply strolled on in deadly silence nor did he profess the slightest interest in any of the fresh paint which Ellis had slathered over the ship in such profusion except once to comment that the commanding officer had evidently not read a directive on paint as a fire hazard. When he was quite through he went below to the engine room with Foster.

Beverly noticed that Calloriac had a gleam of satisfaction in his eye when he returned with Ellis to the wardroom. The latter, needless to say, was in a violent rage.

"Son of a bitch!" he exclaimed as he threw himself on

the sofa. "What the hell business is it of his how I run this ship! We're only in here for repairs."

"Any base commander can inspect at will," Calloriac observed.

"But they've got to give you warning," Ellis shouted. "They've got to give you at least a few hours' warning."

"So I noticed."

Ellis glared at him.

"If he'd get off his God-damn ass in Miami and go to sea for once he'd find out how much the fighting men in the Navy care for his silly drills."

Calloriac permitted a barely perceptible smile at the corners of his lips.

"I believe Captain Arnold was on a destroyer in the North Atlantic before he was ordered to Miami," he said quietly.

"Oh, Christ, Calloriac, you're always siding with people like that," Ellis said disgustedly. "Who cares about drills anyway?"

"Well, you know, Captain, this could have been avoided if you'd taken the advice about drills that I—"

"Oh, dry up!" And with this Ellis flung out of the room. Calloriac shrugged his shoulders and returned to the newspaper.

It was too late for Beverly now to get out to the Bath Club in time for lunch with the Strouds but he decided that lunch in the wardroom with Ellis would be too unpleasant and with the Exec's permission he left the ship almost immediately and went to a bar near the docks for a drink and a sandwich. While there he placed a call to his mother in New York. There was little traffic at the time and in a few minutes he heard the operator saying: "Is this Mrs. Stregelinus? I have a collect call for you from Lieutenant Stregelinus in Miami. Will you accept the charges?" and his mother's nervous "yes, yes" followed by the inevitable, anxious: "Beverly, darling, are you all right?" which always irritated him.

"Yes, I'm all right, Mother," he said a bit crossly.

"How's Miami?"

"Fine."

"Do you still think your boat's going to be there for a while? Or can't I ask?"

He chafed at the continued anxiety in her tone.

"Yes, you can ask," he said. "I think she'll be here for a couple of weeks."

"Then I can come down?"

"Well, that's what I called about—"

"Oh, Beverly, I warn you, I'm coming, no matter what you say. I've got to see you, darling. It's been a year!"

"Yes, Mother dear, I know. But here's the thing. I think I can get leave and come to New York—"

"Oh, that would be lovely!"

"I'm not sure, but I think so. So don't come down yet. I'll call you tomorrow. And Mother," he continued swallowing hard, "I've got some other news for you. Who do you think is down here?"

"Who?"

"Syvvie and her mother and Arlie and Helena."

"Oh!" Her surprise sounded genuine. "Well, that must be fun for you. Is Arlie at the school?"

"Yes. And Mother—"

"Yes, dear." He could feel the suspense in her tone. Then he blurted it out.

"Syvvie and I are engaged."

There was a breathless second, a second in which, so well did he know her, her disappointment and her quick realization that she must put a good face on it both intertwined, communicated themselves forcibly to him over the wire.

"Darling," she said, "how sudden! But I'm so glad. Is it— is it—"

Something malicious seized him.

"Irrevocable?" he said supplying the word. "Quite."

"No, no," she protested unhappily. "I mean is it definite? Does Mrs. Stroud know?"

"Syvvie was going to tell her last night. I'm going out to the beach in a minute to meet them. But I know she approves."

His mother had pulled herself together.

"Bev, darling, I think it's fine," she said in a more settled tone. "I know you know your own mind and I know Syvvie knows hers. I have every faith in both of you."

"Well, I know you have your doubts—"

"Oh, darling, the war has changed so many things. I'm not the fussy silly person I was. Really. And I have more faith in you than I have in myself. If you're happy about it so am I."

"Of course I'm happy about it." And for some reason he felt that he wanted, all of a sudden, to cry.

"Then there we are," she said. "I'll call Angeline tonight. Where is she staying?"

"At the Miami Colonial."

"Have you any plans?"

"None as yet. We'll talk it all over in New York and announce it there."

"Call me tomorrow, darling, will you?"

"I promise."

In the bus going out to the beach he read a newspaper with forced attention but he gathered only vaguely the drift of the columns. His mind did not revert to his mother and Sylvia, but only because he had closed that door tightly and was still leaning against it, pressing his shoulder there until he could feel the strain on the panel. The effort cost him all his attention; he had no mind for anything else and he almost leapt from the bus when it stopped at the corner by the Bath Club. It had started to rain during the trip and he hurried in the door to find that most of the members were flocking into the club house in various stages of beach costume and that the bar was already jammed. He finally discovered the Strouds gathered in the far corner of the main lounge; they were not in bathing suits and he supposed they had come out just before lunch. Arlie and Helena were listlessly reading a pile of Sunday papers; Mrs. Stroud was working on her needlepoint. Sylvia was looking out the window at the rain; she got up when she saw Bev and came towards him.

"At last, darling," she said. "We missed you so at lunch."

While he explained about the inspection Arlie and Helena came over to him and congratulated him very warmly and shook his hand. He beamed at them all and moved slowly over to where Mrs. Stroud was sitting. She had taken off her glasses and was holding them in one hand while she offered him the other with the pleasantest of smiles.

"Well, Bev, my dear, I hear it's all settled," she said. "I couldn't be more pleased. Come and talk to mother now." She indicated a seat beside her. "And the rest of you run along to the bar. I want to talk to my new son-in-law alone. Yes, even you, Syvvie."

He gave Sylvia a kiss and sat down by Mrs. Stroud. She waited until the others had gone and then picked up her needlepoint. She put her glasses on and placed a needle firmly in the material, drawing it through from the other side.

"Syvvie tells me," she said, "that you're not planning to get married for a while."

"That's right."

"May I ask why not?" She raised her needle to the light to rethread it.

"Oh, the war," he answered generally. "I have to go back to Panama. She couldn't go down there."

"I understand that," she said. "But I mean if you got some leave now. Or even if you went back to Panama and then got some leave. After all, you've been away quite a bit. I should think you'd have some coming up."

"Quite possibly. But it's not altogether the leave—"

"What is it?"

He hesitated.

"Well—it is war you know, and I suppose I could get killed."

She disposed of this point rapidly.

"Fiddlesticks," she said. "Nothing's going to happen to you, Bev. Not in Panama surely." Then noticing how obviously this irked him she went on: "And even if the worst did happen, how could it be any sadder for Syvvie married than unmarried? It isn't as if she were a blushing eighteen, you know. Let's be frank about things. Syvvie's almost thirty. She'd never marry again anyway so you couldn't say that you'd be ruining her life. I know my daughter, Bev, and I know that you're the only person she ever has been or will be in love with."

He felt that Angeline for once was probably right, and he felt strangely guilty that what she said should be so. He reached for a cigarette and lit it slowly. She stopped her needling again to look at him and he felt the penetration of her eyes.

"If I had my way I'd have you married next week," she continued. "It's nonsense to talk about war marriages when you're as old as you two. I tell you what. I'll find out from Captain Arnold how long your ship will be in Miami and arrange for you to come to New York. I know he'll be only too glad—"

"No, don't do that," he said laughing at her impetuosity, "I can get leave without your going to all that trouble. But I haven't finished all my reasons. I can't support Syvvie the way I want on a naval salary."

"Beverly Stregelinus!" she interrupted in her highest, firmest tone. "Don't talk nonsense. Let's be grown-up about this thing. I can take care of Sylvia and you know it."

He looked at her in dismay, not so much at the offer which he had never pictured his married life without but at the absoluteness of her assumption that he wouldn't mind.

"Angeline," he protested, "I don't want to live on your money."

"My dear Beverly," she insisted, "I never thought I'd have trouble with a man of your intelligence on that point. I have definite views on this subject. I've never adhered to the school of thought that believes in giving a young couple an enormous wedding reception and tons of presents only to dump them in a two room apartment right afterwards to teach them some silly notion of independence. If people have money or are going to have it the earlier they learn how to use it the better. That sort of independence isn't real anyway. Suppose you and Syvvie tried to live on your pay. Who'd pay her doctor's bills which I can assure you come to a pretty penny? She's hardly strong enough to do all her own work. And is she to be deprived of happiness for a few scruples?"

"Well, no—"

"I'll show you what I mean," she interrupted sweeping on, the needlepoint now entirely laid aside. "Suppose I were to die and leave Syvvie some money. Would you let her spend it?"

"Why—I suppose that would be different. It would be hers then."

"So it would be all right," she exclaimed. "Don't you see what a premium that puts on my death?"

He held up his hands.

"Angeline, you're too much for me. I guess there's no logic in my attitude. Just a little instinct, that's all."

"Oh instinct!" She dismissed the word. "I believe my dear that you know my reputation for being definite?"

"Yes."

"I would like to tell you exactly what I'll do for you and Syvvie when you're married."

"Please," he protested. "It isn't necessary."

"Really, Bev! You're too funny today. Now listen will you?"

He nodded obediently.

"You win," he said.

"Syvvie has very little of her own," she began, picking

up her needlepoint again and adjusting her glasses. "Her father was badly off when he died. I believe she has an income of fifteen hundred. I have about two hundred thousand a year from a trust which my father left me which goes outright to Syvvie, Arlie, and Beatrice when I die. There won't be any tax on that either. Then, of course, my husband earns a great deal every year, though most of it goes in income taxes. He doesn't have anything like the capital I have but he has something. By rights he should leave it equally to Arlie and Beatrice, but in view of the fact that they will be so exceedingly well off—really much too much so—when I die he has decided to split it three ways in his will and leave Syvvie a full third."

"Oh, he shouldn't!"

"No, I've consulted Arlie and Beatrice both and left it up to them, and they want it that way."

"Of course they'd give away anything. They're so good."

"Yes, they're good children," she acquiesced, "but it's a sacrifice they'll never notice. Now in addition there's my sister who has no children and whose trust will be divided among all her nephews and nieces when she dies. So you can see, my dear, that even with taxes what they are I can easily afford to guarantee you and Syvvie an income of fifteen thousand a year to be increased as time requires."

Beverly sat back in astonishment and stared at her. There was something wonderful about the way this woman enumerated the items of her wealth, utterly without self-consciousness or false modesty, utterly without pride or even the faintest trace of conceit. She rather enjoyed it, it was true, but it was the enjoyment that a mind like hers could take in any sort of inventory. He could fairly hear the ring of the cash register as she drew her list to a close. And then it was so open and generous; so few people would be so frank to a new "in-law." He felt a little sick about the whole affair and wondered miserably how much the prospect of all this had been in his mind. He had always thought of Syvvie as one of the Strouds but also as a poor relation and though he must have always known that her mother would look after her he had never allowed his mind to play with any definite sums. And now here it was, stripped of equivocation.

"I don't know what to say," he stammered, "—"

She patted his hand.

"Say nothing, my dear. What are parents for anyway?

But promise me this. Promise that money won't stand in the way of your getting married."

He looked at her, his face full of emotion and he felt the tears in his eyes. She smiled so kindly; she was waiting; he knew how impossible it would be not to rise to this.

"I'll tell Syvvie," he burst out, "that we'll get married as soon as I have leave!"

He hurried into the bar and brought them all back with him, and properly symbolical the sun came out at the same time. So they all changed into bathing suits and went to Mrs. Stroud's cabaña and ordered two bottles of champagne. It was a wonderful afternoon. Sylvia was to happy to say much of anything; she sat quietly and smoked an occasional cigarette. Most of the conversation was carried on by her mother and Bev who seemed in the highest spirits; they got together on the topic of everyone they knew and brought each other's gossip up to date. Arlie from time to time would supply information as to this or that friend who had gone to the Far East, and Helena supplied the necessary questions to keep Mrs. Stroud at the height of her form. There was the sea and sun and the sparkle of the wine and everything to make life perfect; to Beverly for the moment it was perfect, and it took the late afternoon with the realization that he had promised Calloriac to be back early to give him a vaguely uneasy feeling that what he had enjoyed was an anodyne, a postponement. When he got out of the Stroud taxi he felt the beginnings or rather the reappearance of his morning headache; he waved good night and walked sadly down the pier.

Pete was sitting in the wardroom when he came in. He looked up and exclaimed:

"Where the hell have you been? Take a gander at that and see if you don't think it's the dirtiest trick you ever saw pulled."

Beverly took the blue dispatch form which Pete handed him. He examined the heading quickly. Yes, it was from the Fifteenth Naval District, addressed to the *Sardonyx:*

"LT. (J.G.) PETER STONER, USNR, 116324, AND LT. (J.G.) BEVERLY STREGELINUS, USNR, 117322, HEREBY DETACHED. PROCEED BY EARLIEST AVAILABLE GOVERNMENT TRANSPORTATION TO BALBOA, C.Z., AND REPORT TO

COM 15. AIR TRANSPORTATION HEREBY AU-
THORIZED."

"They've got the ship's damage report I assume," Pete
went on, "and Darlington wants to make sure we don't get
a chance at two weeks' leave. Typical of the old s.o.b. And
with my wife coming down. God-damn it all!"

Beverly said nothing as he folded up the message. He was
afraid that if he so much as trusted a sound to emerge from
his lips his tone might betray to the other in some unaccountable way no matter what control he exerted, the fact,
the distressing, grisly fact, utterly unanticipated and unwel-
comed by himself, that this news far from filling him with
ponderous and profane chagrin was already seeping through
every pore of his body in a rising tide of relief.

Part IV

Panama

CHAPTER ONE

AUDREY HAD A dull time during the cruise of the *Sardonyx* to Miami. Section Blue lost its atmosphere of gaiety with Beverly gone and Esmond had been transferred to the State Department in Washington for reassignment. She had only seen Bev once after that night at the Union Club and that was on the following Monday morning when he had come into the office to say good-by before leaving for Colón. He had spoken to her very pleasantly and there had been no mention of the bitterness of their Saturday night conversation. He had even promised to write her from the first port he touched, and she found herself in the ennui that followed the termination of those well-ordered dinners at El Rancho hopefully examining her morning mail, but nothing came.

It was entirely possible, she reasoned at first, that they had not stopped at all. Then word came that the ship had gone to Florida and she gave up hope of ever hearing from him again. He would telephone a friend in Washington, she felt sure, and get himself transferred. He would never come back to Panama. She tried to think that she was resigned to it, but the work at the office had never been more tedious and at home Aunt Betty and her mother never more exasperating. Her mind kept revolving on the problem of whether he thought of her with bitterness or never thought of her at all. It was probable, of course, that he really had been offended by her sharp words at the Union Club, but on the other hand he must have realized that his own attitude had been ungracious. What seemed most likely, and it filled her with gloom, was that Pete had bragged about the later events of that evening and that Bev had been shocked to the point of refusing even to correspond. This idea was constantly in her mind. She had been ashamed of what she had done, but it was not a moral shame. It was not the fact that primarily bothered her; it was the place, the time, and the man, the fact that she had been a pushover to an utterly unprincipled person. She felt uneasy when she imagined what the reaction of certain people whom she knew would be: Aunt Betty's gasps and appeals to a virtuous past; Mrs. Livermore's quiet, half-sneer, her "Well, of course. Just what I suspected. Thank heaven, Bev's gone"; Laura's delighted maliciousness, and Beverly's utter disillusionment. For she was sure that despite everything he had respected her and somehow this respect meant more than anything now. It was all very well for her to tell herself fifty times a day that everyone was immoral in time of war, but the ghost of puritanism was not so easily laid. She even felt a return of her sense of guilt towards Helen who was rather prematurely expecting a baby, but after a single visit to this radiantly proud friend she realized with a funny little pang that Helen was far beyond sympathy. Helen was positively smug in her triumph.

Then Laura returned suddenly to the Canal Zone from her grandmother's and lost no time in telling her how she had been out with Bev and a "dreary female" called Sylvia Tremaine.

"They seemed very twosy," she commented. "She's some sort of relation to Arleus Stroud, so I guess there's money. Trust old Bev not to fall on the buttered side!" ·

This put a different face on his silence and her mind was filled with suspicion. She remembered his lofty attitude and wondered suddenly if he had been engaged to this girl before he had come to Panama. But it was hard to believe anything quite so insincere of Bev. He might have fallen suddenly in love with the "dreary female"—not that this thought was much consolation to her—or else, as was the case nine times out of ten, Laura might be entirely mistaken. She brooded over the matter, approaching it from every angle, even viewing it from the standpoint of Bev being truly in love with herself but feeling himself too poor for commitments but she arrived at no satisfactory conclusion. She did discover, however, an interesting sidelight on the *Sardonyx*'s trip one day when she was helping Mr. Gilder open a large stack of official mail.

"I heard some scuttlebut about our absent friends today," he told her with the confidential wink that he always used when dispensing semi-official information to the prettier girls in the office. "Apparently their ship's in Miami for repairs. Think of it. I'll bet they spend every night out at the beach. I've sent a dispatch directing them to return immediately."

"They'll love you for that."

"But there's a war going on. I can't do all the work in this office myself," he protested. "Even with your help," he added with another wink. "Besides, I'd rather not have any of the boys from this office mixed up with that ship at the moment."

"Oh? What's wrong?"

Mr. Gilder glanced over the office to see if anyone was listening.

"Don't noise it about," he told her in an excited semi-whisper impossible to reconcile with his dignity, "but there's something rotten in the state of Denmark up that way. I was just up in the Sea Frontier office and they told me that the Captain of the Naval School in Miami had sent in a bad report on the *Sardonyx*. I gathered it panned Ellis up and down the block."

"Who's Ellis?"

"The skipper. Or perhaps I should say the present skipper."

"What's he done?"

"A little of everything. Sloppy ship, improper watches, that sort of thing."

"Can they hang him for that?"

"Probably not. But if we could get some more it would make a good start."

"We?" she asked in surprise. "Why should *we* be interested?"

Mr. Gilder leaned back in his swivel chair and looked at her with a foxy little smile.

"Now wouldn't you like to know?"

She almost laughed aloud at the way he shifted the burden of curiosity.

"Well, it's not a matter of life and death," she said.

"Ah, but it is!" he exclaimed. "I'll let you in on a little secret, my dear. How much do you think a man of my rank enjoys being stuck in an office like this under a senior officer who—well, let's say has the uncertain temper of advancing years?"

Audrey suddenly did become interested. It had never occurred to her that Mr. Gilder wasn't entirely satisfied with his present job.

"So you want the *Sardonyx!*" she exclaimed.

"Ssh!" He looked around nervously. "Not so loud."

"It's nothing to be ashamed of."

"It isn't, is it?" he answered eagerly. "She's a dandy little ship, very comfortable, and they're going to send her down to Salinas to train Ecuadorean midshipmen. Excellent duty. I know the Chief of Staff will let me have her if Ellis ever gets transferred."

She stared at him with new interest.

"Why, Mr. Gilder," she said, "you're a regular Machiavelli!"

"Now don't go telling everyone," he said fussily, afraid that he had gone too far. "These things take arranging you know. Of course I'm not trying to start any trouble. But if the man is incompetent it's for the good of the Navy that he be replaced, isn't it?"

"Absolutely," she agreed. When later she gathered up her papers and returned to her desk she thought very little more about the matter, reflecting only that it would make a good topic for jokes when Beverly came back.

When Beverly and Pete did return, however, a few days after this conversation had taken place she found herself suffering from constraint with each. She wanted to make it clear to Pete that what had happened before he left was not to be regarded as the opening chapter of a long and cozy relationship, but he gave her no opportunity, greeting her simply with a rather suggestive smile of easy familiarity and going about his business. With Beverly she wanted to be properly aloof until she had a more definite clue to his silence, but it was difficult to be aloof with Beverly. Who else was there in the office to talk to? After a few days moreover she began to be afraid that he was going to be aloof with her; she had to admit to herself that he showed symptoms of shyness of which there had been no trace before. He did not immediately ask her out to dinner as she had rather expected he would to tell her about the trip, nor did he buy her Coca-Colas during the morning with the frequency of old times. Whenever he passed her desk or his eye caught hers across the room he would flash her the old smile, but there was something about the promptness with which he observed this little courtesy that suggested a break of which he was conscious even if he was not in accord with the reasons for it. She wondered if he knew what Pete knew; she wondered about the girl in Miami; she wondered about him in general until she could put up with it no longer. Coming into the office one Saturday morning two weeks after his return and happening to be the first of the girls to arrive she caught him alone, writing his log, for he had been on watch the night before.

"Good morning," she called cheerfully across the room.

"How are you this morning, Audrey?" he asked politely, looking up for a moment to smile at her but going right on with his work.

She went over to his desk.

"What's wrong with you these days?" she demanded. "Don't you love me any more?"

He looked up.

"Whom else?"

"A certain Miss Somebody with very dark hair and very high heels whom Laura saw you with in Miami."

He laughed, but she could see he was blushing.

"Oh, that's my other life."

"Your real one?"

"Well—you know what they say about sailors."

She made a little face.

"She can have you. But later on. Don't drop me. I won't bite."

He got up at this and sat on the edge of his desk looking at her.

"Audrey," he said earnestly, "I'm not dropping you. I'm not that sort. I thought after our tiff at the Union Club you might have had about enough."

"Oh, that." She laughed in relief. "But you see you won. I gave you up." She turned her palms outward in a gesture of withholding nothing.

"I was such a prig. And you were wonderful. I wish I—"

She stopped him by putting her hand up.

"No, Bev. Let's not go into it. Let's just be friends."

"What about the beach tomorrow morning? It's Sunday."

"I'll be there."

He finished up his log and went back to his quarters to sleep after his watch, but even after pulling down all the shades and tying a pair of black socks over his eyes he found that although his body was relaxed his mind was still racing up and down over the topic of this little conversation.

Audrey drove her Pontiac over to the beach at ten o'clock the following morning. The strip of sand which they all used was on an island off Fort Amador reached by a road that passed over the top of a long breakwater. It was a pleasant fifteen minute drive from naval headquarters with a very blue sea on either side and the high hills of the bay islands looming ahead. That morning an aircraft carrier, a heavy cruiser, and three destroyers having transited the Canal during the night were standing out to sea, and Audrey watching their great bows slide through the water felt one of her rare moments of pride at the importance of the little isthmus to which she had been so long confined.

When she had arrived at the little club house and changed into her blue and white bathing suit, she strolled down on the beach looking for the office crowd. Someone waved at her. It was Pete, sprawled out by himself on the sand in a rather ridiculous pair of bathing trunks with red and black dots. She waved back and went over and sat down by him. It was still early; there couldn't have been more than a dozen couples on the beach and perhaps twenty children; the raft was empty and beyond it she could see the lifeguard rowing his little boat lazily out towards the protective shark net on which a row of large grey pelicans were quietly perched.

"Where's everybody?" she asked.

"Oh, they'll be along," Pete drawled. "Amos makes Beverly go to church."

She nodded in approval.

"That's where we all should be."

"Even atheists?"

"Are you an atheist?"

"I am."

"You don't believe in an after life?" As usual the idea appalled her.

He laughed at the serious pucker on her brow.

"Isn't one enough?" he asked. "I'm not so greedy. Heaven must be full of Amoses and Beverlys."

"What do you mean by that?"

Pete rolled over on his stomach and propped his chin on his hands. He squinted up at her.

"I mean, my chick," he continued in his lazy tone, "that heaven is for people who don't live in this life. People like that dried up Boston bean and that New York geranium. If they miss heaven they'll have missed everything."

Audrey thought this over with a little shudder.

"But you of course have your heaven here," she retorted after a moment. "Or wherever your wife doesn't happen to be."

"Ow!" He ducked his big head, the defensive, crushed mien on his countenance that he loved to adopt with women. "Why are you like that, Audrey?" Then he reached over and tickled the bottom of her foot. She drew it away quickly.

"Don't!" she snapped. "Behave yourself."

"I'm not going to get fresh," he said. "You needn't worry. I know you 'virtuous' girls," he continued with a sneer. "What are you going to look for in heaven?"

"You'd be too earthy to understand."

"I guess I was earthy enough for you on one certain occasion a few weeks past."

She stared at him in disgust.

"What a low personage you really are, Pete," she said cuttingly. "I don't suppose I need answer that. I just don't suppose you'd understand."

He rolled over on his back and put one arm over his eyes. He was smiling still but he said nothing.

"You know, Miss Emerson," he said at last in a tone of reflective speculation, "I guess you're about the most disagreeable girl I've ever known. What men see in you is a mystery to me. You've got a nasty temper, you're a snob—"

But his inventory of characteristics was interrupted by the arrival of Amos and Bev, already in bathing trunks, who sat down on the sand beside them, the former concealing a thermos bottle of mixed Bacardis and paper cups under his towel.

"I see," said Pete, "that you've brought the communion cup."

Amos had already started pouring.

"But only for believers," he retorted. "The heathen have

no right to divine refreshment. How about you, Audrey?" He offered her a drink.

"No thanks."

"I've seen everything now," Pete drawled possessing himself of the rejected cup. "Someone from the Naval Information Office refusing a drink."

Amos poured cups for himself and Bev.

"Mr. Stoner is very insulting today," Audrey said in a flat voice.

"Mr. Stoner is always insulting!" Bev exclaimed wondering what had preceded their arrival to cause the set look on her face. "As our poor, dear, helpless friend, Laura, discovered when she went out with him in Miami."

"Indeed?"

"Helpless!" cried Pete rubbing his shins. "That girl ought to be a marine!"

"Mr. Stoner," observed Audrey, "has all the subtlety of a Neanderthal."

"Beverly's one to talk about what went on in Miami," Pete retorted.

"Oh?"

"And pray what do you mean by that?" Bev demanded.

"Helling around with Ellis. Up all night." Pete turned to the others and winked.

"Very interesting," Audrey commented.

"Ah, sea duty," exclaimed Amos. "Why don't they send me to sea!"

Audrey watched him finish his drink.

"You're doing all right here," she said.

"Amos ought to be made skipper of the U.S.S. *Bacardi*," suggested Pete.

"Of course all this is very amusing," broke in the exasperated Bev. "And completely untrue. My conduct in Miami was faultless to the highest degree. It—"

"I admit you ended up well," interrupted Pete. "You finally did sow your wild oats." He turned to the other two. "He must have finally decided that the wild life was too much for him and it was time he settled down. That's why he got engaged."

Audrey pressed the bridge of her sunglasses tight against her nose.

"Oh, did you get engaged?" she heard herself ask him. Again she could see he was blushing.

"As a matter of fact I did."

"To Miss Tremaine?"

"To Miss Tremaine."

"I'm afraid my congratulations are a little bit late. Why didn't you tell me?"

"Well, you see, it isn't to be announced for a while."

"Of course. Naturally I won't tell."

"I guess Pete's told about everyone already."

"What a friend Pete is."

"Hey now!" Pete protested. "I didn't know it was a secret."

Amos felt the uneasiness in the atmosphere and made an effort to change the conversation.

"This Ellis must have given you quite a time up in Miami," he said.

"He gave us all the liberty we wanted," Beverly answered.

"Himself included," added Pete. "I don't suppose he ever saw his ship while we were there except when he was leaving to go on liberty. He was too blind when he came back."

"Really?"

"He's a disgrace, Amos. A disgrace to the Navy."

Pete said this seriously and Bev was surprised.

"Come now, Pete. What do you mean?"

"What the hell do you think I mean? Women on board all night."

"Tsk! Tsk!" said Audrey looking at Pete.

"I'm no puritan," he said shaking his head, "but when it comes to ships I draw the line." He was sincere in this. Pete had the highly departmentalized mind where virtue and vice were concerned that for centuries has characterized the bourgeoisie. Life was business and life was sex but never simultaneously.

"How do you know?" Bev demanded.

"Are you kidding? When he asks a floozy on board after midnight and disappears below?"

"A charming fellow," said Audrey. "No wonder people love him so."

Pete turned to her.

"Listen, Audrey," he said, "that guy would do anything. He was gumming up the repair work on the ship so he'd have more time in Miami. I wouldn't be surprised to hear that she'd sunk at the dock."

"Oh, Pete!" Bev protested.

"I mean it. Why are you sticking up for him? I suppose

he was polite to you in the wardroom? I suppose you thought he behaved like a hero during that submarine alert?"

"No," Bev admitted. "He was yellow. But what do you expect of a guy who goes into the Navy at the age of seventeen? Think of his background."

Pete jumped on this.

"I see," he said sarcastically. "He never went to Chelton. He never went to Yale. *Ergo,* he must be a coward and a louse. How can he help it?"

"No I don't mean that. I mean he was so young when he went in—"

"He was a rat when he went in," Pete interrupted brusquely, "and he's a rat now. You can't get away from it."

"He may be a rat but whose fault is it?"

"Gentlemen!" exclaimed Amos. "Keep your voices down. This is not the way to be talking about your former commanding officer on a naval beach."

They all looked around at this.

"Nobody can hear us, Amos," Bev said. "And Audrey knows better than to repeat this sort of talk."

"I live with secret and confidential material," she said. "And as a matter of fact I haven't heard anything I didn't know."

When the men went in swimming she simply lay on the beach alone and looked up at the sky. It was like being alone on a long platform at the station after a train has pulled out, a train filled with vociferous, vacation-minded friends. It was like standing in front of a broken Coca-Cola machine with a useless nickel. It was like—nothing. It was Panama. There was not really any pain but a deadness, as if some tissues about her heart had atrophied and only reminded her of their continuing presence by the felt pressure of their heavy if decaying weight. She had never known desolation so utter and complete.

She stayed on at the beach after the other three had left —junior officers in information had to work on alternate Sunday afternoons—and lunched disconsolately by herself on a sandwich. She was still there at two o'clock when Mr. Gilder strode down the beach, resplendent in white trunks and a dark sun tan. He came over and settled himself with dignity on the sand beside her. His talk was full of an embassy dinner that he had been to the night before. Apparently Mrs. Livermore's curiosity had at last got the best of her and she had included Mrs. Schmidt in the party.

"Esmond would have enjoyed it so," he told her. "I wish he was still here."

Audrey frowned. Dinners at the embassy were the last thing she wanted to hear about.

"It's nice to have Beverly back," he said.

"Is it?"

"Don't you think so?" he asked in surprise.

"It makes very little difference to me where Beverly is."

"Oh." He hesitated, but she could see that he was consumed with curiosity. "I always thought that there was something there between you two."

"Not any more."

He looked baffled but tried again.

"I suppose you and he didn't quite see eye to eye on certain things."

"That's true I'm sure, Mr. Gilder," she answered a bit sharply, stung at last into further explanation. "But I might as well tell you that that had nothing to do with it. Beverly did ask me to marry him and I declined."

Gilder sat up in surprise.

"But why? I should have thought it was an excellent match."

She felt his genuine bewilderment and her irritation subsided.

"Maybe," she conceded. "If I only hadn't been so wildly in love with you." She picked up a handful of sand as he snickered at this.

"No. Be serious."

She thought for a moment and let the sand run between her fingers.

"Oh, why do we do anything we do?" As she looked at his confused, handsome, empty face all her own thoughts, once so clear, collapsed in an absurd little mess. She had been living on theory and this was her reward, the hard, glaring, empty Isthmus. Sheridan Gilder. How could he ever understand her jumble of pros and cons? She continued her pointless lie. "I thought it was rather noble of me to let him go at the time," she continued. "But I guess some people are beyond such gestures. They can't live up to them. Like me."

"Well I'm glad you're still available, Audrey," he said comfortingly.

"But I'm not glad!" she exclaimed with sudden vehemence. "What sort of a life is it?" She lay back on the sand with a wild, trapped feeling. "You know how it is. With Daddy so old and dull, yes dull, Sheridan—you know he bores you to distraction—and Aunt Betty so alcoholic—"

Gilder looked shocked and then giggled.

"She does tipple," he observed.

"I'll say she does." With a sort of fierce satisfaction she threw discretion to the winds. "She lolls around the house uselessly and complains about the heat. Then a big swig every so often and she's off on a series of meandering reminiscences about beautiful old 'homes' with Mother supplying a kind of dirgical chorus. Sometimes I wish I were dead."

But Gilder was only shaking with laughter.

"Go on, Audrey. This is a panic."

She paused but only for a moment.

"I hope I'm not embarrassing you," she said in a tone of absolute indifference. "I guess I'm just desperate today. But after all, Sheridan, who can I ever marry down here?"

"Anyone you choose."

She reached over and squeezed his hand.

"You're an absolute dear. And if it weren't for all these people around who know you're a lieutenant-commander I'd give you a kiss. You're the only person down here who treats me like a human being," she continued bitterly, as her mood sharpened. "As for that screaming, social-climbing flower with his darling ambassadress and his drivel, drivel—"

"You don't mean Beverly!" he exclaimed with a shout of laughter.

"Yes, I mean Beverly. Sea-going Beverly." She snorted. "Gossiping, interfering, desk-ridden Beverly. Not that there's anything wrong with desk work," she added in sudden compunction. "A man like you, Sheridan, who's been to sea and who's a little older than the others obviously has to spend some time in an administrative position. But Beverly! That little convoy trip was just perfect, wasn't it? Short and safe and spicy, and now he can tell everybody he's been to sea!"

Gilder produced a pipe from a little canvas pouch that he carried and started carefully to fill it with tobacco.

"So long as you really don't like Beverly," he said in an easy, satisfied tone, "you might be interested to know that he and his darling ambassadress, as you call her, had their heads together about you."

Audrey sat up suddenly and stared at him.

"What?"

"I heard them talking about you at the Union Club one Saturday night. She asked him if you were with him and he said no. Then she congratulated him. And, Lord, how he smirked!"

She turned away from him, her pulse pounding. Her hand reached out, almost instinctively, as if in search of a weapon.

"Are you sure?"

"I tell you I heard him." He looked at her in sudden alarm. "Now don't go running and tell him I told you. I can't have a lot of office feuds!"

"Don't worry." The picture of Bev and Mrs. Livermore laughing at her, discussing her as if she were a nervous habit that he had to be cured of throbbed side by side in her inflamed mind with the memory of his sanctimonious attitude. God! And then as she looked at Gilder and the worried expression of his foolish face, she remembered in a sudden, inspired flash what he was after and what Beverly had said. "Sheridan," she said, "I want to tell you something."

CHAPTER TWO

AUDREY WAS NOT altogether comfortable when she got home that afternoon, and the full realization of what she had done dug into her. There would be an investigation now or a court-martial; of this there could be no doubt. Gilder was not a man to let such an opportunity slip. Pete and Beverly would have to repeat their casual gossip before some kind of legal board and would have to make it good. She had no doubt that they could prove their statements; she would have been horrified had she been told that possibly they couldn't. Her only thought had been to stick them both with the discomfort of going through with the legal form; it boiled down really to the fact that she had told because Beverly had told her not to. She had not stopped to visualize the full potentialities of the situation's unpleasantness. At home she mixed a stiffer than usual cocktail for herself and Aunt Betty and tried to believe that she didn't care if Beverly never spoke to her again.

Nevertheless, when she saw the foxy look that Mr. Gilder was wearing the next morning she became more nervous than ever. And when at ten o'clock the Chief of Staff of the Sea Frontier, the grey-haired, hook-nosed, dictatorial Captain Michalis entered Captain Darlington's office followed by a lieutenant whom she recognized as the assistant legal officer of the district, her heart almost stopped. Then Mr. Gilder went in and closed the door. For forty-five minutes nobody entered or left the Captain's office. At a quarter to eleven Mr. Gilder opened the door into Section Blue and called to one of the yeomen.

"Ask Mr. Stregelinus and Mr. Stoner to come in, please."

For a moment she struggled with a desire to rush in and tell them it was her fault, that she had lied abominably. Then she decided she couldn't bear it and went out to get a Coca-Cola.

Neither Beverly nor Pete suspected their betrayal when

they went into the office but they could immediately see that something out of the usual was brewing. Captain Michalis was a sea-going man who much resented his present shore assignment; he hated the Naval Information Office and hated Captain Darlington, calling the latter the Navy's "arch paper shuffler," and never went near him if it could be helped. As he was junior only to the Admiral he didn't have to fear Darlington as the rest of the District did and his contempt seemed sufficiently expressed by the way he lolled in the swivel chair drawn up by Darlington's desk, his shirt open at the neck, his fingers drumming on the arms. Mr. Gilder and the legal lieutenant stood respectfully behind the two captains' chairs like a pair of butlers.

"I have called you in here, gentlemen," began Captain Darlington in the low, purring voice with which he always commenced a dangerous interview—dangerous that is for the visitor—"to ask you a few simple questions in the presence of Captain Michalis. I need hardly state that he will expect answers that are accurate." Here he glanced around at the Chief of Staff with a small nod. "I wish you to state whether or not you have any complaint to lodge with reference to the conduct of Lieutenant William Ellis, United States Navy, as commanding officer of the U.S.S. *Sardonyx* during the time that you were aboard that vessel on her recent cruise to Miami."

Beverly drew a quick sharp breath but was afraid to glance at Pete.

"None, sir," he said.

"Mr. Stoner is senior," snapped Darlington. "Let him answer first."

Pete was silent.

"I have no complaint, sir," he said at last.

"In your opinion he performed his duties properly?" the Captain pursued.

"So far as I could see, sir," Pete answered.

"Yes, sir," said Beverly.

Captain Michalis gave a snort at this and turned around to glare at Mr. Gilder.

"Then, Mr. Stoner," continued Darlington, an ugly rasp appearing in his tone, "you will perhaps be good enough to explain certain quoted remarks of yours to the effect that Mr. Ellis was—" here the Captain glanced at a sheet of paper—" 'a disgrace to the Navy,' 'a coward,' and a man who committed irregular acts aboard ship?"

Beverly glanced sideways at the thick reddening neck of his companion, the firm solid set about the jaws. Pete seemed as hard and motionless as a mass of mineral, and Bev watching him almost forgot for a second the sickening impact of Audrey's treachery. He knew what was going through Pete's mind. Pete was weighing his chances. If he decided that he could substantiate his statements he would reassert them and attempt ruthlessly to crush Ellis. If not, he might deny making them at all. In any case truth would count for nothing.

"May I know who quoted me, sir?" Pete asked.

"You may answer the question," snapped the Captain.

Pete seemed, almost imperceptibly, to stiffen.

"I made those remarks, sir, and they are true."

"I see," snarled Darlington. "And what about your earlier statement that you had no complaint to make? Or do you think a man such as you described is a proper commanding officer?"

"I didn't want to see a fellow naval officer get in trouble."

"That's sometimes inevitable, Lieutenant," Captain Michalis interrupted in a booming voice. "At any rate it's much better to make such remarks to the proper authorities than to go spreading them around in public. Of course if the remarks are untrue it's inexcusable."

"The remarks were true, sir," Pete answered now fully repossessed of his confidence. "It is my opinion that Lieutenant Ellis is a coward and unfit for command and I am prepared to testify to that effect. I regret extremely, sir, having made the statement 'in public,' as you put it, but to tell the truth at the time that I made it I was among people all of whom were connected with the Navy and supposedly trained in handling secret and confidential material."

There seemed to be a general feeling in the room that Pete had reestablished himself.

"Well, that's all right I guess," said Captain Michalis nodding at him. "As to your testifying I'm afraid that it will be necessary. I have decided upon a board of investigation. The *Sardonyx* arrived in Balboa yesterday."

Captain Darlington looked up at Beverly now who stared straight back at him. He felt an independence that he had never felt before. The thought of Audrey, her tales and her lover, of Pete's ugly hardness, the sight of Sherry Gilder's small lips so primly closed and of old Darlington's mean little eyes were enough to decide him. It was with a certain exhilaration that he planned his response.

"Mr. Stregelinus," Captain Darlington was saying. "You are quoted as having been in essential agreement with Lieutenant Stoner."

"But I was not, sir."

"How's that?"

"I did not agree with Lieutenant Stoner's opinion of Lieutenant Ellis."

Captain Darlington glanced again at his notes.

"I understand, Mr. Stregelinus," he said icily, "that you said Lieutenant Ellis was 'yellow,' a quality that you attributed to his long enlistment in the United States Navy."

The assistant legal officer gave a little gasp.

"It appears that Miss Emerson had a dictaphone concealed on her person," Bev answered almost cheerfully.

"Do you realize that you are insolent?" shouted Darlington.

"I'm sorry, sir."

"Did you make the quoted remark?"

"Some such remark, sir."

"And do you now retract it?"

"It was made, sir, without serious consideration at a time when I thought I was among friends and allowed myself, I fear, to talk a bit glibly."

Here Captain Michalis interrupted.

"Do you realize, sir," he thundered, "the impropriety of making such remarks about your former commanding officer?"

But Bev felt strangely uncowed.

"I do, sir," he answered quietly. "But it's better, is it not, to confess my exaggeration and foolishness now than to get another officer into serious trouble?"

"You persist in your good opinion of Ellis?" Michalis snapped.

"I didn't say it was a good opinion, sir. I said that the remarks made about him were never meant to be taken seriously. I have no complaints to lodge at his door."

Captain Darlington threw up his hands.

"All I can say is you're in a pretty pickle, Stregelinus," he snapped. "Calling an officer a coward and then saying it was all in fun. You'll hear more of this. Go on back to your work. Stoner, you wait here."

As he walked slowly back through Section Blue he saw

Audrey coming in the doorway. She looked very scared and white and said nothing as he passed her and went out into the passageway. But a moment later he heard her behind him.

"Bev," she said, "what happened?"

He turned and looked down in her wide brown eyes.

"How could you?"

"Could what?"

"How could you?" he repeated.

She stared at his blank distant face.

"I didn't know what I was doing," she cried nervously. "Mr. Gilder told me something about you and Mrs. Livermore conspiring about me and I got mad. I didn't know what I was doing," she repeated. "Bev, is it so bad? Tell me, Bev."

He looked at her incredulously and then shook his head slightly as though to wake himself up.

"Don't speak to me," he said and went on down the stairs.

It was his day to act as officer messenger and he spent the afternoon being driven around in a station wagon from army post to army post, his lap filled with large sealed envelopes. All through his body there was a funny numb feeling. Mechanically he collected the initials on the receipts at his different stops and uttered those routine humorisms of greeting and departure that make speaking American so effortless a proposition. It was a day of equal levels. Even Audrey's abominable treachery seemed drab and matter of fact. That was just the way people were and what was the point of getting mad at them? Audrey and Gilder and Pete and Captain Darlington. They couldn't really help their appetites; it was their destiny to gobble away at the cellar walls until the attic fell in. Not with a crash but in a cloud of dust like an Egyptian mummy or a deep sea fish suddenly exposed to the air. As Mr. T. S. Eliot would put it, "with a whimper." The fact that the vision of Audrey filled him with distaste in no way rekindled his dying thoughts of Sylvia. The fact that Panama seemed such a little belt of evil in no way revived his nostalgia for New York. It was the sense of sameness and lowness in things that oppressed him. His mind kept throbbing with *The Waste Land* and the "red sullen faces" sneering "from doors of mud cracked houses." It was a poem that he had thoroughly explored by his standards. But he had still been far from understanding it; such a bleak picture of modern aridity had not been sympathetic to his way of thinking. Now, he found, the haunting rhythms of those lines kept returning to him. Surely these people fitted more into Eliot's world than they did to his own former vision of actuality. But, after all, did it matter so terribly? There was a remedy.

They were now driving back to naval headquarters.

"Driver, leave me off at Pier 18," he said. It was already after three and he had finished his deliveries. There was no point in going back to the office. He hopped out and passing through the gate strolled down along the piers to look for the *Sardonyx*.

It was not long before he spotted her tied up outboard of a large mine sweep and he hurried across the two gangways.

"Is the Captain aboard?" he asked the gangway watch.
"Yes, sir."

In the wardroom he found Calloriac reading a magazine.
"Stregelinus! How are you? Back for another cruise?"
"I wish I was," Bev answered. "Is the skipper in his room?"
"Where else? He was up at the District this morning and came back in a foul mood. Go ahead down if you want."

Below he found the door of Ellis' room half open and through it in the dark he could make out the Captain's figure in underwear reclining on the large bed. "Captain," he said.
"Uh?"
"It's Lieutenant Stregelinus. Can I talk to you?"

Ellis reached up and turned on the light over the bed. He squinted at the figure in the doorway, and Beverly noticed the tired hostile look on his face.

"What do you want?"
"May I come in and sit down?"

Ellis grunted, and Bev taking this for assent closed the door behind him and sat down on a chair by the bed.

"I wondered if you'd been up to the Sea Frontier office yet," he began.
"Why?"
"I thought I might be able to be of some assistance to you."
"How?"
"If you were in any sort of trouble."

Ellis' brow was puckered with suspicion.
"What makes you think I'm in trouble?" he snapped.
"Because I was interviewed by the Chief of Staff this

morning," Bev answered calmly. "He wanted to know if I had any criticisms to make of your conduct during the last cruise."

Ellis scowled even more deeply.

"I suppose you had a nice little story for him."

"On the contrary, I said I had none."

The man on the bed looked at him blankly.

"I thought you were the guy that tipped him off," he said in surprise.

"Well, I wasn't," Bev retorted. "You can give that credit to Mr. Stoner. I may have made a remark or so privately that was misconstrued but officially I have stated my belief in your competence."

Ellis didn't quite follow this but the expression on his face softened.

"Well—thanks," he said. Then he sat up abruptly. "Stoner did you say?" he cried angrily. "The son of a bitch! What did I ever do to him?"

"He didn't mean to really," Bev explained. "He made some remarks which got repeated." He paused. "If you don't believe me you can ask Captain Michalis, you know."

"That bastard. Sure I believe you." And here Bill Ellis' features suddenly relaxed into that lazy smile that was so unexpected a part of his attractions. It was a smile that seemed to say, as its wearer always said, "What the hell?" just when things seemed most confused and tempers most excited. It was certainly not devoid of charm; it made him seem pleasant and boyish. "But so what?" he asked. "What's your angle?"

"I thought I could help. They seem to be ganging up on you."

"You're telling me!"

"Have you seen Michalis?"

"I saw him this morning. I'm going to be relieved by a guy called Gilder. A lieutenant-commander. And then there's going to be an investigation. They'll probably hang me. Let 'em."

Beverly gasped. Even in his wildest imaginings he had not supposed Gilder capable of this.

"Did you say Gilder?" he asked.

"Yeah. Works in your office I think."

"He certainly does. Captain, what are you going to do?"

Ellis shrugged his shoulders and reached for a cigarette. "A hell of a lot I can do," he said morosely. "What chance have I got? A mustang. Why they spit at guys like me."

Bev produced the idea now that had been lurking in the back of his mind.

"Nonsense!" he exclaimed. "We'll fight them. I'll be your counsel."

"Aw, what's the use? You don't know those guys like I do."

Ellis was rapidly sinking into complete defeatism. Bev got up and walked around the cabin.

"I'm learning," he said excitedly. "Let me defend you, will you? I had a year in law school and I've been taking a correspondence course in naval law." He didn't add that he had only completed three assignments. "I know I'm not too good but the point is I know the whole dirty deal in this case and I'll make it stink all the way to Washington!"

Ellis looked at him with a vague curiosity.

"Why do you care? How do I know you're really on my side?"

"You've *got* to believe me," Bev insisted firmly. "I tell you, it's your only chance."

Ellis looked at his watch and got up. He slipped into a shirt and buttoned it slowly.

"I don't know what you're up to, Stregelinus," he said after a few moments, "but if you want to help me I'm sure as hell not going to stop you. I know one thing. I could do with a friend in this naval district."

"Then it's a deal?"

"What?"

"My defending you in the investigation?"

"Do I have to have a lawyer at a board of investigation?"

Bev laughed.

"You don't have to," he said. "But it doesn't hurt. Much."

Ellis shrugged his shoulders.

"Have it your way, partner," he said.

As Bev walked back up the dock towards the main gate his heart was pounding, but this time he knew it was exhilaration. There was surely only one clear road to take and the finger was pointing to it with remorseless clarity. It would ruin him to be sure; he got a pleasure almost sadistic as he visualized the fury that would sweep over the office and burst on his own head. It would mean disgrace and probably transfer to some Pacific atoll; it might mean worse things for there was no telling what Darlington might not do when aroused; but wasn't this the best way after all, after the commission so politically pursued, after the falseness of his hankering for sea duty and his play acting with Sylvia, after the years of non-living in a jungle of about-to-be-purchased canvases, wasn't it best—even if it did smack of false heroics, and what if it did?—to jump down off the plane of the observer and do or rather be one real and unappreciated thing?

He turned out the main gate and wandered into the little town center of Balboa but he couldn't make up his mind to go back to his quarters. He wanted to· talk to a friend, but who was there now? Lydia would never understand his mood. Amos? No, Amos would be horrified. Gladys. Yes, Gladys might see. He hailed a taxi and directed the driver to the American Embassy in Panama City.

Mrs. Livermore sat back in her wicker chair and stirred her tea with a gesture of preoccupation. She was sitting alone with Beverly on the veranda; she had by rare chance nothing else at the moment to do and she should according to her usual formula have been having a pleasant time. But her jaw, usually so firmly set, was relaxed into what might almost have been called a suppressed yawn and her eyes wandered. Really, what *was* Beverly talking about?

"But if you say the man isn't worth saving anyway," she said vaguely, "I don't quite see—"

"That's just it!" he interrupted excitedly. "He isn't. That's just the beauty of it."

"Beauty—?"

"He's so rotten. But he's so misused. Which means if I save him I won't get any credit for it. I won't even be sure in my own heart if I've done the right thing!" He was leaning forward in his chair, his eyes big with enthusiasm. "Gladys, if you only knew what was going on. It's not Ellis I'm really worried about. It's the filthy way that the gold braid is trying to get rid of him."

Gladys, however, was not a person lightly to espouse the cause of the trampled. Hers was a background of "tramplers," and her faith in "whatever was" was strong. The Army, the Navy, the Diplomatic Corps, the police were to her the legs, spindly perhaps but still the legs, on which her money rested. She didn't doubt that her money would survive their crumpling but so long as they were there, there they were. Where did one get by pulling them apart?

"I can hardly believe that the Navy would be so down on him without a very good reason."

"There is a good reason. Somebody else wants his job."

"But if he's not fit to handle it——"

"That's not the point. And anyway, I believe he can. The point is, how can one stand by and watch such things going on without doing something about it?"

Gladys did not like this form of approach at all. Beverly had always been one of her most reliable dinner guests; he could be counted on for humor and occasionally wit. Decidedly it was going to be different if he was turning into a Buchmanite. She recalled now her husband's criticism of his manner of speaking about Latin-American relations.

"People have always walked over other people, I suppose," she said a bit wearily. "I think you've picked a rather poor issue to make a stand on."

This was undeniable.

"I've got to find myself," he said rather incoherently. "It isn't what you do, like fighting in a war or asking someone to marry you or making money. It's what you are. The inner life—it—that's what living is."

She stared at him with rising impatience.

"Really, Bev. Try to make some sense."

"I am!"

"Don't be so extreme about it all."

"That's the old tradition," he said with sudden rudeness. "Nothing in excess. That was America. But it meant nothing *worth while* in excess. It meant not too much beauty or art or love. It never applied to money!"

At this Gladys mentally but irrevocably crossed him off her list. He knew it though. He was perfectly aware of her hostility, just as he was aware of the Ambassador lurking in the living room waiting till he should have gone before rejoining his wife. He was aware also that he had never existed for them as a person with problems and a heart. They had such friends, to be sure, among their contemporaries but he was not one of them. He was Beverly, the extra man, the person one giggled with as the cocktails were passed around. And for all he knew it had probably been the same way everywhere. Somehow he made his escape from the house; somehow he got back to his quarters.

"I want to congratulate you on your new command, Mr.

Gilder," he told the head of Section Blue later that evening when he got him on the telephone. "I just heard."

"Oh, thank you, Bev," the other purred back. "And about this morning. I was very sorry. I had no idea you'd go back on what you said. I hadn't meant to get you in dutch."

"Well, we'll fight it out in court. It ought to be fun."

"We?"

"Yes. Bill Ellis has asked me to defend him."

"What? You can't do that!"

"It has already been cleared through the legal office."

Gilder hardly had the receiver back on the hook before he was dialing Captain Darlington's number. Breathlessly he told the old man the news.

"You idiot, Gilder!" came the angry retort. "You've done it again! Don't you ever get anything right? Well, it's your fight this time. I won't be involved in it."

"Can't you stop him, Captain?"

"Stop him? Certainly not. How can I stop him?"

"But it's so outrageous. So disloyal."

"The disloyalty I am quite aware of, Mr. Gilder," the old man snarled. "I'll take care of that. Afterwards. But this investigation is all your affair. I wash my hands of it."

Mr. Gilder was about to protest once more but he heard the decisive click from the other end and sadly he placed his phone back on the receiver.

CHAPTER THREE

LOCATED IN BACK of Navy Headquarters on a rough grass lot adjoining the neat cultivated area assigned to quarters for lieutenant-commanders and those of higher rank was a small frail structure called the "Recreation Hut." It was nothing but a wooden pavilion, a shingle roof supported by poles and completely screened. Inside was an old upright piano, a large victrola-radio, a ping-pong table with a string across the center to serve as a net, and an odd assortment of wicker chairs and tables. It had formerly been used by enlisted personnel but since the erection recently of a much larger and better equipped building on the other side of the Headquarters, it had fallen into abandonment and was already earmarked for destruction as soon as the plans for a bomb-proof operations office that was to occupy its site should be complete.

In the meanwhile it was a handy place for the courts-martial and boards of investigation which took up so much of the District's time, and it was here that at eight o'clock a few days after the happening of the preceding events a commander, a lieutenant-commander, and a lieutenant gathered at one end of the oblong table that served as the bar of justice. They constituted the board of investigation convened by the admiral-commandant to inquire into the conduct of one Lieutenant William S. Ellis, USN, and to determine whether during the recent trip of the U.S.S. *Sardonyx* to Miami, Florida, and during said vessel's period of availability in said port he had shown himself to be unfit for his command by his behavior on the bridge during general quarters, and whether he had furthermore shown himself to be unfit by delaying the accomplishment of ship's repairs and by bringing women on board at night for lewd and immoral purposes. The yeoman first class who was to act as reporter was arranging pads of paper, pencils and copies of *Navy Courts and Boards* on the table.

The senior member, Commander Leslie Benson, USN, a tall straight man with receding sandy hair and a well-trimmed mustache which he was always fingering, sat at the head of the table. There was no conversation. He sat there waiting for things to get started, one hand on his mustache, the other firmly on the table to maintain the balance of his tilted-back chair, his grey eyes staring absently across the room. He despised courts and boards; he despised Panama, and for that matter he pretty much despised the two other members of the board, Lieutenant-Commander Cheney, the Chief of Staff's favorite, and the officious, bright-eyed, stout Lieutenant Stowell whose delights in points of etiquette and points of law had made him the favorite choice of the legal office for junior member. But Commander Benson's dislikes though evident in the coldness of his manner and the harshness of his tone were not of a demonstrative nature. He had learned to take Panama in his stride and to go through the pattern of a life which disgusted him through the application of a self-discipline as rugged as any found among the tragic heroes of Corneille. For his was a tragic story.

He had graduated from the Naval Academy seventeen years before with a love for the Navy that was almost idolatrous. His very personal ambition had been blended with this love and when promotion had come half his pleasure had lain in the increased opportunity of contribution. He had always been quiet and humorless, but his fellow officers did not have to become intimates in order to discover the deep kindness of his nature and the courage of his soul. His rise was steady and his future seemed assured; his work for fifteen years was totally satisfactory. And then just before the war, as navigator of a new heavy cruiser the then Lieutenant-Commander Benson had been responsible for the ship's going aground off the coast of California, an accident which though it cost the vessel only a few weeks of dry dock repairs was decisively fatal to the navigator's career. He had made no elaborate defense; he had admitted the erroneous fix which had caused the accident. He knew it was the crime unpardonable to touch the hull of a capital ship to submarine earth and he uttered no complaint at what he knew would be his fate. He lost no numbers; he received no court-martial; he was even, in fact, promoted to Commander a year after the war began. But he had been stationed for the past two years, ever since the fatal day, not in the turbulent waters of the Far East where his heart had been every instant since Pearl Harbor, but with implications so deadening to a man of his caliber in the Naval Ammunition Depot of the Isthmus of Panama. He had done his job well and the District had reported of him favorably to Washington. There was even hope for a transfer. But a life sustained entirely by a sense of duty has its effect on personality. He never under any circumstances smiled. He had become incapable of small talk and was rarely to be seen except in his office or his quarters. And he was impatient with those who worked for him. He turned suddenly now to Stowell, the junior member and recorder.

"Go and round these people up, will you? Let's not be here all day."

Stowell hurried out of the hut with a quick "Aye, aye, sir." The Commander knew perfectly well that he wouldn't hurry things up any, but it relieved him to send people to and fro.

"I think this should be an interesting case, Commander," Cheney began. "I've thought for a long time that we ought to do something about checking up on our sea frontier skippers. Some of these guys have been getting away with murder—"

"I don't choose to discuss the subject before we're convened," Benson interrupted roughly. Cheney shut his jaws with a click and eyed his senior malignantly. Nobody could be quite as rude as Benson, he reflected, but Benson might live to regret it. Even a commander might some day need something from the Chief of Staff. So many of the regulars failed to appreciate that all reserves weren't alike, that there were any number of lieutenant-commanders but only one Hiram Cheney. They'd learn.

Benson picked up his copy of *Courts and Boards* and scanned the pages on boards. It was wearying but familiar stuff, the type of extra duty that he continually drew, for it was well known in the District that the Ammunition Depot was overstaffed. He had sat on perhaps thirty boards or courts in the past two years with offenses varying from unstenciled clothing to rape. The shore Navy passed before him and he judged it, conscientiously and fairly but with little if any compassion. His mind and heart were always a thousand miles off. And now the commanding officer of a ship, a man who was lucky enough to have sea duty even if only in the Caribbean, was apparently mixed up in some filthy mess. He puckered his brow. Strange how ungrateful people were. There had been none of this on that sparkling day when the cruiser, *Montauk*, had pulled up her hook and sailed for San Francisco. He could still hear the rhythmical clamp-clamp of her chain as each link ascended to the hawse pipe.

The screen door opened with a twang and Stowell returned followed by Ellis and Beverly. Ellis was very pale and nervous; he had a khaki overseas cap tightly clutched in one hand and a pad of paper in the other.

"Good morning," the Commander said gruffly. "You can sit down at the other end of the table. You're Ellis, aren't you?"

"Yes, sir."

"What are you doing here, Stregelinus?" Benson went on.

"I'm Mr. Ellis' counsel, sir."

"Oh. Well, you sit beside him. Are we about set?"

Stowell hurried to his seat on the Commander's left, and the yeoman with his shorthand pad sat down at the center of the table dividing the board from the defendant.

"Board meets," Benson announced. "Enter that as 0820," he added to the yeoman, "and put in the 'those present' later. Introduce the reporter, Stowell."

Stowell sifted through his little pile of notes.

"You just tell us the yeoman's name and then introduce him," the Commander said impatiently.

Stowell pushed away the notes.

"I introduce Frank Watkins, Yeoman first class, United States Naval Reserve, as Reporter," he said hurriedly. He deplored the Commander's familiarity with legal procedure; it enabled him to keep telling the recorder what to do before he did it, thus reducing the latter's carefully planned little effects one by one to a series of stammering ejaculations. This was not their first board together.

The Commander picked up the precept and started it off in a quick but audible and distinct voice.

"From: Commander, Panama Sea Frontier.

To: Commander Leslie Benson, USN.

Subject: Board of Investigation to inquire into and report upon the conduct of Lieutenant William S. Ellis, USN, while on board the U.S.S. *Sardonyx* during that vessel's voyage from Guantanamo to Miami, Florida, *via* Key West and during that vessel's availability at the United States Naval

Section Base, Miami, Florida, with the purpose of discovering if his conduct during this period was properly that of a naval officer and of a commanding officer and to conduct the examination with specific reference to his conduct during a submarine alert at sea, to his attitude towards the supervision of repair work in Miami, and to the question of having brought women aboard the vessel at night for purposes of fornication."

The precept went on to enumerate the members of the board and to direct that Lieutenant Ellis be notified of the time and place of meeting and of his status as defendant. Commander Benson read swiftly and clearly; when he had finished he said to the yeoman:

"Make the entry that the defendant has entered." Then directing his glance at Ellis he said: "Do you desire counsel?"

Ellis leaned forward nervously.

"Excuse me, sir?"

"Do you want counsel? A lawyer?"

"Oh, yes. Mr. Stregelinus is representing me." The pompous verb gave Ellis a slight reassurance and he settled back in his chair. To hell with them he said to himself for perhaps the hundredth time that morning. To hell with them. But he knew in a minute the panic would return and his intestines would start jumping about. Bev had told him that the worst that could happen would be to be busted down to ensign or even chief quartermaster again, but what did Bev know about old birds like that Commander? And he was filled with a yearning for the carefree days as a chief with liberty every night and Honolulu—

"Remember not to interrupt the witnesses," Bev whispered to him. "Just talk it over with me first. We'll get through." He smiled nicely and made the V for Victory sign under the table, but Ellis could see how taut he looked.

The first witness whom Stowell called was Ensign Quimby, the Communications Officer of the *Sardonyx*. Beverly knew what to expect here. Quimby, a plump little martinet and violently anti-Ellis, would give damaging testimony but would be strictly truthful. He would emphasize also the wrong things and could be made to look foolish.

Stowell opened the examination after Quimby had seated himself at the middle of the table opposite the yeoman with the necessary question: "State your name, rank, and present station." He then informed Quimby generally of the subject of the investigation. The ensign turned and as he did so gave Ellis a quick but comprehensive look, completely without timidity, as though to say: "At last they've caught up with you! And about time too."

"Tell us what you know," Stowell said, "of Mr. Ellis' conduct during the *Sardonyx*'s stay in Miami."

"It was much the same there as anywhere else."

"What do you mean by that?"

"Abominable. Nothing but paint and dirty talk. By which I mean he never took the slightest interest in anything on his ship except painting the bulkheads and telling lewd stories about his naval past in the wardroom." The most damaging part of this, Beverly quickly realized, was the cold way that Quimby kept looking Ellis up and down. Most ensigns would have been bashful before their former captain. But not this little bag of ice. His whole air seemed to say: "I've waited for this." Ellis' eyebrows slanted more and more; he stared unhappily into his lap. Beverly knew that he would be surprised at the way people turned. Ellis had no malice and expected none; nor did he have the imagination to conceive of the hatred that his irritability could arouse in the hearts of more educated but lower ranking officers.

Stowell was not doing too well with Quimby. The latter had not been on the bridge the night of the submarine alarm; he had not seen any women on board in Miami, and his only contribution to the charge of Ellis' delaying repairs in Miami was his statement that Ellis had told him in answer to report on radio defects "to let the God-damned Section Base worry about it." Stowell, with a nasty little smile, returned to the "lewd stories."

"Could you be a little more explicit on Mr. Ellis' wardroom conversation?"

"I don't know that's so important, Stowell," Commander Benson interrupted.

"But I'd like to examine, sir, the implications. If a man discusses nothing but pornography how can he be fit for a rank or a command?"

The Commander waved his right hand impatiently but told him to proceed.

Mr. Quimby picked up his cue.

"If any officer in the wardroom brought up a non-pornographic subject, whether it was Shakespeare, modern life, the war, or how to get a naval sound recorder, the Captain was invariably disgruntled." Beverly noted here that

Quimby was probably reciting from memory. "He would fall into a sort of black and disapproving silence, supposing, I guess, that we were making fun of his lack of education, and sometimes leave the room. The only topics that interested him were discussions of the sexual portions of a woman's anatomy and detailed versions of his numerous fornications. These were occasionally varied with accounts of his venereal troubles. He even went so far as to describe to me the intimate moments that he enjoyed with his wife, sparing me, I can assure you, no slightest detail."

Beverly could reflect during this curious recitation which so obviously caught the attention of all but the Commander how dreadful it was for any man to be enjoying himself as much as the cool, collected, soft-spoken little ensign so obviously was. It was evidently to him the summit of satisfaction to spew out the garbage that had offended his sensitivity so long in front of this shocked and august audience, and above all in front of the perpetrator. It was a moment that he must have rehearsed by himself for days. And how Ellis writhed! He stared at Quimby at first in astonishment, and then shaking his head in what appeared to be sincere bewilderment, put one hand over his eyes.

Stowell wore an expression of exaggerated disgust.

"Did any of you remonstrate at this?"

Ensign Quimby shrugged his shoulders.

"He was the Captain. You know how a commanding officer dominates on board a small ship."

Mr. Cheney leaned forward and asked:

"Was this confined to talk or did you observe him on board in any acts that could be described as indecent?"

"So far as I know it was only talk."

The board had no further questions; they seemed, indeed, anxious to be through with the witness. Beverly cleared his throat.

"Mr. Quimby," he began, "how long have you been in the Navy?"

"Six months the day before yesterday."

"And what had you been led to suppose were the topics of conversation to be avoided in the wardroom?" The nervous tremor left Bev's tone as he spoke; he leaned forward and tapped the table with his pencil.

"At indoctrination school we were taught the old Navy rule that one avoided three topics: women, politics and religion."

"Exactly. And *were* those topics avoided at the mess at the school?"

"Religion, yes. I guess it doesn't interest people. But women and politics, frankly no."

"No," Beverly repeated. "Particularly women, I'm sure. And have you ever been at any officers' mess where the topic of women was avoided?"

"Almost all my duty has been on the *Sardonyx*. But I can certainly affirm that it wasn't avoided there."

"Your duty has been limited to the *Sardonyx*, has it?" Bev asked. "I see. Not the widest field of experience, is it? But is it your general impression that Navy officers avoid—"

"Where are you getting, counsel?" came from the Commander. Bev leaped at the opportunity to elaborate.

"Commander, I'm only trying to show that naval officers as a rule do discuss sex at the mess. It may be deplorable but how can we deny it? And if trained officers are guilty, how can we hold it against Mr. Ellis, a former enlisted man, who was given a rank because of his ability to handle ships and men without any indoctrination at all? He was put there to do a war job. No one can expect an ex-chief who's been in the Navy half his life to be able to change his manners to please an ensign fresh out of Harvard—"

"Minnesota," Quimby interrupted angrily.

The Commander brought his tilted chair down on the floor with a bang.

"Consider your point made, counsel," he said angrily. "And let's get on to the next witness. We can't spend all day hashing over what officers talk about when off duty." He proceeded to give the witness the usual warning not to disclose his testimony.

Ensign Winston, the man from Texas, was the next to testify, but very little was gained by either side during the twenty minutes of the interrogation. Beverly remembered how violently he had spoken against Captain Ellis on the ship and had marked him in his notes as a witness to be carefully watched, but the bluff, noisy hostility of the ranchman lacked the sustaining power provided by the venom that animated Quimby and tended to dissipate into a meaningless "I guess he wasn't so bad" in the hushed atmosphere of a legal procedure. And even as Beverly breathed a sigh of relief to hear the equivocal answers of the Texan he noticed in himself the quiver of some sensation that was akin, he felt sure, to contempt for a man whose hostility was so easily overcome.

"Oh, you know how it is," Winston was saying. "Commanding officers have a lot on their minds and they're bound to get excited once in a while. But as a rule he was about as stable—"

"I knew I could depend on Winston," Ellis whispered to Bev. "He's an all right guy. Not like that little snot of an ensign, Quimby. You can bet your last dollar that if I ever tangle with him—"

Beverly put his finger to his lips and did not answer. "No, Ellis," he felt like saying, "you're not going to persuade me that you're pugnacious. You know that chiefs are supposed to be tough. So you put it on. But if you ever ran into Quimby in the street you'd go up to him with a smile because you're yellow." And he suddenly felt dizzy and a little sick. "But I've thought all that out," he reminded himself; "it's all right. It must be."

Winston rambled on, glancing from time to time at Ellis and once even smiling. But like Quimby he had nothing to contribute to the main points of the investigation, though he seemed to love to talk. When Stowell was through Beverly waived his right to cross-examine, and the big ensign lumbered out of the shack.

Two more ensigns followed Winston and then two chief petty officers. Stowell did not add much to his case. It was apparent that the ensigns disliked Ellis and that the chiefs liked him, but this had been the anticipated lineup. Stowell, however, trotted along through his examination, his small nostrils between his big cheeks aquiver for the scent of hidden smut. Tirelessly he pried into Ellis' conversation and habits; incessantly he harped on words like "gentleman" and "example." Twice the commander interrupted to point out that they were looking for faults more serious than the telling of dirty jokes, but Stowell never seemed to lose hope that in this oozing and promising mud his little snout would ultimately come up against a solid object, one that wouldn't just bury itself deeper as he rooted. Beverly hardly cross-examined at all. Ellis once asked him nervously if he didn't think he ought to.

"Our time is coming," Bev assured him.

The investigation really began when Calloriac was called. He looked uncomfortable, as if the whole affair was highly distasteful to him; his was too large a nature to take any pleasure in the discomfiture of his old antagonist. He shifted in his seat; he folded and unfolded his hands. His large and sympathetic grey eyes roamed curiously over the people at the end of the table and finally rested on Stowell who was searching through his notes. So this was it, he seemed to be thinking; this was the end of the hunt. This was the corner into which the poor, weak, pitiable Ellis had been hounded. A sensible world would have shrugged its shoulders, opened the door to let him out, and forgotten. But the Navy must persecute; bureaucracy must persecute; they have their records. When his eyes met Ellis' he gave him a little smile and a nod, kindly, but not without self-consciousness.

Stowell started.

"You were the executive officer and navigator of the *Sardonyx?*"

"I was."

"You reported on board at the time Mr. Ellis took command?"

"That's correct."

"You have been able then to observe him at all times and in all situations in the performance of his command?"

"Pretty much."

"Tell us how he acquitted himself in his job."

Calloriac paused.

"That depends on so many things," he said slowly. "For example, am I to compare him with the captain of an aircraft carrier or with the average small ship skipper of the Panama Sea Frontier?"

Stowell's eyes snapped impatiently. He felt, and he felt correctly, that Calloriac meant to include the whole board of investigation in his vaguely derogatory category of "small ship skipper."

"You're not to compare him with anybody at all," he said tartly. "You're to tell us if he was a commanding officer according to the standards of the United States Navy."

Calloriac looked at him with just the suggestion of a smile.

"And what are they?"

But Stowell was ready for this.

"I'll read you a paragraph from Commander Ageton with the permission of the board." He opened a large blue book at a place that he had marked. "'The commanding officer must, at all times, present in himself an example to his subordinates. He must endeavor to cultivate in his subordinates a seamanlike and military spirit, a proper sense of duty and honor, and a careful observance of professional etiquette, so as to develop them into well-rounded naval officers and men.' Let's try that as a starter. Did Mr. Ellis qualify under such a description?"

"No."

"In what way did he fall short?"

"I haven't seen anyone around here yet who could qualify as a skipper under one of those fairy tale definitions."

Stowell glared and Mr. Cheney looked anxiously at Commander Benson, a dog straining at his master's leash, his mouth dripping.

"Remember, Mr. Calloriac," the Commander said ominously, "where you are. I am very close to holding you in contempt."

"Excuse me, sir."

"To return to my 'fairy tale definitions'—" Stowell was beginning with emphatic sarcasm.

"Enough of that, sir," the Commander thundered. "My remarks apply to you too."

"Yes, sir." The recorder was unnerved by this; his voice trembled for several seconds. "To return," he continued, "to navy standards. Would you please tell the board if Mr. Ellis' behavior in the wardroom of the *Sardonyx* was the behavior of an officer and gentleman?"

Calloriac appealed to the board.

"Commander," he protested, "I've always thought that the wardroom was a place where an officer could say and do pretty much as he liked. I know it's better to act like a gentleman there but I thought if an officer didn't, he should be spoken to by his superior, not court-martialed."

The Commander nodded, and Beverly spoke up.

"I agree with the witness, Commander," he said. "This board was convened to investigate the conduct of Lieutenant Ellis during one particular period of the ship's activity—the Miami trip. I cannot see the relevance of this highly generalized line of attack."

The Commander turned to Stowell.

"Confine your questions to the period indicated by counsel," he said gruffly.

The recorder with a hurt look reshuffled his notes. After a few seconds he looked up.

"You had the 4:00 to 8:00 watch, I believe, on the morning of October 11th, when the U.S.S. *Norris,* escort commander of Convoy WEH112, dropped a depth charge on a submarine contact?"

"I did."

"Will you describe to the board the action you took before the Captain relieved you of the conn."

Calloriac described the second depth charge concussion, the general quarters, and how he had put the speed up to flank and engaged in zig-zag maneuvers. In telling this he used careful, deliberate phrases, lingering over the few facts as they appeared as if he had a premonition that the security which they afforded would soon be dissipated in the fog of rumor and spite which he could feel gathering in the air.

"When did the Captain come up to the bridge?"

"When I sounded the general alarm."

"Did he take the conn immediately?"

"No."

"What did he do?"

"He asked several questions and tried to find out what was going on."

"Would you say that he had control of the situation?"

"No. Definitely not."

"How did he behave to give you such an impression?"

"He was very excited and lost his temper at me. He said he should have been notified earlier, which wasn't possible. I got a bit angry myself and told him that if he spent more time on the bridge he wouldn't always be taken by surprise."

Mr. Cheney drummed his fingers on the table and smiled.

"You seem to have changed your ground, witness," he interrupted. "A minute ago you were on his side."

The Commander was about to reprimand his fellow member when Calloriac, now thoroughly angry, did it for him.

"I don't know what you mean by that, Mr. Cheney," he retorted, turning his broad flushed face to the offending member, "but I suppose you regard me as a witness who is on one side or the other. In other words, a witness who will lie for one side or the other. Let me inform you, sir, for the benefit of all here present, that I am *not* such a witness; that strange as it may seem to you I came here to tell the truth; that I'm not on anyone's side and that furthermore your question makes me doubt the integrity of at least one member of this board!"

There was a moment of the tensest silence. Beverly felt that he could never admire Calloriac enough; it was clear beyond all doubt now that he was Byronic. There was in his truculence, in his defiance something that smacked of the sublime, and it was inevitable that Beverly should feel that Calloriac was not being treated as fairness required when Commander Benson, ignoring the witness quite as much as he ignored Cheney's nervous whispered appeal for "contempt," gave a laconic "proceed" to Mr. Stowell.

As the recorder again fumbled with his notes, however, Benson filled in the gap:

"The board is not questioning your integrity, Mr. Calloriac," he said dryly. "And I would advise you not to worry about ours. Mr. Cheney's question was unfortunately phrased. We will have it and your protest struck from the record."

Cheney leaned towards him but he waved him off. Then the Commander passed his hand over his eyes to avert a sensation of giddiness. To be there this way, in a land of Stowells and Cheneys, was more and more like a nightmare of flight through a marshland at night. He seemed suddenly to hear the cacophony of croaking; he closed his eyes tightly behind his hand. He looked at Calloriac and almost smiled; he thought for a moment he had. He knew now anyway that he would believe anything that this young man told him.

Stowell proceeded.

"Would you say that Mr. Ellis was scared on that occasion?"

Calloriac hesitated a few seconds.

"Possibly—yes. He was highly confused and seemed intensely nervous."

"How long did he keep the conn?"

"About thirty to forty minutes."

"And then what did he do?"

"He secured from general quarters, returned the conn to me, and left the bridge."

"Was the emergency, in your opinion, over by that time?" Beverly interrupted.

"I object to the recorder's asking the witness' opinion, sir."

Stowell reached for his copy of *Navy Courts and Boards* and opened it at another of the many markers which he had stuck there.

"I refer the board," he said briskly, "to Section 733. It states here that where a Board of Investigation takes testimony not under oath this testimony cannot be introduced as evidence in a subsequent court-martial; hence a wider latitude is permissible in observing rules of evidence. Let me point out that as the defendant cannot be subsequently prejudiced by anything that is allowed here we would simply make the matter easier for ourselves by hearing everything that is relevant to the case without doing him the slightest harm."

"It would do the defendant harm," Beverly protested, "to be recommended for court-martial by this board. The board should realize that like any group of men it is subject to being influenced by unsubstantiated testimony. It should take steps to protect itself. The board should make up its own opinion and not take Mr. Calloriac's."

"Mr. Calloriac," Stowell pointed out, "is an officer with considerable sea experience and has, as I've brought out already, seen Mr. Ellis under all situations at sea. I am sure the board will find his opinion both helpful and instructive."

The board adjourned to debate the point, and Bev and Ellis left the shack to walk across the little plot of grass to the Ship's Service Store for a Coca-Cola. Stowell came slowly after them and stood rather self-consciously apart to drink his.

Ellis was taking it hard; he alternated between dejection and bravado.

"Jesus!" he exclaimed, after drinking half his bottle at a gulp, "I never saw a rigmarole like this in my life! Seems like half the Navy down here is got together to see if I had a jump in Miami. Take me back to Chief. I never wanted this job."

"We're doing all right, Bill."

"To hell with it! What's the damn use? That bunch of pansies mincing in there and warbling about how I shocked them. Deary me! I'd like to shock them with a kick in the ass!"

"I thought you wanted to win your case," Bev said dryly. Ellis gripped him by the shoulder.

"Don't take it personally, old man. I think you're doing a swell job. And I'm damned if I know why you bother."

Bev walked away without answering to smoke a cigarette by himself, but as he did so he saw Audrey, who had obviously been waiting for him, detach herself from the counter of the Ship's Service Store and hurry after him.

"Mr. Stregelinus," she said hurriedly. "Mr. Stregelinus!"

He stopped.

"Yes, Miss Emerson?"

"Could I please have a word with you?"

He slightly raised his shoulders.

"Why not?"

She followed him over to a spot shaded by the overhanging roof of the shack.

"Well?" he said.

"I know what you think of me, and I haven't come to say anything about that," she began, the words tumbling out one over the other in her nervousness. "But isn't there something I can do to help you? Can't I make it up in any way?"

He looked at her coldly.

"How?"

"Couldn't I come in and tell them the whole story? How I got mad at you and went to Mr. Gilder and blabbed everything because I knew he wanted Lieutenant Ellis' job? Wouldn't that help to discredit the whole procedure?"

He stared.

"You'd really do that?"

"I would!"

"But, Audrey, don't you know what it would mean?"

"What do I care what it would mean?" she answered impatiently. "Suppose I lost my job? That would be terrible, wouldn't it? Give me a chance, Bev. Don't hog all the nobility for yourself."

He looked at her gravely and felt an easing of all the tension in his body. He had not known till this moment how tight his nerves had been. She was staring back at him with earnest, imploring eyes.

"Audrey, I think I could love you for this," he said at last.

"But will you let me testify?"

"Oh, that." He seemed to dismiss it with a shrug, continuing to search into her face. "You're a funny girl," he said gently. "You don't know what you want, do you? Or you do and then you don't. You build something up with every kind of care; you put a lot of passion and planning into it and then you kick it all over in a flash. Why? What really makes you want to?"

She was less complicated.

"Conscience."

"Conscience?" he repeated. "Is that it?" He sighed and looked at the grass, appearing for the moment to forget all about the girl so excitedly expectant. "A belated, destructive conscience. A sudden sense that the world isn't worth it. That you can't go on living and be yourself. And who else can you ever be? All you can do is kick over the ladders that you've taken such trouble to put up. But even the kicking doesn't do it. So back we go to the job of putting them up again. I don't know. I suppose it's all right."

"But don't you think I should?"

He smiled at her.

"No one could answer that but you, Audrey," he said with more decision. "But I'll call for your testimony if you want. And it will come in handy too. I think I can make Gilder look like a fool with it. Yes. I guess it's all right."

"It must be all right," she said stoutly.

He reached out his hand.

"Well, anyway," he remarked, "it's all right between you and me. You once said we were real friends. We are."

She put her hand in his.

The marine was standing beside them, very stiffly. He saluted Beverly.

"The board's reconvened, sir."

Beverly nodded and went back to the Ship's Service Store to get Ellis.

CHAPTER FOUR

COMMANDER BENSON ANNOUNCED that the board had decided to allow Mr. Stowell's question. The recorder with a hardly suppressed smile of satisfaction repeated, emphasizing the first three words:

"In your opinion, Mr. Calloriac, was the emergency over when Mr. Ellis secured the ship from general quarters?"

"It was not."

"Will you explain why?"

"Certainly. There was every reason to suspect the existence of a submarine in the area and no reason to believe that it had been destroyed by the *Norris's* attack. While at battle stations the ship's port shaft went out of commission and we were forced to drop behind the convoy. This information was transmitted to the Escort Commander on voice radio and there was every possibility that it might have been picked up by the lurking sub. At the time we secured from general quarters we were proceeding alone some miles astern of the convoy in disabled condition. I hardly think the emergency, under such circumstances, could be called 'over.' "

Commander Benson grunted.

"Hardly is right," he said. "What was the idea, Ellis?"

This was the first question that had as yet been directed at the defendant. Ellis was much startled.

"I didn't see why I should keep the men up all night," he stammered. "Lots of times destroyers drop cans on a school of fish or on a whale."

The Commander looked at him coldly and nodded.

"On this occasion then, Mr. Calloriac," Stowell continued, "would you say that Mr. Ellis was definitely lacking in the qualities requisite for a commanding officer?"

"On this occasion," Calloriac repeated, "I definitely would."

Stowell seemed to have an instinct that he had done as well with the witness as he could expect.

"That will be all for me," he said.

"Mr. Calloriac," Beverly started right in, "at the time that all this took place do you remember how the visibility was?"

Calloriac looked at Beverly for a long moment and then smiled. It was just a little smile and seemed to convey: "I still don't know why you're mixed up in this, but good luck to you anyway. He's not worth much, but still."

"It wasn't dawn. It was pretty black," he answered.

"When Mr. Ellis came on the bridge wasn't it to be expected that he would need some time to acquire night vision?"

"Yes."

"Mightn't thirty or even forty minutes be needed?"

"Oh, no. Possibly fifteen."

"What's the point of this, counsel?" Benson asked roughly. "Any officer at sea whose duties may take him to the bridge during the night ought to wear red goggles and keep ready."

"But in a general alarm," Bev protested, "mightn't he dash so hurriedly to the bridge—"

"In a general alarm he ought to be doubly careful not to let a white light catch his eyes," the Commander answered. "And if his ship is properly darkened there should be only red lights on below deck anyway."

Bev looked at the Commander for a second and decided that this line of interrogation was decidedly unsafe. A plea of extenuating circumstances to excuse misconduct in the possible face of the enemy immediately had the board alerted. They knew all the answers to this, and all the war cries of history seemed marshaled in the muggy atmosphere of the little shack to descend upon him. It was unfortunate, he clearly saw, that the mention of this submarine, if submarine it was, had ever come up. Even Stowell and Cheney were dimly aware that behind all the mimeograph machines, behind the courts-martial and the saluting marines, behind the whole fantastic paraphernalia of Panama, there was a war and there was a sea that was the enemy's too. The mammoth defenses of the Caribbean had little enough chance to prove themselves; everyone had to depend for actual engagements on the few little ships that were so heavily over-administered. If these should fail, what an indictment!

No, his only chance was to skip over as much as possible this incident.

"No more questions," he said quietly.

The board asked Calloriac a few questions, but nothing significant was developed. He was finally dismissed and Mr. Foster was called. The little engineer walked in quickly and sat down in the wrong chair. When Stowell told him where to sit he looked at the other chair as if it were a trap. Then quickly he glided over into it and hunched himself up, looking anxiously to his left and right like a guilty thing pursued. He hesitated for a moment when asked for his name and rank and then gave them in a tone of more assurance than could have been expected.

"Mr. Foster," Stowell began, "would you describe the damage that existed in the engineering department when you arrived in Miami? Was it extensive?"

"I would say it was, sir. One of our generators had blown out and the bearings on the port shaft had been pried out of line. Then there was a piece out of one of the props. And all kinds of small things wrong."

"What did you estimate would be the time necessary for repairs?"

"Oh, depending on what they did in Miami. Maybe two or three weeks."

"And how long did it take?"

"It isn't done yet. It'll be a month altogether by the time it's finished."

"To what do you attribute the discrepancy?"

Foster's jaw dropped.

"To what do I what?" he asked.

"How do you explain the fact that the repairs took longer than you expected?"

"Oh. Well, there was more to do."

"What?"

"The steering gear was out of whack for one thing."

"You didn't tell us about that."

Foster flared up at this.

"It belongs to the deck force!" he exclaimed indignantly. "It ain't an engineer's job."

"Your engineers didn't work on the steering gear, then?"

"They certainly did not."

Beverly glanced at Ellis, and for the first time during the investigation the latter smiled. They both knew that if Stowell made the engineer angry his entire testimony would be colored in the defendant's favor. It was not that Foster was dishonest. He believed everything that he said with a passionate intensity. But his inconsistency was as complete as it was ludicrously unconscious; he was utterly without a coördinating principle, unless his strong sense of injustice meted out to engineers by the Navy could be called one. He would surely, Bev reflected, have baffled even Socrates, and Plato would have had to tear up his notes.

"Did your men work on the port shaft and the generator?" Stowell continued.

"They did."

"As hard as they could?"

If Foster had flared up before, he exploded now.

"My engineers always work as hard as they can!" he rasped. "They're not like deck hands who lay about topside in the sun. And then criticize a machinist mate if he pokes his nose out of a hatch once in twelve hours for a breath of air."

Stowell stared at him in perplexity.

"I don't mean that. I mean, did they work long hours?"

"Certainly they worked long hours!"

"No liberty?"

Foster turned furiously to the Commander.

"Commander," he protested, "does this modern Navy expect a man to work all day in a hot engine room and go without liberty in port? That's worse than the old Navy!"

Benson almost smiled.

"Engineers work very hard, I know," he said. "They surely rate as much liberty as anyone."

"I knew you'd realize it," Foster said triumphantly, "but some of these 1942 officers who spend all their time on the beach—"

"You're missing the point, Mr. Foster," Stowell interrupted.

"Oh, I am! What is the point? That my motor macks don't do nothin'. Is that it?"

Stowell looked very stern. He realized that the witness was out of control but he was baffled.

"No," he said sharply. "The point is this. Did Captain Ellis, by declaring too much liberty, cut down the repair work that his own crew could accomplish?"

"I object," Beverly interrupted. "The recorder is obviously leading the witness. Mr. Foster has stated clearly enough, it seems to me, that his men were working full time. I cannot see why the recorder should be allowed to badger and pester him until he has put words in his mouth."

"Haven't we already decided, counsel," Mr. Cheney put in, "that there's wider latitude in the rules of evidence in boards? A man can't suffer for what he's said here so there's less danger in using strong measures to get at the truth."

Benson whispered for a moment with the other two.

"Objection overruled," he said.

"I hope, sir," Bev protested, "with all due respect, that the same latitude will be allowed the defense on cross-examination."

"It will." And Benson turned to the witness. "Answer the question, sir."

Foster looked blank.

"What question?" he asked.

Stowell repeated the question. Foster appeared to give it some thought.

"Well—yes. I think maybe he did. We had 1300 liberty every day for half the crew and he gave a huge number of forty-eights and seventy-twos besides that."

"Did this delay your repairing the engine damage?"

"Oh, that was meant to be done by the Yard in Miami."

"All of it?"

"Yes."

Stowell mopped his brow with a large silk handkerchief. It was easy to see that he was not enjoying himself.

"Then what, if you'll be so good as to tell me, were your men doing?"

"They were helping."

Mr. Cheney here whispered to Commander Benson and the latter nodded.

"I'll take over the examination, thank you, Mr. Stowell," Cheney said smoothly. "It's my understanding, Mr. Foster, that with certain types of repair work it's obligatory for the ship's company to do as much of the work as they are able. Wasn't that the case in Miami?"

Foster looked uneasily at the red round face of this far more assured as well as higher ranking officer.

"Yes," he said. "We were supposed to do as much as we could."

"To set everybody's mind at rest on that point," Cheney went on, "I can read a portion of the letter Captain Arnold wrote the ship when she docked at Miami." Here he produced a letter and read a short passage describing the shortage of personnel in Miami, the heavy program of work, and the necessity of ships' coöperation. Beverly stirred uncomfortably; he was quite aware that the reading of this letter by a member of the board was an improper introduction of evidence but he knew it could be introduced in some other fashion and he saw no real reason to object. It was, however, embarrassing, for he could see that Stowell would think him a poor thing to take it silently. To Stowell law was a little game of objections and tricks; to miss any of them regardless of its bearing on the case was to lose a point on a large, invisible but carefully maintained balance sheet.

Foster nodded his head repeatedly during the reading of the letter.

"That's right. That's right," he kept saying.

"Well, then, Mr. Foster," Cheney concluded, "let me put you the question again. Did the Captain's leave policy interfere with the part of the work your men were meant to be doing?"

"No doubt of it."

"Did you point this out to him?"

"Repeatedly. I told him his deck hands weren't doing nothin' while my engineers did all the work."

It was now Mr. Cheney's turn to look confused.

"Was that usually the case on your ship?"

Foster was emphatic.

"That's the way it is on *all* ships," he roundly declared.

"Do you mean that the leave policy did not affect the work that your engineers did?"

"My engineers can do their work and go on liberty both," Foster said proudly.

"Then they weren't affected by the leave?"

The Engineer almost smiled at his simplicity.

"How can men do a day's work and knock off for 1300 liberty every day?"

"That's what I'm asking you," Cheney insisted in exasperation.

"It's simple. They can't."

Cheney tried a new line.

"You protested, then, about the amount of leave granted to the men?"

"No. I figured if the deck hands rated it my motor macks certainly did."

"Then you didn't protest?"

"Why should I?"

"Well, the work wasn't getting done."

"That was the Yard's fault."

Cheney began to get angry.

"I thought you said, Mr. Foster, that you had told the Captain that he was giving too much leave."

"So he was."

Here Cheney risked a bold stroke.

"What did he say?" he asked.

"Oh, he said what did it matter whether we got out of Miami in two weeks or a month. He said it was a good liberty town."

Cheney smiled in satisfaction and quickly signed off.

"I have no more questions," he said.

Beverly sat back and tried to look composed.

"Mr. Foster," he began in a quiet and friendly tone, "you told us just now that your engineers always did a good day's work."

"That's so."

"I don't doubt it. I've been on board your ship and I know." He saw Stowell look around and hurried on: "A hard working man needs a certain amount of liberty, doesn't he?"

"He can't work around the clock continual."

"Certainly not. How long would you say that the average man in your engineering department had been out of the States?"

"Oh, at least a year and a half. Some more."

"They were pretty excited, I guess, when they heard they were going to Miami."

"Like wild cats." Here Foster, half placated, stole a smile at the board.

"Don't you think," Bev continued earnestly, "that it was natural for Captain Ellis to want to give the men a break during the little time they had in their own country?"

"I guess so."

"Don't you think he was thinking about the—"

"I object," Stowell exclaimed. "There must be a limit, even in investigations, to the extent that a witness can be led."

"Overruled," the Commander grunted.

"Don't you think, Mr. Foster," Bev imperturbably continued, "that he was thinking about his men when he told you that a little more time in Miami wouldn't make so much difference?"

"Sure."

"He never tried to go on leave himself, did he? I mean he never left the ship for more than 24 hours at a time?"

"No, he didn't. Of course he—"

"Thank you, Mr. Foster."

Bev knew that the whole thing would really begin when Pete was called and he felt his heart tighten uncomfortably when this happened. As he had expected, Pete came in with his most solid, most set expression and seated himself truculently in the chair. He gave Bev one look and then fixed his attention on the board. It was perfectly clear in every inch of his thickset figure that he was tensely and firmly resolved to go through with his role as originally contemplated. There would be no quarter in this fight. Bev felt the dryness in his throat; his heart pounded but he kept telling himself: "You've got to go through with it; you've got to be tougher than he."

It began uneventfully enough. Stowell opened with questions about the night of the supposed submarine attack, and Pete was not able to contribute materially to the picture of incompetence already drawn by Calloriac. He was less familiar with the background here than the Exec and he answered usually with a brief "yes" or "no" in a tone that seemed to assume that this was mere preliminary. Stowell, however, gathered that this was the spot in which to hit Ellis and to hit him hard, and it was not until he had approached the night's events through a series of different channels that he finally switched to the less naval aspects of the defendant's misconduct, aspects which he knew that Commander Benson regarded as crude irrelevancies. But he came to them.

"What have you to tell us," he said casually, "of Mr. Ellis' conduct while not actually on duty in the strict sense of the word? In the wardroom for example?"

Pete's features seemed to congeal. He reminded Bev of something Asiatic, something ruthless if lazy, something massive and lizardlike that blinked in the sun.

"It was a disgrace," he said shortly.

"A disgrace? To what?"

"To the Navy."

"Would you elucidate?"

"Certainly. The language he used was invariably disgusting. His mind was always in the gutter."

"What subjects did he talk about?"

"Subjects? Subject. Sex, sex, and more sex."

Stowell hesitated before putting the next question. He wanted to follow out his original plan and draw the witness out to explicit details but he had the Commander under observation and he could see that the latter was already restive. He cut short his project and came to the point.

"Did he ever indulge in irregular sexual activity on board?"

"He did."

"Under what circumstances?"

Pete shot a glance at Ellis and Beverly and then proceeded, in his heavy, definite voice:

"In Miami he brought a woman on board and slept with her."

Bev heard Ellis' snort and under the table put a hand on his knee to steady him.

"Who was this woman?" Stowell asked.

"I don't remember her name. I saw him bring her on board late one night after everybody had turned in and although I didn't actually see her leave, I understand it was a couple of hours later."

"Where were you when they came on board?"

"I came on board at the same time. It was about 0200."

"Was there anyone up?"

"Only the gangway watch."

"What about the officer of the deck?"

"Oh, Ellis let him sleep all night."

"What did they do after coming on board?"

"Well, I didn't tuck them in if that's what you mean, Mr. Stowell," Pete drawled; "I had enough tact to go below and leave them alone in the darkened wardroom. After all, he was the Captain and it wasn't up to me to spy on him. But when a man of Ellis' nature brings a floozy on board a darkened ship and she leaves a couple of hours later, I assume it's not to play double solitaire."

Bev didn't have to object; the Commander did.

"We're not interested in your assumptions or your opinions, witness," he said sternly. "Stick to the facts. I might warn you now that your answers betray a disrespect for this board which I will not tolerate."

Stowell cursed inwardly. Abruptly he turned to Bev.

"Your witness," he said.

Bev swallowed twice, hard, and then looked down at the rough surface of the table.

"Mr. Stoner," he began, quickly and nervously, "you stated,

I believe, that Captain Ellis' language in the wardroom was offensive?"

"I did."

"I'm amazed that you could listen to it. Perhaps you indicated your distaste for the topics he seemed to enjoy?"

"Me? No. Why should I? He was the Captain."

"Did you participate in these discussions, then?"

"To a certain extent."

"Do you remember a conversation in the wardroom on the subject of whether or not the United States Government should sponsor houses of prostitution for service personnel?"

Pete paused, staring at him.

"Yes," he answered.

"Didn't you adopt the point of view that such a plan was desirable?"

"I don't remember committing myself."

"You don't?" Bev's voice was clear and sarcastic now; he felt quite in the swing. "Please remember the number of witnesses I can call to refresh your memory. Perhaps you don't remember saying that it would be easy for the Government to find recruits because American women were so loose. Or boasting, as an example, that you had slept with the wife of the President of your company but that you still preferred waitresses—"

Pete interrupted here violently, his face black with irritation.

"I never said I'd slept with the wife of the President of—"

"Mr. Stregelinus," the Commander cut in sharply, "I don't know what you're hoping to prove with this line of questioning. This board was convened to investigate Mr. Ellis' misconduct, and Mr. Stoner's conversation, however unsalutary, can hardly be relevant. Let me remind you also of the dignity of this board and warn you to be careful about the nature of the evidence that you introduce."

"But Commander," Bev protested passionately, "I am conscious of the dignity of this board, terribly conscious of it. It's for that very reason that I so resent the conspiracy that lies behind this investigation and that I want so to show it up. Your time, sir, is being wasted by people who have brought on this whole affair for malicious motives. How can I show this unless I can show the conduct of which some of the witnesses have been guilty?"

The Commander looked very grave.

"These are serious charges, sir," he said.

"I'm aware of it, sir."

"If based on fact they would, it seems to me, be more properly the subject of another investigation. Their relevance here escapes me. Even if some of the witnesses should be maliciously motivated they still might testify truthfully about Mr. Ellis."

Bev had a wonderful excited feeling of being in up to his neck. What could it matter now?

"But Commander," he urged, "this isn't a court-martial, as you yourself have pointed out. Aren't we here to get at the truth? Are we to be bound so as not to get the full picture? I didn't take this case because I like this sort of thing. I took it because I felt so strongly that an injustice was being done and if you let me go on I know I can prove it."

His tone fairly rang with sincerity; he felt it himself and was sure, after a moment of much suspense, that Benson felt it.

"I had rather hear no more about Mr. Stoner's views on sex," he said gruffly.

"May I proceed, then, sir, skipping Mr. Stoner's views, to show why Mr. Stoner's account of what happened in Miami is unworthy of belief?"

A short whispering between the three members followed. Then the Commander nodded.

"You may proceed, sir."

"I'd like to say, Commander," Pete burst out, "that I never slept with—"

"No more of that, sir."

Bev took advantage of Pete's discomfiture to press on:

"You have stated, Mr. Stoner, that Mr. Ellis brought a woman of low moral character on board the *Sardonyx* at night for purposes of illicit intercourse?"

"I have, and I reaffirm it."

"Why are you so sure of her low moral character?"

Pete gave a little snort.

"A woman with morals would hardly have done what she did."

"You beg the question. Were you acquainted with this woman?"

"Slightly."

"Slightly?" Bev looked up at him. "How did that happen?"

"Mr. Ellis introduced us."

"When?"

"At a night club in Miami. The Glass Bucket."

"Oh, were you out with them?"

"More or less."

"More or less?" Bev repeated severely. "Did you meet them there by appointment?"

"Yes, I did."

"Were you alone when you met them?"

"No, I was with Miss Smith."

"Please tell the board who Miss Smith is."

Pete hesitated as he glanced at the three members.

"She's General Smith's daughter."

"Oh." Bev swooped on it. "So you took the daughter of the Lieutenant-Governor of this Zone to dinner with a man whose vile language disgusts you and whose companion you have described as a 'floozy'?"

"I didn't know anything about her then." Pete was sullen now; the big hands in his lap were clenched.

"When did you find out?" Bev pursued relentlessly. "During dinner?"

"Well, she acted rather cheaply."

"How? Did she say or do anything improper?"

"Not that you could put your finger on."

It was Bev's turn to snort.

"You seem to have some trouble with that finger, Mr. Stoner."

"Well, anyone could see what she was!"

"Very clear. Did you drink much during the evening?"

Pete glared.

"No."

Beverly smiled nastily.

"I hoped you would say yes, Mr. Stoner," he remarked glibly. "Otherwise I can hardly conceive of any excuse for what you, a married man, did later. Surely you won't deny that you made a pass at Miss Smith and received a well deserved kick in the shins for your pains? Or will I have to produce her as a witness?"

Pete breathed heavily and looked at Stowell. The latter turned to Benson.

"How much longer, Commander, must we put up with this line of irrelevance?" he demanded.

The Commander frowned.

"Until counsel finishes," he said.

"Oh, I won't deny it," Pete admitted peevishly. "Maybe I was a bit full."

"So you were drunk after all?" Bev continued.

"Not drunk. Just a bit lit. It was Saturday night."

"Do you remember returning to the ship?"

"Certainly."

"Who was with you?"

"Ellis and thàt girl."

"Did he make lewd propositions to her before coming on board?"

"No."

"What did he say to her?"

"Oh, he pulled the old gag about scrambled eggs and showing her the ship."

"And what did you see that made you suspect he had other motives?"

"Any child could see what his real motive was."

"Apparently then, I'm not a child. Did you see them go into his cabin?"

"No."

"Did you see them in a suspicious pose in the wardroom?"

"No."

"What *did* you see?"

"I've already told you. I went to bed."

Bev leaned back and smiled. "No more questions," he said.

CHAPTER FIVE

VERY LITTLE WAS accomplished during the rest of that day and the board recessed early in the afternoon. Beverly, unwilling to associate with his client in non-legal hours, fled to Panama City and spent a long evening on Lydia Schmidt's veranda, sipping rum drinks and making unkind remarks about the Livermores. It was, anyway, a complete relaxation, and he was in a more cheerful mood when he joined Ellis at the table in the recreation shack at eight o'clock the following morning. The board was convening early in the hope of finishing up before lunch, which prospect appeared very likely as there were only a few witnesses still to be heard. Bev was feeling moderately sanguine about the result; little had so far been uncovered to justify the drastic step of court-martial. His hopes leaped even higher, moreover, when Mr. Stowell called Sheridan Gilder to the stand. It was not at all clear what the recorder hoped to prove by this as Mr. Gilder had never been aboard the *Sardonyx*, but apparently the board had got wind of his role in instigating the proceedings and wanted to hear more. Mr. Gilder testified as to his "disagreeable" meeting with Ellis at the Union Club prior to the departure of the *Sardonyx* for Guantanamo and mentioned his "distress" at tales that he had subsequently heard. His sentences were moderate and restrained, his attitude to the board deeply respectful. Stowell did not press him.

Beverly gripped the arms of his chair tightly as Stowell turned to him with a clipped:

"Your witness."

"I have some questions I'd like to ask Commander Gilder," he said in a strained, unfamiliar voice. Commander Benson nodded and Bev turned to Gilder who looked at him with just a trace of a smile as if to encourage any friendliness that might still exist. All traces vanished when he had taken in Bev's expression.

312

"Mr. Gilder," Bev began, "would you tell the board under what circumstances you first became aware of any suspicious conduct on the part of Lieutenant Ellis?"

Mr. Gilder appeared to reflect and then answered stiffly:

"It was reported to me shortly after the return of the U.S.S. *Sardonyx* from her last convoy."

"You use the word 'reported,' Mr. Gilder. Perhaps you will explain the exact circumstances of your learning the details."

Gilder moved uneasily and glanced at Commander Benson.

"Is your question relevant, Mr. Stregelinus?" the latter demanded gruffly. "Why is it of interest to us where this information came from?"

Beverly suddenly realized that his whole shirt was wet. His voice shook.

"It bears on the motive with which this whole investigation was started, Commander," he said, "and I think it will throw some light on the value of Mr. Stoner's testimony."

"Answer the question, Mr. Gilder."

"I heard this information from a source that an information officer is not privileged to reveal," Gilder said shortly.

All nervousness left Beverly in a great surge of wrath. He turned to the board.

"I should like to ask Miss Audrey Emerson to testify. And as her testimony is relevant to Mr. Gilder's last comment, which I maintain to be a deliberate falsehood, I would like Mr. Gilder to remain in the room."

The members looked at each other in surprise. Commander Benson whispered with the other two for a moment.

"We will adjourn to discuss the point."

The board rose and Beverly followed them out of the shack. He hurried down the walk to the Administration Building and up to Section Blue. Audrey was sitting at her typewriter. She jumped up when she saw him.

"Come on," he said.

They left the room together and went down the stairs.

"Are you ready for it?" he asked.

"Ready for anything," she answered.

"Good girl."

The board was reassembling when they entered the shack.

"Miss Emerson may take the stand," Commander Benson announced, "and I will ask Mr. Gilder to remain and hear her testimony."

Audrey took her seat at the long table and gave her name to the reporter.

"Miss Emerson," Beverly began, "do you recollect a conversation with Commander Gilder at Fort Amador Beach two weeks ago on the subject of Lieutenant Ellis?"

"I do."

"Miss Emerson, you work, I believe, in the Information Office?"

"Yes."

"Were you and Mr. Gilder at the beach for official reasons?"

"No."

"I take it, then, that it was a purely social occasion?"

"That's correct."

"Do you recollect the exact nature of the conversation?"

"Perfectly."

"Was there anything confidential about it? I am using the word 'confidential' in its naval sense now. Was there anything mentioned that had been derived from information sources as such?"

"No. It was gossip, pure and simple."

"I see. Would you tell the board the nature of this gossip?"

Audrey paused, but only for an instant. Looking Bev straight in the eyes she said:

"I gave Mr. Gilder a somewhat colored version of Mr. Ellis' activities as they had been told me by yourself and Mr. Stoner."

The members of the board exchanged glances and even the reporter looked up.

"Describe that in more detail, please, Miss Emerson," the Commander said. "Tell us exactly what you told Mr. Gilder and where you learned it yourself."

Audrey proceeded to tell of the conversation that she had had on the beach with Pete and Bev and of their adventures in Miami.

"Did you feel, Miss Emerson," Bev interrupted, "that these tales were to be taken seriously?"

"No. Not entirely. We all had a bad habit of exaggeration," she explained to the board, "which we used to make allowances for among ourselves. I supposed that the *Sardonyx* was not perhaps the tautest ship in the Navy, but I knew too that Pete and Bev were talking loosely with regard to the more serious things and did not mean to be taken up on them."

"I am sorry that it should seem so natural a thing to you to hear junior officers insult their superiors," the Commander broke in gravely.

"I fear I must share the blame," she said quietly. "Perhaps I encouraged an atmosphere of loose talk."

"But when you repeated these things to Mr. Gilder," Commander Benson continued, "did you indicate that they were not to be taken seriously?"

There was a pause.

"I'm afraid not."

"Why?"

Audrey looked out through the big screens at the grass lawn. It was dark outside and, as always in Panama, it was beginning to rain. The green plant by the door looked very green. Suddenly her eyes filled with tears, but unembarrassed she looked back at Bev.

"I was angry at Mr. Stregelinus for personal reasons," she said calmly. "I knew that Mr. Gilder hated Mr. Ellis because Mr. Ellis had once been rude to him at the Union Club. I knew that Mr. Gilder would not let this rumor die and that Mr. Stregelinus would get in trouble."

Beverly looked away. There were a few more questions from the board and then he heard Commander Benson say:

"I must tell you, Miss Emerson, that I take a very grave view of your conduct."

With that she left the room. Bev could not see the expression on her face.

The recorder recalled Mr. Gilder who had preserved an absolute silence during the foregoing. He looked very pale and fidgeted. Bev breathed hard.

"You have heard Miss Emerson, Mr. Gilder," he started. "Have you anything to dispute in her statement?"

"It isn't true that I hated Mr. Ellis," he protested angrily. "I had always had the highest respect for him until I heard the gossip relayed by my junior officers who, I gather, are unable to tell the truth or to keep their mouths shut." Here he turned to Commander Benson. "Commander," he said respectfully, "even if I have been grossly deceived as to the character of Mr. Stoner and Mr. Stregelinus, must I be questioned in this way? I had thought that my junior officers were trained to observe accurately and to report accurately. I find they are gossip-mongers. Proper action will be left to Captain Darlington. May I be excused?"

"The defendant has the right to cross-examine you, Mr.

Gilder," Commander Benson rejoined sternly, "whatever discipline in your office you take later on."

"Is it true, Mr. Gilder," Beverly continued inexorably, "that you first learned of the activities of which Mr. Ellis now stands accused in the fashion which Miss Emerson described?"

A long pause was followed by a reluctant "yes."

"What action did you then take?"

"I took the matter up at once with my immediate superior, Captain Darlington."

"What was the next step?"

"Captain Darlington went to the Chief of Staff and this board of investigation was convened."

"Did Lieutenant Ellis have a commanding officer?"

"He did. Naturally."

"Who was he?"

"Captain Lawrence of Inshore Patrol."

"Is Captain Lawrence not competent to handle the discipline of the officers and men under his command?"

"Why, I suppose, of course, he is."

Beverly paused for emphasis.

"Then, tell me, Mr. Gilder," he continued, "is it one of the duties of Naval Information to investigate the private activities of line officers which may appear unbecoming?"

"It is the duty of any naval officer," Gilder related pompously, "to investigate conduct of a brother officer which may be a disgrace to the uniform we all wear."

Beverly gave a wry smile.

"I didn't know," he said patronizingly. "Then you would regard Mr. Ellis' Miami activity as a proper field for information?"

Even Gilder could not go this far.

"Maybe not exactly," he answered, "but—"

"But you showed a remarkable zeal in prosecuting this case," Beverly finished for him. "Two last questions, Mr. Gilder. Would you tell the board what position Mr. Ellis occupied when this investigation began?"

Mr. Gilder looked about him suspiciously.

"He was the commanding officer of the U.S.S. *Sardonyx*."

"Right. And would you now say for the record what position you have recently been ordered to take?"

There was an embarrassed pause.

"I have been ordered to take command of the *Sardonyx*," the witness answered in a muffled voice.

Commander Benson read the findings of the board. He read them in his slow, deliberate voice, pausing at times over the construction of the sentences. He didn't look up more than twice. The opinion was not long but it was to the point. The board, in brief, failed to find that the misconduct of Lieutenant Ellis was of such a nature as to justify court-martial proceedings, but Mr. Ellis was sternly reminded that his personal language and looseness of attitude by no means measured up to the standards which the Navy laid down for its officers and he was advised to give the deepest consideration to these findings. He was exonerated, however, for lack of proof, of the particular issues raised. The board proceeded to find that Lieutenant Stoner, though not a defendant, had been lacking in loyalty to his erstwhile commanding officer and to recommend strongly that Lieutenant-Commander Gilder be given an official reprimand for his officious and malignant interference in bringing the whole matter to the attention of his superiors. Lieutenant-Commander Cheney dissented from the board's conclusion, being of the opinion that Lieutenant Ellis' conduct merited a general court-martial.

When the board had adjourned and filed out Beverly and his client sat facing each other as the yeoman busied himself clearing the table and emptying ash trays.

"Well you did it, Bev!" Ellis cried after a moment in affected heartiness. "By God, you showed them!"

Beverly gathered up his papers in silence.

"Is there anything I can do for you?" Ellis continued.

Bev turned on him in cold exasperation.

"Yes," he retorted. "If you ever get a ship again, which God forbid, you might show some consideration for the feelings of your junior officers!"

With this, his books and papers gathered under his arm, he turned on his heel and walked out.

CHAPTER SIX

AUDREY MADE VERY little trouble for the Navy about her own resignation. Shortly after the investigation Miss Stirling, the Admiral's secretary and senior civil servant of District Headquarters, a large, square-faced woman whose whimpy Georgia drawl served as a cover for Panama's most heavily motored power of organization, summoned her "topside" for "a little private chat." Audrey went up to her office through which passed a constant file of wheeled trays, heaped with mimeographed material and pushed by yeomen, and listened calmly while the senior servant explained. It would be undesirable for obvious reasons, the voice whined, for Miss Emerson to continue working in the Information Office just at present. She (Miss Stirling) wasn't going to go into any pros and cons; the matter was not her affair except insofar as it affected the redeployment of personnel. Personally, she thought Miss Emerson would be well advised to take a non-naval job, but in the event of her not caring to do so it could be arranged to have her transferred across the Isthmus to some naval activity at Coco-Solo—

"There's no need of that, Miss Stirling," Audrey interrupted abruptly. "I'm going to resign. I assume there'll be no difficulty about my getting a release?"

The older woman stared at her, debating if sympathy would be in order. But Audrey simply stared back.

"None at all," Miss Stirling answered crisply. "I'll have it ready this morning. You can pick up your check at noon. Good day, Miss Emerson."

She told nobody in the office about this conversation and she said good-by to no one when she left. She could trust the girls in Miss Stirling's office to get the news around fast enough. At noon she went up to get her check and turn in her identification card; she then walked out of the building and drove home. She had a stunned, unhappy feeling and a rather defiant sense of being in disgrace in the eyes of the world.

Her family had to be content with the briefest account of what had happened. "I've lost my job," she told her mother abruptly as she went through the living room; "I won't be down for lunch." Up in her room she lay on her bed and stared at the ceiling, resolutely ignoring her mother's occasional timid knocks. She appeared at dinner, however, in time to mix them all a cocktail. She seemed in a better mood but continued to limit her explanation to the statement that she'd been "fired" for "talking too much." For the next two days she sulked around the house, her only visit outside being a short walk part way down the hill to the Zone Administration Building to ask for her old job back in the library. When Aunt Betty asked her if she had been successful, she mumbled something about being "told to come back later" and intimated darkly that she had been "black-listed."

Of course this was nonsense. Audrey knew it herself and in a few days she actually did get the job. Most of her friends and acquaintances were in utter ignorance of any unpleasantness with the Navy and saw nothing unusual in her switching positions. The Zone needed more help and the Navy got new enlisted men for clerical work every day. But she persisted in her attitude that the world frowned. Actually she wanted it to frown. She wanted to perform some sort of public penance for what she had done and thought. She felt clotted and her tired imagination revived only at the idea of a spiritual chipping hammer such as she had so often seen used on ships in the yard to bore down below the surface and leave her thin but cleansed. Like all her ideas it became an exclusive preoccupation. She had come up against a wall in her life and dimly she felt that it was a chance that she mustn't lose to learn to climb. Ladders she scorned, she simply stared and stared at the top until it blurred and seemed higher than it was. But it was there.

She assigned herself little tasks in self-discipline. She wanted to call up Beverly and find out what had happened to him, and assiduously she kept away from the telephone. She had always found it next to impossible to be even civil to her Aunt Betty, so she now rigorously if mechanically assigned herself the job of pleasing. This was made even more difficult by her aunt's lavish and unwelcome sympathy.

"Don't fuss, dear," she would say constantly. "We all have our ups and downs."

"It isn't quite as simple as that, Aunt Betty," she answered once with a patient dignity that verged on the sharp. "In wartime it's not particularly pleasant to be ousted from a job serving the armed forces. It's a sort of dishonorable discharge."

"But it was the sort of thing that could happen to anyone, my dear," her aunt implacably continued. "A few loose words. You always did speak up when you were mad. After all, you're a Miles. It's a family trait. And that's nothing to be ashamed of," she concluded with a toss of her head that almost upset the bowl of peas she was shelling.

Audrey stared quietly at the ravaged old woman and reflected with a new amazement that her aunt really believed this. That in any set of circumstances she could always derive comfort from the contemplation of the lower branches, imaginatively viewed, of the ritualistically watered family tree. How it would have staggered Aaron Miles, the bankrupt Orange County politician whose legislative committee work in Richmond during the Civil War had been rated by General Stuart as "worth two divisions" to the *North,* to hear his granddaughter and great-granddaughter thus deriving sustenance from his name! And when Aunt Betty dies, she reflected, no doubt Mother will construct some legend about her.

"If Great-grandmother Miles had lost her job during the War Between the States," she pointed out, "the family would have worn sackcloth and ashes, and you know it."

Aunt Betty blinked uncomprehendingly.

"Ladies didn't have jobs then," she said evasively.

"Oh, well, her place in the bandage rollers or whatever it was."

"You mean her position as Chairwoman of the Keswick Society of Sisters of Mercy for the Cause? But that could never have happened."

Audrey gave it up.

"The immunity of that generation must have been delightful," she snapped.

"Don't be bitter, dear."

She started working at the library again and was happy to be occupied. The girl whom they had got to replace her when she had gone to work for the Navy had been a poor substitute, and they were glad to have her back. She was at her most efficient with cards and books; she gave good advice, if a little on the heavy side, to service men who came in looking for something to read, arranging special shelves of "suggested non-fiction." She had time to read too, and started once again to assemble material for the biography, long delayed, of George Eliot.

The first Saturday afternoon that she got off she left Quarry Heights, to which she had clung since resigning from the Navy and walked down to call on Helen. Her friend, who was now back with her parents, as her husband had gone to the Solomons, was sitting on the porch as placid as a Giotto Madonna, the very symbol, as no doubt she felt herself to be, the very essence of the mysterious process of maternity. She asked about the office and listened rather perfunctorily while Audrey explained the circumstances of her resignation.

"I never did like that place much, anyway," she said at last. "I think you're well off."

"But it makes all the difference how you leave it, don't you think?" Audrey regretted this after she'd said it, afraid that Helen would think she was drawing a parallel between their cases. But she need not have worried. Helen's obsession with her marriage was such that she couldn't even imagine any criticism of the circumstances leading up to it.

"Not really," she answered. "I think there were some very bad people there. How can it matter how you're out as long as you're out? I'm sure you're more useful to the war in the library. Think of all the lonely soldiers who like to read. And with all that you've read, Audrey! You must be a great help." But she wasn't thinking of Audrey or the office at all. The little brawl there had no significance to her. Audrey was understandably provoked. The smug isolation of an expectant mother was hard enough to take, but when it was combined with the smugness of the service wife it was almost unbearable. She remembered, however, her good resolutions. When she spoke she was mild enough.

"I can see how trivial it all looks to you, darling," she said with a rather wry smile, "and why shouldn't it? Your well is overflowing. You make me feel as dry as an old twig."

But Helen was quite unconscious of malice.

"You ought to get married, Audrey," she said. "Really."

"Just married or to anyone in particular?"

"Well, I've always been fond of Tommy Sondberg myself, and everybody knows he likes you."

This remark revealed a lack of familiarity with Audrey's affairs so abysmal that the latter was genuinely stung.

"Really, Helen," she retorted, getting up; "you must think any man would do for me. Babies aren't that important in everybody's life."

As she walked back up the long hill to Quarry Heights she was bristling. She stopped and pushed back the hair that was slipping over her forehead and to rest for a moment in the little breeze that suddenly fluttered across her path. And just then she caught sight of Laura's yellow roadster turning into the road above her by the Governor's house. Quickly she glanced around, but there was no place to slip away. What annoyed her about Helen was the latter's lack of interest, but Laura's prying curiosity was far worse. The roadster was already upon her and there was a sound of brakes.

"Audrey, my dear, do you know I haven't laid eyes on you since all this happened? Where have you been?" One hand lay somehow ostentatiously on the wheel, the other dangled a cigarette out the window, but her eyes snapped with excitement. "Really, I think it's all been too beastly. Of course, as Commander Robinson says, we can't afford that kind of thing, but in Operations we all feel they could have strained a point with you. I hope you're not too down."

"Not at all."

"That's good. I was worried. All the talk and everything."

"It doesn't bother me a bit, Laura," she continued calmly. "I was sick of that office anyway."

"I wouldn't take that tone if I were you, dear." Laura's voice had a slight edge. "Some people might say those grapes were just a tiny bit sour."

"I know. I ought to wear a hair shirt."

"Oh, you! But the whole thing was rather a scandal and if I were you I'd take the humble line. Just for a little while, you know. It pays off with the Navy."

"Show me the nearest hole. I'll go crawl into it."

Laura shrugged her shoulders.

"Well, I tried," she said. "But, Audrey," she continued, "I don't want you to think this is going to make any difference between us."

"I don't."

"That's right." Laura looked just a bit nettled.

An MP drove up behind them on a motorcycle.

"You can't park here, sister," he shouted. Immediately all her temper was transferred in his direction.

"Sister!" she repeated in horror. "Sergeant." she exclaimed in a high imperious voice, "how would you like following me up the hill for a little interview with Major-General Smith?" But it was lost on the MP who had started up his motor again while she was talking and now drove on.

"What a damn rude creature!" she snapped. "Did you see his number?"

"No."

"Lucky for him!" Laura stared angrily after him. "Well, I'm on my way. Will you dine with us tomorrow night? Nothing grand. Father and a few friends."

This would have described even the grandest evening at Laura's, but Audrey accepted.

When she got home she went straight to her room and slammed the door. She leaned against the bureau and stared at herself in the mirror. She pulled her hair back straight with one hand and placed the other on her hip. "Laura Smith?" she queried in a vague tone. "Do I know you?" She was clad in a long white gown; she had diamonds in her hair. "Oh, yes"—as she swept on from the street to the crowded lobby—"*years* ago in Panama." And turning abruptly from the mirror she threw herself down on the bed. "How can I go on this way? How can I?" she moaned.

If only she could go to Beverly and throw herself on her knees and ask him if in all fairness she hadn't done enough to be forgiven. She felt capable of any abasement that would enable her to tell him how she loved him. Loved him? Adored him. "Yes, Bev, why should I conceal it? You'll never care." The tears came again with the agony of emotion trying to push its way out between the choking branches of sentiment. She felt so riddled with the hackneyed attitudes of her own desperate monologues that she wondered in despair if she really felt anything at all. "Do I love him? Am I sorry?" she asked. If she shook herself and put a meter on her heart and focused her mind on everyday things would there be anything different? Wasn't she still she, the Audrey who always knew what she was doing? "But I want to love him!" she cried aloud; "I've got to love him."

But it was her own emotion that preoccupied her. She didn't think that anything would come of it; she had no hopes of attaching Beverly in any permanent fashion. He was attracted to her, she knew, but events had come between them, and anyway he was engaged. She didn't really think he was in love with Sylvia; he had shown her a picture of her once in the office and she had thought her very phthisic. Beverly always said she was "wonderful" and "magnificent" but he used these words to describe such varying personalities as Lydia Schmidt and Mrs. Livermore, and she couldn't feel they meant much. No, it was an eminently suitable marriage, and that was that. And like everything else, she decided in her fit of melancholy, it served her right.

As she stared steadily and blankly at the ceiling she thought regretfully of her religious phase at thirteen when she had been able to squeeze her eyes tight shut and pray very hard and feel that warm glow all through her that we interpret as the nearness of God. It seemed a little base to turn now to the long abandoned deity; it seemed to put him in the position of a doctor or lawyer summoned only in trouble. She closed her eyes, however, and repeated the Lord's Prayer. But what was the use? She could hear herself say it, knew herself attitudinizing; she could feel only a vague fear at the hypocritical and pompous reverence of her tone as the words fell out and wondered if her instincts of faith, long unused, had not atrophied beyond hope of revival.

CHAPTER SEVEN

BEVERLY'S FAILURE TO call her was intentional. He wanted time to pull himself together and adjust himself to his new circumstances. The simple facts of his situation were bad enough as he reluctantly reviewed them: in love with one girl, engaged to another, and deep in the bad graces of a military organization that in the twinkling of a carbon could whisk him off to almost any one of the world's less attractive atolls. He was already out of the Information Office; that had occurred immediately after the board had adjourned in a brief sharp interview with Captain Darlington. Miss Sondberg had then typed him a set of orders to report for temporary duty to the commanding officer of the District Headquarters area pending his further disposition by the Bureau of Personnel in Washington. Washington would make its decision on the basis of a letter that the Captain was writing which described Beverly, Amos confided to him, as "unqualified for information duty." In this way, Amos pointed out bitterly, the office could knife Bev without giving him a chance to make a statement as would have been his right had they followed the more routine method of an unsatisfactory fitness report. Bev and Amos talked till late one night as to the possibility of defensive measures, but everything seemed more dangerous than to do nothing.

"After all," Amos told him, "this letter doesn't attack you on any points of morality or conduct. The Bureau wants to weed out unqualified information officers and send them to sea, and Captain Darlington's description of you simply implies that you're not quite bright enough for your present job."

Beverly smiled sourly.

"Not bright enough to be a file clerk."

"That's one point the Captain and I agree on!" Amos cried with his squeaky laugh. "Anyway, if you try writing to Washington about this Gilder business you'll hang yourself higher than a kite." He raised a hand to demonstrate how high. "Even if he hangs with you."

So Beverly submitted meekly. The lieutenant-commander who was in charge of the headquarters area was a genial and talkative man of fifty, regular Navy but much passed over, and he seemed quite unconscious of there being anything irregular about Bev's transfer. He made him one of the six rotating officers of the deck of the headquarters building which involved sitting four hours a day in a small office off the main lobby and solving the small problems that arise at the main entrance of a naval shore establishment: examining questionable passes, receiving routine sentry reports, and speeding up the despatching of station wagons. It was not disagreeable work; there was a pleasant hum of activity and even a slight feeling of importance to it, and he had lots of time off. The only thing he minded was his own acute self-consciousness each time anybody from the Information Office passed through the lobby. He felt that they viewed his present position as the depth of degradation and that they were profoundly sorry for him. Had he not himself in former days referred to it as a "janitor's job"? Everyone, except, of course, McShane, Gilder, Stoner, and the old man, was nice enough to him; with Amos he was as intimate as ever, but he was sure he was looked on as one fallen from the skies and he found it galling. He spent longer before supper now at the little naval bar and his afternoon quota of martinis rose from three to four.

He had no idea what sort of orders he would get and his imagination, active as ever, sometimes visualized the direst proceedings. The vision that haunted him most was the picture of himself in bell-bottom trousers, reduced to the rate of seaman second class and assigned to the New York Naval District where a ghastly fate might throw him the job of swabbing decks in an office filled with his commissioned acquaintance. His heart would stop at the thought, though in nobler moments he saw himself calmly indifferent to the whispered sneers around him as he plied his swab. At other times he fancied himself ordered to a scantily defended island in the Pacific and starting a rubber of bridge after the exhaustion of all ammunition and prior to the final assault. But why poison the present, he would tell himself? Wasn't one meant to live in the present during war? And he would become almost gay and drive into Panama City for an evening at a bar with Amos.

His most persistent source of unhappiness was the intensity of his feeling for Audrey. He was resolved not to call her up until he had come to some sort of decision but as the days passed he seemed to make no further progress in his dilemma. Sometimes it seemed to him that he wasn't engaged to Sylvia at all; as he looked back on the Miami interlude it seemed as unsubstantial as the subject matter of one of his poems. The engagement had not been announced and in his world such matters almost required the sanction of the New York *Herald Tribune*. He was totally unable to picture himself in any relation to Sylvia other than that of protective brother, and her letters, so frequent but so brief and strangely impersonal, did nothing towards any new sense of intimacy. Somehow he had kept the sexual forces of physical desire at bay over a period of years; he had consistently dressed up that emotion in romantic tresses until, a large, inanimate tasseled doll, its very artificiality had made it an easy prey to the forces of acquisitiveness that had been sharpened by his own wishful thinking. Indeed, his "beautiful" friendship with Sylvia seemed to have turned into an ugly and ordinary engagement for money. To this he had sunk. Painfully he recollected the gradual degeneration of his life and his own desperate efforts to survive. The Beverly of twenty-one would surely have gaped incredulously could he have seen his counterpart of thirty-one clutching at an easy commission and a semi-invalid heiress. He didn't need a portrait like Dorian Gray; he could see it now in the frazzled corners of his eyes in a mirror. And now that he saw it and wanted to turn, the past seemed to be in a position to hold him. This was proverbially the case. It made him sick to realize that he loved Audrey as he never believed he could love a girl; he wanted her enough actually to lose sleep. "When I remember how irritating she can be," he told himself wryly, "I just want to slap her and then—why, I'm nothing but a cave man after all!"

More often he thought of her strained white face at the board and her clear, unevasive testimony and loved her for it. How perfectly she knew how to take the consequences; how many girls would have wriggled out of the whole thing! Oh yes, when he thought of her as his wife he was still capable of squirming at the idea of being related to people like the Emersons and Miss Miles. He gave himself bad moments at the thought of Bella Stroud on the subject of "poor, infatuated Beverly," and it was torture to picture what

her smile would be like when she heard Aunt Betty shake
the branches of the moldy family tree. But there were things
more important than Bella's point of view, and weren't these
the crossroads? He was bringing himself, gradually to be
sure but steadily, to the point of view that Sylvia would
mind the severance as little as he. She had refused him
once, he reasoned; perhaps it was his turn now. He shrank
at the prospect of Angeline's anger; when thwarted she never
forgave and she had been trying to get Sylvia married for
years. He knew what a good hater she could be when aroused
and that the Stroud world would be closed to him as hard
as she could close it. But he reflected, also, that nobody
now could close many more doors than their own; society
no longer acted with any unanimity, probably because society
no longer existed. And, anyway, he was wondering if he
would live in New York at all; he had little enough to go
back to. He might realize his old ambition of teaching at
Chelton School. Audrey would hardly mind this; it was out
of the Canal Zone and near Boston. An academic life would
provide ample opportunities for scholarships for their children. Children! He had always wanted children; he loved
children. And he was quite sure, really, that Sylvia could
never have any.

Such was his nervous train of thought one morning as he
sat at his desk glancing occasionally at an open copy of
Better Left Unsaid by Daisy, Princess of Pless, which he had
only partly concealed under a map of the headquarters area
that he had been told to study.

"Don't you even stand for the Captain of the Marine
Guard?"

Steve Kennan, the diminutive Marine officer who occupied
this position and who bullied everyone at Headquarters, was
standing in front of the desk. Steve's men were popularly
supposed to be devoted to him, but then, as Bev often
pointed out, nobody ever asked them.

"Occasionally." Bev slipped the map over the exposed pages
of Princess Daisy as he leaned forward on his elbows. "But
not while I'm OOD."

"Any orders?" This was a daily reference to the possibility of Bev's departure.

"None."

"I have a suggestion."

"For me?"

"You'll see what a friend I am. Commander Benson is leaving."

Bev looked at him for a second.

"You think I ought to get his job?"

Kennan coughed with dignity.

"Very funny. The Commander hopes to be placed in charge of a group of LST's. To an ignorant desk hugger such as yourself I may as well explain that an LST is a landing ship designed to carry tanks to the enemy beachhead—"

"I know," Bev interrupted impatiently. "Large Slow Targets."

Kennan made a little bow.

"The usual joke. I'm so glad to see you have as yet acquired no wit. A dangerous thing in the Navy. In any event I would suggest that you ask him to take you on his staff. They say the amphibs can use anybody."

Bev stared, but with interest.

"Amphib!" he exclaimed. "I might get killed."

"The plan has many advantages."

"Do you think he'd really take me?"

"I have every reason to believe him unbalanced. Anyway, he can only say no." The Marine's tone became friendlier. "I don't like to see you sitting here like a milk toddy waiting for those anemic bastards in Darlington's office to ship you off to the Galapagos. Act!" Here he pounded his fist on the desk.

The upshot of this was that after some coaching from Kennan which he later disregarded he sat waiting that afternoon in the bar for a chance to catch the Commander alone. Benson arrived at five, his usual time, and took a seat at a table in the corner with a glass of beer. Diplomatically Bev substituted a beer for his usual martini and approached the table.

"May I sit down, sir?"

The Commander simply waved at an empty chair.

"I hear you're leaving us," Bev started off cheerfully, a confidence in his voice that he did not feel. Benson looked at him coolly for a moment.

"Not that I've heard," he said.

"I thought you were getting an amphibious command."

The Commander snorted.

"The way scuttlebutt flies around this place is something that beats me. I'm not getting anything," he retorted. In a moment, however, he added more politely: "I don't mind

telling you, though, that it's true that I've applied for amphibious duty."

"Well, they say that's one request that's always granted,"
Bev said with a laugh.

"Possibly." The Commander was uncommunicative.

Beverly hesitated. Oh what the hell, he thought.

"Commander," he said bravely.

"Yes?"

"Do you mind if I ask you something?"

"What?"

"I'd like to go with you."

There was a silence.

"That's a nice thing to hear," Benson said pleasantly
enough, "but you know I can't pick my own—"

Bev was so excited now that he interrupted him.

"Please let me explain why first."

There was another silence, this time one of surprise.

"Go on."

"I suppose you guessed that I was sticking my neck out
in acting as Ellis' defense counsel. Well I was. I knew he
was getting a dirty deal and I thought it was up to me to
do something about it. Now, of course, Captain Darlington
is out to get me."

The Commander looked serious.

"And that's why you want amphibious duty?"

"One reason."

"I can hardly discuss the personal animosity that may exist
between you and your superior officers." He was very stiff,
very correct. "Still, if you're qualified for the job there's no
reason you shouldn't apply. Have you had any sea duty
or communications experience?"

"None. That's just it," Bev confessed. "But I could learn,"
he continued desperately. "I'd start studying right away. I
hear that in amphib they take lots of beginners."

"That's true of all branches now, but even so—"

"Oh, please, sir!"

"You'll have to learn not to interrupt all the time, Mr.
Stregelinus," the Commander said sternly.

"I'm sorry, sir."

"What do you think you could do?"

Bev rushed into an enthusiastic description.

"If you became an LST group commander I could be your
personnel officer. I know quite a bit about rates and personnel reports. I used to have to check all those things for

Captain Darlington. And then I could be useful to you in all sorts of odd jobs. I'd be a sort of maid-of-all-work."

He hadn't meant to use this expression but it slipped out. Fortunately the Commander smiled.

"Why pick on me?" he asked.

Again he hesitated.

"Can I tell you?"

"Can you?" Benson repeated in surprise.

Bev staked his all.

"Because you're the one officer down here who seems to me to have every quality an officer should have," he said in a strained voice. "You're the only one who really cares about getting on with the war. You're—"

"My gosh, man, what brought all this on?"

"Oh, I admired the way you presided at that board. And I—well I—" He stopped in confusion. "Well, everyone knows how unfairly you were treated in the *Montauk* case," he blurted.

The Commander looked up sharply.

"That'll be enough of that," he said angrily. "In fact I guess you've said enough of everything. You seem to have the makings of a trouble-maker, Stregelinus."

"Oh, no, sir. Not for you."

This time there was a long silence. Then the Commander got up.

"I tell you what you do," he said gruffly. "Send your full name and service number over to my office on a card. I'll write a letter about it. And I suggest you put in as much spare time on communications as you can. I won't be leaving for a few weeks."

Beverly was so surprised he was barely able to thank the Commander properly before the latter walked away. Then he hurried over to the bar for a martini.

"Amos!" he cried to his friend as he caught sight of him in the doorway. "Amos, I'm going to sea!"

CHAPTER EIGHT

WHEN AUDREY ARRIVED at Laura's on Sunday night she found that she was the first of the guests. Laura came down in a few moments, her tall figure snappily crackling in black satin, and exclaimed in admiration at Audrey's green and white dress.

"And the coral necklace! Except you're really not the aloha type," she added in afterthought. A Filipino brought in two cocktails and the girls sat down together on the big sofa.

"Who do you think's coming tonight?" Laura asked brightly.

"The Admiral?"

"My dear, I told you this was just a tiny affair," protested her humorless friend. "And as a matter of fact it wouldn't be quite the thing to ask you two together after all that's been, would it?" she continued. "No. Beverly's coming. He still seems to be the favorite extra man."

"He is amusing."

"Oh, maybe." Laura waved an arm indifferently and spilled some of her cocktail. "Damn." She reached for her handkerchief. "I must say I don't see his great attraction. I suppose it's nothing but snob appeal. The way he flings first names about as if he were spraying the room with Flit. I do think that sort of thing is very ordinary."

"Very."

"You ought to see this girl he's engaged to," Laura continued, rubbing away at the spot on her dress. "I suppose she's got family, in a Manhattan sort of way, but that's certainly all."

Audrey put her glass down on the table and lit a cigarette. "She's really that bad?" she asked.

"My dear, she's death warmed over."

"Poor Bev."

"Oh, she's good enough for him."

"I don't see why you ask him if you feel that way about him."

"Oh, why do I ask anybody?" asked Laura again waving her hand. "Don't be dull."

The party consisted mostly of older army officers and a few wives, women who had been in the Zone before war was declared and who had secured permission to remain by taking jobs with the Army. It was not very amusing. Audrey made little effort at conversation during cocktails. Her eye was constantly towards the hall, and it was with a sudden shock that she found herself staring at Bev who had come in with Laura by the porch. He smiled happily and went over to her.

"I hoped you'd be here," he said. "I've been wanting to see you."

"I've been right at home," she answered flatly.

His look of dismay was genuine.

"But you know how things have been," he protested. "I haven't been free to do anything."

"Not even to telephone?" she demanded, and then remembered how little she was entitled to any such attention. She could see too that he understood all that her question implied, for he didn't look hurt in the slightest. He only smiled. Then Laura came crackling over and told them dinner was ready, and, of course, they were seated at opposite ends of the dining room table, but it didn't really matter for all during the tedious meal she had the pleasant and reassuring feeling that he was watching her. She had been put on General Smith's left, more, as she well knew, from his choosing than from his daughter's and she listened easily with an effortless smile to the familiar round of his tales of early Canal days. It was of all subjects the most familiar to her for she had heard it often enough, goodness knows, at home, and her ability to supply comments that actually had some relevance had long made her a favorite with the lieutenant-governor. She had heretic views, it was true, of the American acquisition of Panama territory; she called it a "swindle," and although this would have struck the General as the last outrage coming from a man he positively enjoyed it from a woman. Female opinions had no importance in his mind and Audrey's gave him a chance to expand indefinitely, almost righteously, on the topic most dear to his heart.

"I know, my dear," he said, shaking his head. "You'd

probably have us give Texas back to Mexico. And New York to the Indians."

They always ended on this note.

"Oh, General, the way you men catch us up!" Audrey murmured in one of her rare Southern moments. "I'm so glad the planning of these huge things falls on people like you. We girls would make such a mess of it!"

Bev followed her out to the porch afterwards and they strolled down on to the lawn. The rest of the company was drinking coffee in the parlor.

"You must have something you want to get out of the old man," he said peevishly.

"Me?"

"You had him eating out of your hand all during dinner. I was watching."

"So?"

"What are you trying to do? Marry him?"

She laughed in sheer surprise. He had a stubborn, irritated look that made his sarcasm ludicrous.

"I believe I would if I could!" she cried. "Think how livid Laura would be. Oh, Bev, it would be glorious!"

"I'll never understand you, Audrey."

She had never felt more gay.

"Can't I have my admirers?" she demanded. "You have your wonderful Miss Tremaine and I, it appears, have the General."

He gasped.

"Do you put them on the same plane?" he was starting, but he broke off. "It's just that I hate to see you making up to someone like that. It's not like the real you."

"Oh come!" she protested. " 'To love and be loved yet so mistaken'? That is the real me. The Audrey of a thousand Zones. And ultimately, as you insist, Mrs. Smith. Mrs. Alexander Smith. I might even hyphenate it. Audrey Alexander-Smith. Yes." She turned and looked at the big house triumphantly. "After all he's not more than sixty-two. And a man's only as old as he feels. That's what the General says."

"Then you probably wouldn't mind squeezing him into his corsets."

"Not at all. I'd even swab out his eyes at night."

He burst into a laugh.

"You're terrible!" But Laura was hurrying across the lawn to them. "Oh bother!" he exclaimed.

"Bev, Audrey," she said rather breathlessly, as she came

up to them, "listen, dears, something too awful has materialized."

They stared.

"Too embarrassing," she continued. "Captain Darlington
just called up and Daddy asked him to come round for a
drink."

Bev and Audrey exchanged glances.

"Well?" Audrey asked.

"So he's coming round for a drink," Bev repeated.

Laura smirked.

"Don't you see, my dears? Surely I don't have to explain
to you."

Audrey felt a sudden rush of anger.

"Explain what, Laura?"

"You make it so hard, Audie," her friend said in a meaner
tone. "You can't pretend you don't know how he feels about
both of you."

"Let him feel," Bev retorted. "He doesn't have to talk to
us."

"Well, of all the—" Audrey was beginning. But Laura
interrupted.

"I thought it would be less awkward generally, Bev, if you'd
take Audrey into town. Take her to the Union Club, why
don't you? The bill's on me of course."

"Laura!" came her father's voice from the porch.

"Oh, dear," she said nervously. "I'll have to run in. Do
be angels, though, and do as I say." And she hurried off.

Audrey was speechless for a moment. When she spoke it
was in cold, slow anger.

"Of all the mangy, spiteful bitches," she began, "I'm sure
our Laura is the mangiest and most spiteful. She and her
God-damn military connections and her sacred old cow of a
father can go and jump—"

"In Gatun Lake," he finished for her.

"Well, don't you think it's the limit?" she protested. "Are
you just going to sit there and take it?"

"Who cares about Laura? This is our chance to get out
of the dullest party of the year. Besides, I want to talk to
you."

She contemplated him for a few seconds.

"Well as for getting out of the party," she said slowly, "it's
abundantly clear that I'm going to do that. What I'm debating is whether to seize this opportunity of telling my 'best

friend,' Laura, whom I've disliked intensely all my life, off, and off with a large 'O.' "

Bev didn't like the glitter in her eyes; he shuddered at the prospect of the scene.

"I have a much better idea."

"Yes?"

"Let's take her up."

"Take her up on what?"

"On her Union Club offer. She doesn't think for a second that I'd be enough of a bounder to make her pay. But that's where dear Laura made a mistake."

Audrey began walking again, very slowly, while she gave the most careful consideration to his alternative.

"There's a lot to be said for that," she said thoughtfully. "It hits Laura where she feels it most. Her pocketbook. She's stingy as Shylock, you know. We could run up quite a bill at the club. If I just told her off now she'd have a righteous sense of being outraged. You see, she really believes all the eyewash she talks. She really believes we are in disgrace and she really believes that Captain Darlington would choke if he saw us even across a room, and she *really* believes that she has a social position to maintain. She has no sense of human inertia and indifference. As a matter of fact she just doesn't know anything. She's got the philosophy of a mosquito."

They decided to coöperate with Laura. They slipped back into the parlor and Audrey went up to her hostess and said in not too loud a voice but loud enough to be overheard:

"Darling, you know we told you we'd have to leave right after dinner? Well, here it is."

Laura's eyes flashed with surprise. Then she smiled.

"Oh, yes, your party," she said. "I'd almost forgotten." She followed them out into the hall after they'd said good night to General Smith.

"I'll never forget this," she said sweetly. "You're both dears."

Bev made a little gesture of writing on his palm.

"Have you got that note, Laura?" he asked.

"Note?"

"I think we ought to have one from you to the manager at the Union Club, don't you?"

She stared.

"But you're a member, aren't you, Bev?"

"Certainly. But I'm not paying the bill tonight. Remember?"

She looked from one to the other.

"Oh, yes," she said, "of course." She laughed nastily. "I'll telephone. How will that do?"

"Fine. We'll wait."

They stood at the door of her father's study while she dialed the number and told the manager to put Mr. Stregelinus's expenses for the night on her account. Then they both made a little bow to her and went out the front door. All during the trip to the club they laughed almost hysterically at the trapped expression on Laura's face.

Sunday at the Union Club was pleasantly uncrowded. It was ideal for the cool, quiet drinking that can be such a mellifluous aftermath to the robuster festivities of Saturday night. They took a table outside on the patio which they had almost to themselves. Through the French doors leading to the conservatory by the oval bar they could see Lydia Schmidt presiding over a party of twelve.

"Let's go straight to work," Bev said cheerfully. "I know what I'm going to start with. Champagne cocktail with a stem of crème de menthe. And some of those small *pâté de foie gras* sandwiches.

"You've been planning this!" she cried.

"Only in the car. Will you have the same?"

"The very same."

The waiter nodded and went off.

They drank cocktail after cocktail that night and talked of everything except what was most on their minds. They both had the same feeling of relaxation and infinite time; they both knew they would come eventually to the painful point; they both wanted to extend the interlude, filling it in happily with champagne and gossip in the most idle and dreamy of drifting evenings. He talked a lot about his family and told her ridiculous anecdotes of Bishop Means and his lady parishioners; he laughed at his Stregelinus grandfather even and described the little privately printed memoranda that each showy generation produced for the next. She in her turn talked about Aunt Betty's boardinghouse and what the students used to say behind her back and entered into the mysteries of General Smith's dyed hair. They lost track of time and people, and both got rather tight.

Lieutenant-Commander Gilder's pleasure in Lydia's dinner party was largely spoilt by the unwelcome sight, so directly before his eyes across the floor, of the couple who had recently plunged him into such painful embarrassment. He stiffened noticeably when Lydia waved at them.

"There's Bev," she told him. "Yoo hoo, dear!" she called.

"Out with that little Zonite again, I see." He couldn't keep the venom from his speech even though Lydia might take offense. But she didn't notice.

"So he is. That nice little Emerson girl. Cute but intense, don't you think? Modern. Young people don't have that 'give' we used to have. But poor dears, with the war and everything—"

"There seems to be plenty of 'give' over there," he said nastily, further irritated by Lydia's presumption in lumping him with herself in an older generation.

This time she understood.

"And why shouldn't there be?" she demanded.

"Well, Lydia, when you see an engaged man out with a girl who's not his fiancée and both drinking quantities of champagne, what do you think?"

"I think there's a war going on and they're having a swell time and it's nobody's damn business but their own!"

"You don't think it makes it rather obvious that he's going to marry the New York girl for her money?"

Lydia brushed it off with a laugh.

"Someone's got to support Bev," she said. "Anyway, how do you know he's engaged?"

"Stoner says so. He was in Miami with them."

"I think it's all very encouraging. I thought Bev was afraid of girls."

Gilder sniffed disdainfully.

"Sometimes those people are heterosexual," he said.

Lydia turned on him angrily.

"And what are you?"

"Oh, I go in for anything," he answered with a weak smile.

She snorted.

"I believe it! But what beats me is this righteous attitude about Bev and that girl when everyone in the Zone knows what a philanderer you are. And you with a wife in the States!"

"A wife expects that sort of thing," he said coolly.

"I should write her about you! I'll bet I could say a few things she wouldn't expect."

Gilder let it drop, for Lydia's rising heat was beginning to attract the attention of the others at the party, but he retaliated as best he could by avoiding all further conversation and brooding unsociably for the rest of the evening.

"Sex is like a silly school game," Audrey was saying as she looked down the empty stem of her glass. "Nobody really believes in the rules. But they hang on to them just the same. It's only human. We love our rules. They give us a chance to make a distinction between those who get by and those who don't. And that's fun. But as far as morals are concerned—well, there's not a moral in the whole picture."

"I have morals," Bev protested.

"Morals, dear? Or are you just timid?" She looked at him questioningly over her champagne glass.

"Both," he answered promptly. "One can be both. I'm no believer in modern freedom. I'm a Victorian," he emphasized with a toss of his head, "and there are certain things which should only be discussed behind barn doors."

"And this, I take it, is not a barn."

"I didn't mean that as a reproach."

"Oh, you men," she retorted. "I know you. The girl's got to be wrapped in cotton but the boy can play——"

"Not at all," he interrupted with dignity. "I'm not that old fashioned. I don't believe in a double standard. I believe in a man keeping himself pure for the girl he intends to marry." He said this with quite an air. "That was the way my old headmaster at Chelton put it. It was good enough for him. It's good enough for me."

"You're drunk," she said firmly. But she didn't smile. She knew perfectly well that he expected her to and perfectly well that he meant to be very funny about his New England church school idealism, but at the moment it made no difference. She felt stung.

"I guess your Chelton's too good for me," she said.

"But you believe in morals," he protested. "Really."

"I don't even know what they are," she burst out; "I wouldn't know how to be good if I tried. I'm one of those people who's half full of this and half full of that and I end up by making everybody miserable."

"You haven't made me miserable."

"Of course, I have," she continued unhappily. "You got thrown out of Darlington's office on your ear, didn't you? And Laura won't even have us in her house."

"But Audrey, you know what a fool Laura is!"

"I know what a fool I am!" she went on excitedly. "I

should never have got mixed up with you in the first place! I haven't done a single thing that's made sense since then. I ought to lock myself up somewhere where I wouldn't be always trying to hurt someone."

"Except George Eliot," he said with a smile.

"Oh, she can look out for herself."

"I daresay. But who in the name of heaven, my dear, is going to look out for me?"

She looked at him in despair.

"Don't, Bev!" she said vehemently. "Don't. What's the use?"

He tried to take her hand but she pulled it away. For a moment she covered her face in her hands.

"I'm not any good," she said morosely. "I don't know what love is. I've even been one of Pete's girls!"

"I know that."

Her eyes stared.

"You know!"

"He told me."

She gasped.

"Oh, the snake!" she cried. "The abominable, bragging, loathsome—" He interrupted her with a roar of laughter.

"There you go again," he said, this time taking her hand. "Listen to me, Audrey. I love you. I know that now. God knows it's taken me long enough to find it out and stick to it. But there it is. I don't give a damn about Pete. Or any of the others, if there are any."

Again she stared.

"You're awful!" she said breathlessly. "Quite awful."

He laughed again.

"I still love you," he repeated. He knew what he was saying, and he knew that it was all right. It was all right, he repeated blissfully to himself; it was completely, it was entirely all right. He was doing it, he even told himself in some remote corner of his mind, because it was something that he wanted to do, not because he wanted to look forward to it or back upon it, not because it was any part of any pattern.

"Thank you, Bev," she was saying. The storm had entirely passed. "Thank you, Bev dear, a million times."

"Don't say that," he said smiling. "That's what girls say before they turn you down and say let's be the best of friends."

"And you're afraid I'm going to say that?" she asked.

"Not for a minute."

"You're not?"

"No."

She looked at him quietly for a moment.

"Are you as sure of Sylvia as you are of me?" she asked deliberately. Her eyes, however, looked frightened as soon as she had said it.

But he was ready for this.

"There isn't anything to that at all, Audrey. You know that."

"Does she?"

"That's what's so wonderful about her," he said warmly. "I believe she does. I'm not saying she doesn't care about me a little. That wouldn't be true. But she knows—oh how well she knows—that with me it isn't the real thing. She asked me all about you in Miami. I guess I must have mentioned you in my letters. She knew. She knows everything. And, darling, I'm not exaggerating when I say that I truly believe she would rather have it this way. She's always wanted me to be a more complete person. And she never could really stand being second best."

He believed it now that he had said it. Sylvia retreated from reality and took up a disembodied pose of omniscience and sacrifice. He was ready to worship her for the tolerance with which he so wishfully endowed her. Audrey didn't believe it but she was too tired to worry about Sylvia. That was after all not her responsibility. He filled their glasses again and they drank a toast to each other. For a few moments they said nothing. It was too serious and she changed the mood.

"Why don't you tell me that I'm going to love your mother?" she asked. "I thought all men said that sooner or later."

He made a face.

"What a cat you are."

"Think how happy she'll be when she hears you've broken off an engagement with a rich girl to marry a Zonite."

He laughed.

"Mother won't mind," he said. "Get this straight. I'm the only one who's going to mind that."

"Do you mind so awfully?"

He gave her hand a squeeze.

"Frightfully. I'm such a snob."

She sighed.

"Poor Bev," she murmured. "But think how good it'll be for you."

"Shall we get married here?" he pursued. "Before I go off?"

"You'll never go," she told him. "Nobody ever gets out of Panama. Yes, let's get married here."

"In the Balboa Episcopalian Church?"

She shuddered.

"Anywhere," she answered closing her eyes. "Anywhere you want."

"And bridesmaids and all?"

"God forbid!" She opened her eyes in horror. "Though I suppose you'll have to ask Mrs. Livermore and Mrs. Schmidt."

"Cat!"

"And maybe that magnificent Mrs. Stroud you're always talking about can come down from New York to be your best man!"

He looked shocked.

"She's Sylvia's mother," he said in a serious tone. But she laughed at the look on his face.

"Oh Sylvia's going to give me away!"

There was little enough sense in their conversation but each hardly heard what the other said. He was going to sea, and they were engaged, and a day before they had been poles apart; there was the night and the champagne and Laura's unpardonable behavior and Sylvia's remote but brooding presence. It wasn't like life at all any more; it wasn't even like a dream. When they finally went home Audrey insisted on driving and Bev fell asleep on the seat beside her.

CHAPTER NINE

THE FOLLOWING MONDAY morning found Lieutenant-Commander Gilder back as usual at his broad and empty desk in the corner of Section Blue. The petrified routine of the day went on as it had always gone; the typewriters hummed, the "in" baskets filled; the incessant stream of cards was separated and they were stamped, but everyone knew that since the ominous day of the publication of the findings of a certain board of investigation the atmosphere in the Section had not been the same. Not a soul but was uneasily conscious of the vacant desk near the Captain's door so recently occupied by that funny, unpredictable Miss Emerson and of the presence on the floor below in strange new duties of the popular Mr. Stregelinus. The sun had quite left Mr. Gilder's personality. No longer did his eyes have the sparkle that visitors were used to as they came through the door that he so constantly watched, and when his name was screamed from the Captain's adjacent office it was not with a springy bounce that he left his seat but with a weary shove. For Sherry Gilder was scared. Barely could he concentrate on the memoranda that fluttered into his basket and rarely now did he have an answering wink for Miss Sondberg's smile. His shirts were still crisp and starched, his trousers ruthlessly pressed; his gold maple leaves shone as brightly as ever but he passed a restless hand more often over his black hair and his big fraternity ring was twisted round and round. For the Admiral himself, the mighty Commandant, had torn up Mr. Gilder's new orders when he had read the Ellis case; he had muttered, too, something about "a vicious bunch of old women," and Mr. Gilder had returned in ignominy to the office that he had left so breezily for his first command.

He feared himself a ruined man. How could he now transfer over to the regular Navy upon the return of peace? This had always been a problem, for he was over forty, but

344   *The Indifferent Children*

now it was a clear impossibility. His vision of shore duty in a postwar world in the New York Navy Yard with a nice white house near the Yard Captain's and a friendly bartender at the officers' club faded away before the grimmer picture of a return to the condescending charity of his wife's brother's stock brokerage firm. There was no consolation in Section Blue. His desk was heaped with the papers that Beverly had formerly taken care of; he understood nothing about them and Amos was completely uncoöperative. Nobody could take a letter as well as Audrey, but worst of all by far, bad enough to dwarf these other factors, was the wild violence of the Captain's irritation. The old man could never refer to the morrow now without adding viciously: "If I'm still a Captain in the Navy tomorrow —if they haven't broken me for Gilder's wretched botch in the Ellis affair." Poor Mr. Gilder shuddered to think of his next fitness report. It was all so bad. And he had tried so hard.

This morning he sat for a solid hour brooding about Beverly and his cross-examination. Beverly was in dutch, of course, but how much did that really matter to a man who would get out of the Navy the moment war was over? Beverly would eventually laugh at the whole matter in the sleek penthouse of his rich New York wife while he, Sheridan Gilder, a lieutenant-commander who had always tried to do his duty, would be doing odd jobs unbecoming to his age in a brokerage firm that might even some day—Heaven forbid!—be handling gratefully a tid-bit of the lucrative stock sales of a Mrs. Stregelinus who would probably have shares in everything on the market. Could it be borne? Ugly indeed were the thoughts that crawled like grubs through the dim passageways of his little mind.

Yet even so he might not have reached in his pocket for the scrawl that he had worked over the night before had it not been for the telephone call that now shattered his contemplation.

"This is Lieutenant Stregelinus, Mr. Gilder," the hated voice squawked in his ear. "Good morning."

"I have nothing to say to you, Stregelinus," he snapped.

"But I have something to say to you, Mr. Gilder," the voice went provokingly on. "As District OOD I must inform you that your car has been parked in an unauthorized lot. Please see that it is moved this morning."

All the most irritating things in life are trivial, and irrita-

tion has never been awarded its full credit as a promoter
of tragedy. With the click of the receiver, so smartly smug,
Mr. Gilder vibrated in an ecstasy of hate. His imagination
went out of control. It was a conspiracy, the whole thing,
a plot between the Emerson girl and Stregelinus! Of course!
A plot to ruin him! Craftily he glanced about the room and
reached into his pocket for a missile that he now had no
further doubts about launching.

Written on the back of a Union Club menu was Mr.
Gilder's unfinished symphony, hastily jotted down in the comparative seclusion of the men's toilet. It was not addressed
or signed; it was simply a paragraph, a jumble of words
thrown together to convey uneasiness and suspicion across
hundreds of miles without incriminating or identifying the
sender:

"There are those of us in Panama who think you ought
to know that your fiancé, Stregelinus, is playing a double
game. While he makes no secret of his engagement to you
and the financial security that this guarantees, he can be seen
nightly in the company of a Canal Zone girl, Audrey Emerson by name, with whom he was recently associated in an
ugly naval investigation. It is common knowledge that their
relationship is not a platonic one. They are kept from marriage only by lack of means. Don't be their goat."

He put the note back in his pocket and set his mind to
work. Obviously it would have to be typewritten; he would
wait until the girls went for their lunch and then dash it
off on Miss Sondberg's machine. He often wrote letters at
her desk; it would not appear unusual. The envelope was
the problem. He knew Miss Tremaine's address; he had
seen it on many of Bev's letters and he was very address-
conscious, but naval censorship required the sender's name
to appear on the upper left hand corner of the envelope
where he was unwilling to put anything. There was also the
matter of the censor stamp. In the Information Office all
letters had to be read by skinny Ensign Malory in Section
Blue, and although he could on occasion be induced to place
his stamp on an envelope already addressed without reading
its contents, it was going to be a tough problem to get
him to put it on an envelope that was totally blank. Certainly it was humiliating for a lieutenant-commander to be
turned down by an ensign, but he also had to consider that
if he made too much of an issue of the thing in getting
his way Malory would remember it, and if Miss Tremaine

should write the Commandant about her anonymous letter (one could never tell what women would do) he might be able to provide a clue at a possible subsequent investigation (Mr. Gilder was very much aware of investigations). He shivered at the idea of how the regular Navy would view an officer who engaged in such letter writing activity, yet never once did it occur to him to write the epistle under his own signature. Of such is the underworld.

All during the morning he turned the case over in his mind until, when Miss Sondberg actually got up to go for lunch, his heart was beating in near panic. He looked carefully around the office and then slipped over to the typewriter. Inserting a white card in the machine he slowly typed his message, making several intentional errors to give the impression of an amateur.

"Do you want these reports to go out now, sir?" came a voice from close by and before he could stop himself he had placed a hand over the card in the typewriter. But Ensign Malory did not appear to notice anything. He stood with his usual indifference in front of Mr. Gilder, holding a large handful of long sheets.

"Er—yes. That's right." Gilder sat back in his chair and tried to look composed. "And, Frank," he continued, taking the bull by the horns with sudden courage, "stamp three or four envelopes for me, will you? I want to write some business letters during my lunch hour about reinvestments. Nothing particularly secret except I hate to have anyone know all about my little property."

"You know I'm not supposed to do that, Commander."

"Of course you're not. But give a guy a break, can't you? There's nothing in these letters that Hirohito would want to see."

"Have you addressed the envelopes?"

Mr. Gilder shook his head impatiently.

"No, I haven't. If you won't, you won't. I just thought you might do me a little favor." And he turned angrily back to the typewriter.

But Ensign Malory had a date with a Panamanian girl the following afternoon and wanted to get off early from the office. Like so many of the sexually inadequate he put his lovemaking on a definite schedule; he mapped out ahead of time the moment for the first pass and the time of night for the ultimate success. It was very important for him to take her to the beach the next day at three. He said nothing but when he left the office for lunch he deposited four envelopes at Mr. Gilder's elbow, each bearing the round, red censor circle about his blue initials.

Beverly looked up from the desk in his little narrow office just as Mr. Gilder passed through the corridor on his way to his quarters for lunch. Instinctively he nodded, and smiled to himself when he received a brief, cold stare. The smile disappeared, however, a second later; it was only a short interruption to his miserable concentration on the hardest letter that he had ever had to write. Everything on the page before him and on the many that had preceded it, now crumpled in the waste basket, seemed either unbearably priggish or insufferably sententious. He had tried a terse, abrupt note; he had tried a flowing confessional; he had tried self-condemnation and self-justification. And what did it add up to except that he was somebody that he himself didn't like? In sheer desperation he relapsed into a hollow imitation of his old lyrical style, and hating every word of it while admitting that at least and at last the words came easily, he wrote:

"As I look back on Miami I don't think of a city but only of light and color. It was indeed an enchanted period. Perhaps we were recapturing some of the sparkle and blue of Long Island that was no less precious for being unreal. And, alas, being unreal that sparkle and blue seems to vanish into memory with the approach of exile. My return to the heat and the desks and the paper of Panama, my return to this 'ditch' that doesn't really connect two worlds or any worlds, seems to have brought with it an unholy disillusionment. I am not what I was—"

CHAPTER TEN

As soon as her maid had removed her breakfast tray, Angeline Stroud tightened the belt of her pink silk kimono, ran a hand over the hair net which fitted so tightly on top of the tin clips that held her wave, straightened the sheets on her huge neat double bed, and reached for her mail. This was the part of the day that was most her own, and alone with her impressive pile of letters and circulars for an hour before her secretary came in with the "plan of the day" she came as near relaxing as she was ever able. There was almost nothing in the mail that she didn't enjoy. The most dreary advertisements of summer camps for boys, the stuffiest appeals of alumni organizations she dipped into with delight; her sharp buzzing mind darted in and out through this mass of printed exhortations with the relentless monotony of a speeded-up electric train for children which runs hotly up and down its little track on the carpet, whizzing again and again through the same painted tunnel and past the same station of tin. The war had brought new types of appeal couched in sterner tones; large long fingers pointed out of envelopes at her; starving Polish babies with spindly limbs and round distended stomachs illustrated her circulars. Angeline read it all, looked at it all; she separated the pile into smaller ones and dropped them into little boxes on a tray by her desk marked in Gothic letters "Answer" "Keep" and "Destroy." But none of it was quite so much fun this morning, for there was no envelope in Arlie's neat handwriting. None, it was true, had been expected; he was off on a training cruise from New London in a submarine and would probably call up when he got back, but still it was a week now and she didn't quite like it. She got out of bed and went across the soft white carpet of her recently modernized bedroom, glistening with big mirrors and glass, to the windows that looked over the East River. It was a frigid wintry day, dull and cloudy; the water looked very dark and cold and the freighters infinitely shabby. She shuddered slightly and turned away.

She had intended to telephone for half an hour; she wanted to call her brother-in-law, Goodhue, about securities; she wanted to notify her caretaker in the Long Island house to have it ready for the weekend, but to her own dread she found herself immobile before the window. Yes, it was one of her private moments, the kind she dreaded, that hit her every few months, a moment when she saw with an absolute clarity, down to the last little perfectly placed peg what a thing her life had become. She was a brave woman but such visions depleted her. She saw the whole beautifully erected structure of her existence, elaborate, organized, with fountains symmetrically plashing and gravel walks carefully raked. She saw its order and its immobility. Its uncompromising attitude of dissent. Yet being a structure unshared, when anything threatened her children, their lives or their loyalty it collapsed like Kundry's palace without even a clap of thunder, and she was left in the void. She shook her head as if to avoid a buzzing insect and went back to sit on her bed.

"Come in," she said loudly when she heard Sylvia's knock. "Good morning, my dear. Did you have a good night? No, I see you didn't."

Sylvia did look very white and sleepless. She kissed her mother and sat down at the foot of the bed.

"I slept badly," she said tersely. "Anything from Arlie?"

Angeline looked away from her with sudden, tense irritation.

"Why should there be?"

"It's been eight days now," Sylvia went on with a tremor in her voice. "You know the cruises are only meant to last five."

"Don't be absurd, Sylvia," Angeline retorted cuttingly. "You always take on so about trifles. They extend those cruises all the time." She was sharply aware that any insistence on Arlie's silence was going to make her cry and she was furious at the idea of her own daughter being the agent of any such unprecedented collapse.

There was a silence for a minute.

"Have you heard from Bev?" she asked more pleasantly. Sylvia shook her head.

"Not directly. Since last week, that is."

"Not directly?" her mother repeated. "Oh, you mean, his mother."

"No," Sylvia answered with a queer little smile, "not his mother. I've heard from friends of his in Panama."

"Oh, you write them?"

"They write me."

Angeline looked slightly puzzled.

"Well, how is he?" she asked.

"I should say he was very well. Very well indeed."

Angeline nodded.

"Good. I must write him soon. I wonder though that he can stand a sedentary job like that. Don't you think we ought to help him get something more active? Bella tells me Malcolm Dangerfield's in Washington now and a commander. I know he can do something in that line."

Sylvia stared at her for a moment and then laughed out loud.

"Mummie, you're priceless!" she said in a strange, bold tone quite unlike her.

Angeline was nettled.

"What do you mean?" she asked crossly. "Don't you think he wants something more active?"

"I'm sure he doesn't," Sylvia answered quickly. "And so are you if you'd stop to think. Bev's no soldier. He'll be quite happy in Panama for the rest of the war. Even without Bella and the gang."

Angeline noticed with surprise the touch of bitterness in her tone but she was still rather too provoked to investigate it at the expense of the main topic.

"Well I wouldn't be proud of it," she said with some scorn. "I can't imagine being a young man and not wanting to be in it. Mark my words, Syvvie, he'll regret it for the rest of his life. What'll he say at parties when other men are talking about Guadalcanal?"

Sylvia laughed again in that irritating way.

"Beverly?" she exclaimed. "I can't see anyone talking *him* out. He'll match them story for story, and before the evening's over everyone there will be under the impression that most of the major campaigns of the war were fought between Balboa and Colón."

"Oh. And what do you think of all that?"

"Me? What earthly difference does it matter what I think?"

Angeline stared.

"What's the matter with you?"

Sylvia's breast heaved with something like a sob.

"Oh, Mummie—" she began in a different voice.

Their eyes met, full of surprise and alarm, for a full second.

"Nothing," she said.

There was a knock at the door.

"Come in," Angeline called. And Miss Greenough, the secretary, came in.

"Good-by, Mummie. I'll see you later." Sylvia gave her a quick kiss and hurried out.

Angeline and Miss Greenough started on the day's work, reviewing the list of the former's engagements, planning methodically meetings and telephone calls, going over bills and servants' wages, discussing ration points, Red Cross meetings, prisoner of war bundles, and whether or not it was too inopportune a year to redecorate the parlor in the country. Angeline prided herself on her ability to supervise each smallest detail.

The winter sun sparkled on the pavements of Fifth Avenue and on the big windows of the second story of Gerard's office building. It cut shining squares on the floor and made the metal objects on the big desks seem to jump up and down; it penetrated the large colored posters but only made their tints more vivid. The nurse holding up the bleeding child, the wounded Marine, the grinning Oriental were alive; wherever the posters were wrinkled, they twisted and writhed; they almost screamed. The other posters, the ones without pictures, were appeals for blood donations, but as their black and red emphatic letters leaped off the white sheets, the chemist sunlight seemed to turn them into cells of the liquid they asked for and to fill the large room with their thick crimson fluidity. The sun flashed too on the neat hair waves of the voluntary workers who now occupied the office; it made them all glossy and sleek, but on no head did it rest with a greater halo effect than on the long, flaxen, smooth, golden hair at the central desk, the crown of Bella Stroud herself. Her long, thin, oval face, framed in so pre-Raphaelite a fashion by her glorious hair, may have had the placidity of a Renaissance Madonna but it was nonetheless the face of the busiest and most executive of all these uniformed women. Her desk was always neat and unlittered; she was never cluttered with files and memoranda, and she was quick with telephones and bells. She remembered everything and delegated quickly. The only notes that she made were jotted down in a tiny, leather-covered pad with an elaborate monogram which always accompanied her on her many comings and goings. She never seemed to read correspondence or even to listen; she simply emanated through the telephone, the dictaphone, and the interview—emanated quite without fuss or preparation, quite without the smallest appearance of effort all that kept the large office so humming and ticking.

"You can have a parade for two reasons," she was telling one of her many ex-debutante assistants. "One, you have it for the people who march, like a Veterans' Parade. They have a glorious time blowing trumpets and stumping about, and nobody cares much who sees it or laughs. But if you have a parade like ours to raise money and get people to give blood it's first and foremost for the onlookers. It's got to be impressive. Now, Lila, I simply can't have Mrs. Emden in it with that frowsy organization of hers. You know how they'll be—panting and puffing and looking a million."

"But she's so set on it, Mrs. Stroud," the girl protested. "She just phoned that she's got a special pair of double-soled shoes so she won't have to drop out at Fifty-ninth Street with the Junior Girl Scouts."

"Oh." Bella reflected for a moment. "Well, I'll fix her. Don't worry. Once I've got her out it won't be hard to dispose of her group. Get my sister-in-law on the phone. Mrs. Arleus Stroud."

The girl dialed the number quickly. Like all Bella's debutantes who were selected, it would seem, for their looks and popularity, she adored her boss and loved to watch her manage.

"Will Mrs. Arleus Stroud speak to Mrs. Goodhue Stroud?" she asked into the phone. She handed it to Bella. "She's coming."

Bella took the phone.

"Angeline," she began, "sorry to bother you. It's about Lucy Emden and the parade. Naturally I can't have her in it. But you know how people's feelings are. Doesn't your Bundles Committee have some extra seats on the Mayor's stand? Yes, I'll hang on." With her left hand she opened a drawer and shook a cigarette out of a pack. The girl lighted it for her. As she inhaled she caught sight of Sylvia standing at the other end of the room, looking out the window down at the avenue. Sylvia was not in uniform; she was dressed very simply in dark brown and seemed totally inactive. Bella felt that little clutch of irritation that always accompanied the sight of her husband's stepniece, but as always she tried to ignore it. She would have been entirely happy to help Sylvia, to "take her over," to make something of her, but since the earliest days of her marriage she had been uncomfortably conscious of the girl's aversion. "Hello, Angeline," she continued into the phone. "Oh you have? Good. Now would you be an angel and see that Lucy gets on the Mayor's list and gets a bid to sit there? Oh, Angeline, you're wonderful. Thanks. Syvvie has just come in. Yes, she *does* look tired. I'll send her home early. Any news from Arlie? Well I guess it's too early to expect that. Good-by, dear."

She hung up and winked at her assistant who went off full of admiration and gratitude. A wink looked very odd on Bella's pale face, but it was just one of the inconsistencies that she liked to affect. Then she called up her husband at his office and reminded him of the dinner for General de Gaulle which he had, of course, forgotten. Goodhue had little of the quality of being definite that she shared with her sister-in-law. Bella and Angeline had always been the best of friends despite fifteen years difference in age. She had used her sister-in-law's money and place in the world, she reflected, but she had always used it for good things, and Angeline loved the smart younger throngs that came to her house when Bella borrowed it for this or that charity. No, she thought, I have never done anything to Angeline that hasn't helped her. And she fell into a moment's contemplation of how large a number of people it was whom she *had* helped.

The little silver hand of her diamond watch pointed to three. She pushed a bell and a stenographer took a seat silently beside her desk with pad and pencil, ready for the speech for the graduation of Nurses' Aides at Hampstead to be delivered the Friday after next. She dictated quickly, pausing only between completed sentences. The general tenor of the speech she had already mapped out; it was sprinkled with her forte: anecdotes, amusing and always new, about the great men of the war, but she was searching for just the right concluding fillip, one that would check any atmosphere of the humorous that might have been created and crack the room into a respectful awe of the mission before them like a charmingly belated but perfectly appropriate bugle call.

"It seems to me," she went on, "that we couldn't do better than emulate the spirit, or at least something like it, of a little British Ordinary Seaman whom Admiral Sir Henry Wilson-Brown was telling me about at our last big rally at the Waldorf—"

Sylvia, she noted, had left the window and had come all the way across the room; she was standing by a desk near Bella's and gazing at her. Bella didn't turn to look at her, but she felt her there, felt her close by like something moist and passive and sticky, and a little shudder of dislike ran through her as she turned her swivel chair more away.

"He was just a seaman and not quite seventeen," she continued in a hard firm tone, "one of those blonde, freckled, charming lads from the Midlands who, even in England, had never seen the sea until war came."

She would have to tell Angeline, she reflected, that unless Sylvia showed a little more initiative she simply couldn't continue to have her in the office. Really, the way she mooned about! Completely unappreciative of the fact that it was only because she was a niece that she had been allowed to work in the outfit at all. A niece of Bella, who had been kind enough to take her back after Arlie's wife had moved to New London!

"In the great action off Crete, Seaman Toms, for that was his name, was on the wheel of a destroyer that took a bomb hit on the bridge. Every officer and man on the bridge was killed except Toms, who although mortally wounded stood by the helm and kept the ship right on her target until the torpedoes could be launched. Admiral Brown went to the hospital in Africa to see Toms before he died. The poor little chap was in a coma but the doctor said he might still be conscious, so the Admiral bent down and whispered in his ear that it was through his courage and persistence that his ship had managed to torpedo a large German transport. Toms didn't seem to have heard; he was perfectly quiet; then suddenly in a hoarse, barely distinguishable tone he murmured—"

"Damn the torpedoes! Full speed ahead!"

Unbelievably, it was Sylvia who had said this, not loudly but distinctly. Bella stiffened with exasperation and amazement.

"Do the speech as far as it goes," she told the stenographer in clipped tones. "That will be all." She slowly turned her chair to face Sylvia who had slipped into the chair beside her desk and was sitting there, her feet crossed, her hands in her lap, her chalky face intent on her aunt as though awaiting consequences that were inevitable, interesting, but in the last analysis utterly without significance. Bella stared back.

"What's wrong with you?" she asked in a grating tone.

Sylvia said nothing for a second.

"Have you given up the London Blitz anecdotes, Auntie Bella?" she demanded suddenly. "I really liked them the best. Your old cockney women with their ruined houses in the East End. You always made them show the wisdom of the ages. But I guess they're out of date now that we're doing the blitzing."

Bella's anger was too much tempered by surprise to be violent. It really was extraordinary to listen to this creature who was usually so scared of her own shadow. She examined her up and down; she stared. Then she smiled.

"You think it's wrong of us to blitz Germany?" she asked.

Sylvia shook her head.

"I don't think anything's wrong over there," she said quietly. "It's here that everything's wrong."

"What do you mean—everything?"

"I mean it's wrong for us here to talk about things in the same terms they do out there. We don't have the passion and the agony. We don't have the excuse."

Again Bella stared.

"Syvvie, are you feeling well? I've never seen you act this way."

"I know. That's the trouble."

"Well, I haven't time for this sort of talk," she said briskly. "I have a million and one things to do. All I know is that there's a war going on and I'm trying to do my part. That's good enough for me. I'm sorry if it's not for you. Now, have you got that list of applicants I interviewed yesterday?"

"No." Sylvia looked sullenly down at her lap.

"Where is it?"

"I don't know."

Bella shrugged her shoulders.

"I don't know what I can do with you, Syvvie. You don't seem to 'take' here at all. I'll have to tell your mother—"

Sylvia looked up wearily.

"You don't have to tell Mother, Bella," she said. "After all, I'm twenty-nine. You can tell me."

Bella looked and felt flustered.

"I only meant that it was because of your mother—"

Sylvia nodded.

"Because of Mother that you wanted me in here," she finished for her. "Except it was more than that. You never could bear to think of Helena and myself doing really useful work away from you. You wanted to have the family all around you in this precious organization of yours." She waved a hand vaguely to indicate the room, and Bella glanced nervously about to see if anyone was watching. "The war's nothing but a football game to you, Bella. You wear the colors of your side and adorn the grandstand and cheer people on and buy all the souvenirs they offer you. You do the whole thing with great *éclat*. I admit it's an impressive job. But I can't stand it any more. That's all. I can't endure it."

To Bella's great relief Sylvia's voice dropped almost to a whisper as she spoke. It wasn't to avoid being overheard though; it was more as if the animating flame of her ideas was flickering lower and lower. She sat rigidly still, apparently unconscious of her aunt; her eyes looked straight ahead; she seemed to be talking to a third person sitting somewhere behind Bella.

"I'm sorry you feel this way," she told Sylvia dryly. "I can't help but think that it's because you're not well. I think I'd better call your mother."

Sylvia looked at her for a moment.

"I've never been well before, Bella," she said slowly. "I suppose I have been very rude. I'm not sorry. I feel as if I owed it to Arlie to make myself crystal clear on what he'd left behind."

"Arlie!" Bella exclaimed. "What's he got to do with it?"

"As if you'd ever understand!" the girl answered scornfully. "As if you could understand anything with your Seaman Toms and your old London crones!" Her tone was suddenly of an intense bitterness. "Bella, I tell you he's down in a submarine, under the water, and you—oh, what *is* the use?" She took her bag and hurried out of the office almost on a run.

Bella stared after her. She was still thunderstruck at the attack, but the bitterness behind it had at last seeped in and she felt sharply stung. She had never before in her life been "told off" in any such fashion and she was very much aware how little she liked it. Of course the girl was demented; she had always known that. She thought of the long cycle of depressions that Angeline had told her so much about and she herself remembered days at her sister-in-law's when Sylvia couldn't even be induced to leave her room. But the hope had been general that she had outgrown these phases and that, particularly with the new element of love in her life, she would straighten out into something more or less normal. And now—ah well, one couldn't worry too much about it. In a great war with great work, and it *was* great, to do, there was a limit to the time that could be given to the whinings of a repressed and frustrated neurotic. She decided, however, to call Angeline, and dialed the number herself.

No, the butler told her. Mrs. Stroud had just gone out and wouldn't be back until dinner. She was going to several places; it would be hard to locate her. Bella hung up and rang for the stenographer and dictated as the concluding sentence of her speech so unfortunately interrupted the heroic remark of little Toms.

Mrs. Stregelinus sat on the big sofa before the fire in her Lexington Avenue apartment gazing at the crackling logs. There were no lights on in the room which was slowly being obscured in the early winter twilight. It was an attractive room; when lit up it showed a pleasant array of flowers and chintzes. The large comfortable stuffed furniture of Mrs. Stregelinus' family life mixed pleasantly and harmoniously with the more rigid Louis XV pieces that had come from her mother-in-law's house. Over the cluttered mantel was a large gilt mirror that by reflection greatly increased the interior. From her seat she could see in it the face of the grandfather clock that dominated the little hallway outside. It was five o'clock. As the hour struck she got up to pull the curtains. Then she opened the dining-room door and called the waitress who a second later emerged from the pantry.

"We'll have tea at a quarter past, Miriam," she said. "Miss Tremaine is coming. Never mind the front door. I'll let her in."

She went back to wait in the living room. Ordinarily she would have been reading or knitting, but today she had just had a letter from Beverly and she couldn't think of anything else. It was not that it contained anything startling; it was just that she had been very much worried about the board of investigation that he had written so much about. She had no idea what the consequences would be, but she was filled with vague dreads about his happiness. It all seemed to stem from that brief period in Miami which she knew so little about. His sudden orders to Panama, arriving only a few hours before the time she had fixed for her own departure to Florida, and his subsequent flight back had been a shocking disappointment. To have had him so near and then to have had him snatched away had given her a sense of embittered frustration that had lingered for weeks. The feeling grew in her that had she only been there she could have somehow straightened everything out. Somehow the whole nasty business, together with his sudden engagement, might never have been.

She hated to admit to herself that she didn't like the engagement, but a hundred times a day she was forced to. Sylvia was such a queer, maladjusted creature. Her sympathy went out to her but never her love. She couldn't understand anyone feeling a passion for her. Angeline Stroud she had always liked and respected and laughed a little at, but the glare and notoriety of the Stroud name she shrank from as much as she feared her son embracing it. Poor Beverly. Her heart ached at his constant mistakes and her own agonized self-reproach. It was darker now, and she turned on a light by the sofa.

The door bell rang, and she got up and went into the hall. When she opened the door Sylvia walked quickly in.

"Good afternoon, Mrs. Streg," she said in a dull voice. "How nice this is." And she slipped off her coat and dropped it carelessly on a chair.

Mrs. Stregelinus led her into the living room. "But, Syvvie, my dear," she exclaimed as she got a better view of her tense pale face. "You *do* look badly!"

Sylvia sank wearily into a chair by the fire.

"I've been shopping," she said. "It's the crowds you see and all the buying. It's so abandoned, so—"

She put one hand over her eyes.

"I know, my dear," Mrs. Stregelinus broke in with sympathy. "I know just how you feel."

"New York is so callous," the girl went on. "All those pushing, half-shaven faces, so set on their own little affairs —how I hate it!"

"I suppose they don't see that it helps the war to sit around and cry about it." There was a note of reproach in the older woman's tone, but Sylvia wouldn't accept it.

"It does do good to cry about it!" she exclaimed in sudden excitement. "To mourn for it. To mourn for years if necessary. Anything to avoid indifference! I'd rather have the world in black than see it obsessed with pleasure while people are dying!"

Mrs. Stregelinus looked at her in alarm.

"Syvvie." she said. "You're worried about something."

Sylvia looked at her for a moment and suddenly burst into tears. She put a handkerchief up to her eyes and sobbed quietly. Mrs. Stregelinus didn't move.

"My poor child," she said softly. "What is it? Won't you tell me?"

Sylvia stopped crying but she kept her eyes covered.

"I'm so worried about Arlie," she murmured.

"About Arlie?" Mrs. Stregelinus looked at her in perplexity. "But your mother told me this morning that it was too soon to expect to hear from him."

Sylvia nodded and dried her eyes.

"It is. Much. But it haunts me just the same." She wiped her eyes, but did not apologize. "You see, Mrs. Streg, Arlie stands for everything that's good and fine to me. He's our great hope. I don't believe you know him well enough to know how good he is. How idealistic. How kind. When I think of the shoppers in New York and then of Arlie fighting for them out in the Atlantic, I just know that if anything happened to him I couldn't go on."

Mrs. Stregelinus said nothing for a minute. There was something in the girl's violent attitude that appalled her, almost repelled her, but above all perplexed. She knew that Sylvia adored her half-brother and his wife but she knew too how Sylvia clung to Beverly. There was nothing insincere about either relationship; in fact she suspected that together they made up the girl's entire emotional life. She had few friends and there was obviously a psychological barrier between her and her mother which no amount of mutual good will could quite overcome. The complete absence, therefore, of reference to Beverly in this sweeping declaration of despair was not, could not be, without some significance.

"My child, what are you saying?" she asked gently. "Couldn't go on? Alone you mean?"

"Oh, what would it matter?"

"If Arlie stands for all this to you, my dear, may a mother ask where her son stands?" She said this with a little smile as if anticipating a rapid rush of explanation. But Sylvia only looked at her, expressionless.

"Beverly?" she said, with the faintest note of surprise. "You know what he is to me!"

"I thought I did."

"I haven't changed," she murmured, looking up as the waitress came in with the tea tray.

There was silence while the tea things were arranged and until the maid had returned to the dining room and closed the door. Mrs. Stregelinus while pouring decided to try less personal ground.

"I've been worried about Bev's last letter," she said with a shake of her head. "I can't make out what's going on. I gather that that awful trial is over and that he's been switched to a different job, but whether or not there'll be other consequences I simply don't know. What's your thought?"

Sylvia stirred her tea and then put the cup on a little table beside her.

"I don't know," she said. "I have a feeling he'll be all right. I don't see very well what they could do to him."

"How do you think he feels about it now?"

"You mean the trial and his bucking all those officers?"

"Yes."

Sylvia thought for a moment.

"I think he enjoyed it thoroughly," she said at last, looking up steadily into her hostess' eyes. "He has a lot of good friends down there, you know, and they probably backed him against the bad ones, and he must have had the time of his life running from one to another and getting everything arranged."

Mrs. Stregelinus shrank before the coldness of her tone.

"He said, though," she protested, "that he was quite wretched."

"Ah, but that was half the fun."

The older woman said nothing; then she smiled, a bit self-consciously.

"How well you know him," she confessed.

Sylvia rested her head against the back of the chair. Her fingers slowly clasped and unclasped the arms.

"But think," she answered, "how long I've loved him."

There was in the apparent coolness of her tone just a

tremor, or perhaps it was in the way she timed the words, a suggestion of great convictions behind, that went far to reassure Beverly's mother.

"Tell me, my dear," she asked, "how long you have loved him."

Sylvia rested her eyes on the ceiling; she seemed utterly unconscious of Mrs. Stregelinus as a hostess. It was so unlike her usual self, full of quiet, frightened timidity and manners.

"Ever since I first met him," she replied at last, "eleven years ago. The summer he came down to us on Long Island to tutor Arlie. You remember. My step-father had been acting up and he and Mummie were having an awful row. The house was full of doors that were always being closed and Mummie was very unlike herself at meal times, not speaking at all and sometimes crying. I felt terribly alone and miserable. I was seventeen and Mummie wanted me to go to parties and I hated it. Oh how I hated that! I remember one dance when I crept up to a bedroom and hid until it was all over—"

"Poor child," Mrs. Stregelinus interrupted. "Why do we torture our children so?"

Sylvia shook her head.

"Mummie thought I had to get used to it. But I didn't. I would go all alone in the back of a big car which would wait for me. And then Auntie Bella came down to cheer things up. It was almost more than I could bear having two of them after me. And Bella is so remorseless about making people enjoy themselves." She stopped and wiped her eyes again with a handkerchief. She seemed quite controlled now. "But Bev was grand," she went on. "He insisted on taking me to a few dances and watched me all evening. He introduced people, and I know he never danced once himself with any other girl for fear of getting stuck and not being able to help me. I know he did it mostly because Mummie asked him to, but I thought it was just a little bit for me too, and that little bit was enough."

Mrs. Stregelinus leaned forward and patted the white thin hand that clung so limply to the arm of the chair.

"I'm sure a great deal of it was for you, my dear," she said.

Sylvia shook her head again.

"No you don't, dear Mrs. Streg," she said with a tiny smile, "but that's all right too. The little was enough. And, of course, now," she continued, "it's quite different. He cares enough now."

"Of course he does."

"If this wretched war is ever over," Sylvia went on, "I'm sure we'll be ever so happy. I want to go home now, Mrs. Streg." She stood up. "I'm very tired."

"Why not stay for dinner with me, dear? I'm all alone." Mrs. Stregelinus got up and looked at her with intense sympathy in her eyes.

"No," Sylvia answered, "I shall go home and take a nap. And then I'll be so much better." She smiled again and kissed Mrs. Stregelinus. "Dear Mrs. Streg, I admire you so, and I do wish you liked me more. Perhaps you would if I weren't going to marry Bev. But then didn't it have to be someone like me or else someone like Bella? Who can tell?"

Mrs. Stregelinus looked at her with eyes filled with tears. There was a definiteness, a certainty in the girl's tone that precluded the smallness of denials and reassurances. She felt the pressure of Sylvia's misery but her alarm was gone. In some queer way Sylvia was now the firmer of the two, and a sense of inevitability had settled in the hallway when they went to get her coat.

"My dear, my dear," she murmured as Sylvia left. "Please come back soon. Soon!"

When she was alone again, her mood changed back to alarm. In a few minutes she was moving uneasily up and down the room. She went to her bedroom and tried to lie down, but she felt a chill in her veins, a chill of absolute horror. She got up and went in to dinner; she sat amid candles and pretended to drink her soup. It was no use. She went back to her room; she stared at herself in the mirror and was surprised at the vapid look that she saw there. Switching the light off she lay down again and stared out the window at the lights opposite. There was no reason or logic to it, but there was no reason or logic in anything now. Suddenly she sat up, rigid and erect; she turned in agony to the telephone. Her fingers shot nervously into the dial circles; she dialed once, incorrectly. The second time she got it; she heard the soft, rich buzz of Angeline's telephone. Again, again, and oh in that house they *never* took so long, never, and finally the rasp of the displaced receiver, and she heard the shrill tense "hello" of Angeline herself.

CHAPTER ELEVEN

Mrs. Stroud, never evasive, minced no words in her cable to Beverly.

"Sylvia killed in window fall from our apartment Friday evening. Was worried about Arlie. Telephone me. All my love and sympathy in this terrible hour. Angeline."

Beverly was just going off watch when this was handed to him; he didn't open it until he had been relieved and was walking up the little hill to his quarters. It would be from Sylvia, he was quite sure; it would be her answer. He opened it, read it, and slowly froze on his feet.

His stomach shriveled up and he felt a queer dryness under his tongue. He began walking again, mechanically but very fast. For a moment he broke into a run and then stopped. His face was covered with sweat. It was his letter, it was his letter, kept booming in his ears. It was murder. Nobody would speak to him. He would be ostracized. He had to think. He hurried through the door and the joint living room that he shared with Amos and locked himself in his room. Then he opened up the cable again and stared at it.

No.

There was certainly no mention of his letter, nor would Angeline have sent her "love and sympathy" had she known of it. Perhaps Sylvia, always considerate, had destroyed it first, destroyed it before she—oh horror! Perhaps it would be found on her person! Rapidly, feverishly, he began to figure out who in Panama would hear about it and how many knew he was engaged. In his panic he pictured everybody as knowing about him and Audrey. They would eventually hear —somehow—Amos would read it in his *New York Times*— and then they would put two and two together—oh why had he ever breathed that he knew Sylvia Tremaine? With a start of agony he remembered his friends in the Balboa office of cable censorship. They read everything; they had seen his cable!

There was a rapping at his door; he jumped up and opened it. It was a messenger from the District.

"Two cables, sir."

"Thank you."

He slammed the door and tore them open. One from his mother: "My darling boy, my heart is with you. Can you come home?" and the other from Bella, more dramatic and of course less genuine: "Bev, what has happened to us all? I'm with you, my dear, always."

He was not even making sense to himself. He flung himself on the bed face down and listened to his beating heart. They didn't know yet, that was clear. They didn't know, he repeated. But they might at any moment. If he called Angeline now he might encounter only the butler's frosty dust-off. He wouldn't go home. He wouldn't ask for leave. He wouldn't even telephone. He was conscious only of an angry independence now, a basic animal instinct that was snarling: "So what? So what can they do to me?"

Hurrying out he got into Amos' car and drove to Cable Censorship. He saw by the expression of one officer's face that he knew.

"Gosh, Bev, I'm sorry."

He turned on him with a nervous stare.

"Help me to get some cables out, will you?"

"Sure."

To Angeline he sent: "God help us. Am praying for you. Will write. Afraid leave impossible"; to his mother: "Know you will help Angeline all you can." Bella's he did not answer.

Coming out into the midday heat he stared blankly for a moment at the car he had borrowed and then got in. He drove off in what did not appear to be any particular direction; he drove slowly and carelessly; he lit a cigarette. The squeaky horn of a Panamanian jitney bus sounded angry and close in his ear; he swerved to the side, pulled himself together. Then he drove on to Panama City. He parked the car in a dirty little side street; he wandered into the area which, in heavy Tennysonian parody, he had always described as the "bubbling of innumerable bars." And at a little round table in a cool dark corner he ordered double brandies and rested his head in his hands in classic pose of despair.

Sylvia had done it, and why shouldn't he? But even as

he allowed the dull, cold idea to settle slowly in the lumpish ooze that all his thoughts had become, he knew with a sickening little twitch in the recesses of his consciousness that that was a step that he, Beverly, would never imaginably have the fortitude to take. No, his only remedy lay in distance; he prayed now that amphibious orders would come soon and would take him far. As the second double brandy sped hotly through him he formed a picture of his redemption through fire. He saw it sadly: the atolls, the great beaching ships, and himself after the invasion, sitting in the thrown-together shack that was the Navy Officers' Club and telling a stranger over a precious jigger of rye why it was that he failed to share the universal urge for home.

The swing version of an old song rasped from the juke box.

Maybe he *was* cracking up, he thought suddenly; maybe he wanted to. Maybe he had never written that letter. Maybe it really was anxiety for Arlie that had done it to her. Certainly she adored him. Almost too much, he thought with a swift sly nastiness—yes, almost too much. After all, he had only been her half-brother. And who could deny her neuroticism? He waved to the bar for his third brandy.

He wanted to get away from himself more than from the fact of her death. His head throbbed with the stunned realization of his own sordidness. How could it be he? He had lost all track of time when he heard his name.

"Bev."

It was Amos, of course, Amos standing by the table, his funny, hawkish face drawn tight with a sympathy so intense that Bev felt ashamed.

"I'm all right," he murmured. "Have a brandy."

"You can be sure of that."

Amos sat down on the other chair by the table and signaled the bar.

"Who told you?" Bev asked sullenly.

"The boys at Cable. They thought I ought to follow you. After all, it is my car."

Bev smiled.

"Yes." Then his face darkened. "I suppose they all think I'm a stinker."

Amos blinked in perplexity.

"In God's name, why?"

"Oh—Audrey."

"What about Audrey? You can't think Sylvia did it because you had an occasional date?"

Bev noticed, as always, the slight self-consciousness with which Amos used the word "date." It was not a word for Lawrences or Stregelinuses. He smiled again.

"Well that doesn't really matter now, does it?"

He wasn't surprised that he didn't want to see Audrey. Too many of his foundations were gone for him to have anything left to give her or even to get from her. He simply had to be alone. Whether or not there would ever be a time for Audrey or his mother or anything resembling his old New York life seemed problems as insuperably irrelevant and distant as borders to large plains on which, in a dream, one stumbles.

Amos was more than a friend. They drank brandy for a while in silence, and then slowly and quietly he began on the practical problems. All matters about being relieved from watches or emergency leave he would handle for Bev. The latter shook his head so violently at the mention of leave that Amos dropped the subject; he insisted instead that they both go up to a little hotel in Baia Honda for a couple of days where they could sit on the sand and do absolutely nothing. He would make all arrangements at the District. Bev felt the relief that one feels in a fever when a competent nurse takes control and firmly steers one into a clean bed in a darkened room. They drove back to their quarters where Bev waited while Amos went over to Headquarters.

He had little difficulty there. He explained the situation to the District commanding officer, pleasant Commander Timothy, who quickly removed Bev's name from the watch list for a whole week. He was surprised that Mr. Stregelinus did not ask for emergency leave but he made no inquiries. A man's way of facing sorrow was surely his own affair. Amos then went to Mr. Gilder to ask for leave for a couple of days on his own part, a request that he expected to have difficulty with. His surprise was great at the reaction. Mr. Gilder perceptibly started and paled when he heard the news.

"Miss Tremaine!" he exclaimed. "Are you sure?"

"Beverly had a cable this morning from her mother."

"But why? Do you know?"

"I believe she had been worried about her brother whose submarine was overdue."

"Is that so? Dear me." Mr. Gilder drummed on the desk with his fingers. His eyes shifted back and forth.

"I want the weekend off if possible to take Beverly up to Baia Honda. He's in a bad way."

"Oh, by all means. Poor fellow! Of course he and I have had our disagreements, but do tell him how sorry I am. Such a bad business!"

Amos drove back to his quarters with the feeling that he had been misjudging Sherry Gilder.

Within an hour he and Bev were speeding northward along the winding, new, empty road to Baia Honda. They listened to Spanish music on the radio and occasionally discussed the sordid life in the little villages through which they passed. When they got to the hotel two hours later Bev felt as if he had really died and stepped into a limbo that was vague and painless and full of cotton.

For two days they sat under palm trees on the beach near the little, almost empty hotel and drank copiously from Amos' constantly replenished thermos of martinis with interludes of scotch. Bev told Amos a good deal; he did not, however, mention the letter that he had written. But he told him of his difficult relationship with Sylvia, his two proposals; he mentioned that his letters had not been kind; he explained the dark unhappiness of her nature. He didn't reveal his engagement to Audrey because it didn't seem important at the moment. He was thinking very little of Audrey. Nothing that Amos said was of the slightest consolation, but he didn't expect that. He only wanted to talk about himself and even to hear Amos tell of his own life. They had an orgy of reminiscence. When it was time to go back to Balboa he felt considerably more adapted to face life, though he had to confess to himself on the ride back that his courage shrank with every mile that they left behind. He did not speak, however, of his sinking heart, for by now it had penetrated into his own self-absorbed state that Amos was being the best of friends.

As soon as they arrived in Balboa Bev asked to be dropped at their quarters. He was sure there hadn't been time for mail to come in from his mother or Angeline and anyway he was too nervous to find out. Amos went over to his office where he found some accumulated work to keep him but he sent a messenger to inquire about Bev's mail. Hence, fifteen minutes after he entered his room Bev was interrupted from pacing the floor by a knock.

"Come in."

Again there was a messenger, but this time with several

letters and three more cables. Bev grabbed them, went into his room and locked the door. Viciously he tore the cables open. They contained only further sympathy: one from Helena Stroud, another from Mrs. Emden, a third from an aunt. And the engagement hadn't even been announced, he reflected feverishly. He opened a letter from his mother; it antedated Sylvia's death, and he threw it aside unread. He glanced at one or two others; they were irrelevant; then he drew his breath and opened the bulky one covered with air-mail stamps with an address written in what he suddenly recognized as Angeline's secretary's handwriting. The first object he drew out was a sealed envelope; incomprehensibly he stared at his own handwriting. As his heart stopped he opened it.

It was his letter to Sylvia.

He fell on his bed and lay there in the wildest, most impossible ecstasy of relief. No one had seen it! But a second later in a sudden agony of doubt he jumped up and seized the outer envelope. His fingers slipped in and searched wildly. Yes, there was a note. He took it out and uttered a quick prayer before he read it.

"Dear Mr. Stregelinus," it began, "Mrs. Stroud is too occupied to write you at the moment, as she knows you will understand, but she asked me to send you back this unopened letter which arrived for Miss Tremaine the day after the terrible event. We're all thinking of you—"

Bev dropped the note and sat down again on the bed. For the first time since his receipt of the cable he saw past his own hideous sense of guilt. As the sweat once again started from his forehead he saw in terrible outline the gawky crumpled body on the pavement. He lay his head on the pillow with a heart-felt moan, and then he discovered that he was sobbing with shame at his own selfishness. But the grief which now swept over him in such an overwhelming tide was too genuine to leave any room for the egotistic concept of shame; he was weeping for Sylvia, weeping the most deeply felt tears that he had ever experienced. He knew now that the world would never blame him; he knew too that he was still as basically at fault as though she had read his letter, but these realizations seemed of little significance against the sickening tragedy of this wretched climax to a wretched life. Sylvia was dead, and she should have lived. It was a reflection on the nature of the whole world that she had found no place in it.

CHAPTER TWELVE

"BEV," AUDREY SAID firmly, "I can't sit here and see you destroy our one chance of happiness. I just can't bear it. Poor Sylvia is dead and that has to be that. Can't you see?"

"Poor Sylvia. Exactly."

They were sitting alone on the Emerson's porch with the view of Balboa basin before them. Beverly seemed apathetic; he was staring moodily down over the little town at the crowded harbor and the long battleship tied up to Pier 18.

She sighed and shook her head. It had been of all weeks the most trying. First the silence—right after his promise to call her every day. Then, when she had phoned the District, the abrupt news from the officer on watch that he was on leave in Baia Honda. After that she had called Amos only to find him also gone, and when she had at last swallowed her pride to the extent of asking Miss Sondberg she had had the disagreeable experience of hearing the appalling news from someone whose superior tone had made it clear that she regarded Audrey's curiosity as the most vulgar of intrusions. After that there had been nothing to do but wait and think. Quite naturally she thought of the tragedy only insofar as it affected Beverly, but she feared the worst from this and the moment she heard his voice on the telephone she knew that her fears had not been groundless. The vibrant energy that had always been the great characteristic of his tone was gone. He had come around to her house and they had been sitting for two hours in the late evening twilight while he went over the whole history of his relationship with Sylvia. She was quite unable to cope with him. Ordinarily so persuadable, he seemed now to have retired into impregnable isolation.

"She was neurotic," she persisted. "You've told me so a hundred times. Darling, can't you see that with her type of ailment it would have been only a matter of time?"

He appeared to give this due consideration.

"That's what Mother wrote me," he answered after a few moments. "Only a matter of time. She said that Syvvie saw life from too many points of view. She had no center, no base. It was all shifting sand."

"She would have wanted you to be happy."

He shrugged his shoulders.

"No doubt. But she didn't tell me how. And I don't know. That's for sure."

"Bev, you've got to be sensible," she urged desperately. "Your letter never reached her. And everyone says she was distracted about her brother."

"Maybe," he conceded with a discouraging calm. "But I know one thing, Audrey. I've got to see this thing clearly. I can't go through life never knowing anything. What's the use?"

She stared at him.

"I don't see what you mean."

"I've got to face the fact that my letter's not having arrived doesn't make any difference. I've got to live with at least one thing that I know. And I *know* I could have saved her!"

"How could you have?"

"By sheer devotion and love. I'm sure of it, Audrey," he said as he noted her gesture of impatience. "And, oh what wouldn't I give on earth to be able to write to her or see her and be able to tell her: "Syvvie, my own, don't worry about anything under the sun. I'm in it with you and for you, and it's going to be all right.' "

There was a shocked amazement in her stare.

"You are in love with her!"

He shook his head patiently.

"No. If you don't see that, how can I explain? But she was my responsibility, all mine, no one else's. And it's my sickening tragedy that I failed her."

"What good can that do her now?" she protested almost in anger.

"None. There's no logic in it. I just can't start a life with you on top of it. That's all. Renunciation may be a fruitless gesture, but sometimes it's all that's left. Do you see that?"

"No, I don't!"

Her tone was bitter now. That after the pain and disappointment of her wartime life in the Zone she should lose the one thing she had left over a scruple that sounded to her as tinny as the dialogue in a love picture was simply too much. A while back she had had a certain dry courage to face a bleak future, but Beverly had changed that. And now he was sitting there as frozen as a gargoyle, mouthing empty sentiments.

"I certainly don't!" she exclaimed. "What's your Sylvia to me? What's she to you, for that matter, except a ghost? She's dead and I'm not. But you can't think of anything but your obligation to her. Don't you owe *me* anything? Didn't you lose my job for me? Didn't you ask me to marry you?"

To her great irritation he only smiled.

"You never depended on me, Audrey," he explained. "Besides, you always knew my hand. There was nothing covered. Nobody in the world owes you a thing. You're independent. You'll never believe I still love you, but somewhere in the bottom of me I do. Maybe this mood won't last. But I find it in me not to want it over."

She stood up in a final burst of anger.

"Don't expect me to be waiting when you finally come out of the clouds!"

Again he smiled.

"I wouldn't have the presumption."

She stamped her foot.

"Isn't it about time you told me," she said sarcastically, "that you'll never marry anyone else? Or have we had today's quota of ham?"

But he met her at the same game. "I put it more subtly. 'It's better this way.' "

She sniffed.

He made a little bow.

"Dialogue complete," he said and held out his hand. "Good-by, Audrey. I'll be leaving soon. And I'll write you whether or not you answer. Some day I'll come back. And I certainly won't expect you to wait."

She looked at him for a long five seconds. There was a baffled, almost frightened expression in her eyes.

"Oh go to hell," she said.

As he walked through the hall to the front door and paused to turn the handle he heard the sound of her angry weeping.

CHAPTER THIRTEEN

As IT TURNED OUT, it was only a few weeks after this interview that Commander Benson and Beverly got their orders to report for training at the Amphibious Base at Solomons, Maryland, on the Chesapeake Bay. From this point on Bev's life moved at a swifter tempo. Beverly was profoundly relieved; he looked forward with an intense longing to the chance to alter his mode of life and frame of thought. He and Amos had a farewell dinner together at the Union Club, but other than this he did not punctuate his final departure from Panama. Early one morning with a large suitcase in one hand and a brown envelope containing his orders in the other, the heavy, inevitable, unworn bridge coat over one arm, he clambered into a station wagon with the Commander and drove to the airport. He hadn't even said good-by to Mrs. Livermore. The motors roared, the fuselage vibrated; it was only a matter of minutes before Panama had been left miles behind. The dramatic moment was over before he had settled himself with any comfort in his seat and with a little shrug of the shoulders he opened the pages of his airmail copy of *Time*.

It had been agreed between him and the Commander that they would stay at Solomons for a few weeks before putting in for leave. Beverly didn't want any leave at all but he knew that he owed it to his mother to spend some time with her. It was now the summer of 1943, and she was staying at a little cottage on the North Shore of Long Island. It would be quiet and peaceful there; it would not hurt him to stay a couple of weeks.

They arrived in Miami and changed planes for Washington and from there took a bus to Solomons. With the return of temperate air and the sight of the east-coast countryside, with its vision of farm houses and road stands, billboards and fields, Bev felt—undeniably—the jump of his pulse. Slowly and almost unpleasantly it dawned on him that he was coming back to life.

The Navy at the beginning of amphibious warfare had been inclined rather to condescend to the new amphibious ships. The world of battleships and destroyers was hardly large enough to contain these slow and ponderous beaching craft. There was even some talk of placing them under Army jurisdiction. But it was soon realized that amphibious ships were going to be needed on a giant scale and the Navy moved quickly to make this important field its own. The planning and production of the ships was ably handled. The selection and training of the personnel was less so. The idea spread quickly throughout the Navy that selection to amphibious meant that one was not only incompetent but expendable, and no amount of popularization programs, and many there were, could ever quite clear it of this vaguely scrofulous atmosphere. A stepchild it was born and a stepchild, despite cajolements, it stubbornly remained.

To Beverly, with Miami still fresh in memory, Solomons came as a surprise. It was hard even to believe he was in the same Navy. The Department had taken pains with the Miami sub-chaser school. Its publicity was good, its students well selected; its atmosphere almost that of a liberal college. The graduate wanted to try his hand at sinking subs; he genuinely feared an assignment as billeting officer in one of the big hotels, the sure hallmark of failure. But not so Maryland. There the officers were mustered three times a day; they slept in long, cold, dirty barracks; they were forced to attend a monotonous routine of classes which repeated themselves every week. The constantly voiced yearning for permanent shore duty was more than an affectation.

But to Bev the atmosphere was not unpleasant. Attached to the Commander he was better quartered and fed than most, and though the courses were dull and badly taught they had much to offer his own great ignorance. He worked hard. He wanted to be uncomfortable. And for the first time in the war he had the blissful sense of at last being attached to an activity that was obviously indispensable to victory, that didn't have to be "explained" to dubious listeners as having a vital if indirect effect on the outcome. He began to love the big LST's that nosed their way into the anchorage near the base like sluggish sea cows; they were so homely and helpless and useful. Their very lack of glamour seemed to make them a more homogeneous part of a most unglamorous war.

To his disappointment it appeared that the Commander would have to wait several months before his "group" was ready. In the meantime he would be obliged to do a good bit of roaming around between production points and shakedown centers, Beverly, of course, in tow, ending each tour with another visit to Solomons. It was the kind of work, however, where Beverly could be very useful, buying tickets and running errands, and it looked as if, before their departure to Europe, he would be almost an expert on the commissioning of LST's.

First, however, as planned he went to Long Island for three weeks. This was not an easy time. His mother, though pathetically glad to see him, was at the same time anxious not to irritate him by making too much fuss, and the obviousness of her little self-restraints he found more trying than he would have an outburst of emotionalism. Then too, he knew that she was full of ideas about Sylvia, and although it was clearly his own fault that this subject was little discussed he resented her silence and was ashamed of himself for resenting it. His sister, Madeleine, irritated him by being too much the same; besides, she was taken up with a dull young man whom Beverly, reverting to form, regarded as most unsuitable. When he was asked out to dinner, which was not infrequent, he didn't want to go; when he had to stay home, he was bored. He thought a good deal about Audrey and what fun they could have together if she were in New York, but in the background was always the gaping hole of Sylvia's absence. He drove over a couple of times to see Angeline Stroud in Westbury. She looked as big and healthy as ever, knitting on the autumn lawn by a marble basin in solemn black. Arlie was safe, and after all, he reflected quickly as he approached her, Sylvia had never been a congenial child. She was properly affectionate, kissed him and all that, even managed a tear, but he thought he could feel in their talk the pound, pound of her passionate belief in the present and future, and what indeed was he but a parcel of her dead daughter's past? As he was taking his leave there was a flare-up of her old, eager personal curiosity, for she asked him suddenly if there had been anything wrong between him and Sylvia. He looked her straight in the eyes and said no. He saw her nod her head with the decision of one who is quickly satisfied.

Bella called him up many times and took him to lunch at the Colony and talked about Sylvia with a surprising amount of feeling. He listened sympathetically and nodded at the right times, but when they reverted to topics of conversation that they had enjoyed at the Colony in former days it was so perfunctory that they looked at each other in dismay.

It was with relief that he returned to the Commander and went off on a trip to examine the LST's building in Evansville, Illinois. Benson, usually taciturn and often impatient, was still a pleasant man to work for because he was so entirely honest and so entirely fair. Although Bev never succeeded in breaking through his reserve to any real intimacy, they developed a pleasant working relationship. Bev learned to handle all the staff details and maintained his position as the Commander's right hand man even after two more officers had reported for duty with the group flag. His promotion to senior lieutenant came through at this time and he began to feel a revival of his self-confidence. He still had awful nightmares when he dreamt of Sylvia's leap; he would wake sweating and then, just as he was allowing that familiar tide of post-nightmare relief to sweep over him, he would stiffen. It wasn't just a dream! But the agony lessened as he concentrated on new work and new places. He had not reached the point where he much wanted to see anything out of his past but he knew that would come. Even Audrey. He would be more of a person, surely, if he went back to her now. The months sped by and in March the Commander's group of LST's, at last organized, set sail from Norfolk on a calm, wintry day, forming up in tubby lines behind the long columns of Liberty ships and tankers, a vast panorama of assembly with destroyers darting to and fro on its outskirts. Bev, standing beside the Commander on the bridge, watched the receding coast line with absolute resignation.

EPILOGUE

THE SUMMER OF 1944 in England was a cold summer, cold and misty. Beverly walking down Piccadilly one morning in July was glad he had changed before leaving the ship from his khakis to his blues. There was none of London's summer color in the streets; the city was grey and impersonal under a cloudy sky. "Unreal city," he quoted to himself as he swung along, "under the brown fog of a winter dawn."

The sirens howled continually as each "buzz bomb" clattered through the mist overhead; occasionally he could hear the distant muffled rip of a detonation. He could actually be nostalgic for the London of the preceding May which, with the blitz buried in the past beneath its own rubble and the V-bomb not yet anticipated, had been flushed and expectant with a sense of great things to come. The streets had been filled with familiar faces and the Ritz bar had rattled with an almost "pre-war" chic while the sun danced on the grass in the crowded parks. Now the familiar faces were in France and the Ritz bar strangely dead. He felt as if he were revisiting the empty streets of childhood. Yet it had been only two months since he had come up from Southampton for a few days' leave and stayed with the Duchess of Baymeath. It had been a fantastic and wonderful few days. There had been nothing in London to remind him of Sylvia or Panama; he had seen only his old English friends. They had dispensed with all reminiscence; he had circulated happily in the brisk little current of pre-D-day gaiety. And then quickly back to the ship and to Southampton and conferences. And finally on June 6, to France. It had all been of so overwhelming a nature that he felt about his reactions as one does towards a diary in which for many weeks one has neglected to make an entry.

It had not been tough physically. He had actually seen not a single German. His mental picture was one of an infinite armada anchored off a long beach from which came occasionally little puffs of smoke and at night great arcs of red AA shells streaming pointlessly skyward, and then soon after, the tiring job of shuttle between Normandie and the English Channel ports, the constant opening of bow doors, the clanging rumble of trucks and tanks moving into the ship. His dominant impression was of the magnitude, the incredible magnitude of the undertaking. It was on a scale that seemed to make everything else about the war somehow absurd; the little Congressmen who debated so ignorantly about movements that were to them inconceivable, the babbling of commentators, the chatter of the Nazis, the cant about freedom. No one seemed to fit the cosmic scale of the undertaking except the mighty and ever-photographed Allied heads of state. Was Spengler right after all, and was this the rise of the Caesars?

He had not been thinking for weeks; he had been receiving only vague impressions. He had felt the odd blankness that comes with the intellectual's consciousness of history in the making. He didn't know if it was magnificent or absurd. Things were just "big," and their very bigness seemed rather awful to him. The past had dwindled suddenly into a little jumble of marionettes; he felt cold and strangely sterile when he thought of home. This, he was sure, was not how men were intended to live.

Amos was in London now, transferred from Balboa to Grosvenor Square, and he was looking forward to meeting him at the Ritz for lunch. He always managed to get both feet on the ground with Amos and he wanted them firmly there before returning to his ship which was now at Victoria Dock waiting for its next load.

He heard the whistle which meant bomb overhead and looked up. There was nothing to be seen or heard. Some others in the street stopped, but most people ignored it. Then he heard a faint rumble over in the Buckingham Palace area and walked on. The bomb was far away. Directing his steps towards Trafalgar Square, he decided to spend the hour before lunch at the National Gallery. The pictures were all, of course, in safe keeping except for one a week that was hung in the entrance hall, a sort of defiant taunt to the Hun, but today in the empty galleries there was an exhibition of war painting that he wanted to see.

As he suspected the gallery was not crowded. The exhibition, however, was very large, and he felt slightly im-

patient as he passed from room to room with no prospect
of an end. Little knots of service men stood critically before
some of the larger pictures trying to translate the blurs into
experiences that they had felt. There were hundreds of water colors that occasionally, to his rapidly moving eye,
materialized into shapes that he supposed were cruisers or
heavy bombers. He had wanted a small exhibition with a
few distinct impressions that he could carry off; here was an
amorphous mass of the third rate. Stuffing his catalogue in
his pocket he was turning to leave when he became suddenly aware of a large oil painting presented to his vision
in a distant gallery at the end of a series of parallel door-
ways. He could not make out its subject, but an object in
the foreground struck him as possibly an LST, and loyalty
compelled him to investigate. He quickened his step and in
a few moments he stood before it. The reward was his,
for it turned out that there was not one but several LST's
in the picture and all of them beaching on what was presumably the coast of France, for the title in the catalogue read: "Normandie—June 6."

Ten minutes later he was still there. In fact, he had
hardly moved. Then he glanced around and, finding a bench
close enough to the center of the room from which he
could view the picture at not too oblique an angle, he sat
down to continue his study. It was funny, but he knew
right away what had happened to him. This was the first
time he had ever "seen" a picture. Never before, he realized
with sudden rapid conviction, had an artist's angle of approach to phenomena mutually observed by him and his audience been apparent to him. He had spent years with the
technique of art, the technique and the trivia; it was as if
he had spent his life in a library, stroking the leather finish
on the backs of the volumes. Salberg's appeared in his mind
as a great, gilded, mid-Victorian frame enclosing not a
Gainsborough portrait of some eighteenth century Bella
Stroud, but a large, smudged mirror in which he stared at
his own reflection.

Yet there was nothing so remarkable about this picture.
He knew that. It would be on display for a week or so because its artist was in the service; it would be returned to
him and ultimately find it's way to the hodge-podge of the
small auctioneer's shop. But he knew what the artist *meant;*
that was all that made the slightest difference. Art was
nothing if not communicated, and was it necessary to judge

it by the number of communicants or their spacing in time during the artist's life or after?

The painting showed a long stretch of beach with six LST's, high and dry, their bow doors open, in the process of discharging tanks, trucks, and jeeps. Further down the beach other landing ships of a smaller type could be seen. Each unit of the picture stood out clearly and crudely; there was no finish but there was no blur. The light and color gave an effect that was cheerful when viewed at a slight distance. There were several fighter planes in the air, one apparently German as it was being fired on by an AA gun down on the beach. There were individual groups of soldiers all over. In one spot a wounded man was receiving first aid; in another some officers were examining a map beside an empty command car. And so on. But the thing that struck Beverly so forcibly was the lack of integration in the picture, the lack of any unity other than that supplied by the unvaried cheerfulness of the French sky and the colors of the beach and sea beneath. There was no common denominator—there were no *relations* between the units: that was it. Each group of men, each ship, each plane was utterly independent and self-absorbed. If the artist had smudged out every sign of activity in the picture except the officers looking at the map, they would have gone right on looking at their map. They appeared to need no support; they existed quite independently of the ships and the planes; like the other units they existed independently of the "invasion." Yes, he saw it now. The title of the picture was not "D-Day" or "France Liberated" or anything of that nature; it was purely and simply "Normandie —June 6." The artist had divorced himself from motives and consequences, from politics and propaganda; he had taken as his subject a strip of beach at a certain point in time and broken it down into its component parts as he saw them. Excitement crept over Beverly as the idea grew. No wonder it had caught his attention. His idea of invasions had been more along the line of those Navy Department posters which in a riot of exaggerated perspective show great fleets in sweeping parallel lines heading into an enemy beach under belching fire. The essence of such posters is the feeling of unity, of history, of mighty teamwork. The military mind in essence sees only the poster. He recollected strongly the odd feeling of chaos that he had experienced in Normandie. It was, he understood now, because he had seen the units. And once they are seen the conviction is forever lost that they add up to the total which the reading public calls "invasion," "liberation," or "victory." For everyday life labels are necessary, and these approximations must do. He didn't dispute this. But if he was ever really to get to the bottom of fact and experience, if he was ever to kill the little observer inside him, that duplicated self whose prying gaze made his every act vicarious, then he had to separate himself from generalities; he had to concentrate on the fact that the whole can't be more than the sum of its parts. One could start, he reflected, by dispensing with the Hollywood superlatives of war reporters, those town criers of Western self-consciousness who babble and babble: "This is it; this is the day; this is history; this is liberation; you are participating now, now, *now . . ."*

He turned away from the picture, tired with the very intensity of his analysis, and wandered slowly back to the main hall. As he stood there undetermined whether to go on to lunch or take another turn in an unvisited wing, he became aware that somebody was waving at him from one of the desks where uniformed women sold bonds. He recognized the lanky, well-muscled figure of Lady Sybil Brandon, oldest unmarried granddaughter of his friend, the Duchess. He went over to her.

"Bev!" she cried, with a friendly smile that showed all her large, perfect teeth. "I thought you were away at the wars. What a lovely surprise!"

"I have been. We're just back in London for another load."

"Bully for you! How is it? France and all that?"

"Quieter than here."

"I shouldn't wonder. Can you come round this afternoon? Granny will be mad to see you. I'll rustle up some gin and we'll have a cocktail."

"I thought you were all in Kent."

"We were. But trust Granny. She's found a government-in-exile to buy the house, so we came up to sell."

They heard the ugly rumble overhead and stopped talking until it should pass. Suddenly the noise stopped. Bev clenched his fists tightly; Lady Sybil just glanced to see if they were far enough from the glass doors. Then the dull "boom." It was blocks away.

"What a damn bore they are!" she said impatiently. "Granny says they're worse than the bombers because you don't kill a Hun if you shoot one down. But I showed her a clipping from the *Times* that said the ground crews sometimes get killed when they launch them. Misfire or something. She feels *much* better now."

There were some people waiting behind Bev.

"Look here, I must work," she said abruptly. "Can you make it around five? Princess Adelaide may be calling on Granny, but you like the ancient?"

"Adore them. I'll be there."

And he walked out into the square.

The people who formed the queue by the bus stop on Trafalgar Square outside the National Gallery that day just before noon aroused the curiosity in much the same way as do the people who crossed the bridge at San Luis Rey. Each one may have been ready for death for some reason unknown to the outside world and been selected by divine interposition to take his place in that patient English line of newspaper readers. Such speculation may furnish the novelist with a handy skeleton around which to orient his tale; in practical life it is futile. The actuality was simple enough. A buzz bomb, its motor having cut off perhaps a quarter of a mile away, glided noiselessly and suddenly over the top of the Newnham Building and dropped directly upon the waiting queue. How many of them looked up at the last moment and saw the terrible winged machine headed for them at so short a distance is once again a source of idle speculation. The blast completely atomized the bus that was just coming to a stop at the corner where the queue was waiting; it stove in the side of a corner store, and it shivered most of the glass on the square. Lord Nelson, serene above the lions, might have felt his column tremble but he remained secure. The Rembrandt on display in the gallery was shaken askew but undamaged. Lady Sybil dropped the change she was handing a customer and murmured: "That was close!" And a naval identification disc, found on the sidewalk a hundred yards from where the bomb landed, together with an oddly undamaged blue overseas cap bearing a lieutenant's insignia, was the only evidence that could be gathered by American naval authorities at Grosvenor Square to explain the disappearance of Lieutenant Beverly Stregelinus.

We'll never know if Beverly had time to picture the climax of his search for real experience. We can hope that he was conscious of nothing or else had only a moment of frozen suspense; I can even picture the words of Henry James flitting through his consciousness: "So it's come at last—the distinguished thing.", I could possibly find significance in the fact that all during the war he had never seen the enemy and that the bomb which destroyed him was a pilotless machine, or that he died, after all, on his way from an art gallery to the Ritz, but, oh, these speculations! Death seems to mock them. All I know is that Amos waited until two o'clock in the Ritz bar and consumed more than five martinis, and that later that afternoon, in a giant Medicean house in Kensington Gardens, boarded up except for the superb, high-ceilinged parlor, the old Duchess snapped her eyes at her worried spinster granddaughter and murmured deferentially to the Princess: "We needn't worry about him, Ma'am. He's all right. It's some girl, I'll be bound. Beverly is my favorite American, but on leave they're *all* the same!"

Audrey was terribly upset when she heard the news from Miss Sondberg; for two days she stayed in her room except for the necessary hours at the library. Nevertheless she accused herself of not feeling it poignantly enough. Then she realized that this was uncalled for. Her pain was genuine. In a world of death one couldn't mourn forever. The following autumn her father retired, and the family returned to Charlottesville as Mrs. Emerson had always dreamed of doing. They rented a small house near the University and took in only two boarders. Audrey continued work on her life of George Eliot with the University library at her disposal, and, when last heard of, was engaged to an attractive and sensitive college undergraduate, a Richmond boy, a few years younger than herself.

Mr. Gilder received a promotion to commander and went to sea as amphibious flag officer. He had a highly competent staff and received a letter of commendation of his handling of his ships at Leyte. But one wonders if in all his journeyings in the wide Pacific he has ever been quite free of a sick, little apprehension, buried in the recesses of his small, objective mind, that among the many papers and documents in the estate of the late stepdaughter of Arleus Stroud there might not turn up, sooner or later, a small typewritten card which in turn might be traced—for one hears the police can do *anything* these days—to the big, green Naval Headquarters building on the Pacific side of the Panama Canal.

Other SIGNET Books You'll Enjoy

THE NAKED AND THE DEAD   by **Norman Mailer**
The famous bestseller about fighting men sent on an impossible mission in the Pacific.   (#Q2460—95¢)

THE DEER PARK   by **Norman Mailer**
A shockingly realistic novel which exposes the private and public lives of the Hollywood film colony.
(#Q2197—75¢)

THE AMERICAN DREAM AND THE ZOO STORY
            by **Edward Albee**
Two remarkably successful off-Broadway plays by the author of the current hit, *Tiny Alice*. .. (#P2292—60¢)

THE GROUP   by **Mary McCarthy**
One of the most talked-about novels of recent years, this is the daring and brilliant story of eight Vassar graduates trying to cope with life and love during the turbulent depression years.   (#Q2501—95¢)

A CHARMED LIFE   by **Mary McCarthy**
A worldly, vivid novel about the inhabitants of an artist's colony in a bleak New England seacoast town.
(#T2416—75¢)

THREE   by **Gore Vidal**
Vidal's novel, *Williwaw*, his book of seven short stories, *A Thirsty Evil*, and a section of his latest novel, *Julian the Apostate*.   (#T2131—75¢)

ONE FLEW OVER THE CUCKOO'S NEST by **Ken Kesey**
A powerful, brilliant novel about a boisterous rebel who swaggers into the ward of a mental institution and takes over.   (#T2240—75¢)

A FINE MADNESS   by **Eliott Baker**
The widely praised satiric masterpiece about a middle-aged poet whose ribald misadventures prove no less mad than the world around him.   (#T2610—75¢)

To Our Readers: If your dealer does not have the SIGNET and MENTOR books you want, you may order them by mail enclosing the list price plus 10¢ a copy to cover mailing. (New York City residents add 5% Sales Tax. Other New York State residents add 2% only). If you would like our free catalog, please request it by postcard. The New American Library, Inc., P. O. Box 2310, Grand Central Station, New York, New York 10017.

THE BEST READING AT REASONABLE PRICES

signet paperbacks

SIGNET BOOKS *Leading bestsellers, ranging from fine novels, plays, and short stories to the best entertainment in many fields, as well as timely non-fiction and humor. Among Signet's outstanding authors are winners of the Nobel and Pulitzer Prizes, the National Book Award, the Anisfield-Wolf award, and other honors.*

SIGNET SCIENCE LIBRARY *Basic introductions to the various fields of science — astronomy, physics, biology, anthropology, mathematics, and others—for the general reader who wants to keep up with today's scientific miracles.*

SIGNET REFERENCE *A dazzling array of dictionaries, thesauri, self-taught languages, and other practical handbooks for the home library, including nature guides, guides to colleges, bridge, job-hunting, marital success, and other personal and family interests, hobbies, and problems.*

SIGNET CLASSICS *The most praised new imprint in paperbound publishing, presenting masterworks by writers of the calibre of Mark Twain, Sinclair Lewis, Dickens, Hardy, Hawthorne, Thoreau, Conrad, Tolstoy, Chekhov, Voltaire, George Orwell, and many, many others, beautifully printed and bound, with handsome covers. Each volume includes commentary and a selected bibliography.*

The SIGNET CLASSIC *Shakespeare presents Shakespeare's works in separate volumes, each edited by an outstanding scholar, with introduction, notes, source material, and critical essays.*